HIGHLAND PASSION

His boots crunched on the ground as he walked closer to her.

"Please," she whispered, "I wish to be alone."

"Aye, that's the problem, lass. You've been alone too much. 'Tisn't healthy, this maudlin obsession with a dead man."

"And I suppose you know all about morose things, do you?"

"Aye. At least I'm not turning into a fixated virgin who lives through her romantic pinings for faded memories."

Spots of crimson blossomed on each cheek. "Oh, well, if it's just a matter of having never been with a man, I can solve that quick enough."

"Nay, Sassenach, do not do that," he said, as he took her into his arms.

"Why not?" Myrtle challenged, but she couldn't explain the reason her knees suddenly weakened and her blood fired at this man's touch. His warm breath fanned her cheeks.

"The laird would nae like it."

"As you are fond of pointing out, the laird is dead."

"Aye, but I'm flesh and blood enough," he said, gently but firmly, pressing her close against him. . . .

PASSION BLAZES IN A ZEBRA HEARTFIRE!

MARY BURKHARDT

HIGHLAND ECSTASY

ZEBRA BOOKS
KENSINGTON PUBLISHING CORP.

ZEBRA BOOKS

are published by

Kensington Publishing Corp.
475 Park Avenue South
New York, NY 10016

First Printing: April, 1993

Printed in the United States of America

To Alan.
You lighten my sorrows and increase my joys.
Best friend, dear husband—thank you.

and

With special gratitude to Susan James, my agent,
and Beth Lieberman, my editor at Zebra Books—
I continue to appreciate your talents,
hard work, and encouragement.

Chapter One

Northeast Scotland,
February, 1747

The winter wind stung his eyes. Standing along the tower walk, the highest point at the edge of the castle, Ian Sinclair peered down at the icy blue water crashing against the back of the fortress far below. The tan stones and bricks of Kilmarock Castle had been home to the Sinclairs for hundreds of years. In summer, sheep grazed on the rolling green plains at the front of the keep. This was smaller than most castles in England, and it was this parapet, where he could watch the jagged rocks below, that always fascinated him. The sound of the waves and the dark sky fitted his mood this morning. He walked farther to the right and looked down at the black iron gates in the distance that led to the family crypt, final resting place of generations of Sinclairs. Bracing his fingers against the rough stones on the high ledge, Ian shut his eyes for a moment. He thought he heard his younger brothers joking as they practiced their claymore skills in the hallways below and in other inappropriate places, like Katie's kitchen.

If only it could be that way again. Laughter came easily to all of them in those days. Lost in his troubled thoughts, Ian ignored the biting air that loosened strands of his reddish-blond hair from the leather thong at the back of his neck.

"Ahem."

Ian turned.

"My lord, yer guest has arrived."

"Yes, I'm coming down, Angus. And I am just Ian Sinclair now."

The older Scot frowned at the reminder that Ian's title had been taken away. "Aye, laddie, but I canna change my way of speaking just to suit the Sassenachs."

Ian's golden eyes became unusually stern. "My father trusted Jonathan Prescott. So far, the earl has proven a good friend to the Sinclairs. And God knows we need him now."

"As ye say . . . Ian."

He walked over and placed a comforting hand on Angus's bony shoulder. "Please try to understand. Prescott is my last hope."

"Dinna forget Katie's dreams about the blue-eyed woman. Remember, the name the same as the symbol," Angus repeated his wife's phrase.

The Sinclair sighed with exasperation. While used to his housekeeper's seeing visions for as long as he could remember, this last year she'd become more verbal in prophesying about a tall, blue-eyed woman who would either destroy or save the Sinclairs. And it was beginning to annoy him. "Angus, we'll not be saved through superstitions, like peering at badger entrails. It is what I can arrange with Jonathan Prescott that will decide our fate." Ian could tell Angus was still unconvinced. "My tastes usually lean toward dark-eyed Scottish girls, if you remember. I don't even know any lass with blue eyes, name same as the symbol," he finished good-naturedly.

*　　　*　　　*

This was Jonathan Prescott's first visit in four years, and Ian was shocked at the change in his late father's friend. When Angus took the Earl of Hartford's traveling cloak, Ian saw how much weight the elderly Englishman had lost. And there was an unhealthy pallor in his sunken cheeks.

"My lord," Ian greeted him. "It was kind of you to make this difficult journey."

At the sound of an unfriendly animal's growl, the earl stepped back quickly when a large dog approached him from the shadows across the room. Jonathan did not miss the canine's sharp teeth.

"No, Robbie, doon. Sit."

The gray-haired dog went down on his haunches immediately at his master's command.

The earl's powdered periwig moved when he shook his head with nervous relief. "Would that my wife obeyed me so readily," he murmured.

Concerned Jonathan's voice was so weak, Ian returned the older man's smile with difficulty. "I feared Robbie might pounce on you. He does nae take to strangers. Even Angus and Katie are a bit afraid of him. Robbie's still too wild for their tastes."

The dog's tail thumped on the wooden floor as his master patted his large head. Brown eyes gazed upward in obvious appreciation as Ian began scratching him behind the ears.

"One of Robbie's ears is much smaller than the other," Jonathan observed aloud. "A fight?"

"Nay. Robbie was born with one floppy ear smaller than the other. To look at him now, you'd not know he was the runt of the litter. No one else wanted him, and—well, we suit each other." Ian could tell the Englishman needed to sit down. Offering his arm to his guest, the Scot accompanied the earl closer to the fire and gave him the more comfortable overstuffed chair.

If Jonathan Prescott noticed the missing furniture

and valuable artwork, he made no comment. Dressed, as his host was, in dark knee breeches, white hose, and outer velvet coat, the Englishman took a few minutes to catch his breath.

"Your note arrived only the day before yesterday, my lord." Distress tinged Ian's words. "I assure you, sir, I would gladly have come to see you rather than have you make such an arduous journey in the heart of winter. Or perhaps in the spring you—"

Prescott raised a veined hand. "No, Ian, this could not wait, for two reasons. The first I will go into later. The second," he added, focusing his gray eyes on the tall Scot sitting across from him on the straight-backed chair, "leaves no option. My doctor tells me the cancer will ensure I never see another spring."

The Scottish chief's golden eyes mirrored his sorrow at this news. He remembered years ago when a robust earl had visited his father every year. The two men went fishing and hunting, laughed, and told stories about their Oxford days. They had met as boys, and the kindly English lad had taken pity on Murdoch Sinclair, a young Scottish nobleman away from home for the first time. And as a boy himself, Ian had delighted in Jonathan's summer arrivals. The earl always treated Ian and his younger brothers as family—presents on their birthdays and Christmas, and letters when Ian was away at school in Edinburgh, then France. Jonathan Prescott was the only Englishman of honor and kindness Ian had ever known. "My lord, I am truly—"

"Of course, no need to say anymore about it, Ian. Know how you feel. Spoke to the King. Had to see you straight away." Gravely, the older man bent his frail body forward. The light from the marble fireplace gave the Englishman a better look at the tall Scot. He did not miss the lines of strain at the corners of eyes once more accustomed to laughter. The earl

10

thought, for a man of only six-and-twenty, Ian Sinclair had been forced to shoulder too many burdens this last year.

When Ian saw pity on Jonathan's thin face, he cleared his throat and sought a lighter topic. "Your wife, I trust she is well."

The Earl of Hartford gave a snort of disapproval. "Barbara is always in excellent health, especially now that the three younger girls are entering their first London season." Devilry again in his eyes, he chortled, "Only your dear father knew how delighted I was to get away from my pretty but shrewish wife each summer to come here to Scotland. Even an Englishman can take just so much twaddle about the right color for gown sleeves." His features became more serious. "The three younger girls will be fine. It's my oldest daughter I'm concerned about. Twenty-three, and still not married. If only she'd take more interest in clothes and parties. Of course, Addison doesn't seem to mind," the earl mused aloud. "Suppose that's why she favors him." His voice became more raspy. "She's so like her mother," he said, thinking of his first wife, who had died when Myrtle was a baby.

"My daughter has little patience with the foppish swains who come to call," Jonathan admitted to his politely listening companion. "Says they're after a rich heiress. Only one she seems interested in is Addison Barrington, yet . . . can't put my finger on it, but I don't trust the fellow. I've nothing against his Cockney origins, but the man's a bit too smooth, if you get my meaning. My little girl has a mind of her own, though, one reason why I never criticize Addison in front of her. Of course, time is running out, and I wanted to see her wed before I . . ." His words drifted off as he glanced into the crackling flames of the fireplace. Like his sweet-natured first wife, Jane, Myrtle was not a classic beauty. What

11

would happen to the girl after he was gone? Wealth she would have, but . . . "Damn it, the girl should be married," he blurted to his surprised host. "Never wed a woman just for her looks," he advised Ian, then colored at his uncharacteristic outburst. A fit of coughing kept him from saying more on the subject.

Too polite to comment, Ian guessed why the oldest girl was unmarried. When Prescott said she was like her mother, the shrewish Barbara came to Ian's mind. Yes, he could imagine a pretty, pampered Englishwoman rudely sending bumbling suitors packing, their ears scorched from her sharp tongue in the process.

"Sorry, Ian, I did not come here to waste valuable time fretting about my eldest daughter. Poor girl, I've never been very astute about helping her."

"Aye, bairns can be a trial at times," was all Ian would say on the matter, irritated a slip of a girl could cause her dying father such worry.

Sitting forward on his chair, the earl told Ian, "Now, to the first and most important reason for my visit. When you wrote me you had received official notification Kilmarock Castle and all Sinclair lands were now forfeited to the Crown, I went immediately to His Majesty. George II owes me a favor, and I requested his leniency in this matter."

Ian's body tensed as he waited for the earl's news. Something lurched in his stomach at the sudden grimness on Jonathan's gaunt face.

"He would not relent on that point, Ian."

"George of Hanover knows I have worked years to keep Clan Sinclair out of local and English skirmishes. When the Knoxes, our clan rivals, stole some of our cattle last year, I forbade my clansmen retaliation, for I'll not give the King any excuse to send more redcoats to our borders. I've never raised so much as a claymore against England. On countless occasions I have spoken out to all my clansmen to stay out of the King's quarrel with Charles Stuart."

"Yet His Majesty takes note you never fought for the Hanovers."

"Aye, and never will," countered Ian. "I am Episcopalian, not Catholic or Anglican. Neither the Hanovers or Stuarts care tuppence what happens to the Sinclairs. We're one of the smallest clans in Scotland. Being left alone to live in peace is the only way we can survive. My late father never fought for the Old Pretender, nor did I fight for his son in '46."

"But your brothers did, God rest their young souls."

Ian bounded from his chair and began pacing back and forth in the large sitting room, his hands thrust behind his back in agitation. "What more does the King want, Jonathan? Father was against the Act of Union from the beginning, for all Scotland received was more taxes and less say in how we are ruled. I've closed most of the castle off to save money, yet my tenants still starve. England rules it is against the law to wear the plaid. My piper canna play for me; the bagpipes are now seen as an instrument of war. And now I am informed I canna act as judge over my own clansmen. By hell, German George knows nothing of honor."

The earl got shakily to his feet. "Ian, you cannot fight battles alone any longer. And there is more," he added, clearly disliking his task. "Both Hugh and Malcolm killed many English soldiers before they perished at Culloden. The King holds you responsible, as their elder brother and laird of the clan. Because His Majesty owes me a favor, he agreed to let me speak with you before action is taken. If you step down as laird, the King promises me your clansmen will not be driven from their lands."

Wary, Ian continued to listen.

"If you step aside, I give you my word the new owner I choose for Kilmarock Castle and Sinclair

13

lands will have a care for your clansmen. But the King orders you to leave Scotland forever."

"Leave Scotland?" Ian echoed. He'd expected the possibility of losing his earldom and his wealth, but never did he consider he would have to leave his beloved homeland. "And if I do not leave?" he demanded, trying to keep the desperation from his voice.

"You will be tried as a Jacobite traitor. Then, the King has told me he will accept the offer of Squire Barrington to buy the castle and lands, thus cutting off my ability to help the Sinclairs."

"You know this Englishman? Is he related—to that Addison Barrington you mentioned before?"

The earl nodded. "Yes, Addison is the squire's son. I know the squire by reputation. In his late fifties, he is a tradesman. Coarse, newly rich, ambitious, wants the land to graze sheep. Old Barrington has been after me for years to arrange a marriage between his son, Addison, and my oldest daughter. To put it bluntly, my boy, Addison's father cares more about money than people. I firmly believe the Sinclairs would suffer greatly from such an owner."

Ian was forced to turn his back on his old friend, lest the Englishman see the extent of his anguish. "I should have raised my claymore," he said, the words sounding bitter. "For all my efforts to keep us out of wars, the end is the same as if I'd fought for Bonnie Charlie. It's come to this. All is lost, then," he finished, his back less straight when he turned to the earl.

"No, we must salvage what we can." Struggling, Prescott walked over to the towering Scot. "My boy, I know how painful it will be to leave Scotland. But think, Ian: all the King demands is that you leave and that no Sinclair ever rule here again. I have friends in France. You could make a life for yourself, marry, raise a family."

14

"Skulk back to France like Jamie Stuart?" Ian demanded with disgust.

"You must leave," the earl said again. When he saw the firm line of Ian's jaw, he felt weaker and pressed a shaking hand on Ian's arm. "George II told me if you do not comply with this agreement, not only will Barrington become the new owner, but you'll be hanged for treason. Please, you must accept the King's word for justice."

"Aye," the younger man muttered, disengaging his arm easily from the old man's grasp. "I've had a bellyful of English justice. Did you know Gavin Mackenzie, my tacksman, was also at Culloden? A ball grazed his temple and the English thought him dead, but it was a temporary paralysis from his injury. Though he knew Malcolm was dead, Gavin saw Hugh, who was merely wounded in the shoulder. Unable to speak or move, Gavin could only watch in horror as that butcher Cumberland ordered an officer to shoot my youngest brother to finish the job. The battle was completely over, Jonathan," Ian emphasized. "The officer refused to kill a wounded man, but an English soldier from the ranks offered to perform the task. Hugh was only eighteen; he was merely wounded in the shoulder, and the battle was over." Ian's voice broke. "A common English foot soldier murdered that unarmed boy. I tell ye this, Prescott, if ever I find that Englishman, he is a dead man. So, dinna lecture me aboot English justice."

The earl's face became paler. "I . . . did not know. I never realized—my God, what barbarians we have all become over this fear of the Stuarts. I . . . please, Ian, I must rest. No more now. Tell me your decision tonight."

Immediately Ian reminded himself that Prescott had come here to help and so deserved better treatment. The laird placed a supportive arm about his companion's shoulder. "My lord, I am truly sorry

15

for my horrid manners. My outburst was inexcusable. Come," he added, forcing a lightness he did not feel. "Angus will prepare a room for you on this floor so you will not have to climb the stairs. And Katie is cooking your favorite lamb stew tonight. After you rest, tell Angus when you are ready, and he will direct you to my library. I will give you my answer then." He was relieved to see the strain leave the earl's thin face.

"It is good to see you again, Ian. Murdoch knew I envied him his three strapping sons," Prescott added with a sad smile. "Ah, well, a man cannot always have what he wishes."

Ian did not miss Jonathan's meaning. But, he thought, helping the Englishman to his room, he'd bent so many times to keep his clan safe, stifled his instinct to fight back. Hadn't his own brothers called him a coward for refusing to fight for Bonnie Charlie? Neutrality, Ian had always believed, was the only logical course for his small clan's survival. Now, he wondered if it all had been for nothing. The King promised his tenants would not be displaced. Yet, how could Ian be certain the King and Jonathan Prescott kept their word if he were miles away in France? And the thought again of leaving Scotland made him feel closer to tears than he had since childhood.

It was evening before the Earl of Hartford awoke. When he arrived at Ian's library, Jonathan peered into the darkened room. He noticed a candle on a bare wooden table. At first he thought the room was empty. After he turned to leave, Ian's voice stopped him. Jonathan walked slowly into the room. The Englishman saw Ian get up from a chair and come over to the table.

He noted Ian now wore the outlawed tartan—a

16

dark green and black crossbar pattern on his kilt, plaid fastened at his left shoulder with a circular silver brooch, white ruffled shirt, badger skin sporran below his waist, tartan hose above black leather shoes. With his unpowdered reddish-blond hair tied neatly at the back of his neck, Ian Sinclair looked every inch a Highland chief, and the Englishman understood the significance of the proud Scot's choice of attire on this solemn occasion. "Your choice?" he asked, apprehension for the young man's safety evident in his barely audible voice.

Choice? Ian thought. The word implied alternatives. No, the Scot saw only one way through this dilemma. And even that desperate act might not be enough. "Yes, my lord. I will relinquish my title, castle, and lands. There is no more Sinclair laird."

Jonathan knew how deeply this decision cost the man before him. Clearly, he tried to relieve the tension in the room. "The Count of Chevreny and his family are wonderful people. Their son remembers you from your university days in Paris. They assured me they would welcome you for a lengthy stay until you decide where in France you wish to set up permanent residence. I will see that a sizable amount is deposited in a Paris bank for your use."

Ian's military posture became even straighter. "No . . . I thank ye, sir, for that generous offer." As always happened with strong emotion, his Scottish accent became more pronounced. "However, I will nae add to my indebtedness to ye by accepting money."

"But your father was my best friend. Murdoch Sinclair would have done no less had things been reversed." He saw the unyielding determination on Ian's face and decided not to belabor the point now. Sighing, the earl smiled up at the handsome Scot. "I am relieved you agree to the King's conditions."

17

Ian couldn't share the older man's mood yet. "There is something more I require before this business is ended. I know you respect our ways." He pulled out a dagger from a leather strap beneath the plaid covering his chest. "If I leave with you on that ship for France in the morning, you must promise me that my people will not be driven from Sinclair lands." Solemnly, he held up the dirk. Light from the candle sparkled from the red ruby at the center of the hilt. He thrust the ornate silver handle close to Jonathan's face. "The Scottish promise, my lord, upon my father's dagger."

"Yes, Ian, I give you my solemn promise, and I will choose the new English owner myself."

"A champion, a man of strength and honor who will have a care for the Sinclair tenants?"

"Yes." The Earl of Hartford already had his choice in mind. "I will send your people a champion. By my life and honor, I swear." Knowing the custom, he brought the handle of the knife to his lips, sealing his vow in the Scottish tradition.

Satisfied, Ian replaced the dirk. "Thank you for being a friend, my lord. I have . . ." What lay ahead daunted him for a moment. "Until tonight, I almost believed God had abandoned the Sinclairs."

"Come," the Englishman managed, "let us go into dinner and talk of brighter days to come. You know," Jonathan continued as they walked out into the light of the next room, "the ladies of Paris will swoon over your stalwart good looks. You'll have to bring along that claymore, lad, to keep them at arm's-length."

Ian tried to match his old friend's attempt at cheerfulness. "I dinna think arm's-length is where I'd want the French lassies."

His companion's smile turned to a grin, then he laughed outright. "Gad, I see a few years hasn't changed your prowess with the fairer gender. I'm sorely tired of seeing nothing but fops paying court

18

to my eldest daughter. A pity you will not have the chance to meet her."

Ian pretended regret. "Yes, a pity." Inwardly, he was relieved. If the earl hinted his wife was a shrew and the daughter was just like her, by St. Andrew, why the devil did he think Ian would want to meet the disagreeable chit? His own father had never mentioned the earl's wife or daughters, probably too discreet to disclose any private conversations he'd had with his English friend. Until today, rarely had Jonathan talked about his family to Ian, but the Scot was now certain this unmarried Lady Prescott must be a real tartar. Best change the subject, he told himself, before he gave this kindly gentleman some blunt advice on how to handle the harridan spinster. He cleared his throat. "I hope you will not mind, my lord, but I take my meals in the room we were in earlier. It is warmer than in the formal dining hall."

Instantly, Jonathan recognized the younger man's embarrassment over his home falling on hard times. "Actually, I like the informality. One more evening soirée at home, and I think I'd trade my wealth to have all four girls taken off my hands."

Ian shortened his stride to accommodate his sickly guest. As they made their way back toward the sitting room to eat, Ian prayed his plan for the morning would succeed. It was his last hope. Would the Englishman the earl promised to send be up to the difficult task of defending the Sinclairs? And the fellow had better be able to handle his fists in a brawl, Ian mused, if he hoped to gain the respect of his proud, stubborn clansmen.

"My lord, we cannot wait, or we'll miss the tide."

Irritated, Jonathan Prescott scowled at his employee. "Captain Rogers, he said he would be here. We will wait." Ignoring the other man's grumbling, the earl peered into the morning mist. Before Jonathan retired last night, Ian had told him they would not meet again until he arrived at the dock where the earl's ship was anchored. It wasn't like the Scot to be tardy. He knew the importance of their leaving early, for Jonathan had to get word to London that the laird had complied with the King's directives.

The sound of horse's hooves in the distance brought the earl's attention back toward the dock. He slapped his right hand against the curved wooden railing of his ship. "See, he comes, Rogers. Get ready to weigh anchor as soon as his trunks are aboard."

But where was the coach with his trunks? Prescott wondered. A lone rider got off a large, barrel-chested horse. The man was too beefy to be Ian.

As the dark-bearded Scot walked up the gangplank, the earl recognized the man in his fifties when he shouted something to Cyril Layton, the earl's timorous clerk.

The befuddled Englishman rushed over to his employer, his white wig askew from the exertion. "My lord, this man says he's come with an urgent message from the Sinclair. He says he's the laird's taxman. Is he here to collect funds?" Puzzlement showed on Cyril's chubby face as he readjusted the round spectacles across the wide bridge of his nose.

Patiently, Jonathan explained, "The tacksman refers to the laird's second-in-command. Please show him aboard, Cyril. And don't look so terrified of Mackenzie. I'm here to protect you."

Dressed in plain coat and breeches, his shoulder-length gray hair whipping about his wide shoulders, Gavin Mackenzie stalked across the deck to the Earl of Hartford. He thrust a sealed parchment down at him. "Last night the Sinclair ordered me to give you this letter before you sailed." Grimly, the Scot waited for the man in front of him to read the short missive.

The frail Englishman's face crumpled as he perused the letter. "My God." Tears swam before his eyes, and his body swayed forward. Cyril caught him about the waist. "A . . . chair," Jonathan rasped.

Cyril's face reflected his distress, for it was clear he did not wish to leave his master to retrieve the requested chair, fearing the earl would drop to the hard wooden deck. Cyril's squeaky voice did not carry to the crewmen working far away from the three of them.

"Och, they'll nae hear ye. Fetch a chair for the earl! Be quick aboot it," bellowed the fierce-looking Scot.

In seconds a wooden chair materialized for their weak employer. With a growl of impatience, Gavin reached for something in the pocket of his outer coat. He thrust the silver flask under the seated man's nostrils. "Take a wee drop."

Jonathan shook his head. "No, thank you, Gavin. I cannot even swallow food with ease these days, let alone your powerful Scottish whiskey." He brushed a bony hand in front of his eyes. "I never wanted it to end this way. Never. Did you find him? How did he—?"

"Nay." Gavin squared his shoulders, his voice giving proof of his own pain at this turn of events. "Angus and Katie found the lad's body, or what was left of it, this morning. He'd plunged the dirk into his heart before throwing himself from the parapet to the jagged rocks along the loch below the fortress. He told me last night I was to assist you with the sale of the castle and lands," Gavin added, unable to disguise his dislike of this directive. "All the Sinclair's personal possessions fit into one small trunk; he sold the rest long ago to help us." Gavin's voice cracked, and he was silent for a moment. "But the lad said nae a word aboot what he planned to do. To die like that, not even a warrior's death . . ." He bit back a growl that on a smaller man might have sounded like

21

a sob. "The laird said I was to offer the trunk to you. It contains two suits of English clothes, a portrait his father made him promise never to sell, some books—Robbie, he said you would understand I'm to take care of him now. My lord, do ye wish me to fetch the trunk aboard?"

"God, no, I don't want . . ." he waved the man away, clearly unable to speak for a moment. "Give the things to his clansmen if you wish." Ian was the descendent of Scottish nobility, Robert the Bruce. His ancestors went back further than the Hanoverians, Jonathan mused, and all that English King's policies had left Ian Sinclair were a few pieces of clothing, books, a painting, and his dog, Robbie. Jonathan buried his face in his hands. "Why didn't he just come with me to France?" he asked aloud. "There was no need for him to die."

"Englishman, ye still dinna ken our ways," Mackenzie told the earl. "The letter says it all."

Jonathan's eyebrows rose. "You read this?"

"Aye. The laird had Angus deliver it to me at dawn, along with his note of instructions. Ian wrote I was to close the letter with the Sinclair seal after reading it."

"My lord," Cyril interrupted, looking more worried. "The captain says we must leave immediately. He wants to know if we sail for France."

It took a moment for the earl to answer. "No, we . . . we have no passenger for France. We are returning to London." Still sitting in the chair, the earl's hands shook as he read the letter once more:

My lord, I thank you for making this arduous journey to assist the Sinclairs. You are the only English aristocrat I have ever known to care what happens to us. You must realize, however, I can never leave my homeland. While King George is adamant that I step down as laird of the Sinclairs, I have done so in my own way, on my own terms.

Gavin Mackenzie is my trusted second-in-command. All documents of sale for the castle and lands should go through him.

Finally, I remind you of your Scottish promise made to me last night. By my blood, I now seal your oath, Jonathan Prescott, Tenth Earl of Hartford. If you do not abide by it and send a champion to watch over my clansmen, I swear my ghost will haunt Kilmarock Castle forever, and no Englishman will find one night's peace within its walls.

Ian Murdoch Sinclair

Horrified, Jonathan then noticed the rust-colored stains on the paper. With his own lifeblood the laird had scrawled his signature. A gust of wind on the back of Jonathan's neck chilled him to the bone. Sick at heart, the earl got to his feet. He brushed aside Cyril's offer of assistance and walked alone toward the curved rail of the ship. There was only the sound of water lapping against the wooden hull. He spoke aloud as Cyril and Gavin looked on. "I did not save your son, Murdoch, old friend, but I vow I'll save your clansmen. Squire Barrington will not have Castle Kilmarock or your lands. I will send you that champion."

Chapter Two

When the closed carriage hit another deep rut, Lady Myrtle Prescott lurched forward and would have been hurled to her knees if the scarlet-uniformed officer sitting across from her hadn't reached out automatically to catch her about the arms.

The handsome Englishman frowned, puffed a little with exertion, then placed her carefully against the leather upholstery of the coach. "These Sinclair roads are deplorable," he muttered. "Lud love me, you'd think Ian Sinclair would have seen to the roads before he killed himself. Damned inconsiderate of him."

Lady Myrtle overlooked his last remark. She tried to straighten the gray traveling cape over her plain wool gown. Shuddering, she recalled the laird's last letter her solicitor had given her at the reading of Jonathan Prescott's will. The unfortunate Scot had had more on his mind than mere roads, she thought.

Captain Addison Barrington moved forward on his seat and took one of the lady's gloved fingers in his hand. "Dearest Myrtle." He winced, then managed a half-smile. "You know, I shall never feel

25

comfortable about your name. It's more suited to a dairymaid or country housewife than the daughter of an earl. You should be a Cynthia or Marigold."

When she attempted to retrieve her hand, her companion would not have it. "Well, Myrtle was my mother's favorite name. I was christened after her beloved sister, who died when they were children." Myrtle's gaze focused on her lap. "I am sorry my name displeases you."

"Well," said Addison, "I suppose it isn't your fault. However, we have more pressing matters to discuss, for we are coming to the spot where I must leave you to join my men. Surely you have seen enough of this godforsaken land to realize it is no place for an English lady, no matter how tall and robust you appear," he teased. "Please, why will you not allow me to arrange your escort back to London?"

The pleading in his hazel eyes was tempting, she thought. Immaculately groomed, in a scarlet coat, breeches, shining black boots, sword at his left hip, powdered bag wig with fashionable side curls, and black ribbon at the back of his neck, of all her suitors, he was still the most persuasive. Her stepmother told Myrtle she was a fool to refuse his offer of marriage. "Please, Addison, try to understand. I promised Father on his deathbed I would make this visit. He left the castle and Sinclair lands to me with the understanding I would carry out certain obligations. And from the looks of what I've viewed thus far, I only hope I'm not too late."

With minor impatience, Addison let go of her hand and sat back against the plush cushions of his coach. "But it is too big a task for a woman alone. To come out here, not even your maid, Bess, with you—"

"It was my stepmother's doing. At the last moment, Barbara said Bess was needed to help with my three stepsisters and could not come with me. It

26

was too late to hire anyone else. I am certain one of the local girls can see to my needs. Besides, it will only be for a few weeks, until I can hire a suitable overseer, then I'll be able to leave Scotland."

"If you married me, I should be pleased to take all such burdens off your fragile shoulders." The officer let her see the open affection in his eyes. "You know the Barringtons all adore you. Mother and I could use your help with Twilla. My little sister still resists the polishing attempts to make her into a proper lady."

Myrtle thought of all the Barringtons, Addison had been the most successful in overcoming his East End origins in manner and speech. "Twilla is doing fine, Addie," she assured her companion. "She's just in that rebellious stage many young girls pass through on their way to womanhood."

"You were never rebellious," Addison pointed out.

"Probably because my father usually let me do as I pleased," she replied with an impudent grin.

Addison continued to study her. "You are too beautiful to be appreciated among these bucolic louts."

Pushing back a strand of her straight brown hair that had come out from the practical bonnet she wore against the crisp March wind, Myrtle said, "Please, Addison, I must see to this duty before I can return to London, let alone consider marrying."

"Does that mean there is hope for me, Lady Myrtle?"

She fidgeted. For some reason her late father had never taken to Addison or his family. Yet Myrtle found this Englishman's manners exemplary. Had the earl been against Addison because the captain's father was in trade and not an aristocrat? At the unfairness of such prejudice against Addison's Cockney origins, her blue eyes warmed to the man across from her. "Yes, there is hope, Addison, but I must honor this promise first. I shall need a friend during the weeks ahead. In truth, sir, I am a little uneasy about taking over these responsibilities. Since you were stationed here before, your candor about the deceased laird and these Scots would be most helpful."

Addison appeared reluctant to speak. "Well, I did try to warn you in London that this is sheer folly, but I can see you will not be dissuaded. Better have the whole truth, then. As you've probably guessed, the Sinclair tenants hate the idea of their landlord being a Sassenach—their name for the English. What is more humiliating in their eyes is that the new owner is a woman. They are taking it as a deliberate insult. I should not expect a warm welcome at Kilmarock Castle. This is an uncivilized country. The Scots in these highlands are ignorant, filthy brutes who cannot be trusted. I'd keep a pistol handy if I were you."

Myrtle could not hide her shock. "While he never told me much specifically about Murdoch Sinclair and his family, Father used to have such wonderful things to say about the Scots and the highlands." Even now it affected her to think about the last letter the laird had written her father. "The despair Ian Sinclair must have felt to be driven to such a state, in which suicide was the only way to save his beloved tenants . . . That trip here in the heart of winter last year hastened Father's death, yet I now understand why he made it. He was heartbroken over the young laird's death."

The Englishman snorted. "I should not waste my sympathy on the likes of Ian Sinclair. Your father was a fine man, my lady, but he was blinded by his desperate need for reprieves from your stepmother, if you can forgive me for being so blunt. These highlands offered him a chance to recapture his lost youth. Jonathan was always too romantic for his own good, a trait you've inherited, it seems. However, you told me how much it vexed you when he refused to take you on what turned out to be his last trip."

Nor had her father taken her on any others, but she shoved the thought aside. Never having visited Scotland before, Myrtle was trying to stay open-minded, to find out the truth. "What do you know of the dead laird?"

"Enough that I could never tell you all, for much of it is not fit for an English lady's delicate ears."

"He never married?"

A shout of unpleasant laughter filled the coach. "From what I have heard, Sinclair was having too good a time wenching his way across Scotland to settle down with one woman. No doubt you will see many of his bastards running about these hills with the Sinclair reddish-blond hair and those distinctive golden eyes the superstitious Scots talk about."

Color stained Myrtle's smooth cheeks. "You mean Ian Sinclair was a . . . a libertine?"

Addison appeared even more amused. "For a woman of twenty-four who ran her father's town house and country estate for years, you are such an innocent in the ways of the world. Ian Sinclair was a cruel rake, ignorant, preferring the baser pleasures of life. Yet like many braggarts, he lacked courage. That vulgarian never fought for King George or the Young Pretender, preferring to squat here on his Scottish highlands to indulge his lewd tastes. And when things got a little difficult, he took the coward's way out and threw himself from the tower of the fortress. His church denied him burial on the consecrated ground of his family crypt. Just some stone marker outside the gate. His clansmen say his ghost still haunts the castle, while he seeks revenge against the English he blames for all his mis-fortunes."

"Stuff," Myrtle countered. "There are no such

29

things as ghosts. Probably a servant in the whiskey."

The captain's eyebrows rose. "To hear your two clerks tell their stories, the ghost is real. The bloodied head of that sheep Tom found in his bed was no illusion." Addison's sharp features became more relaxed at the sudden paleness in her face. "And Cyril Layton had been your father's right-hand man for thirty years. Not like him to speak of a ghost without a face roaming Kilmarock's halls after midnight."

Myrtle couldn't keep the defensiveness from her voice. "There is a logical explanation for those occurrences, and I intend to find out who is harassing my representatives. Both gentlemen were apprehensive about coming here in the first place, all that talk about the ghost of a dead Scot. I will see to this matter myself," she added, her lips pursing to a stubborn line.

"Well, my lady," Addison added in earnest, "last month some of my own men told me they spotted a white-faced phantom on a demon black horse charging across the moors after midnight."

Silence.

"Hmm . . . I can tell by your expression you will hear no more about ghosts. The cursed cad's sins probably keep Ian's black spirit wandering these highlands at night."

Again, Myrtle made no comment. Yet as she sat gazing out the window, she could not help being appalled at Addison's revelations about the true nature of the former laird. Ian Sinclair now seemed a figure to hold more in contempt than pity. Had her father been blind to the truth, as Addison said?

When the conveyance slowed, Lady Myrtle smothered the temptation to ask Addison to come with her to the castle. Of course it was out of the question, she told herself; he'd explained that his military duties meant he had to leave her here. Arrangements had been made.

After assisting her out of his coach, the captain had his driver remove her two bags from the back of the carriage. They only had to wait a few moments before another carriage approached at the prearranged spot.

The brown-haired woman swallowed and mentally recited her promise to her father once more. She saw Addison blanch when he took in the condition of the worn coach arriving for her.

Myrtle had to stifle her own surprise that such an ancient, unkempt means of transport had been sent to take the new owner to Castle Kilmarock. She placed a hand on Addison's arm, giving him a pleading look in hopes he would not make things more difficult for her.

A man of medium height and short-cropped white hair jumped from the driver's seat with surprising dexterity for a person in his mid-sixties. Ignoring Addison, the Scot focused his unsmiling features on the tall young woman. "Ye be Prescott?"

"'Ere, Lady Myrtle Prescott to the likes of you," snapped the English officer, his speech slipping over to the Cockney side. Addison took in the shorter man's muddy boots, and his frayed coat and breeches. "And have a care of her ladyship's two bags. Be quick about it."

Unmoving, the Scot took a closer inventory of his new employer. "From the looks of the lassie, she could verra easily heft both trunks herself."

Perhaps it was release from pent-up nerves, but an outright chuckle escaped Myrtle's lips at the Scot's outrageous remark. He was quite correct; it had to be her too generous figure, she told herself. Still giggling, she leaned down and gripped the handles of one of the leather bags.

"Put that down at once! Blimey, Myrt—my lady,"

the captain corrected in front of the others. "It is not proper for you to be addressed or treated in this surly manner."

Holding onto the satchel, Myrtle laughed again when she had to use both hands to lift the bag. Apparently, it had never occurred to Addison to solve part of this awkward situation by helping her with the luggage. "I am not a fragile English rose, Addison," she added with amused exasperation for his continued insistence over such a trifling matter. "Oops," she said when she almost tripped over a stone on the dirt road. "More a sturdy—urk, if somewhat clumsy—boxwood hedge." When the Englishman did not return her humor, she sighed, grateful for the sound of approaching horses. "It appears, Captain Barrington, your men have arrived just in time."

Dressed in red coat and breeches similar to Addison's, a young lieutenant gave a smart salute to his superior. "Sir, there is a storm coming up, and we should return to the fort as soon as you are ready. These stone-covered hills get more treacherous at nightfall. We shot one of those heathen Scots stealing food from our supply wagon yesterday."

"Very good, Lieutenant Johnson," Addison replied. "My carriage will follow you presently." The same height as Myrtle, Addison turned around to speak with her. "You will write to let me know how you are doing, my lady?"

At the moment she wished they were alone so she could tell him the prospect of becoming his wife appealed to her very much right now. After his frank comments about this area and the late laird, she was feeling more apprehensive about taking on this task alone. Yet responsibilities were to be faced, not run away from, her father'd often told her. Of course, he'd managed to escape his sharp-tongued wife, Barbara, often enough. She looked down at the leather satchel at her feet. "Yes, I will write you as soon as I get settled."

"And keep my picture on your night table, so I'll know you will think of me just before you sleep?"

A pinkish hue washed across her face. "Yes." Myrtle felt uncharacteristically small right now. "Thank you for your escort. It made the journey more pleasant. Your kindness meant a great deal to me." She held out her right hand, unable to keep it from trembling.

Formally, Addison bent down and placed his lips briefly on the smooth brown leather covering the back of her fingers. "Please take care of yourself, Lady Myrtle," he whispered.

She attempted a reassuring smile. "I . . . I shall be fine," she added, with more bravado than she felt.

"Johnson," the Englishman said over his shoulder. "You brought my extra sidearm, as I ordered?"

Instantly the young lieutenant was at his superior's side, handing him a flintlock pistol.

"Here, I want you to take this. It's been with me since I entered His Majesty's service. God willing, you won't need it, but by having it you'll allay my fears."

"But I . . . I've never even shot one of these things." She stepped back, only to have the captain follow.

He placed the silver handle of the pistol in her hands. "Since you have set your feet upon this ill-advised course, my lady, it is time you learned. Take it," he commanded, for the first time addressing her in the demeanor of a military officer.

"Very well, since you insist."

Addison had ball and powder brought out and showed her how to load the pistol.

Then, standing in the middle of the road, holding a loaded pistol, a scuffed portmanteau at her feet, Lady Myrtle Prescott watched as Addison's carriage

33

and his men made their way back down the steep hill.

When the English soldiers were out of sight, Myrtle turned to the Scot. He was watching her. "You are Angus Thomson?" she asked politely.

The older man nodded. "Aye. We'd best be off, lass."

She agreed. As it was clear Angus still expected her to carry one of the bags, she grabbed for the piece of luggage at her feet. The physical activity helped restore her usual good humor. "In my spare time I shoe horses and fell trees."

Angus blinked, then peered over his shoulder at the taller Englishwoman. He read the twinkle of mischief in her bright blue eyes, just before she screwed her face up with determination to begin lugging the bag behind her, while still holding awkwardly on to the pistol the redcoat had given her. No one had told him this Sassenach possessed a sense of humor, he mused. Then he brushed the thought aside, reminding himself he, Katie, and Gavin had their orders.

When Mr. Thomson made no attempt to assist her into the rickety carriage, she bit back a request for help. It was now clear she was as welcome as plague. So be it, she decided, raising her chin. Used to fending for herself, it would be no different here.

Nearly falling forward in a heap on the dusty floorboards in the process, the Englishwoman heaved the bag into the opened coach, then grabbed the sides of the dilapidated conveyance and hoisted her frame inside.

Her cheeks pink from exertion, she managed to inquire, "How long will it take to reach the castle, Mr. Thomson?"

"As long as it takes," came the dour Scot's answer.

"Oh, I thought it took an hour more than that."

Without comment on Myrtle's rejoinder, the Scot tossed her second bag on the bare wooden seat across

34

from her, slammed the door shut, then went back atop the coach. With a speed less prudent for the state of the carriage and the threatening weather, let alone his female passenger, Angus flicked his driving whip near the ears of the two horses, and they went storming up the perilous road.

By the time they reached Kilmarock Castle, the rain pelted driver, horses, and carriage. Twice Myrtle had to get out to help dislodge the almost springless coach from the mire that bogged down the worn wooden wheels. However, she had little occasion to feel relieved when she walked up the gravel path to the crumbling stone steps that led to the entry hall of the castle. Her muddy shoes squished with every step.

"The Sinclair shut up most of the castle to save money," Angus told her without preliminaries. "Katie!" he shouted. "Where are ye, woman?"

A small, plump woman with gray hair tucked under a white pinner came from a room to their right. She was dressed in a blue wool gown with embroidered apron tied behind her waist. "Saint Andrew, protect us," she said aloud, then quickly crossed herself. "'Tis her, Angus." The older woman's shocked eyes took in Myrtle's appearance. "The one with eyes the color of the loch in summer, the straight brown hair. Your name, lass? What is your name?"

What the devil was going on here? While Myrtle knew she was no beauty even under the best conditions, why was this Scottish woman looking so terrified? "I am Lady Myrtle Prescott, and I—"

"God have mercy on us," interrupted the Scots-woman. "The name same as the symbol. I dinna think it would be a Sassenach."

Myrtle's slender chin jutted north for a second. "Madam, it has been a tiring journey. I assure you, I

35

mean you and your husband no harm. Despite my imposing appearance, most of my friends consider me rather gentle natured. Local children do not race from me in terror when they see me approach."

As if not hearing her, Katie addressed her husband again. "Gavin only said her name was Lady Sinclair."

"Surely Mr. Mackenzie told you I would be arriving tonight, and I wished to—"

"Angus, it is *her*, I tell ye."

"Well," Myrtle grated as the woman's odd behavior continued, "since we've established that I am here and the torrent of mud and water I am leaving on this floor is no illusion, let us all assume it is me, shall we?" She took a deep breath to squelch her growing irritation. "I assume you are the housekeeper, Katie Thomson?"

Katie's eyes seemed to clear as she took in Myrtle's bedraggled appearance. "Aye, lass, I am that now."

The younger woman's features relaxed with the faint hope she'd finally met the first friendly soul in Scotland. But then Katie appeared to remember something, and Myrtle saw the warmth in her eyes depart.

The woman gave Myrtle a mechanical curtsy. "The room is ready, my lady. Your maid will be lodged next to you."

"I have no maid with me at this time, Mrs. Thomson." Right now, Myrtle had no desire to go into the details of why Bess wasn't with her. "Perhaps you can recommend a local girl I might employ as my maid."

"Well," Katie offered in a more friendly tone, "Fiona Ross is the best seamstress in these parts. The Rosses always served the ladies of Kilmarock Castle as personal maids, and—"

"Be still, woman," Angus ordered. "That traitor bitch Fiona is nae fit to return to this castle. She and

36

her devil's spawn can stay right where they are."

Myrtle saw Katie open her mouth to protest, then look meekly at the floor. "My room?" the English-woman repeated, to guide these two away from the obviously heated topic of some Sinclair clanswoman out of favor. Of course, right now she wasn't exactly Queen of the May with these Scots, either, Myrtle reminded herself.

"Aye," Angus said, "and 'tis the best room in the place."

Knowing the importance of first impressions, Myrtle forced herself to smile. "Thank you both for looking after things until I could make the trip here. I understand Mr. Mackenzie will be showing me about the estate in the morning." When both Thomsons looked uncomfortable, she added, "He did receive the letter with my instructions?"

Angus spoke first. "Aye, he got it. Said he'd see you at seven. Of course, this is our rainy season. The weather doesn't look too promising. Gavin said if ye feel unable to go aboot, since the ride is long and hard, he'd understand."

Myrtle understood all too well. She looked across at the deceased laird's manservant. "I shall be ready to inspect *my* property no matter the weather. Now, if you will kindly direct me to my room, I would like to wash before retiring."

For the first time Angus looked pleased. "That we will." Katie followed behind them.

Led downstairs, she made no comment that most master bedrooms were usually above stairs from the main floor. However, after Angus opened a heavy oak door to reveal a dismal, dank room, it took all her self-restraint not to voice her shock and outrage. Instinctively, she now realized these two were testing her mettle. Well, if they wanted her to beg for simple courtesy, they'd have a long wait, she decided. Not even the help in the scullery at home had such deplorable quarters. She gave her new servants an icy nod of acceptance. "This will do. Goodnight."

It was clear Katie Thomson was uneasy about the arrangements. She looked at her husband, but his scowl seemed to quell anything she was going to say. Both servants left.

As she closed the door, Myrtle was disappointed to notice there wasn't even a lock on it. The room was lighted by only a single candle on a table. Her nose wrinkled as the musty scent of damp linen, stale air, and something she didn't even want to contemplate assailed her. Unfastening her wet traveling cape, she folded it neatly over the straight wooden chair next to the rough oak table that slanted to the right, the result of the fact that two legs were shorter than the other. She put her ruined bonnet and gloves on the table. There was also a wooden crate. The dresser? she asked herself. After pacing over to the low cot with its straw mattress, she held up the greasy quilt between two cold fingers. Yes, she knew there was little money, but couldn't they have at least cleaned this . . . cellar room for her?

Her gaze went back to the door. Looking down, Myrtle almost expected to see a square cutout where the prisoner's food could be shoved at her across the wet floor. A squeak, followed by a scurrying sound along the edge of the gray blocks of stone at her feet, made her vault back. Was it a mouse or a rat? Hiking up her skirts in her hands, she walked to the center of the room and forced her thoughts elsewhere. A chipped basin and a pitcher with the handle missing were on the table. There was no water, of course. Her stomach rumbled, reminding her she'd had little to eat since breakast many hours ago. The sound seemed to echo off the damp stone walls. Angus and Katie hadn't even offered her a cup of tea. "No bread and water for the prisoner," she quipped aloud. Talking to herself was a habit she'd often used since childhood to steady her nerves in times of difficulty.

She went over to one of her suitcases and managed to get it on the bed. Were the Thomsons living like this, too? she wondered. Katie had been wearing a homespun dress with an apron over it. Their clothes appeared clean, if not fancy. What was going on here? After opening her bags, the Englishwoman decided the room's condition made unpacking implausible. Things would stay cleaner and drier in the leather cases. She took out a bar of her favorite soap and a linen towel Bess had had the presence of mind to pack, bless her. Then she grabbed the empty pitcher and the lighted candle from the table.

After opening the door, Myrtle went carefully back up the stairs to the hallway. She listened and looked about, trying to ascertain the best direction. Right led only down a dark hallway. She turned around and headed back. God, what a desolate place, she thought, feeling another wave of homesickness for the English countryside. A clap of thunder from the storm outside made her jump. It was then she saw light under a door ahead. Taking a deep breath, her hands still occupied with the pitcher and the candle, Myrtle raised her right foot and banged on the wooden door with the tip of her muddy shoe.

She heard voices, hasty movements; a dog barked, then the door opened. Angus had his outer coat off and Katie, also still dressed, peered around her husband.

A huge gray dog bared his teeth at Myrtle. Instead of stepping back, she walked slowly into the room, keeping her blue eyes on the long-haired beast, who stood with his wary brown eyes focused on her.

"Robbie does nae take to people much," Angus explained. "He tolerates me and my wife. The Sinclair was the only one he cared aboot. Near broke the beastie's heart when the laird died."

39

"Poor thing," Myrtle said, instantly feeling sorry for the wild dog. It was then she noticed how uncomfortable Angus and Katie appeared.

As well they might, Myrtle thought, for she saw blazing logs in the red brick fireplace, and over-stuffed chairs on the worn but clean rug over the wooden floor. A plate of ham and cheese sat on the clean mahogany table, and the smell of baked bread permeated the cozy room. Steeling herself, she managed to show little of her feelings, a habit learned in childhood dealing with her demanding step-mother. "Excuse me for bothering you again," she explained politely. "I wonder if you could tell me where I might obtain some water to wash my face before I retire."

Something in her manner must have touched a chord in Katie, for she brushed past her husband and bade Myrtle sit down while she got the water from the next room herself. It was clear the Thomsons' bedroom was in the adjoining room. Everything here was clean and orderly.

Angus said nothing while Myrtle sat on an overstuffed chair, the lighted candle still in her right hand. Blast them; they knew by the terms of the sale contract she could never fire the Thomsons or that Mackenzie fellow. It was her father's doing. Looking at Angus now, she knew he expected her to rant and rave, or demand to be given a better room. Damned if she would, she told herself, the Prescott pride floating to the surface. Never would she ask these two Scots or any of the Sinclairs, alive or dead, for anything.

Used to animals, to keep herself occupied while she waited, Myrtle called the dog. After a few uneasy seconds, Robbie sauntered over to her. She let it sniff her left hand. Then she slowly petted its broad head. With more confidence, Myrtle began scratching him behind his shorter ear. "Why, Robbie, you are not as

40

ferocious as you look. You're just a big puppy at heart."

Robbie thumped his tail loudly on the floor while making soft whimpering noises of pleasure at being fussed over.

When Katie returned with the pitcher of warm water, Myrtle stood up, thanked her, then went toward the door, which Angus opened for her.

"Dinna worry if ye hear the Sinclair's ghost, or see anything not of this world," Angus said by way of a parting word.

When her empty stomach gave a loud growl, the Englishwoman squelched her embarrassment and gave Angus a measured look. "If he's got a muffin in his sporran, the laird's ghost may get more than he's bargained for if he tangles with me this night." Back straight, Lady Myrtle Prescott swept regally out into the cold hallway.

"All the congeniality of Newgate," she muttered, stomping back down to her quarters. "Laird's ghost? They'd have to pay a specter to haunt this dreary pile of stones."

After washing her face and hands, Myrtle decided the conditions warranted sleeping fully attired on the wooden chair. She donned her woolen cape again. With the door open, she marched about the room and was rewarded to see two gray mice scamper out into the corridor. Then Myrtle shut the door quickly, assured she was now the only live thing in the room.

It took over an hour of fidgeting on the uncomfortable chair before she dozed for a few minutes, only to be awakened with a start when she heard sounds emanating from the walls.

The rattle of chains was followed by another low moan. She clutched her fingers about her arms.

When she peered out the door, she saw nothing. After placing the candle on the flagstones at her feet, she struggled and pushed, and managed to get the

41

wooden table up against the closed door. At least if anyone tried to come into the room, she'd be alerted. As the moaning continued, Myrtle went to her second bag and pulled out the flintlock pistol that Addison had insisted she take. For the first time, she felt reassured by a firearm.

"Leave Castle Kilmarock before you die," said the rasping voice that seemed to come from the other side of the room. Then the moaning started again, this time behind her. The sound changed direction. She sat back in the chair, the pistol in her right hand. After a while it got too heavy and she rested it on her lap. Her head slumped against her shoulder when things grew quiet.

Once again it seemed she was only allowed but a moment's repose before an unholy sound screeched through the room. "Mother of God," she swore, jerking awake so quickly that she dropped the flintlock pistol on the floor. Thankfully, it did not go off. Bagpipe music? she asked herself, first thinking she was losing her wits. Yet the notes were in no way related, just a cacophony of loud, whining noises. "By hell, that's enough," she said aloud.

Grabbing the candle, Lady Myrtle stormed from the room and back to the Thomsons' door upstairs. So, she fumed, they'd thought with their cheap theatrics to harass her into leaving.

It seemed a long while before anyone came to the door.

However, when Katie Thomson opened it, Myrtle was taken aback to see the sleepy visage of an old woman. Angus came stumbling out in a dressing gown tied hastily over his long nightshirt. It was clear both had been fast asleep. They could hardly have been carrying on below stairs with chains and bagpipes. She felt a fool and could see Angus's pleased expression, as if he expected her to cry about ghosts any second. Instead she asked, "Are there any other servants living in this castle?"

"Nay, my lady. Angus and I are the only ones who live at Kilmarock Castle now," Katie answered.

Despite herself, Myrtle wanted to believe the woman. She read something in Katie's eyes when she realized Myrtle was still in her traveling clothes, but the Englishwoman was too upset for concessions this night. She straightened her back. "It must have been the storm. I thought I heard a voice. Sorry I bothered you. Goodnight."

Katie's glance reproached her husband when they were alone. "'Tis no Christian way to treat the lassie. Did ye nae see the fear in her eyes when first I opened the door?"

Angus put a bony arm about his wife's plump shoulders. "Dinna fret, woman. The laird suffered much from these English. He's no one but us to count on. Those redcoats would kill him if they knew the truth. Besides," he teased, "you've already lied for him tonight."

Pulling away, Katie looked affronted. "I dinna lie. I said we are the only servants in the castle. 'Tis the truth. Ian Sinclair is no one's servant."

"Aye," Angus agreed with a smile. "I give ye that."

Chapter Three

God, she'd played right into their hands, Myrtle told herself after arriving back at her room. Her show of weakness was probably just what they'd hoped for. Plopping down in the straight-backed chair once more, the silver-handled pistol across her lap, Myrtle suddenly wished she'd demanded some kindling from Angus Thomson. Of course, if she got desperate, she could always put the table out of its misery and give it a Viking funeral to warm herself.

While she believed Katie about there being no other servants in the castle, wasn't it possible one of the clansmen had snuck in to frighten her? Probably just the culprit who'd scared the daylights out of Tom and Cyril. Neither of them had lasted one evening in this place. Well, she told herself, soon she'd get to the bottom of these events. However, she could not think about it tonight. Sheer exhaustion won out after a few restless minutes, and she scrunched her body into a ball on the wide seat of the wooden chair, with her hands holding onto the only two remaining slats at the back.

When she heard something scurry across the stone floor, Myrtle peered down to spot a tan-coated mouse near the candle on the gray flagstones. He sat up on his hindquarters and gave a squeak. The animal must have remained when she'd chased his kin away earlier. Too fatigued to get up again and haul the table from the door to toss the unwelcome guest out, Myrtle gave the small creature a baleful stare. "As long as you don't play the bagpipes out of tune, you can stay." Then she closed her eyes. At least the "ghost," or whoever it had been, had ceased making noise.

It was after three in the morning when Ian Sinclair made his way down to the new owners' quarters. Silently and easily he managed to open the door and squeeze his muscular frame into the damp room. Without making a sound, he hoisted the square table in his large hands, lifted it out of the way, then set it down quietly to his right. He wanted to get a look at this Englishwoman. At his orders, Gavin had found out all he could in his travels about the area. It seemed this Sassenach was wealthy and arrogant; she intended to dispose of Sinclair lands quickly to the highest bidder, then expel all the tenants from their crofts. Before the ink dried on the bill of sale, they said she'd be back in her town house in London.

The mouse stirred near his boot. "Come on, Mortimer," he whispered, bending down. Ian picked up his pet with care, then stood up to slip Mortimer into the soft lining of his coat pocket. "Guess you didn't frighten the lass, either."

Curse Jonathan Prescott, Sinclair thought, his fingers tightening on the candlestick he'd retrieved from the floor. The dead earl had betrayed him. Prescott had not sent a champion, a man of strength and honor, to look after his clansmen. Instead, he'd sent his English daughter, the same one Prescott had hinted was such trouble to him. What a fool he'd been to believe Jonathan, curse his soul to Hades.

46

Never again would he trust anyone English, he promised himself.

It only proved he'd been right to arrange his death to comply with the King's demand that he leave Scotland forever. How could Prescott or the King imagine he'd abandon the Sinclairs to the whims of any Englishman? They'd left him no choice but to become a man of shadows, never leaving the castle except at night. The money still came from Prescott's estate to pay the English taxes, but now would that stop with the arrival of this woman?

Jonathan's "champion," the Scot mused with bitterness . . . he looked down at the girl sleeping in the chair. He had to go around to see her face, for she was curled up like a barn cat near a hearth. He saw pale skin, long brown hair that billowed about her shoulders, a straight nose, and spiky dark lashes fanned against dark smudges under her eyes. It was those rings under her eyes that nudged him for a moment. She seemed in need of rest. And her dreams were not happy ones if he could read the strain distorting the creamy smoothness of her face. Was her conscience bothering her about her greedy plans against the Scots? he hoped. Yes, she deserved every inhospitable act he'd planned. Yet . . . When he heard a soft cry and looked back to see her troubled features, he found himself replacing the candle on the table before returning to her. Keeping his eyes on her face, Ian took the pistol from her lap and placed it on the table.

He was a fool, he told himself. Yet the Scot reached about her shoulders carefully, then placed his left arm under the expanse of petticoats, wool gown, and traveling cape. Holding her against his chest, he walked slowly over to the cot. For a second he felt something gnaw inside when he spotted the rag covering the poorly made cot, but he thought her traveling cloak and clothes would keep her more

47

comfortable here than on the chair. Actually, he'd never expected her to stay the night in this room. Her two employees had lasted but one hour in the better rooms upstairs before they'd gone racing from the fortress, convinced the brutal ghost of Ian Sinclair was going to murder them in their beds. It amazed him when Katie and Angus told him Myrtle had not spoken a word of complaint about this treatment so far.

When the lass stirred against his chest, Ian bent his head. The faint scent of tea roses greeted him. For an instant he wanted to soothe her, whisper she was safe; yet he did not. Katie had to be wrong about her dreams of a blue-eyed lass. He didn't believe in fey or ghosts. The woman in his arms was his enemy; it was all he was certain of now. She'd come here to destroy the Sinclairs.

Ian placed the sleeping girl on the cot, relieved when she murmured something, then settled to a clearly more comfortable position on her side. He took a critical look at her from this new angle. She was tall, with a buxom figure, from the feel of her. After a restive movement toppled her cloak to the floor, he could not suppress an appreciative grin at the outlined view of a well-formed bottom. She made a shivering motion and Ian went over automatically to retrieve her cloak. He wrapped it about her.

Why had Prescott betrayed him? he shouted inwardly. Instead of a champion, he'd sent his pampered English daughter to ruin the Sinclairs. By God, Ian told himself, he'd use every means available to scare this Sassenach wench from Kilmarock Castle. He heard the dark-haired girl whimper in her sleep. Well . . . starting tomorrow, after she'd had this one night's rest.

Going to the door, Ian told himself he had no choice. The Sinclairs were his responsibility, and he would protect his clansmen with his life. It was all he had left to give them.

The next morning Lady Myrtle, disconcerted, found herself on the cot with her pistol placed on the table next to her. How she'd gotten there or the table had come away from the door, she had no idea. Angus didn't seem strong enough to have lifted her without waking her. But who was lurking about? Was it the same fellow who'd serenaded her with that eerie bagpipe solo during the night?

Dressed in riding boots, wool skirt, and gray riding jacket, felt tricorn under her arm, the English girl sniffed appreciatively as the delightful aroma of frying ham assailed her. Upstairs, when the dish of weak tea and stale oatcake was offered her by Katie with an almost apologetic expression, Myrtle said nothing.

After taking part of this meager breakfast, she rose and went out to the entrance hall. In daylight things looked a little better, but not much. It was clear, though the late owner had tried to bring some parts of the house into the eighteenth century with upholstered furniture, molded plaster ceilings, brocade draperies, and rugs covering the wood floors, during the last few years things had gone unrepaired. There were numerous outlines on the walls where paintings had been removed, obviously to pay the bills.

She jumped when the entry door in front of her crashed open. A brawny Scot with long gray hair about his shoulders stalked into the keep as if he owned the place. He was dressed in worn brown breeches, laborer's shirt, frayed coat, and scuffed black boots. His full gray beard covered his cheeks and chin, except where the jagged line of a scar ran from temple, across the wide bridge of his nose, to end down the left side of his face.

When she realized the bold fellow was looking her

up and down, Myrtle allowed him to see her displeasure. From her father's description, she knew this had to be Gavin Mackenzie, the trusted second-in-command of Ian Sinclair. "In future, Mr. Mackenzie, you will kindly knock before entering this—my home." She refused to be intimidated by the bearded giant.

Frowning, Mackenzie stared down at her. "Aye, but ye must remember, 'tis a verra long time since we had any gentry within these walls. Ye still intend to ride oot this morning?"

"I do."

"'Tis fixin' to rain. Ye'll get soaked within an hour, then I'll just have to haul ye back here. I've nay patience with blubbering females."

Her expressive eyes turned to blue chips. "Then I promise, you shall not have to haul me home. Now, let us be off. I assume you have a horse for me?"

"Aye, but I doubt ye'll like Sian. We have no docile mares for a lady's canter, like in Hyde Park on a Sunday."

"Mackenzie," warned her ladyship with tight control, "cease that condescending tone if you wish to stay in my employ, my late father's signed contract with you notwithstanding. As long as the bloody beast has four legs, I shall be able to ride him. Do I make myself clear?"

Surprise showed for a brief second in the Scot's dark eyes. "Aye, my lady. Seems yer not like those sheep-herding Knoxes with barley water in their veins."

Puzzlement showed on her face. "Knoxes?"

"Aye," said Mackenzie. "Clan Knox, the Sinclair enemies for years. If ye ever see those oak-wearing Knoxes in the forest, run."

"They wear oak leaves?" She hadn't meant to sound so prudish, but there it was.

50

Gavin gave an impatient snort. "Insignia on the bonnet is an oak leaf for the Knoxes. They're a weasely sort of bunch, and ye'd best never turn yer back on them, for those Knoxes would just as soon slit yer gullet as ask ye for porridge." He reached into the sheath of the leather belt around his waist and pulled out a black-handled dagger in his beefy right hand. He made a slicing motion in the air, clearly as a demonstration.

"Hmm," was all Myrtle would say about rival Clan Knox. Right now she had the same trepidation about Clan Sinclair.

A few hours later, Myrtle had to admit, while she expected a cool welcome from her new tenants, she had not anticipated this open hostility from all the men, women, and even the children. As Gavin and two of his sons led the way up the winding, rocky terrain of Sinclair lands, she wondered why they didn't realize she was here to see they were taken care of, not to harm them. Her purpose today was to gain information of what was needed so she could formulate a logical plan of action. Yet the treatment she'd received so far shouted they wanted nothing but her absence. As she made a careful inspection of the people, livestock, and cottages, Myrtle made brief notes with a wooden pencil in a small notebook so that later she could use quill and ink to write more detailed listings in the leather journal in her luggage at the castle.

And there was much to do. Stone and sod cottages had thatched roofs needing repair; there were only a few emaciated-looking cattle, and the clansmen were in tattered rags, the children listless from lack of food as they stared wide-eyed at the Englishwoman their parents had obviously told them was their enemy. Myrtle asked pointed questions of Mackenzie and his two handsome sons, Andrew and Lachlan. Both dark-haired young men, only a year or two older than

51

her, smiled at her once, before a gruff word in Gaelic from their father returned their attentions to the road ahead.

When the rain began to fall, Myrtle's equanimity became more strained. What else could happen? she asked herself, getting a firmer hold on her horse. The feisty stallion pawed the earth, evidently wishing to pick up the pace. Not the best horsewoman, she would have preferred a little mare, not Sian. The Gaelic word for "storm" suited him. With difficulty, she tightened her leather-covered fingers on the straps.

Stopping for a second, she made more notes. "Yes," she said aloud, "the roads are in a deplorable condition, more cattle will be needed this spring. I shall want to hire all the able workers you can recommend to begin the repairs on the croft roofs as soon as the weather clears. You must tell me how much seed we will need for the first planting. Barley and oats are fine, but if we add potatoes, turnips, and wheat, it will help supplement our diet, along with rotating the crops. Those measures increased the yield at my Chelmsford farm. I have people in Edinburgh and England waiting for my letter of how much and what I need. They will send the raw materials to us quickly. I made preliminary arrangements before I left London."

She could not tell what Mackenzie was thinking, but he growled something to his sons, then all three men raced ahead when the rain turned into a downpour. As they neared a denser wooded area, Myrtle wanted to hurry to catch up with the others, but prudence made her keep Sian's pace slower to control the irksome black devil. "You ride ahead, that's right," she shouted outrageously. "You may lead the way." Giving Mr. Mackenzie permission to desert her made her feel better. The scowl the elder Scot shot over his shoulder increased her satisfaction.

She gave him a jaunty wave. "No, no, don't wait for me. I insist you ride ahead." This ill-mannered Scot had a surprise coming if he thought she'd crumble at the thought of riding through a dark forest by herself. Little did they know she's grown up used to adversity and rejection. However, thoughts of the past as well as this recent treatment, including lack of sleep, were beginning to take a toll on her usual even-temperedness. Her father had to be wrong, she told herself. Not one Scot had shown her an ounce of kindness, let alone the briefest civility, since her arrival.

Suddenly, something sharp and hard hit her left temple. It happened so quickly she never knew where it came from. The Mackenzies were out of sight. Thick shrubs and trees could hide anything. One minute she was on Sian's back, the next she went crashing to the muddy ground, landing hard on her right side. Flashing lights and searing pain shattered within her skull. It took several minutes before she realized what had occurred. The rain pelting her face was tinged with red as it ran down the left side of her face to splash the front of her wool riding skirt. At first she could not move or call for help. A buzzing sound reverberated in her ears. Her tricorn was a few feet away, covered with mud, ruined beyond salvage, so she made no attempt to retrieve it. When she saw the heavy, sharp stone next to her leg, where it had obviously fallen, fire surged through her veins. She grabbed the offending rock and tossed it hard, then heard it hit the base of a tree. Ahead she made out the three riders returning. At least one of them had presence of mind to look behind to see the new owner wasn't following in the distance.

Or were they returning to be certain she was dead? Myrtle wondered, sparks of fear and rage warring within her.

Lachlan Mackenzie was at her side instantly.

She almost thought she saw concern in his dark eyes. "Och, lass, let me help ye. Da," he shouted to his father above the pelting rain, "I think she's hurt bad."

If Gavin was surprised, he showed no emotion. "Come, we must head back to the castle."

Had these Mackenzies planned this "present" for her? Myrtle brushed Lachlan's hands away. "I can see to myself, thank you," she said with barely controlled fury. By God, she'd had enough of these Scots. Struggling to her feet, she ignored the pain on the left side of her head, the bruised right side of her body, and walked slowly over to Sian: This time she mounted him astride, arranging her sodden skirt about her as best she could. "Hold still, you damn black nuisance," she snapped at the stallion, "or I'll turn you into a gelding right here." She was in no mood to allow more rambunctious behavior. Sian appeared to recognize the tone if not the words, for his ears pressed back against his head, and then he quieted and stood still.

"That's better," Myrtle said, briefly patting the horse's muscular neck. "Now, then, let us proceed," she ordered. "I will finish this inspection of my lands."

For the first time Gavin looked as flustered as his two sons. "Things have changed, my lady, and we must return to—"

"Damn it to hell, Mackenzie, nothing has changed," she countered in a voice that must have carried to the next farm. "The crofts still need fixing, the roads need repair, the marshes still need draining, it is still raining, and I intend to finish this inspection. The only difference is that now I have an abominable headache." Without another word, she pressed her legs to Sian's flanks and went charging ahead of the three astonished Scots.

For the next three hours in the rain, Myrtle forced

54

herself to continue her detailed inspection of her property. If any of the wary tenants felt shocked to see their new owner riding astride, mud-covered, and hatless, with a bloody and bruised face, they said nothing.

Doggedly, Myrtle kept pace with the three men as they made their way back to the castle. After sliding off Sian's back, she refused to allow the young men or their father to assist her up the stairs to the entryway. "You must tell me in future if there is a back door to the cellar. It will save me a few steps if I can enter through a servant's entrance to my suite," she added with asperity.

"The Thomsons have put the lass in the cellar?" Lachlan demanded of his father.

"See to the horses," growled Gavin. "Help your brother," he ordered the equally astonished Andrew.

Without a backward glance, Myrtle went to her quarters. Every muscle in her body ached, and she felt hot, despite the chilly air of the cellar and her sodden attire.

"Then she says, 'And the only difference is that now I have an abominable headache.'" Gavin Mackenzie could not hide his admiration. "For a Sassenach, the lass shows a lot of mettle."

Ian stood up. "I had not counted on this. Are you sure none of my tenants threw that stone? I gave specific instructions she was not to be harmed in any way."

"Ye know they've always done as I've asked in the past. Of course, your death tore the heart oot of them. And the talk in the pub was all aboot the pampered English bitch and how she was going to drive us off the land."

Ian frowned. It went against his code to have any woman, even an English one, attacked this way. His intent was only to frighten her into returning to England. Gavin was correct; she could have been killed. "Please try to find out all you can about the incident. Now, where is the lass?"

Gavin shrugged his broad shoulders and leaned closer to the blazing fire to warm himself. "Would nae hear of anyone helping her. Och, she dinna look verra good, if ye ask me, but the lass is stubborn, I'll say that. And braver than many a Scotswoman, for I canna list one who would have insisted on continuing that ride in the pouring rain. Think the blow to her pate rattled her wits?"

A white full mask over his face, a powdered white wig covering his reddish-blond hair, Ian Sinclair went quickly down the stairs toward the cellar. As instructed, Katie followed close behind. If the girl was in as bad a condition as Gavin had hinted, pride or not, she needed attention.

Ian opened the door slowly, then motioned Katie to enter ahead of him. "Wiser if the lass sees a familiar face first."

Katie Thomson went into the room. "Lady Myrtle?" she called in her motherly tone. "Lass?"

Standing with her back to the threshold, her hands pressed against the edge of the rough table, Myrtle turned about quickly. "Katie, I told Gavin I do not require—" Dizziness assailed her. She took a step forward, not aware there was someone standing behind the door with Katie. "I can see to myself." However, her body had a mind of its own. Hot and lightheaded, Myrtle never felt the strong arms that caught her, saving her from hitting the gray flagstones at her feet.

Through the holes in his white leather mask, Ian saw the blood running down the side of the girl's pale face. He looked at the filthy bed, then cursed pointedly in French and Gaelic. "Come," he ordered Katie. "Sassenach traitor or not, she'll nae spend

56

another night in this dungeon of a room." Still holding the unconscious girl high against his chest, Ian left the room and moved swiftly up first one flight of stone steps, then the next that led to his rooms above. Katie followed more slowly behind him.

Entering his spacious rooms, the laird went immediately beyond the sitting room to the bedroom. He placed Myrtle in the center of the clean down coverlet.

His concern increased a few moments later when he felt the English girl's forehead. "God, she's burning up. Katie, please send Angus to fetch her luggage up here. There must be something we can put her in after we get her out of these wet clothes. And bring me the box of medical supplies. I'll clean the wound on her temple." Immediately he focused his attention on the bloody side of her face and saw the dark blotches on her right arm where her elbow-length sleeve ended. "Damn it," he cursed aloud, "if I catch the bastard who threw that stone, so help me, he'll feel my fist. She's just a lass, after all."

"'Tis what I tried to tell ye that first night she arrived," Katie countered, giving her employer a censuring look. "Men. Ye always think ye have the answers." Then she left to carry out the laird's directives.

A frightened moan came from the girl. She began babbling words he could not make out. Was she trying to ask for something? He bent his ear closer to her face to catch the word.

"Bar—barians," pushed its way between her cracked lips.

"Easy, lass, you are safe." He couldn't tell if she'd heard him. Yet part of him was relieved she was still unconscious. He'd taken the precaution of the mask tied behind his powdered wig, yet Ian felt suddenly ashamed for his earlier behavior. The Thomsons and

57

Gavin Mackenzie were following his orders. All the information he'd been able to glean about this woman led him to believe she meant to harm the Scots. They said she was nothing but a wealthy, cold-hearted bitch. Yet as he looked down at her on his bed right now, he began to wonder about the accuracy of all those reports.

He cleaned her face, tended to the deep gouge on the left side of her head, then bandaged it. Stitching was not needed, but she would require a few days in bed, at least. It was her fever that worried him most. He'd seen similar cases where the sickness settled in the lungs.

Angus returned with the lady's bags and left. Katie began undressing Myrtle, while Ian pawed through her two bags, searching for a bed gown. He pulled out a gray flannel garment. A cursory look through her belongings surprised him. He'd expected Paris frocks, a dozen trunks, at least two boxes of jewelry. For such a wealthy heiress, she'd only brought four rather dowdy gowns, three pairs of serviceable shoes, a wool traveling cape, two bonnets more suited to a dowager, writing paper, portable inkstand, quill pens, and a notebook. Her toiletries included bars of pleasant-smelling tea rose soap, but no pots of make-up, hair powder, or jewelry—the only nonessential item was a silver-framed picture.

Ian peered through the slits in his full mask at the small painting of a man in his late twenties, with powdered wig, the hazel eyes staring ahead, and a beaky nose. Dressed in the scarlet uniform of an English officer, was he that Addison fellow her father mentioned? A sweetheart? Obviously the lady's taste in men was as questionable as her discernment in choosing clothes. Well, none of this was his business, he told himself.

"Have ye found a bed gown for the lassie yet?" Mrs. Thomson asked.

Ian shoved the picture back in Myrtle's leather bag. "Yes, well, I suppose you could call it a nightgown." He held up the high-necked garment. "Reminds me, I must order more seed bags."

"Now, you step outside while I finish getting the lassie out of her clothes."

Amused, Ian obeyed the short, stocky woman who'd once been his nanny. "Really, Katie, you have nothing to fret about. My tastes run a little more colorful than English spinsters swathed in gray flannel." He chuckled at Katie's reproving scowl when he passed her on the way out.

After a few moments, Ian returned when Katie informed him he could come back into the room.

Still wearing the disguise that concealed his face and hair, in case Myrtle awakened, Ian said, "I'll take the first watch with our patient. You and Angus get some rest. I'm used to sleeping during the day, becoming a ruddy vampire. Run along, Katie, for it's clear the lass probably won't be in any condition to eat or talk tonight. She won't even know I'm here."

Katie nodded, accepting the logic of her employer's suggestion. "Poor wee lamb," she muttered, looking down at Myrtle. "I'm not usually wrong aboot people. I told ye she was the one in my dreams. It is her, I tell ye. I canna believe this woman would harm us."

The laird's usual congeniality with the woman became more difficult. "Please, Katie, dinna bring that up again. Gavin heard the truth, along with many of our clansmen. We musna let our guard doon. Too many lives are at stake to trust this Sassenach. She has the ear of King George, high connections at court—nay, we canna risk it. Only you, Angus, and Gavin know I'm alive. It must remain so."

Katie sniffed. "And dinna forget Jean Mackenzie."

Behind his mask, Ian smiled at the mention of

59

Gavin's seventeen-year-old daughter. "Aye, but I gave the black-eyed lass my word we'd never tell her father on her. The nosy one will keep my secret."

"Humph," said Katie, "that forward minx wraps ye and every other mon in the Highlands around her little finger." She looked down at the ashen-faced girl. "Has it ever occurred to ye this Englishwoman could help the Sinclairs?"

Ian shook his white-wigged head. "Never. My father's old friend mocks me with this 'champion' he sends." He could not keep the rancor from his voice. "By St. Andrew, it would take more than this young woman to save the Sinclairs. I tend her now only because her death would bring more English soldiers on our borders."

During the night, Ian sat in a wing chair by his patient's bed. He sponged her fevered face with a cool cloth and checked on the bandage to be sure the cut at her temple had stopped bleeding; mostly he sat watching her, trying to sort out his conflicting thoughts. He had warm tea with healing herbs ready, but not once did the ill woman open her eyes. She mumbled and tossed fretfully. He caught her dead father's name, but he could make little sense of her ravings. When she cried out again, obviously in the throes of some hideous nightmare, despite his resolve, the Scot found himself sitting on the edge of his bed and taking the English girl in his arms. He attempted to quiet her as he might treat an ill child of one of his tenants. "Shh, there now, nothing to be afraid of, wee kelpie. Don't fret, there's a good bairn. No one will harm you. I'm here."

"No, there is no one now. No one," she sobbed.

Ian continued to hold her. He rubbed her neck, the area behind her ears, as if his hands could show her he meant no harm. Then her thrashing stopped; he felt her begin to relax against his chest.

The dream was changing, Myrtle thought. Now

60

there was the feel of a strong chest covered by a soft linen shirt, a faint smell of oatmeal soap. Firm but gentle hands massaged her back, and a coaxing male voice spoke to her in a language she did not understand. But sometimes the pleasant voice said French and English words, too. It made her feel protected, something she'd not experienced in many years. Without protesting, she allowed herself to be settled back against the pillows. "Are you my guardian angel?" she murmured, still unable to make her way out of the fevered delirium. "Papa always said he would watch out for me, but I never believed him." She nestled deeper into the embroidered pillow under her head.

No, he told himself with humor, he was certainly no angel, yet when he answered the sick girl, he said, "I am whoever you want me to be. Now, go to sleep."

Hours later, he felt her face. The fever had broken during the long night, for her skin was now cooler. She stirred. "Rest now," he encouraged, "there's a good lass." He saw a slight smile curve the corners of her pink mouth. Myrtle snuggled deeper against the mattress. He could not help studying her again, this time in a different way. He noticed the gold highlights in the brown hair about her shoulders; the pale smoothness of her skin looked ethereal in the candlelight. Then he saw the white bandage once more. Just who was this Myrtle Prescott? How was he going to find out the truth? "And I'm a bloody ghost," he whispered aloud. In many ways, he lamented, he and Lady Myrtle were both alone.

Before dawn, Ian and Angus gathered up some of his belongings and moved a table, chair, and cot from below stairs into the secret space adjoining his own room, accessed by pressing a panel in his bedroom. Ian's great-grandfather had found the hidden room useful during previous troubles with the English. The narrow stone stairs he'd used last night led to the

61

other floors and outside the castle. Now the room served as a hiding place for the current laird.

Angus had already returned below stairs when Ian suddenly remembered the portrait in his bedroom. It was his mother's favorite of him, and Murdoch, his father, had made Ian promise never to sell it. Even with his disguise, Ian realized it would be wise to hide the picture elsewhere. He pressed the iron button to open the wooden wall panel to reenter his room. Good, she was still asleep. Katie would be arriving soon with her breakfast. Walking quietly over to the wall across from her bed, he tried to lift the heavy painting down. The wire proved difficult. He got a firmer grip on the ornately carved wooden frame.

"What are you doing?"

Ian wondered if she was still groggy enough for him to pull this off. He couldn't disclose his hiding place by racing away. Not moving, he answered with hesitation, "Angus told me to take it down. With all the talk of ghosts, he thought the picture of the deceased laird might give ye more bad dreams."

"Nonsense, a picture cannot harm anyone. Please leave it." The slight burr in the man's accent told her he was a Scot. She noticed he was dressed in simple blue breeches and work shirt. The white wig with something tied behind it confused her. "Who . . . who are you?"

Removing his hands from the portrait, Ian turned quickly to face her.

Myrtle gasped in horror as dreams and reality collided against her. In her weakened condition, all she could make out in the light from the dying embers of the fire was a hideous white mask with slits for eyes, nose, and mouth. She struggled forward and opened her mouth to scream, but no sound came out.

For the second time in two days, sturdy Lady Myrtle Prescott did something she'd never done in her life: she swooned, this time against ruffled pillows.

Now, after he'd given up all deliberate attempts to frighten her, the lass fainted from terror at a mere look from him. "Bloody hell," swore the laird of Kilmarock.

Chapter Four

Ian Sinclair raced out into the drafty hall to get Katie to minister to the fainted girl. He had to leave the troublesome portrait up, for the lass would probably demand to know where it went if he took it away now. If they kept their stories straight, the Thomsons might be able to convince the English-woman she'd merely dreamed seeing a frightening apparition try to steal the painting.

Tired after the long night, Ian pressed the panel to his hidden room after Katie arrived. His former nanny began clucking over the girl, while scolding Ian for his "brutish treatment in scaring the wee lamb." Without comment, Ian entered his hidden sanctuary, removed the wig and mask disguise, dropped on the cot, and fell asleep the minute his reddish-blond head hit the pillow.

By the second morning, Myrtle was a little stronger. Still not up to eating more than steaming porridge and tea, she nevertheless felt the need for some exercise and decided to investigate her new quarters. The canopied bed she occupied was as big as a parade ground. Four men the size of Gavin Mackenzie could have fit on it. Earlier, when Katie

Thomson had come to take the breakfast tray away and Myrtle had pressed her, the Scottish woman had told her Katie and Angus had managed to get her up here to the former laird's rooms after she fainted. The Englishwoman vaguely remembered someone standing near the other side of the room—she touched the white bandage at her temple. Had she been dreaming? The Thomsons now seemed chagrined about their former inhospitality. If this was their way of apologizing, she'd accept it without comment.

The blazing fire in the rose marble fireplace, along with the mountain of blankets covering her, made the room delightfully warm. Myrtle swung her flannel-covered legs slowly over the side of the bed and stood on the soft wool carpet covering the polished floorboards. Looking above the carved wooden headboard, she gasped to see the silver-handled dirk hanging on a leather sheath nailed to the wall—an odd ornament over a bed. Addison told her the Sinclairs were known as fierce warriors, all except Ian. She reached for her paisley shawl Katie must have placed on the bottom of the bed for her. After wrapping it about her shoulders, Myrtle walked over to investigate the portrait hanging over the fireplace. This morning Katie had answered her question, saying this was a painting of the late laird, Ian Sinclair, when he'd been about twenty-two.

Myrtle studied the large picture, noting the artist signature—"Allan Ramsay." It was a time before the tartan was outlawed, and the handsome young man stood dressed in dark green and black plaid, a badger-skin sporran on a silver chain about his waist. His leather belt held a sheath on the right hip that contained an intricately carved silver dirk with a red ruby at the center of the handle. It looked like the one she saw over the headboard. In the strong yet graceful fingers of his left hand, Ian held the claymore as if it weighed far less than fifteen pounds. The artist had painted the thick, heavy blade of the sword so that it gleamed in the sunlight. The top of a black-handled knife was visible at the edge of the late laird's plaid right stocking, above black leather shoes with silver buckles. The targe, a round wooden shield covered with leather and silver studs, rested against the base of an oak tree at the laird's feet. Yes, Myrtle thought, admiring the man's broad shoulders, narrow waist, and muscular legs, Ian must have been a formidable clan chieftain. His reddish-blond hair shone like a copper helmet beneath his round, flat highland bonnet. There was a sprig of something with blue-green leaves and white flowers attached to the wool cap. Katie told her this morning it was not the kilt but the choice of leaf in the bonnet that designated the clans, reinforcing what Gavin apparently meant about the oak leaves the Knoxes wore.

Yet it was the expression in Ian's eyes and the slight curve at the edge of his sensual mouth that intrigued Myrtle. To her, there was humor in those golden eyes. Lion eyes, she thought, then smiled. His right hand rested gently on Robbie's head, while the laird's fingers appeared to be rubbing one of the dog's mismatched ears. She sensed no brutal barbarian in this portrait. Yet Addison had told her Ian Sinclair was a cruel, over-indulged man without honor. It puzzled her.

Not able to explain it, Myrtle liked the feel of the former laird's rooms immediately. After walking slowly about the bedroom, she entered the dressing area before heading to Ian's sitting room. It was clearly a man's domain, with brown leather and sturdy oak furniture, yet there was a warm, welcoming feel about the rooms. A frayed blue and beige Oriental carpet lay on the floor. The small sofa and wing chair were covered in light blue damask. The material had been patched but was as clean and fresh as everything else in these rooms. The woodwork was

67

a lightly stained oak, the carved plaster ceiling painted white. Three large windows let in the morning sun. The room had a white marble fireplace and wooden shelves filled with books. Instantly the Englishwoman decided to use this room as her office. Still weak, she had to cut her tour short and return to bed.

Later that day, when she grew restless again, Myrtle put on her slippers and went over to the carved wooden bookcase against the left wall of the former laird's sitting room. She saw that many of the leatherbound volumes were in French, Italian, Greek, and Latin. Why had Addison said the deceased laird was ignorant, uncivilized? She pulled out one of the books. She could tell from the worn pages it had been read many times. Would a brutal warrior have a liking for Plato and Marcus Aurelius?

Before she returned the volumes to their proper places, the Englishwoman spotted two small books tucked behind the ones she'd retrieved. Reaching back, she took out the volumes. Oh, what was this? She plunked herself down on the carpeted floor. An unhurried translation of a few paragraphs from the first book made it impossible for her to hold back a giggle. Apparently the late earl of Kilmarock had had an affinity for French erotica. While she'd heard of such novels and her father's extensive library at home had always been open to her, never had Jonathan Prescott possessed such books. And there were a few illustrations, she noticed, her blue eyes rounding. They were well drawn, she admitted with an artist's critical eyes, but decidedly improper. There was a drawing of a broad-figured nymph, naked, her face thrown back in ecstasy as a very muscular Adonis adored her with his lips and hands. "Good Lord," Myrtle said aloud, intrigued and feeling delightfully wicked at such an unexpected find among the classics. Quickly she opened the second red-bound volume translated into English and titled *Lisette Meets the Pirate Prince.* "My, my," she said aloud, then placed her hand over her mouth to suppress another fit of giggles. This novel had even more painted pictures of full-figured ladies.

Still smiling, Myrtle rose stiffly from the floor and took the two books to her night table next to the bed. She would peruse them more thoroughly later. When she returned to the sitting room, she went over to a cherrywood writing desk with chair on the other side of the room. The brass-handled drawer was unlocked. She opened it. Only a thick leather volume was inside. Myrtle brought the book out and opened to the first page. Ian Sinclair's name appeared on the inside cover. There were entries and dates. After only a few minutes, she realized this was the late earl's diary. Odd, she'd never considered a man like Ian would take the time to write out his thoughts in a diary. These discoveries were at odds with what she'd learned earlier about the dead Scotsman. She needed to learn more about this elusive laird of Kilmarock if she was going to assist his clansmen. After sitting on the wooden chair, she began to read.

The early entries years ago were brief notes about hunting, fishing, and hawking with his two younger brothers. Ian liked playing a game with a leather ball and a wooden stick that was flat at one end. He called the game "golf." She smiled at the endearing things he wrote about her father and his yearly visits to them, then leafed through these and other pages about his enjoyable university years in Paris—bits of humor, everyday events, scattered entries when he was obviously busy with happy pursuits. Yet the years after his father had died and he'd become laird were difficult ones. From 1745 to 1746 the entries grew longer, darker. Was it that Ian had needed the catharsis of writing his troubled thoughts down during these painful months?

His younger brothers, Malcolm and Hugh, supported Charles Stuart's claim to the English throne. She read how frustrated Ian was that not only his younger brothers but many of his clansmen would not listen to his arguments that their small Sinclair clan could survive only if they remained neutral. With their men away, as the time increased, the rest of his clan needed more food, clothing, and the barest necessities. On April 16, 1746, five thousand weary, starving highlanders fought nine thousand English troops at Culloden moor. Later Ian wrote:

> *Gavin Mackenzie and three of my clansmen brought the bodies of Hugh and Malcolm home last week. I can hardly write about it even now. It is a wound that will not heal. And the manner of Hugh's death still tears at me.*

Myrtle's eyes smarted at the pain and grief visible in Ian's words. She held her mouth in horror at the entry about how the youngest, eighteen-year-old Hugh Sinclair, had been murdered after the battle was over. Ian had sold everything he could to feed his clansmen:

> *Today Jonathan Prescott arrives from London. The old men, women, and children cannot survive another winter without more food. Of the young men still with us, many are too ill to muster enough strength to attempt a cattle raid against the Lowlands. Jonathan is my last hope. I will do whatever is necessary to see that Clan Sinclair survives. Even death holds no horror for me now.*

So moved by the late laird's plight, Myrtle had to stop reading when her tears blinded her to the page. Faced with having to leave his beloved Scotland,

70

feeling despair over his brothers' deaths, knowing the threat of extinction of the clansmen he was sworn to protect, and then ordered by the King to leave his highlands forever—Myrtle finally understood why the desolate laird had killed himself. She only prayed she could fulfill the promise to her dying father. When she went to rub her aching forehead, her fingers brushed the bandage. It reminded her that the people she'd promised to protect despised her. How could she even hope to handle this task alone?

Without windows in his small quarters to help him gauge the time, Ian reached into his vest to pull out his pocketwatch. After midnight. It was now safe to move about the castle. Katie said the lass was feeling stronger, but was still too weak to get out of bed for very long. Yet, he'd observed wryly, the feisty Englishwoman had energy enough to prowl about her quarters and—God! he thought, and sat up on the cot. His diary! He'd been in such a hurry to get the injured woman up here, he'd had no time to take down the cursed picture, let alone remove his diary from the desk. Had he locked the drawer? He couldn't remember.

Taking the chance, Ian pressed the iron button against the wooden wall molding. The panel moved to the right, giving him clear access to his former bedroom. He could tell by her even breathing that it was safe, for the lass was asleep. Tiptoeing across the carpet in his stocking feet, he went to his sitting room. When he pulled back the unlocked drawer, he found it empty. Where the devil was his diary? He walked back to his bedroom and looked down at the young woman asleep in his bed. Her color was better tonight. There were still dark smudges under her eyes, but the clean bandage across the wound at her temple proved the cut was no longer bleeding. When

71

she stirred, the Scot realized he couldn't risk staying in the room a second longer. He spotted the books and his diary on the nightstand but dared not risk reaching across the girl to get the books on the other side. He could tell when her eyes fluttered he had only seconds to get out of here.

Racing for the open panel, Ian just made it before Myrtle sat up. He left the panel open just a crack and saw her get slowly out of bed. She had to hold onto the heavy wooden post of the bedframe to keep herself upright.

"Is someone there?" Myrtle demanded, the hair at the back of her neck ruffling against her skin. She touched the bandage on the left side of her face. She'd been dreaming again about that hideous white monster, the hellish demon without a face. "Who's out there? Answer me."

Ian tried what worked before. He moaned that eerie way, imitating his ghost voice. Luckily, he'd thought to bring up the chains when he'd moved in here the other night, still intent on getting this unwelcome guest to leave. But he stifled a lurid curse when his stocking-clad toe hit the side of the low bed in his impatience to grab the chains off the table. He rushed back toward the nearly-closed panel, but this time he went to the opposite side of the room to face a different direction.

It was that sound again, those clanking chains, followed by the low moan. Uneasy, yet refusing to admit defeat, Myrtle forced herself to walk toward the sound. "Who are you?" she demanded again. "Answer me, I say."

Nothing.

"I do not believe in ghosts," she tossed to the four walls, almost wondering if she was losing her senses at such an illogical gesture. "I'm not afraid of you."

"Liar," came a low masculine voice, followed by a wicked chuckle. Then, from another part of the room came a growled order: "Get back into bed!"

Genuinely terrified now, Myrtle bounded back automatically to the huge fourposter and brought the down coverlet up to her nose. She kept the lighted candle at her bedside, unable to explain why she couldn't blow it out. There are no ghosts, she told her logical mind once more. Yet how could she explain the moaning, the chains, and the bagpipe music she'd heard two nights before in that cellar room when Angus and Katie Thomson were fast asleep upstairs? And the same voice just now came from different parts of her room. Was the castle haunted by the dead laird's ghost, as everyone said?

Though she was tired, her usually calm nerves were too frayed for her to go back to sleep. Myrtle sat up shivering, despite the mound of covers surrounding her in the large bed. Did the ghost resent that she was in his bed? She shook her head, appalled at her own thoughts. It wasn't like her to be frightened by superstitious talk of pixies and goblins. It must be all the trying events. Encircling her flannel-covered legs with her arms, she rested her head on her knees.

Myrtle's head started to throb again. Even if it wasn't a ghost, she'd seen enough angry clansmen's faces to realize they all wanted her dead. Was Addison correct? Was it folly to try to help such strange people with their unfriendly ways? A sound of pain escaped her lips. Not even at her father's funeral had she given in to such despair. She did not want to break her promise to her father, but the thought of staying one more night in this dismal place unsettled her. Hadn't her own father said he wished she'd been a son before he'd asked for her vow? There was no one she could turn to for help, no one she could trust.

From the narrow crack in the open panel Ian continued to stare at the woman in his bed. He tried steeling his emotions against feeling anything but contempt for this spoiled Englishwoman. Yet something touched him, the way she sat there, looking for all the world like a lost, lonely child. Instantly he regretted his teasing just now in ordering her back to bed. He'd obviously terrified her. How would he feel alone in a strange land without kin or friend? In the darkness, he walked slowly over to the opening, aware she would still not see him. "Lady Myrtle," he called softly.

She gasped when she heard her name. Raising her head, fear gripped her. "Mother of God . . . I must be losing my mind," she whispered aloud. "Who . . . what are you?"

"A fearsome ghost to my enemies but a guardian to my friends."

Suddenly she thought she remembered the sound of that voice. "Did . . . you speak to me that night I first came to this room?"

"Aye."

Confusion buffeted her. Now the voice came from the other side of the room. "But why did you try to scare me that horrible night when I was in that . . . dungeon below?"

He did not miss the hurt behind her accusation. "I still do not know if you are a friend or an enemy to the Sinclairs."

"You appear only at night, Scottish specter," she said with feeling, "else you would see I mean your people no harm. I am sworn to protect the Sinclairs."

"As I am, lass." He heard the strain in her voice and knew she needed rest. "We will talk again another evening. Go to sleep now."

"But will you start that horrible moaning and clanking of chains again?"

"Nay, you shall only hear soothing music tonight. Please, go to sleep now."

It was the tender masculine voice of her dreams again. Sighing, not understanding this, yet too exhausted to dwell on it any longer, Myrtle nestled

74

down into the feathery mattress of the comfortable bed. Leaning over, she blew out the candle on the night table but tucked the three books under her pillow. She didn't want to shock Katie in the morning, nor did she want the two lurid novels and the deceased laird's diary to disappear before she finished reading them. "Are you Ian Sinclair's ghost?"

"No more questions tonight," came the voice from within the walls.

"You know," she murmured, "for a ghost, you certainly are bossy." It was only a few moments later when the soft sound of harpsichord music drifted up from below stairs. It was calming, almost a lullaby. He really must be sorry he scared her. Well, if she could talk to the ghost again, she must try to get him to shed light on these strange occurrences at Kilmarock Castle.

The next morning, Myrtle awoke slowly. She felt something cool and wet next to her right hand. Her gaze focused on gray whiskers, big brown eyes, long and short mismatched ears. "Robbie." She patted the dog on his smooth forehead. His low whine as she scratched his ears made her chuckle. "Why, Robbie, you are no fierce beast—just a big baby." His tail thumped against the carpeted floor. After she gave him an affectionate hug, the dog went back over to stretch out near the fireplace. Well, at least she was beginning to make a few friends. Angus and Katie were nicer to her. Then there was the ghost. She smiled. Addison would probably have her committed to Bedlam if he knew she was talking with the laird's ghost.

For the first time since her arrival, Myrtle felt hopeful about the future. She heard the soft knock at the door. "Enter."

After Katie came in with a breakfast tray of eggs, ham, steaming chocolate, and homemade oat bread,

Myrtle could not disguise her delight as she devoured the delicious food. "Thank you, Katie," she said, between mouthfuls. "Never have I had such a feast in bed. You'll spoil me."

The gray-haired woman watched her for a few moments. "We all thought—that is, ye seem more a bonny lass than first we believed."

Her new employer did not take offense. "I am learning, too. For instance, you are wrong to think the Sinclair ghost is a fearful monster."

In the process of taking the wooden tray from Myrtle's lap, Katie almost upset the china cup.

Puzzled by the late Sinclair's retainer, the Englishwoman went on to explain. "Did you not hear the pleasant music last evening? I own this ghost may be friendlier than you and Angus believe. Perhaps poor Ian was unhappy in love."

"Ye dinna see the . . . ghost, did ye?"

"No, but his voice seemed pleasant last evening. He did not carry on as he did my first evening here. I believe he even has a sense of humor," she added, thinking of his pleasant-sounding laughter when she'd defied him.

Clearly not comfortable with this topic, Katie asked, "Would ye like a warm bath by the fire? Angus will have Lachlan Mackenzie fetch the brass tub."

"I should not like to put you to so much trouble," Miss Prescott said, for she knew this acquiescence between herself and these Scots was still new.

"Och, 'tis no trouble. Besides, it will do ye good to bathe, then pop back into bed after I change the linens."

"Oh, I should love a bath," Myrtle answered, unable to hide her pleasure at the prospect. "Then I shall spend just one more day abed, for I must see to my duties here. First off, I intend to hire more servants to help you and Angus. If you have anyone in mind, I will be most pleased to engage those you recommend." She did not mention her intention to hire a Scottish girl to serve as her maid, remembering all the furor the other night at the mention of—what was it? Oh, yes, Fiona Ross, the clanswoman somehow in disgrace here.

"But today ye must rest; the lair—I mean, Angus—and I think it best."

Myrtle smiled at her cosseting tone. "I promise to sit her and read most of the day." Perhaps if she studied Ian Sinclair's diary more thoroughly, she would gain a better understanding of the late laird, which could help her deal more effectively with his clansmen.

While the water for her bath heated below stairs, Myrtle rested facedown on the recently changed linens of her bed. She continued reading *Lisette Meets the Pirate Prince*.

Through the small opening in the panel, Ian watched her with open amusement as she studied the erotic plates of the book.

"Can they do that?" she asked aloud, then turned the volume ninety degrees to get a better view. "They can't do that, can they?" She giggled again.

It was then that Ian realized the outline of her buxom figure in that flannel nightgown was interfering with his need for a cool plan of action. He was going to have to get that diary away from her. It was private and contained information about his clansmen he'd trust with no one, especially this Sassenach wench. He would wait until the recuperating girl was asleep, then get it. He pressed the iron button and shut off this disconcerting view of the Englishwoman.

As Angus and Lachlan brought up pails of warm water, Myrtle poured her favorite tea rose scent into the tub. She looked up to find Angus heading for the painting on the wall, "No, please, Angus, leave the portrait where it is. I like it."

The white-haired man frowned. "We thought— that is, Katie thought the laird's picture might be given' ye bad dreams. The ghost and—"

"Thank you," she assured the shorter man. "But I'm beginning to like the laird's ghost. Please leave the picture on the wall."

Angus shrugged and left.

After Lachlan Mackenzie finished with the last pail of water and stoked the fire, Myrtle thanked him for his help.

His dark eyes crinkled at the corners when he returned her smile. "Ye mustna judge us by our rudeness to ye at first. We were told things aboot ye before ye arrived. It was said ye planned to sell Sinclair lands and the castle to the highest bidder, then drive us off the land to make room for Sassenach sheepherders from the lowlands."

This information puzzled and troubled her. It explained the Scots' open hostility. "Who told you this?"

Near the door, Lachlan wiped his wet hands on the leather apron covering his work shirt and breeches. "My father heard it from a reliable source, though he dinna find out who first started the talk."

"I see."

Alone, Myrtle removed the cloth bandage on the left side of her temple, deciding it was no longer needed. She would wash her hair, too. After pulling the nightgown over her head, the young woman stepped into the scented water. A contented sigh escaped her lips as the warmth from the water and heat from the marble fireplace soothed her. Closing her eyes, she rested her head against the high curved back of the large brass tub.

*   *   *

Aware there was nothing he could do about removing the painting, for the woman seemed determined to keep it in her bedroom, Ian knew this would probably be his best opportunity to retrieve his diary. He cursed himself for not getting it sooner.

With her head facing away from his hiding place, the Sinclair held his breath as he stepped out onto the carpet. He'd seen her put his diary under the pillow last night. The clever minx probably thought Katie or Angus might take it. Without shoes, he was sure he could get over to the bed and pick up the book before she opened her eyes. Keeping his gaze on the back of her head, he reached under her pillow and felt the leather volume. He decided to leave her the two erotic novels. It might just do the straight-laced English spinster good to peruse something besides *Caesar's Gaul Campaigns*.

When he began walking back across the room, Ian could not resist a brief glance at the English girl. He'd not seen her like this before, with damp tendrils of hair about her bare shoulders, creamy skin with a hint of pinkness from the warm bath, lips slightly parted in relaxation. The bubbles having dissipated, Ian saw her full, ripe breasts and the dusky rose nipples. Her figure was ample. Her long legs were bent to accommodate the brass tub. Firm calves, wider thighs—a walker's legs. The heady scent of roses filled the air, making him unusually light-headed. A very pleasant armful she was, he mused, unable to forget the feel of her when he'd carried her. A wave of heat engulfed him suddenly, and his healthy body responded to the arousing vision before him. She was oh so tempting with her Rubenesque figure. It was only going to make his task more difficult. If she'd been the Sassenach wench he'd expected—pale, fragile, coldly English—no, he had not expected this.

The tales he'd heard of this woman's appearance

were wrong, Ian mused. Her hair was not beagle brown. He looked again at it. In the firelight, he could make out the rich golden highlights. They'd told him she had mud-gray eyes. Her eyes were blue as the starlike flowers in the meadow. Her eyes were—God, they were open! he shouted at himself.

Everything seemed out of focus to her at first. Then she made out the white full mask. "You!" she shrieked. "Help! Somebody, please, help," she screamed at the top of her lungs.

Alarmed, Ian stepped back, raising his hand to try and show her he meant no harm.

Grabbing the linen towel next to her bar of soap and brown sponge, Myrtle pulled the scrap of material across the front of her, oblivious that it now was getting soaked. "Who are you?" she demanded.

"I . . . damnation," he swore.

Chapter Five

The door of her room flew open and Angus rushed in.

Wrapping her makeshift covering about herself, Myrtle Prescott stood up. It was not possible to step out of the tub with any modesty while these two men stood in the room, so she had to remain standing in the cooling water of the tub. She read Angus's unease, but he did not look alarmed. It was clear the servant knew this intruder.

"I am waiting," she demanded.

Through his mask, Ian could not hold back a grin, for he knew this blustering Englishwoman did not realize the towel clinging to her wet body left nothing to the imagination. He could see the rose-tipped nipples through the thin material. He also got a perfect view of her delectable pink buttocks in the mirror on the wall behind her, while she awkwardly battled with the scrap of linen held at her back, assuming incorrectly that everything was shielded. For reasons he did not understand, Ian suddenly did not want any other man's eyes on her. He said something to Angus forcefully in Gaelic.

Myrtle saw the older man drop his gaze to the carpet. What was going on here? Then she spotted the book in the stranger's hand. "That volume, sir,

81

belongs to me. You will place it on the table next to this tub immediately."

Even stark naked this Sassenach was formidable. Grudgingly, Ian walked over and followed her directive, for he knew he could not divulge his identity. Not yet, while he still had doubts whose side her ladyship was on. But what to tell her now?

Angus seemed to guess his thoughts and spoke before Ian could. "My lady, this is the late laird's gillie. In the old days, a gillie carried the highland chief's sword and shield into battle. He used to be Ian Sinclair's manservant. The lad acts as a fetch boy now. Stays in the paneled room he occupied when the laird was alive." Angus then explained the history of the hidden room.

"He'll nae harm ye, for the big lad's touched." Angus tapped his white-haired pate. "The laird always took care of the orphan. Kept him hidden here to protect him from the outside world, especially English soldiers."

Myrtle looked at the masked Scot standing silently across the room next to the much shorter Angus. Though less frightened, she was still suspicious. "Why does he wear a mask?"

"Smallpox, your ladyship. Left the laddie's face disfigured somethin' horrible, then all his hair fell out. That's why he wears the powdered wig," Angus offered, cozying to his tale. "Only a bairn at the time, he almost died with his parents. English soldiers caught him stealing a handful of grain and beat him savagely in the head. The late laird's father found him on the road one night and took him in. He and Ian were about the same age, and Ian looked out for the lad. Later, when it became clear his wits were damaged and he'd never be right in the head, old Murdoch decided to keep him here on the estate, hidden, safe."

Something lurched against her heart at this tale.

Hadn't she seen countless children born on London streets orphaned, disfigured from disease? "But my father never mentioned him," she said aloud.

"Only Katie, Gavin, and I know of his existence," said Angus. "Murdoch and Ian protected the lad, fearing he'd be a source of ridicule from outsiders."

She shivered, the damp towel and water cold about her legs. When she looked up at Angus's companion, she could tell nothing. He'd obeyed her command about the diary; that was a good sign. He stood well over six feet, broad shoulders outlined in a workman's blue-gray shirt and breeches, gray hose without shoes. The full white mask tied at the back of his powdered wig had slits for eyes, nose, and mouth. Head bowed, he shifted from one leg to the other, appearing ill at ease. "What is your name and age, lad?"

Angus answered for him. "He's twenty-seven but has the mind of a bairn. His name is Urisk."

At the name, Ian's head snapped toward his employee, but to his credit he said nothing.

Strange name, she thought. When she saw Urisk step back, clearly intent on going back to his room, she spoke. "Both of you, please leave me to finish my bath. Angus, take Urisk down to the kitchen and get him something to eat. I will decide what is to be done with him. Clearly, he cannot stay in that room adjoining mine."

Not certain he liked Angus's attempt to rescue the situation, Ian stood his ground. "Want to stay in this room," he said, using what he hoped was the right tone to play the role in which Angus had just shoved him.

The voice sounded familiar, yet his words were just the sort one associated with arrested mental development. "Please, Urisk," she said, her voice softening. "Go with Angus."

"Can . . . can I keep Mortimer?"

"Mortimer?" She looked from Angus back to Urisk.

The big lad reached behind his back and pulled out a tan-coated mouse. "Mortimer."

Myrtle peered down at the creature. It looked like the one who'd stayed all night with her in the cellar. "Yes," she answered with a smile, "you may keep your pet. Now go along with Angus, there's a good boy." Poor lad, she thought, another casualty of the hatred between the English and the Scots. "I shall be downstairs shortly, and we can sort out this new muddle."

Angus took the taller man's hand and led him out of her room.

Finally alone, Myrtle got out of the tub and toweled herself, all the while thinking of this change of events. She remembered seeing that masked face in her delirium. Could Urisk be the ghost everyone feared? Was the lad so terrified of being tossed out, losing his protection from the castle that he tried frightening away any intruder? It made more sense than believing in ghosts. But how had he sounded so "normal" those times last evening when that masculine voice calmed her fears? Did Urisk have temporary lapses of insanity? God, what a mess, she thought, reaching for her chemise.

Below stairs, in the kitchen, Ian glowered at Angus while Katie finished putting away the uneaten food. "Urisk?" he echoed.

"'Twas the only name that came to mind."

"I can just imagine. Forgive me if I fail to sound grateful."

Angus looked defensive. "We'll have to tell Gavin what has happened. And if you ask me, ye dinna have to skulk aboot her rooms when she was takin' a bath, where she was bound to spot you."

84

Ian sighed. Angus was probably right, and he did appreciate the old Scot's attempt to salvage the awkward situation. How long could he have gone on deceiving a shrewd woman like Myrtle Prescott, anyway? "But I'd have rather let her get to know me and the truth in my own way. Now things have changed. It will not be easy."

"Why not?" Angus countered. "I think I've settled things verra nicely. She still believes Ian Sinclair is dead, and you can live more openly in the castle."

Ian gave an exasperated snort. "Thanks to you, that young Englishwoman now believes I'm the village idiot."

"Weel," said Angus, "since you've been dead, I'd say yer personality has improved."

"Remind me to decrease your wages."

Angus smirked at his masked employer. "Too late. Her ladyship doubled Katie's and my wages already."

"If you think I'll allow you to—"

Ian's words ended when the door opened and Myrtle Prescott entered.

Angus stared at her, clearly aware of the danger if the Englishwoman overheard Ian speaking not as Urisk. "Oh," he whimpered, then clutched his stomach. "Dinna punch me again, Urisk."

Myrtle rushed over to Urisk, unaware of Katie's astonished look at her husband. "No, no, naughty Urisk." She took the towering Scot's right hand in hers and lightly smacked his fingers the way one might correct a baby. "Angus is our friend. You must not hurt him."

The culprit of this distraction turned away from her for a second. "Oh, my lady, I'm sure Urisk dinna mean to thump me. He does love Katie's oatcakes so . . . even the last one on my plate."

Pulling his hand from the lady's grasp, Ian could hardly contain his fury. He was this woman's senior by three years; he towered over her; and she was treating him like ... When Ian spotted Angus Thomson's shoulders shake at the humor of the situation, he growled something in Gaelic.

"What did he say, Angus?"

With the visage of a saint, the white-haired Scot turned to look up at Myrtle. "I dinna think I should translate, my lady. It involves a sheep and my mother."

"Oh, my, ah . . ." Myrtle looked at Katie's face. It was as pink as she knew hers must be. "Well, I—my, my . . ." She then saw the plate of cookies. "Katie, would it be all right if Urisk had another oatcake and milk while you, Angus, and I talk about what is to be done with him?"

Giving her ladyship a shy smile, Katie picked up the earthenware plate and offered Urisk another cookie.

"There now," said Myrtle. "You may have another oatcake while you sit at the table."

Damn it to hell, he didn't want another oatcake, Ian thought. He wanted to find out what this English chit meant to do about Kilmarock lands and her tenants. Through the slit in his mask, the words pushed out between his teeth. "Urisk . . . doesn't . . . want . . . to."

Myrtle patted his arm. "Now, be a good boy, Urisk. Come along." She pulled him gently by the arm toward the flat bench next to the sturdy table.

Aware little would be accomplished until he followed her instructions, Ian went over and plunked himself down on the hard bench.

"You may have two more cookies," Myrtle added.

Irked by her placating tone, Ian said, "Too kind," but knew his sarcasm was lost on the Englishwoman, who now stood on the other side of the room, talking with his retainers. The laird took one of the oatcakes and popped the whole thing in his mouth through the slit in his white mask.

Myrtle addressed the Thomsons. "On my way here, I noticed the unoccupied room next to yours. Do you think that would be comfortable enough for Urisk? When the wagons arrive with the food and supplies I've ordered, we can salvage something to make his room more comfortable."

Katie spoke first. "Oh, that would be fine, my lady. The two rooms face the morning sun. They are clean and dry. They used to be Master Malcolm's old rooms."

"I'll help you sort things out after I post another letter to—" Myrtle had to stop speaking. She shut her eyes, hoping the vertigo would stop. "I dare say, I'm still not over that clout to my hard head," she added, trying to make light of the situation. She heard the wooden bench scrape against the tile floor but was too queasy to look up.

Ian took only a second to reach her. Automatically, he placed his right arm about her waist, his left under the backs of her gown-covered legs. It was like holding a sun-kissed bouquet of summer roses, he thought, inhaling the scent of her upswept hair.

"Really, I am all right," she whispered, though she was forced to place her arm about her rescuer's shoulder for support.

Katie's concerned features came into view. "We can finish talking up in your rooms, lass. Come along, Angus."

Nevertheless, irritated with herself for this unusual show of weakness, Myrtle accepted the logic of Katie's suggestion. Angus opened the door, and Urisk carried her out into the hallway toward the first flight of stairs. "Thank you, Urisk, for your assistance," she managed in a weak voice. The masculine warmth and scent of oatmeal soap brought back a memory. Confusion etched her smooth features. "It was you, not Kate or Angus, who carried me up here from my cellar room when I was ill, wasn't it?"

Holding this Englishwoman in his arms, Ian knew he could not trust her with the truth. She had the power to destroy his entire clan. Rather than answer, he sought to ease her troubled thoughts with humor. Imitating a puffing noise, then a wheeze as they reached the second flight of stairs, he stopped and leaned against a stone pillar. "Ye've the solidity of a good draft horse."

Instantly, Myrtle's face turned ashen. She struggled. "Please put me down. I can walk from here. Please, Urisk," she added, a desperate edge to her voice.

He'd expected her to give him back as good as he'd given. A Scottish lass would have jabbed him in the ribs, and followed with her tart reply. Myrtle's frantic struggles increased, and he was forced to place her carefully on the steps. She raced up the stairs with a speed he knew was unsafe in her condition. He made a motion to go after her, then stopped. Miss Prescott thought he was Urisk, the dull-witted lackey, and he couldn't go after her now as Ian Sinclair. Realizing he'd just humiliated her unintentionally, Ian cursed himself for his careless jest. The young Scot could only follow Angus and Katie up the stone stairs.

When they reached Myrtle's bedroom, he felt even more censured by the Thomsons' look of reproach.

Myrtle directed the three Scots to sit on the sofa and chair in the room. She went over and sank down on the edge of the bed.

"Urisk," Lady Myrtle said, when she felt more in control. "Do your former injuries cause you pain? Has a physician seen you?"

Taken aback by her consideration, Ian at first couldn't answer.

"Oh," Angus piped up, "the dead chieftan once took Urisk to Edinburgh. Finest doctors saw him."

Through his mask, Ian glared at his longtime servant when the little man piled on the manure. "No, my lady, I'm not in pain." At least not physically, he thought, still ashamed for the way he'd hurt her feelings just now. It was clear she had an area of vulnerability he'd never considered before.

"I want you to continue viewing Kilmarock Castle as your home. Will you try the two rooms downstairs for a few days to see if you like them?"

Urisk nodded his head in agreement.

"Good." The Englishwoman saw the Scot shift his position on the wooden chair. "Do you wish to say something, Urisk?"

So much, but in his role as simpleton, intelligent rapport was almost impossible. A thought occurred to him. He touched his mask. "Afraid ye'll try to see my face." This part was true. What if the mask slipped, or she came into his room while he shaved? Things would get awkward if curiosity got the better of her.

Though brain-damaged and unable to verbalize it, Urisk, she realized, was probably worried about his safety now that she was the new owner-in-residence. She tried to think of a way to ease his fears in a way the addled Scot could understand. Something her late father told her came to mind.

Slowly, Lady Myrtle got off the bed and reached above the headboard. Taking the dirk from the leather sheath, she walked over to Urisk. "Will all of you stand, please?"

After the three Scots joined her, Lady Myrtle said, "From what Father once told me, I know how sacred you hold the Scot's oath." The light streaming from the windows danced off the blood-red stone in the hilt of the dagger. She held the dirk like a crucifix in front of her face. "I swear on the cross of my Lord Jesus and by the holy iron which I hold, I will never look upon your face unless you ask me. Also, I swear

89

to protect you, Urisk, with my life, if necessary." She kissed the hilt of the knife, then walked back to return it in the tooled leather sheath above the bed.

Something inside made him realize she took this Scot's promise seriously, and it moved him in a way he thought he was past feeling. From Katie's and Angus's expressions, he could tell they were as moved as he. What he'd heard about her before, along with his awareness that she wrote regularly to that English officer, Addison, and of two letters she'd sent to London, warred with his current emotion. Had Myrtle written Captain Barrington about the attempt on her life? Would Addison now send more redcoats to patrol Sinclair land? Suddenly, Ian felt trapped by his own plan to kill off Ian Sinclair, along with Angus Thomson now putting him in the role of simpleton.

Katie spoke first. "Ye should rest now, yer ladyship. 'Tis sure yer not as sturdy as ye'd have others believe."

Myrtle smiled at the older woman. "Once the wagons of supplies and materials arrive for the clansmen, I'm sure I'll rest easier. Urisk, please go along with the Thomsons and mind what they tell you."

Myrtle didn't see the look of unease pass between Katie and Angus at her directive that the Chief of Clan Sinclair was now to take orders from his two elderly servants.

Misinterpreting Urisk's reaction, Myrtle reached out and gave him a light hug. "Do not be afraid, dear Urisk. I am here to see that you are safe . . . and well fed."

After the three Scots left her rooms, Myrtle felt too agitated to go back to bed. Hands behind her, she paced back and forth between her bedroom and office. She stopped once or twice to draw comfort from the late laird's portrait over the fireplace. "Just who were you, Ian Sinclair?" she asked aloud. Was he a ruthless, ignorant barbarian, as Addison said, or a studious man with a sense of humor who'd tried to rule the smallest clan in Scotland as best he could?

Outside his former room, Ian stood alone, leaning against the closed door frame. He could hear Myrtle pacing back and forth. Used to her habit now of talking to herself, he knew she only did it in times of stress. Shaking his head, he forced himself to turn away and head back downstairs to his new room. How could he give any comfort to this troubled lass? He was a damn ghost. And though he believed she meant her oath to protect Urisk, was Lady Myrtle Prescott intent on ordering wagonloads of supplies merely to fix up her property to get a better price when she sold it in a few months? How could this Englishwoman, a stranger, possibly care for his clansmen when she hardly understood their Scottish ways?

In spite of himself, an hour later Ian knocked at Myrtle's door, carrying a steaming cup of tea.

"Oh, how thoughtful, Urisk." Myrtle showed him her pleasure at the simple lad's gesture. Sitting at her desk, she put down the quill pen and turned the sheet of paper over. "Did you have your supper?"

"Yes. My lady didn't eat."

Myrtle couldn't tell Urisk her worries about Clan Sinclair. She tried to smile. "I wasn't hungry. Besides, as you could tell earlier, I'm quite a hefty armful as it is."

"Nice armful," Urisk murmured through the opening in his mask.

It was sweet of him to say it, she thought, then took a generous swallow of the tea. Unexpectedly, her mouth and throat ignited. Her choke turned into a coughing fit, while her eyes pumped water. Gratitude wasn't the first thought that came to mind when Urisk walked behind her chair and thumped her heartily on the back. He took the wobbly cup and saucer out of her hands. "Wha—what is this?" she gasped.

"Tea and Scots whiskey. Help you sleep."

"Help kill me, don't you mean?" Another cough overtook her before she could speak again. "Mother of God, I think my windpipe's gone. I don't even drink wine at home. Is my throat still under my chin?" she asked, pressing her fingertips to her throbbing neck. "I prefer the barley in my soup, not fermented in a bottle." Instantly, she reminded herself of Urisk's mental deficiency. "No harm done. I know you meant well, dear Urisk. However, next time, if you don't mind, I would prefer just straight tea. I'm not used to that much hard liquor." She saw him nod and prepare to leave. "Goodnight, Urisk. Pleasant dreams. And thank you again for the kind gesture."

Outside her room, Urisk looked down at the cup of tea on the wooden tray in his hands. So much liquor? God, the amount of whiskey he'd put in her tea wouldn't faze a Scots bairn of two. Katie had to be right. This Sassenach wasn't as sturdy as she looked.

Near dusk, still dressed and unable to sleep, Lady Myrtle decided a short walk in the spring air might do her good. Remembering what Addison had told her, she made her way out to the right side of the keep. Before the black iron gates that led to the Sinclair family crypt, she spotted the slab of gray stone. Plain, unadorned, the grave shoved into the earth as Addison said—unconsecrated, away from the Sinclair family's burial spot, as a result of Ian taking his own life. *"In Despair"* were the only words chiseled on the large, crude rock, along with Ian

Sinclair's name and years of birth and death. Sadness engulfed her as she stood staring at his grave, thinking about all she'd recently learned of this noble Scottish chieftain.

How long she stood there she didn't know, but when the Englishwoman looked up, Myrtle saw a silhouetted figure on the parapet, the highest point of the castle. The last rays of sunlight flashed across a white mask. It was Urisk on the castle walk. He looked down at her in the distance. She waved a greeting to him only to have the Scot turn away.

Hadn't he seen her? Or had she intruded on his thoughts? She reminded herself that paying him thirty-five pounds a year, which was more than an experienced valet received in London, did not give her the right to intrude on his private time.

Three days later, Myrtle was delighted when the stream of wagons began arriving with food, warm clothing, tools, seeds, and simple toys for the children. Cyril, her devoted clerk, wrote he thought this last barrel was a needless extravagance, but Myrtle was adamant. When Gavin Mackenzie and his two sons arrived, as Myrtle requested, they brought a large number of the clan with them. She tried to reassure the unsmiling faces.

Dressed in the laundered gray wool dress, her traveling cloak about her shoulders, the Englishwoman noted again how tattered these Scots appeared. "Good morning," she said, adding a smile to her greeting. "Thank you for coming here today. Before the Mackenzies and I set out with my drivers in these wagons, I wish to request your cooperation in distributing these supplies." She pointed to the long line of canvas-covered wagons. "Since many of the older members of your clan, along with the younger children and their mothers, could not come today, please tell Gavin, Lachlan, or Andrew how many others there are at home. We are making a list to assist me in ordering more supplies in the future. Now, the first order of business is to get the food to your crofts as quickly as possible. As instructed, those wagons are the ten in front." The Scots continued watching her—wary, hostile, some just plain hungry. "There is room in the wagons, if any of you would like to ride back to your houses with us."

A Scottish girl, about seventeen, dressed in simple wool dress and shawl about her shoulders, stepped forward. The insolence in her dark eyes told Myrtle she was not the least intimated by the new owner.

"If it's just the same to yer ladyship, most of us would prefer to walk. We're particular about the company we keep, even when there's an offer of food for our starvin' bellies."

"Jeanie!" bellowed Gavin Mackenzie from atop his horse. With the scar across his nose and cheek, he looked even more fierce when the wind whipped his shoulder-length mane about his massive shoulders.

Myrtle noticed that the dark-haired beauty didn't appear daunted by the older Scot's censuring tone.

Gavin looked apologetically at Myrtle. "This outspoken lass is my youngest and only daughter. And without her mother, harder to raise than any of my six sons ever were. She has an aversion to obeying, as well as to wearing shoes."

Automatically, Myrtle looked down to see Jean's small, bare toes beneath her homespun dress. When she saw her blush, then look belligerently back up at her, Myrtle said, "I am pleased to meet you, Jean Mackenzie."

Backing down slightly, Jean gave her dark head a cursory nod. "Weel, I'll wait to return the greeting until I see what ye do for the clan."

Myrtle touched a strand of her straight brown hair the wind had wrenched from her tightly pinned upsweep. Tempted to pull up the hood of her cloak against the morning chill, she refrained. It was more important these clansmen see her expression as she spoke to them. "That seems fair, Jean. I will work hard to make that time soon when you feel you can greet me as a friend."

When the clansmen turned to walk toward the wagons, Myrtle's voice stopped them. "One more moment, please." They scowled back at her. This was not going to be easy. "I . . . I understand about the custom of intercepting Lowland cattle," she said, deliberating not calling it cattle-stealing. The faces ahead became more defensive, but she continued. "In a few days a large herd of long-haired cattle will be arriving here from the lowlands. I have purchased them, along with two hundred sheep, for distribution among the clan. I would take it as a great favor if you would refrain from, that is, if you could—"

"What the lassie is trying to say," cut in Gavin Mackenzie, "is that there's to be no raiding these cattle because we'd be stealin' our own property."

Myrtle gave Gavin a smile of appreciation for his help. After a few of the Scots actually chuckled, she felt some of the tension leave her body.

When Sian was trotted out for her to ride again, Myrtle sighed. She understood the compliment of being given the best stallion on the estate, but she would have given a lot for a docile mare. Later, when Gavin trusted her more, she would tell him how she felt about the magnificent but unruly Sian.

"If it's all the same, Da," Jean told her father as everyone prepared to leave for the crofts, "I'll stay here until ye return so I can visit with Katie and Angus."

"It's up to the new owner," Gavin said, looking across at Lady Myrtle, who sat sidesaddle on her black horse.

Myrtle tried again to coax friendship from the girl.

"Certainly. When I return in a few hours, Katie has promised me a tour of the castle. Perhaps you would like to join us."

"Maybe," said Jean.

Before Myrtle turned her feisty horse to head away from Kilmarock Castle, she looked up at one of the tower windows. For an instant she saw the masked Urisk watching her. Knowing she felt responsible for keeping his whereabouts a secret, she breathed easier when he moved away from the glass panes as their gazes met.

Three hours later, Myrtle was relieved when Gavin said this was the last cottage they had to visit. There was only one wagon left, the rest having been emptied and returned to Kilmarock Castle. She'd been aware all during the trip today that the Mackenzie brothers had stayed close by her side. Had their father ordered them to act as her bodyguard?

Before Myrtle turned with the Mackenzies to return home, she spotted a small cottage in the distance. "Does anyone live there?"

Gavin and Andrew frowned at Myrtle when they saw what caught her attention. However, she saw pain in Lachlan's brown eyes when he stared at the cottage.

"Bah," Gavin blustered, "'tis no one ye need be worried aboot."

Her attention on Lachlan, Myrtle wasn't sure. "Lachlan, does a Sinclair clansman reside there?"

It seemed to take Lachlan a long time to answer. "Aye," whispered the black-haired Scot. "Fiona Ross."

So this was the infamous "traitor" Angus had spoken of.

"Nay," said Gavin, wrinkling his scarred face at his son. "That Ross viper is dead to Clan Sinclair, and her changeling with her."

96

While the last thing she needed was a feud within the clan, Myrtle struggled with her sense of duty to *all* her tenants. Nudging Sian's flanks with her legs, she moved closer to Lachlan's mount. She leaned over and asked, "Lachlan, could this woman and her child use some food and supplies?"

"Oh, aye," he answered, clearly unable to hide the eagerness in his voice. Then his face clouded. "But I dinna think Fiona would let us in. She's proud and quiet. Refuses to live closer to us so we might protect her," he added, his face coloring. "All her close kin are dead now, and—"

"Aye," snapped Gavin, coming over to them. "And dinna forget to tell the Sassenach her father and three brothers died at Culloden, while she was entertainin' a redcoat in her cottage."

Myrtle looked down at her hands. "How can you be sure, Mr. Mackenzie, about such private—"

"Oh, my daughter, Jean, along with three other clansmen, saw a redcoat, dressed in his uniform and all, slippin' into the cottage late at night on at least three occasions," Gavin answered. "Never caught the wily Sassenach. And a few months before Culloden, doesn't Fiona whelp a bastard, her not even promised to any clansman. Even the late laird could nae get Fiona to tell the father's name. The elders voted to drive her oot of the glen, but the laird would nae hear of it. Made us promise to let her stay with us. And didn't the uppity bitch move way out here on her own, as far as she could get from her own." Folding his arms across his barrel chest, Gavin waited for her obvious agreement of his attitude toward the fallen angel.

He would have a long wait, Myrtle decided. In her efficient manner, she directed the driver of the wagon to head over to the solitary cottage in the distance. "Gavin, you and Andrew may wait here, if you wish. It won't take us long." Gavin muttered something in Gaelic, but followed them just the same.

Lachlan reached up to help her off her horse when they arrived at the Ross cottage. "What made ye decide to go against my da?"

Returning his smile, she brushed the dust from the bottom of her skirt. "You know, I'm really not sure. Perhaps it's because I'm also a Sassenach, or I don't understand this strong hatred between the Scots and the English. Perhaps I just want to see this Fiona Ross myself—or I could be a fool, Lachlan, for no doubt your father will tell all the clan about this, which certainly won't make my position here any easier."

"Yer nae a fool, my lady." Lachlan's eyes softened as he watched her. "I think the dead laird would approve of yer actions. He would nae let my da and the others harm Fiona or the bairn, either."

"Fiona!" Lachlan called again when no one answered his knock on the locked door of the stone cottage. Gavin and Andrew helped the driver unload bags of flour, cured meat, and blankets.

Myrtle noticed the rags stuffed in a wide hole where the thatch had worn away. The cow in a recently mended pen looked healthy, in contrast to the mostly emaciated livestock she'd seen so far. This cottage, like most of the others, consisted of only two rooms. One usually served as living room, kitchen, and bedroom, the other as a sort of byre for the cattle. She glanced back at the door when she heard a bolt move near the latch.

The auburn-haired woman was near her own age but shorter, and her smile at Lachlan turned to fear, then anger when she spotted Myrtle. "I'll nae welcome any Sassenach to my home."

Lachlan shook his dark head. "Fiona, Lady Myrtle is nae like the other English. Ye shouldn't live here alone, so far from the rest of the clan. I canna think

98

'tis good for Jamie to have no other bairns to play with."

Fiona's gray eyes narrowed. "'Tis nae yer concern. Jamie and I do just—"

Her words ended when a small boy crawled out from the open door. Too quick for his mother and Lachlan, the toddler raced out toward Myrtle. She smiled and cut off his retreat by crouching down to take the sturdy lad in her arms. "You must be Jamie. What a fine name for a braw lad," she said, remembering some of the expressions she'd heard today at the other cottages. A few months past a year, the child rewarded her by giggling when she chucked him under the chin. He had a mop of his mother's auburn hair. But Myrtle's breath caught in her throat when she saw the golden eyes studying her so intently. She'd seen those eyes in the portrait hanging over the fireplace in her bedroom. Addison's remark about the deceased laird's virility, and about his offspring populating the highlands, buffeted her. It was clear none of the clansmen had spotted this distinctive feature. Of course, she reminded herself, all the clansmen save Lachlan clearly held Miss Ross in contempt for consorting with an English soldier. None of them probably took a look at the "devil's spawn," as they called him. And what of the English soldier witnesses had seen leaving Fiona's cottage? Myrtle blushed at the implication, then told herself Fiona's bedroom activities were none of her business.

"Don't ye dare hurt my baby!" Fiona screamed, charging beyond Lachlan to confront Myrtle. "Didn't ye Sassenachs get yer fill of Scots' blood at Culloden? Aye, ye've come to murder my son then, because I will nae tell who his father is."

Myrtle, horrified this woman could even think she would injure anyone, let alone a child, felt the woman's words pound her like physical blows. "Fiona, I have not come here to judge anyone, and please understand I would never harm—"

"Doon," said Jamie, wiggling his bare toes against the Englishwoman's side. He pushed against her cloak with his smock-covered arms.

Gently, Myrtle handed him back to his mother. "He's a fine boy, Fiona."

Ignoring her, Fiona walked back toward the men unloading the supplies. When Lachlan came over, he looked embarrassed.

"You must nae judge Fiona by her behavior today. I check on her and the boy as often as I can. She's really a verra lovely woman, though mulish where—says she'll nae marry anyone, not even to give her illegi—" Lachlan seemed to catch himself. "Yer pardon . . . ah, after such a long ride, ye probably need to stretch yourself before we go back."

Myrtle forced a half-smile. "I understand, Lachlan. I'll just rest near the large oak over there away from the cottage. Take all the time you need to unload the wagon. Fiona seems more at ease with you than me. Please be sure the stuffed dog is taken out for Jamie. I'll be fine here."

Alone, Myrtle stood resting against the base of the wide tree. She breathed in the beginning smells of spring flowers as the sun peeked out behind billowy clouds. These clansmen had suffered so much at Culloden, then the indignities of having laws passed against wearing the kilt or carrying arms—no wonder they hated her presence here. If Scots had killed her father, she probably would feel the same. Yet why was Fiona Ross so adamantly against her as an Englishwoman when she'd taken an English soldier as a lover? A puzzling business.

Myrtle kicked at the pebbles in the dirt at her feet. Though successful at disguising it in front of the others, right now she admitted it did hurt to be so misunderstood by these people. Of course, it was a start that the clan had accepted the supplies today.

But it was such an uphill battle. She thought of Jamie again. There was little doubt in her mind that he had to be Ian's illegitimate son. The Sinclair features were unmistakable. The diaries mentioned nothing about this. However, she assumed these intimate matters concerning the head of a clan during such tumultuous times were probably best left undocumented for the boy's protection, especially against the English, who might use him as a hostage to bring Clan Sinclair to its knees. It explained why Ian had made his clansmen promise not to harm Fiona or her child: the boy was his.

Both Fiona and her son looked better fed than many of the other Scots she'd seen today. Though their clothes were simple, they weren't patched. Perhaps Lachlan managed to— Myrtle turned her head quickly at the sound of a twig snapping in the dense woods to her right.

Steel hit wood. The next thing she knew, a lethal-looking knife vibrated in the oak barely an inch from her face. Gripping her cloak-covered arms, Myrtle attempted to steady herself. Her throat constricted, making it impossible for her to shout for the men only a few feet from her. Straining her ears, she heard the whinny of a horse in the distance, then hoofbeats. Whoever threw this knife was charging away after the failed attempt. If her assailant hadn't inadvertently stepped on that dry twig, she might never have turned her head, and . . . She pressed her hand to her mouth to quell the threatening nausea.

Something must have alerted Lachlan, for he dropped the sack he was carrying and raced over to her. If he was in on this attempted assassination, he hid it well, Myrtle thought. He looked as ashen-faced as she felt right now when he glanced at the black-handled knife embedded in the tree.

"First a rock, then a knife," she grated, trying to force her Prescott verve to the surface. "If the curse is

101

real, and the laird's ghost is out to make sure I never have a moment's peace at Kilmarock Castle, he's doing a bloody good job of it."

The black-haired Scot did not join in her dark humor, nor did he change his serious expression. "Da," he called to Gavin, "it happened again. Come have a look at this."

Chapter Six

"And you gave the coins to Fiona? How does little Jamie fare?" Ian asked.

Miss Prescott had paid Ian his generous wages ahead of time, and he'd wasted little time making use of them. The Scot backed away from the small, dark-haired beauty in front of him only to have her follow, a flirtatious smile on her lips. He felt his broad back touch the cold stones of the lower room that served as the laundry. "I'll not ask you again, Jeanie Mackenzie," he warned.

The Scottish girl smoothed the wrinkles from the front of her skirt. "Haven't I always done as ye asked, Ian?"

"Aye, but if you hadn't been so nosy when you came to the keep with your father last year, I'd have less to fret about. 'Tis enough your father and the Thomsons know the truth, let alone an impertinent brat who does whatever she pleases."

Jean pressed her ripening breasts into his chest. "I'm nae a child, Ian. If I'm to tell ye what ye wish to know, there is a price."

Ian was still wearing his wig; his white mask was on a low stool next to one of the wooden drying racks. His reddish-blond eyebrows arched. "I am not a wealthy man, Jeanie. Your price may be higher than

103

I can pay," he said, amused by her kittenish ways. However, he knew this seventeen-year old was affecting him physically. He wasn't a eunuch, for God's sake.

Ian escaped to the right. "Your price?"

"Only that you let me kiss you . . . my way."

"First the information . . . then you may kiss me," he answered, going over to sit on a bench near a rough wooden table. He stretched his long legs out in front of him. Dressed in gray breeches and linen shirt, the laird folded his arms across his chest.

Her dark eyes alight with mischief, Jean walked over and flopped down on Ian's lap. "There," she said with a saucy smile, "I'll meet your bargain halfway."

"Tell Gavin his daughter needs a husband— soon," Ian added, only half in jest.

"Och, I'll pick my own when the times comes, and that's a long ways off."

The gold in his eyes brightened with amusement. "Best not wait too long, lassie, else the young bucks here will learn just what a little hoyden they'd be saddled with if they wed you. They might think you'd make a better spinster than a shrewish bride," he teased.

She wiggled her small bottom across his muscular thighs. "Och, I'll wager I'm wed long before that homely Sassenach ever stands in a kirk. Her with an arse the size of a washtub."

A spark of irritation flamed in his lion eyes. "You watch your tongue, lass. And stop that bouncin' about my lap."

Jean looked disgusted. "Blessed Andrew, dinna say yer cozyin' to that English cow? Ready to hand all yer clansmen over to her so she can drive us from the crofts, are ye?"

"I was ten years old when you were born, Jeanie. If knowing me as long as you have leads you to that conclusion, then I'll not say a word to defend myself."

For the first time, Jean appeared chagrined by the laird's soft-spoken rebuke. "Aye, ye've given up more than many a braw lad ever did, Ian." As if trying to show she regretted her groundless accusation, she said, "When I arrived at Fiona's cottage this afternoon, the wagon of supplies had already been delivered. Fiona is still grieving aboot—well, at least Jamie keeps her busy." Jean leaned her face closer to Ian's. "I don't mind the reddish-blond stubble on yer face, though it will probably singe my skin when I kiss you in a moment."

"Serves you right for charging down here and interrupting my shave while the Sassenach is away. Now, tell me, how is Jamie?"

"He's bonny, Ian. He looks just like you, and he's nae afraid of anything. Fiona said he darted from the cottage and crawled toward the Sassenach, not even crying when she grabbed him."

"The Sassenach dinna harm the lad, did she?" Ian demanded, alert at the tone in Fiona's voice.

When she tossed her head, her midnight hair tousled about her slender shoulders. Thoughtful for a moment, Jean said, "Well, Fiona was terrified for her bairn, but I suppose the Sassenach realized Lachlan was in earshot if Fiona screamed for help. The English bit—woman," she amended, obviously remembering Ian's earlier prickliness when she'd spoken of Myrtle Prescott, "finally tossed Jamie back to his mother. He dinna hit his wee head on the hard ground when she threw him back at Fiona, thank the Lord. Da and the others never saw what happened with Jamie, more's the pity."

Ian could not hide his shock. "I never imagined Lady Myrtle would harm children," he said aloud. His distrust of this Englishwoman came to the surface. He clenched and unclenched his right hand.

Had she made the connection with his portrait upstairs and Jamie's features? He'd strangle her if she harmed Fiona or Jamie. "You've done well to tell me this, Jeanie. As I can't go about freely during the day, I rely on you to check on Fiona and the lad. Please tell me if you find they aren't receiving supplies, or if ever Myrtle Prescott touches wee Jamie so harshly again."

"Oh, that I will, Ian." Jean's tone became condescending. "Of course, Lady Myrtle may not realize what strength she has in those hamhock fists of hers. Most Englishwomen I hear are usually paste-faced, fainting creatures. The lowlanders probably never told the Sassenach she's too tall and broad in the beam to be around bairns or breakable furniture."

When her companion appeared too preoccupied with his troubled thoughts to take her to task for another jeering comment about the new owner, Jean rested her curly dark head against the laird's chest. "Ye don't have to let me kiss ye as ye promised," she said, the right amount of feminine regret in her purring voice. "I'd have told you everything without a condition, as I always do. Ye know I'd die rather than give yer secret away, my lord."

Touched by her words, Ian raised his hand to caress her smooth right cheek. "Thank ye, Jean. Oh, lassie," he sighed, suddenly feeling older than his late twenties. "There's been too many deaths of our clansmen already. I dinna want anyone else to die." When she snuggled closer to him, Ian knew he'd have to end this cuddling session soon. His healthy body was missing these times of intimate feminine company. How he longed to fish in the burn at his secret place near the steeper hill of his castle, talk openly with his clansmen, play with their children. Instead, he was forced to walk along the edge of the castle tower at night, or ride Sian out alone across the moors after midnight, skulk about his own castle just like the ghost many thought existed. God, how long could he continue this enforced masquerade as the laird's ghost?

He felt Jean squirm on his lap. "I keep my word, little Scot. You may have your kiss, then you'd best go, before your father and the others return. Gavin still doesn't realize you know about me, does he?"

With a self-satisfied smirk, Jean lifted her head after patting Ian's shoulder. "Da doesn't suspect a thing. The day I can't outwit any mon, 'tis the day I take the vows in a convent."

"You're a saucy baggage, Jeanie Mackenzie," he said, giving her a playful shake.

Smiling, Jean wrapped her left arm about Ian's neck. "Och, I wish ye'd taken off that cursed wig," she complained, "but I guess I'll survive kissin' ye with it on."

"Most kind," said the laird of Kilmarock, stifling his urge to laugh at the way the minx was drawing out the kiss he'd promised. "Please let me know if there is anything you wish me to do."

"Oh, no, I'll do everything. Ye just sit there and keep yer hands at yer sides."

If Ian was surprised or tempted to point out this first kiss between them might be more enjoyable if he used his hands, he remained silent and did as instructed. Having expected just a quick buzz on the cheek or mouth, the laird wasn't prepared when Jean pressed her entire body into him. One of her bare feet entwined about the calf of his stocking-clad leg. It was then that he experienced Jean's determined, warm tongue as it thrust its way between his teeth. He was engulfed by a jolt of astonishment and arousal.

Suddenly, there were noises coming from the hallway outside the laundry room. Alert, Ian pulled away from his amorous companion. "Hell, yer father must be back. Quick, Jean, hand me my mask on the stool."

In the lethargy of an enjoyable kiss, Miss Mackenzie looked irritated at the interruption. However, she leaned over and easily picked up the white leather mask next to her. Clearly amused as Ian fumbled with the leather strings at the back of the mask, she said, "Dinna fret yerself. They've been back for an hour. That's why I first came doon to fetch you. Da wants to see you in your new room upstairs."

Continuing to struggle with the ties behind his powdered wig, Ian swore under his breath. "And ye waited this long to tell me? Jean, I ought to—"

As the door opened, Ian froze at the sound of Myrtle's voice.

Her silver laugh filled the air when Katie asked her something. Then he heard her say, "I've already seen the cellar, thank you."

Katie entered first, followed by Myrtle.

"This is the room we use for washing and drying. Wools and linens are hung on—" Katie stopped speaking at the scene greeting her and the new owner.

Myrtle tried to hide her shock at seeing Urisk sitting on the wooden bench with Gavin Mackenzie's daughter perched on his lap. Jean's hand was caressing an intimate portion of the simple Scot's jutting anatomy. "Mother of God," she choked, her face flaming. "I . . . er . . . I'm sorry, excuse me."

The Englishwoman's feelings of protectiveness toward the brain-damaged young man wrestled with her dismay at Jean's forwardness. Of course, Urisk's hands at his sides proved he wasn't fighting for his life, but . . . "Ah . . . Katie, you can show me the laundry room another day." Awkwardly, she rushed for the door.

"Wait!" Ian made a motion to rise, forcing Jean to

scamper off his lap rather than topple to the flagstones at her feet.

Katie scowled at the pair of them, but Lady Myrtle did not see it.

Myrtle turned slowly back to Urisk. "I . . . I am sorry I intruded without knocking," she said, then berated herself for apologizing again. After all, she'd done nothing wrong. This was her home, her laundry room, and this encounter wasn't her fault. Yet the tall woman reminded herself of Urisk's limited mental abilities.

Hurled back into his role of Urisk, Ian knew he couldn't explain anything to Myrtle now. And what the deuce had gotten into Jean for such a lurid trick after the two ladies walked in? Seeing Myrtle's reaction, along with her apology, Ian could have throttled Jean. He stood there, suddenly feeling the addlepated oaf Myrtle thought him. "My lady, I never meant to—ouch!" he yelped when Jean pinched him hard on his buttock. Even through his breeches it bloody well hurt. He snapped something in Gaelic at her through the slit in his mask.

More embarrassed now at what Jean had just done to Urisk, Myrtle wished she hadn't turned back when he called her. A glance at Katie told her the older Scot was more irritated than shocked by this awkward situation.

Appearing angelic, Jean gave Myrtle a quick curtsy. "I'd best be lookin' for my brothers. Glad to meet you, Urisk," she said to the Scot, before turning back to Miss Prescott. "Good day, my lady." As fast as her bare feet would take her, Jean rushed from the room.

Myrtle saw Urisk shift from one dusty shoe to the other. "I am not angry with you, Urisk," was all the assurance she could muster at the moment. "Come along, Katie, please finish showing me the rest of the castle." Myrtle walked out of the laundry room.

Katie gave the laird of Kilmarock another disapproving look before following the Englishwoman.

"Women," Ian muttered. While irked at Jean, he could not explain why he cared what the Sassenach thought of him.

Concerned after learning from Gavin about the second attempt on Myrtle's life, Ian knocked on her bedroom door later that evening.

"Come in."

Myrtle moved away from the deceased laird's portrait that she'd been studying again. Thinking about Jamie, after reading more of Ian's diary, she realized she would never be his judge. Indeed, she was beginning to admire many things about the late earl of Kilmarock. Shaking her head, she went back to her desk to finish working. She was expecting Katie, and her blue eyes mirrored her surprise to find Urisk waiting for her in her office. "What can I do for you?" she asked, giving the Scot a shy smile. Jean's earlier antics with this slow, hulking lad still gnawed at her. He was under her protection, she reminded herself.

Relieved, Ian saw the knife attack hadn't unsettled her. Though she'd seemed fine when he'd met her in the laundry room, he knew some people had delayed reactions to near-death experiences. "I . . . I heard Gavin talk aboot the knife attack, had to check—"

"Oh, I am just fine." Quickly she sought to reassure him. How unfortunate he'd overheard Gavin. His childlike fretting touched something within her. "Please sit down," she offered, gesturing to the overstuffed sofa to her right.

"I have something for you." She went over to her wardrobe in the next room, then returned. "I pulled these two out of the barrel before we left for the crofts this morning." After he sat down, she handed him the cloth-covered items. "I hope you like them,

110

Urisk. Go on," she encouraged, as she stood looking down at him. "You may open them."

Slowly, Ian unwrapped the items. One was a gray sock monkey, stuffed with cloth, with an embroidered smile sewn on his mouth and two large eyes. The other was a ceramic music box.

Kneeling down on the carpeted floor at Urisk's feet, Myrtle showed him how the music box worked. "You turn this key at the bottom," she demonstrated. "Then watch and listen." Holding the base in her hands, she held it up for him. "When I spotted them, I knew they were for you. See?" She pointed to the tan-colored mouse that ran out from a hole in the wall. "That's Mortimer."

Ian looked down and smiled behind his mask. A gray-haired dog looked up from his relaxed spot on a round rug near the hearth as the mouse made a circle around the rug and returned to the opening in the wall.

Ian didn't know what to say. The box played a simple little tune, one he'd learned as a child. Myrtle's blue eyes watched him with eager anticipation. He fought the urge to caress her sweet face with his fingers. "Thank you . . . my lady. Like the presents."

"Oh, I'm so happy you do, Urisk. I thought Mr. Monkey might be company for you on your dresser. Sometimes we forget how much we all need a special friend, one who doesn't tell us what to do or remind us when we make mistakes, just loves us the way we are."

Through his mask, Ian saw her expressive eyes take on a faraway look. Then she seemed to catch herself.

With a self-conscious laugh, Myrtle got up and joined Urisk on the sofa. "I daresay, I could have used a Mr. Monkey years ago, too."

The music box ran down. He placed his unex-

111

pected gifts reverently on the table. "About the knife attack—"

"Urisk, you must not fret about that accident this afternoon. Things are not always what they seem." She forced a light tone. "It was probably a Scot out hunting or a group of boys practicing their knife-throwing skills. Would you like some hot chocolate and oatcakes?" she asked, to change the subject.

He shook his head. "Had three bowls of stew for supper. Katie's cherry tarts, too. You eat?"

Truth wrestled with her determination to assure this lad all was well. "I've eaten so much of Katie's delicious cooking, I forced myself to skip supper tonight, else I'd not be able to get into the few gowns I brought with me. Unlike you, dear Urisk, all food goes to my waist and hips. As you can tell," she added, with self-deprecating humor, "I am not built like petite Jean Mackenzie."

Through the slits in his mask, Ian took another look at her figure. It was then he decided most of the trouble stemmed from her choice in wardrobe. "Ye dress badly," popped out.

Her body stiffened at the unexpected blow. "Bootblack turned couturier, have you?"

Ian hauled himself back to his role as Urisk. He lowered his bewigged head.

Immediately Myrtle regretted her snappish remark. "Urisk, I know you meant well just now. Forgive me. I . . . it is just that my looks were once a sensitive area for me. I learned early I'm no beauty, and it is partly my own fault for never cultivating an interest in clothes. However, let us talk of other things, all right?"

Ian's head came up. "Urisk thought ye were beautiful in the tub."

Oh dear, for a backward soul, Urisk had a good memory. Then the scene of Urisk and Gavin's daughter flashed across her mind. Had no one ever

112

thought to explain a few facts of life to this poor lad? Responsible for him now, Myrtle came to a decision.

She moved closer to him on the sofa. "Urisk, you do know there are . . . certain differences between boys and girls, don't you?"

"Oh, aye, girls are softer. That's all, isn't it?" he asked.

Her suspicions proved correct; no one had bothered to speak to him. "Well, that is not all, my dear." Nervous, she looked down at her hands resting on her lap. When she saw Mortimer's pink ears and nose peek out from Urisk's outer coat pocket, an idea came to her. "Hello, Mortimer," she whispered, then reached out to stroke the mouse's silky head. "Urisk, have you ever seen Mortimer with other mice?"

Ian couldn't help feeling intrigued to learn where this woman would lead him. He took his pet from his pocket and held him in his hand. With his right finger he petted Mortimer's head. "Well, I've made him a little box where he can play. There's a wheel and ball in it. Sometimes I've found him wrestling with one of the other mice in the cellar. What could have made him so mad to pounce like that?"

Despite her intent, Lady Myrtle's face reddened. "Well, sometimes Mortimer isn't actually angry with the other mouse. Have you ever seen baby mice?"

He shook his head. "Oh, aye."

Relieved, Myrtle asked, "Then you know where the little mice come from?"

"Aye, the pixies bring them at night when we're all asleep. That's the way bairns come, too, isn't it?"

Floundering, Myrtle answered, "No, Urisk. The baby mice come from what Mortimer does to the lady mouse. They . . . that is, they . . . Mortimer takes a certain part of his anatomy—" she pointed to the spot under Mortimer's tummy. "And he . . . he puts it into the lady mouse's . . . umm . . . opening," she finished, convinced she appeared as flustered as she felt.

"He does that?" Urisk demanded in disbelief.

"Yes."

Urisk raised the mouse he held carefully in his hand to eye level. "Mortimer, ye auld bugger." Hiding his grin behind his mask, Ian slipped his pet back into the soft lining of his coat pocket. "And that's how babies are made, too?"

He sounded so crestfallen to learn the truth, she almost regretted having enlightened him. "Yes, Urisk, but men and women are different from animals. That is why I brought this subject up. You see, my dear, I believe Jean Mackenzie took unfair advantage of you when . . . when she caressed you that way this afternoon."

"Took advantage of me?" echoed Urisk. "Dinna ken."

No, of course he didn't understand. Raising her eyes from the lace sleeves where her gown ended at the elbows, Myrtle took a deep breath. "You had just met, yet she must have realized you are—" She would not hurt him by calling him handicapped.

"You mean because I'm stupid."

Her eyes misted. "Oh, no, my dear, you are not stupid." Quickly she reached out and took his hands in hers. "You are special, with gifts many of us do not have. You are kind and helpful. Katie and Angus have told me what a devoted friend you were to the late chieftain. Now, you use your strength and sweet nature to help us. I'll always feel beholden to you for being my friend here."

Moved by her words and the threat of tears in those deep blue eyes, Ian watched her intently through the slits in his mask. He inhaled the scent of roses in her hair, felt her soft hands on his. With her emotion, her full breasts moved against the wool gown. It was difficult to keep from responding to her vulnerability right now. How he wanted to reach up and slip those

114

pins from her severely-coiffed hair for just a moment to see the rich brown tresses about her shoulders once more!

Unaware she'd been caressing his large, yet graceful fingers, Myrtle released his hands slowly. She rested her spine against the patched upholstery. "What I was trying to tell you is that you have a right to protest when someone touches you without your permission, as Jean was . . . fondling you when I came into the laundry room."

"But I . . . kinna liked it."

"Oh, dear. My, my . . . well . . . yes, of course, you are a healthy young man, and your physical response is normal. Nothing to be ashamed of. Our bodies are beautiful creations of God."

"Just as you are beautiful in the tub."

Lord, back to that tub again. "Well, in truth, dear Urisk, I must correct you. I am not beautiful, though it is sweet of you to make such a mistake. Lovely figures like Jean's are considered much more desirable with the ton. In London I am thought overly tall and far too . . . too ample to have that word applied to me. However," she continued, forcing herself back on track, "those intimate touches, similar to Jean's this afternoon, should be between people who care deeply for each other." Myrtle knew he couldn't possibly understand her yet. "You see, Urisk, Jean was merely reacting to your handsome body."

"Aye, a mon likes a lass to tell him he's a bull, that the sun rises and sets on his backside."

"Well, turn around and I'll tell you if it does," Myrtle blurted, then thrust a fist to her mouth in horror.

Unable to fight it, Ian's rich laughter escaped. Automatically, he reached out and gave her a quick hug. He thought Myrtle adorable the way she looked so appalled at her own quick rejoinder.

"Oh, my. Oh, this is frightful. Terrible. I never

115

wish to give you the impression this topic should be treated in a bawdy manner. Marriage is a serious, honorable estate."

"Dinna husbands and wives share laughter with each other?" Urisk asked.

"Yes, of course, but I must insist you listen carefully to what I am about to say." Her failure just now made her more determined to complete this needed instruction. "It is only when we know and love what a person is *inside* that we can experience the highest pleasure in coming together with our bodies. I was upset with Jean this afternoon because she does not know you, so she couldn't care about the fine young man inside who is really Urisk. She was only using your body, and that is a selfish thing for any man or woman to do."

Myrtle stopped, hoping with all her heart she had reached him. If this didn't work, she wasn't sure what other analogy she could use.

Never, Ian thought, had he heard the birds and bees explained in such an endearing manner. For the first time he felt rather ashamed for having coaxed her into going on so long with this topic when it was clearly so awkward for her. "Aye, I understand yer meaning, my lady. I'll bear it in mind if Jeanie ever comes after me again."

Myrtle's demeanor changed back to one in full control. "You tell me if Jean Mackenzie accosts you in the future, and I shall attend to that forward miss."

He chuckled at the determination on her pretty face. Yes, he suddenly realized it was true—Myrtle Prescott was pretty to him.

"Well," Myrtle added, breaking the silence. "It is getting late, and I still have work to do at my desk. I'll be having a visitor arrive early tomorrow to spend the day, so you may wish to stay in your rooms, out of sight, until he leaves the next morning."

"Who's comin'?" he asked, remembering to use

116

his Urisk voice.

She smiled. "You do not know him. His name is Addison Barrington. He is a fine man, and—"

"Urisk does nae want to stay hidden. If I'm verra quiet, can I help Katie in the kitchen?" Ian groaned inside at the thought of this English officer prowling about Kilmarock grounds. However, he wanted to find out any information he could about future British troop movements. And he was curious to learn just what this woman saw in the beaky-nosed redcoat he'd seen from the picture she kept on her bedstand.

Amused by his pleading, Myrtle reminded herself how lonesome it must get without any contact with the outside world. Boys were always intrigued by military things. Surely it wouldn't hurt, once she explained to Addison about poor Urisk's condition. "All right, my dear, you may move freely about. Just mind your manners and obey Katie."

Ian ground his teeth rather than spout the reply on his tongue. Older than Myrtle, at least six inches taller, he was suddenly irritated at her condescending tone. However, he reminded himself, to Lady Myrtle he was Urisk, not Ian. "Urisk will be a good boy," he managed.

"I know you will, Urisk. You go along to bed, now." Rising from the sofa, she took Urisk's hand and walked him to the door. "Pleasant dreams," she added, giving him her usual nightly *adieu*.

His hand on the brass door knob, Ian remembered why he'd come here tonight. Turning to her, he ordered in his normal voice, "If you go out past the castle lands, from now on, take one of the Mackenzie brothers with you."

Her mind was already on preparations for Addison's visit. "Yes, yes. Sweet of you to be concerned," she said, dismissing Urisk with a wave of her hand.

Chapter Seven

Ian could not believe all the bustling going on in the kitchen. A side of beef was turning on a spit in the fireplace, and the aromas of baking bread and fruit pies filled the kitchen. Katie told him Lachlan Mackenzie had arrived earlier with a string of salmon he'd caught for her ladyship's dinner guest. It was the new clothes Katie wore that caught his eye, and he remarked on them.

Katie smiled when she glanced up at the masked laird. "Aye, Lady Myrtle sent to London for our ready-made clothes." A new ruffled apron covered her dress, with a white lacy pinner atop her gray head. Katie touched one of the elbow-length sleeves of the flowered-print gown. "Angus got a new livery set. Later on, my lady says more bolts of cloth will arrive for making new curtains and linens for the hall. But she says the clansmen's homes, food, and clothing must first be met before active repairs are started on the castle."

It was clear to Ian that his former nanny now approved of Miss Prescott. "Yet her ladyship is wasting a lot of food here for just one English officer. And she's made too much work for you by yourself."

"Och, three of Gavin's nieces and two of his nephews will be arriving shortly to help with the

119

extra work. And the leftovers not used at table are to be sent to the nearby crofts. Her ladyship told me she and the captain are going to eat in the sitting room, not the great hall." Katie leaned closer and whispered, "Lady Myrtle is paying those Mackenzies three times what they deserve, but the lass says she's grateful they're willing to help with so much work needed at their own crofts. And they each get a new set of clothes and shoes in the bargain. Daft, she is, to be paying so much. Ah, but she's a kindhearted lassie."

Ian was not so easily won over. "If she doesn't destroy the Sinclairs, as you've pointed out to me so often."

Katie's expression changed to one of sadness. "Aye, there is that. My dreams have nae told me which way the Sassenach will go with us." Then her lined features brightened. "But 'tis a good omen she is having the cattle sent up from the lowlands for us."

Angus came up from the wine cellar with four bottles of Ian's best claret. He set the dark bottles down and brushed a flutter of dust off his brand new coat and breeches before greeting Ian.

"Where's Robbie?" Ian asked.

"Weel," said Angus, rubbing his recently shaved cheek. "As a rule, the beastie usually visits her ladyship early in the morning before she dresses. He should be comin' doonstairs any moment now."

As if he heard his name, Robbie's nails could be heard on the stone hallway as he sauntered toward the kitchen.

Ian could not believe the changes in his scruffy pet. Someone had recently taken great pains to clean and comb his coat. Robbie pranced toward him as if aware just how much his appearance had improved. Instinctively Ian knew Myrtle had transformed his pet. "You too, Robbie," he said, more amused than irked that it seemed his whole household was captivated by Kilmarock's new owner.

As Ian stood playing with Robbie, Lady Myrtle arrived.

Today she wore a tan lutestring dress with small beige bows from throat to waist. It was well made, with Dutch lace at the elbow-length sleeves. While Ian realized this was the best of the three gowns she'd brought with her, he was glad his mask hid his reaction to the poor choice of color and her penchant for pulling her long hair up and back in that severe style. "Good morning," he answered to her pleasant greeting.

Myrtle walked over and handed him a wrapped parcel. "Here, Urisk, this is for you. Open it," she added, smiling at his shy reaction.

But she had already given him the sock toy and music box. Finding a spot on the large work table, Ian placed the brown package down and opened the gift. It was a dark green coat with waistcoat and breeches, and a simple but elegant lawn shirt. There were white stockings, and a new pair of black leather shoes. He felt embarrassed by this unexpected generosity.

Aware Urisk might feel too baffled to say anything, she came over to him. "Here, my dear, let's try on the outer coat."

With a docility that surprised him, Ian let Myrtle help him remove his patched gray coat to slip on the well-tailored green livery coat. Something lurched within his chest when he glanced at the inner lining of the coat. It was a dark green and black crossbar pattern, which would be hidden when the coat was properly buttoned but there for him to see whenever he wished. "'Tis a grand coat. Thank ye, my lady," he said, surprised to find such emotion had not died within him a year ago.

Taking joy that her small gift pleased him, Myrtle touched his arm, smoothing out the material of the

121

jacket. "My, Urisk, you do look handsome. The coat shows off your wonderfully broad shoulders and narrow waist." She saw him look at the lining once more. "I thought you and Angus might enjoy having a little of the plaid for yourself. You understand, of course, I could not openly have any of the clothes, nor bolts of cloth coming later, in any tartan color. I know if any English soldier catches a Scot wearing the plaid, it means six months' imprisonment for the first offense and seven years' transportation to a colonial plantation for the second." She peered up at the slits in the leather that shadowed his eyes. "If any of you Sinclairs were harmed because of me, I should never forgive myself."

The three Scots stood silently watching the Englishwoman, clearly not knowing what to say.

When Robbie nudged her right hand with his cold nose, Myrtle bent down to give him a hug. "Oh, and I love you, too, Robbie, you little darling."

Ian could not suppress a smile as his once fierce dog whimpered and cuddled up to Myrtle like an overgrown pup.

"Well," said Angus gruffly, "best finish getting the liquor. Urisk, laddie, before ye change to your new finery, will ye fetch a small keg of ale from the cellar?"

Remembering his role, Urisk nodded and proceeded to obey. He was halfway down the stone steps when Angus called him back. He could tell his old servant was enjoying their role reversal by the twinkle in the white-haired man's eyes.

Katie and Myrtle were busy sorting through the china, trying to separate the pieces with the fewest chips. Bored with all the activity, Robbie accepted a beef bone with a generous amount of meat left on it, then lumbered past Ian to take his booty outside. Ian waited for Angus to tell him why he'd been called back.

Angus coughed, cleared his throat, then thumped his bony chest with a fist. "Oh, 'tis certain I've taken a chill," he said in a loud voice, clearly, so her ladyship could hear. "When ye haul up that keg, bring me up a bottle of the late laird's reserve cognac, there's a good laddie."

From beneath his mask, Ian blurted a Gaelic expletive.

Katie heard the word. "Urisk," she admonished, which caused Myrtle to look up, too.

"What is amiss?" Miss Prescott asked Katie. "What did he say?" Her blue eyes rounded when Katie translated. She marched over to Urisk.

A halo seemed to hover near Angus's short-cropped hair. "No call to scold the lad, my lady, for I'm certain Urisk dinna mean it."

Mollified, Myrtle took a deep breath. "Now, Urisk, you said you wanted to help serve dinner tonight and set up the archery targets for the captain and me, isn't that correct?"

With difficulty, Ian answered, "Aye . . . Urisk did."

"Well, then, you do what Angus says." She patted his arm. "And no more swearing, especially in front of Captain Barrington. Like me, he would not understand the Gaelic, but I'm certain he wouldn't overlook the tone. Go along now."

The saintly expression on Angus Thomson's face made Ian grind the backs of his white teeth. He turned to do as bidden. Physical labor appealed to him right now, for he hoped it would work off his barely controlled temper.

Ian stood in the shadows of the castle as he watched Myrtle quickly walk down the dirt path to greet the English officer. For his part, Addison swung down from his chestnut-colored mount and swept her into his arms. The kiss he gave Myrtle was short but affectionate. Addison was dressed in scarlet coat and breeches, sword on his left hip, tricorn over powdered wig with black silk ribbon at the back of his neck; and his medals and boots gleamed in the morning sun. It pleased Ian to realize he was at least taller and broader in the shoulders than her military Lothario.

After telling Addison briefly about Urisk, she said, "He's really a harmless lad and helps about the castle with odd jobs. He's so much like a little boy. You must understand the poor dear still has frightening memories from the mistreatment he received by English soldiers as a child. If he could finally meet one like you, I'm sure it would help him see there are kind men who represent His Majesty. For me, Addison? He's standing near the entryway ahead."

Clearly, other things on his mind, Addison continued to look at her. "I love you. Why won't you marry me?"

Myrtle chose her words carefully as she looked across at the Englishman. "Though I am very happy in your company, Addison, I do not know if I love you."

He smiled. "I have enough love for us both. Besides, after we are married, love will come later."

Out of the corner of her eye, she saw Urisk. "Will you meet Urisk . . . for me?"

"How can I deny you anything, beautiful Myrtle?"

Uncomfortable with his adjective, she tried not to show it. "I have missed you."

"Umm, heard about that knife incident."

She couldn't hide her surprise. "How did you find out?"

"Lieutenant Johnson was out on patrol that morning. He came by when one of the Scots was talking with Miss Ross. Of course, they both got tight-lipped when Johnson asked for more details. Was that the first time someone has tried to harm you?"

She looked down at the stony ground, thinking of the rock incident. Addison studied her so intently, she decided not to tell him about this. Would his protectiveness toward her cause him to do something rash against her tenants? "Certainly," she lied, forcing a lightness in her voice. "And I'm not even sure that knife in the tree wasn't just an accident. The Scots really are beginning to accept me."

He appeared unconvinced.

"Urisk," Myrtle called when he started to leave. "Come over, please."

Reluctantly, Ian walked toward the two English people.

"Urisk, I would like you to meet Captain Addison Barrington. He will be staying overnight, and we are happy to have him as our guest."

Automatically Ian put out his hand in greeting, only to have Addison turn back to his horse with a cursory, "How do you do," tossed at the Scot dressed in his new green livery.

Reaching into his inside pocket, the officer pulled out a halfpenny. He tossed the coin to Urisk. "Here, see that my horse is watered and fed after you take my trunk inside."

Ian looked down at the bronze coin in his palm.

Myrtle bit her lower lip. "Oh, Addison, you should not have—well, the Scots are insulted by tipping." She didn't mention that the niggardly amount didn't help, either. Lowering her voice, she added, "No matter how poor a Scot may be, he sees himself as a gentleman."

"Lud love me, what twaddle," Addison blustered. "Big loony's probably glad to get the money. Say one thing, m'dear, Urisk is better dressed than most of the untidy oafs I've seen in this area." He turned back to the Scot. "Here, get along, clod pate, do as you're told."

"Addison, please." Myrtle went over to Urisk to whisper to him. "Urisk, I would be most grateful if you would see to the captain's horse and luggage. I . . . I am sorry if you feel upset by his—you can buy yourself some sweets with the money. Put it in your pocket now, there's a good boy."

Tempted to tell Addison where he could put his coin, Ian thrust the offending copper into his vest pocket. "Urisk won't let the beastie suffer just because his owner's a horse's ass."

His long nostrils flaring, Addison charged over to stand just inches from the taller Scot. He fingered the hilt of his sword. "What did that moron say?"

"Nothing, Addison. He just asked me about your fine horse. He is a beautiful animal," Myrtle added, running her hand along the stallion's smooth neck. Not as impressive as Sian, she thought, but she knew how Addison doted on his mount. Anything to keep the peace. It wasn't like Urisk to be so belligerent. Of course, Addison wasn't helping matters, and he was the adult male in this group.

Though a scowl contorted his English features, the officer moved his hand away from his rapier. "My lady, you have spoiled this Scotchman, just as you indulged your servants in London."

"I'm a Scotsman," muttered Urisk, "nae a whiskey."

"My, my," Myrtle interjected with a nervous laugh, "now that we're all acquainted, why don't you and I leave Urisk to his chores."

After watering and feeding the captain's horse, Ian stayed out of the two English people's way until dinnertime, except to move the blue-and-white circular archery targets outside for Myrtle and her guest. Convinced Addison was showing off when he ordered Urisk to move the targets farther away, Ian congratulated himself on not opening his mouth. The look of appreciation Myrtle gave him made him feel better, but not by much.

Using the hidden stairs that led through the castle to the outside, Ian made it a point to eavesdrop on Miss Prescott's and her visitor's conversation. Though gaining little useful information on her plans for the Kilmarock estate or the redcoats' military intentions, Ian saw and heard enough to realize Addison viewed himself as Myrtle's future husband.

Addison and Myrtle spent the early afternoon in the downstairs sitting room. When he brought in the tea, Ian could not believe Myrtle allowed Addison to kiss her hand two more times, while she sat on the sofa listening to the captain spout such nauseating drivel about missing her, along with why she should marry him. Finally, Myrtle suggested they take a canter about the estate, riding two of the new horses she'd just purchased. Then she showed Barrington his room. Katie or Angus could have done it, the Scot mused, with growing irritation.

After he changed his uniform for riding clothes, Addison led Myrtle to their saddled horses. Ian said nothing as he assisted them.

Two hours later when Ian went over to help Myrtle off her mare's back, he couldn't help wondering what had caused her blue eyes to sparkle with such intensity.

"Out of the way, imbecile. I'll see to her ladyship." Shoving Ian aside, Addison reached up to get a firm grip about Myrtle. "You're not as thick in the waist as you used to be," Addison mentioned, clearly struggling with his load.

Fearful he might accidentally drop her, she reached out quickly for Lily's pommel to steady herself. Sorry for Urisk, who stood holding the leather straps of both horses, his wig-covered head bent, Myrtle patted his arm after she made it safely to the ground. "Thank you, Urisk, for seeing to the horses."

Ian decided his employer probably meant she was grateful he'd kept his gob shut this time. For once he was glad his mask kept his expression hidden.

By dinnertime, Myrtle had to stifle a yawn. It had been a trying few days. She studied Addison, who sat across from her. Dressed handsomely in blue silk evening clothes, with ruffles at throat and cuffs, Addison never seemed to need much sleep. It was probably his years of discipline as a soldier. She gave Urisk an encouraging smile when he deftly poured a third glass of wine for her guest.

"Bring me another bottle, Urisk."

Myrtle nodded to Urisk, letting him know Addison's command was to be obeyed. "Of course, Addie," she said, only half jesting, "if you need fortification to spend a few hours in my company, perhaps you should think twice about your proposal of marriage."

All contrite, Addison reached across the small, square table and took her right hand in his. He kissed the smooth whiteness of her fingers. "Dear Myrtle, you know I adore you."

After Ian returned with the bottle, he went over to stand at attention on the side of the room, as he'd watched countless servants do in the days when he was a boy growing up within these walls. He'd just taken them for granted as part of this castle life—never would he feel the same again. His thoughts shot in a different direction when he saw—how could she let the twit fawn over her like that?

"Dear Myrtle," Addison coaxed, "say the word and I will take you away from this barbaric country."

"Addison, the Scots are not barbarians."

"Don't know how you can defend them after they tried to murder you. Though we English have conquered them, I cannot say we've gained anything of worth. Lud love me, the spoils of war consist of orphans, widows, and rocks. Only thing the dour rabble can converse about is dung and bullocks."

She watched Addison take another spoonful of his crawfish soup. "Oh, but the more I learn of these clansmen and the late laird, the more I am convinced they have many fine attributes."

"Name one."

She thought of how much she'd discovered from Ian Sinclair's diary. "No chief rules except by the consent of his clan. The land here is regarded as property of the clan, with the chief as head and representative. The grazing, fishing, and hunting are open to all clan members. Dues to the laird are not counted in money, but in service and fidelity to the chief."

"Piffle." Addison slurped the rest of his soup. "Though my mother and Twilla are grateful for your kind invitation and look forward to the visit— both are balmy about those bright-colored plaids—I don't trust their safety among these hordes. Without the military escort I intend to provide, they'd be robbed as soon as they reached the border, and not just of their purses," he added with a meaningful stare at her.

Affronted, Myrtle said, "The Sinclairs would never harm a woman or child, nor waylay a coach, as many a London highwayman does in a snap of the fingers. The Scots view such attacks as vulgar."

"Oh, and I suppose brownies stole my father's prize bull last month from the lowlands?"

With the arrival of their salmon, Myrtle waited for Urisk to step back to his post before she answered. "Well, to the highlander, cattle raids are seen as justifiable reprisal. Seventy percent of their farm income comes from livestock because of the mountainous terrain here. Those hardy long-horned cattle

129

are vital for survival of the clan. If I hadn't ordered the first wagonloads of supplies before I left London—my tenants were starving, Addie."

Addison plunked his wineglass on the polished table. "Who's been filling your head with such bunkum about these Scottish vermin?"

His autocratic tone sparked something within her, but she reminded herself Addison had lost English friends at Culloden. "From speaking to some of my tenants, and things I've read recently, I believe the deceased laird was a brave, honorable man who was forced to shoulder more burdens and sorrow than any young man should have to face alone."

Looking up, it surprised her to see how quietly Urisk had returned with the platter of beef and gravy. He stood watching her, which prompted her to say, "Yes, Urisk, you may serve us now. None for me, thank you," she added, before Urisk could place a large slice of beef on her china plate. Her healthy appetite departed. If she couldn't convince Addison of Ian's worth, how did she hope to persuade King George to do as she asked?

Addison frowned. "My dear Myrtle, as a soldier, I can tell you it is folly to ask a conquered race about one of their own. Ian Sinclair spent all his time chasing after light skirts. That buck's single attribute, according to the accurate reports I have gleaned, would have made him suited only for stud service."

"Son of a pox-riddled 'ore!" Addison swore when hot gravy and beef hit his silk-covered lap. He shot out of the chair, his Cockney origins blasting to the surface. "You clumsy bonehead," he bellowed at Urisk.

Alarmed at Addison's fury, Myrtle got up and pushed herself quickly between Addison and Urisk, who was standing with the half-empty trencher in his hands.

"Slipped," Urisk said from the opening in his mask.

"Slipped, my arse," growled Addison as Myrtle took her napkin and began blotting his coat. "'Ell, that moronic swine did it on purpose."

"There, I do believe it's coming out," said Myrtle, then dropped to her gown-covered knees to remove the last vestiges of gravy from her guest's clothing. "This is the first time Urisk has ever served at table." She turned to the masked Scot. "Everything will be all right, Urisk. Go along now and help Katie with dessert." When she turned back to the enraged Englishman, Myrtle gave him her most beguiling smile. "I have your favorite, lemon cream in puff pastry."

The enjoyment of his deliberate assault on this pompous English officer muted when Ian saw Myrtle on her knees, using her white napkin to assuage the damage to Addison's fancy attire. Earlier, he'd been moved by her defense of the Scots and Ian Sinclair. Right now, as Addison looked down his sharp nose at her, smiled, then pulled her to her feet to place a kiss on her lips, something unfamiliar sparked in Ian's veins. He turned on his heel and stalked from the room. What was wrong with him to feel—what did he care whom the Sassenach kissed? She was nothing to him. Yet why did he have an overwhelming urge to rush over and haul her out of that Englishman's arms just now?

After dinner, Myrtle sat on the patched sofa, with Addison across from her on the best overstuffed wing chair in the castle. Without powdered wig, his brown hair gleamed in the light from the fireplace. He took another generous swallow of brandy. "You know, m'dear, I hate the thought of you living here alone for these few weeks. Heard the castle was a dark, depressing place." He looked around the sitting room. "Furniture, pictures gone, yet you have managed to spruce the place up a bit." He raised the crystal glass to his lips again. "I'll say this for him, the dead laird kept a marvelous supply of liquor."

Myrtle stifled another yawn. The bustle of activity today, along with her recent recovery from that rock attack, was making her drowsy. When Addison rose from his chair to come over and sit next to her on the sofa, she managed a smile. It had been a long time since they'd had the chance to talk like this. "It is good to see you again, Addie. You were right about one thing," she admitted, as he moved closer to take her in his arms. "I have been lonely."

"Poor girl," Addison whispered next to her ear. "Thank heavens your enforced prison sentence is almost over." He kissed her cheek. "You must know how worried I've been about you."

Resting her head against his shoulder, she sighed. "I was not looking forward to coming here, but I felt I had no choice." She knew this was a sore point between them, so she sought a change of subject. Looking down at her tan gown, she added, "I had to write Barbara to request that she send more of my clothes along. Hope my stepmother sends them quickly. I do wish to make a good impression on your mother and sister when they arrive next week."

Addison smiled down into her blue-eyed gaze. "Mother and Twilla are excited about the visit. They're bringing you a lovely housewarming present, but I am under strict orders not to reveal it. I can spare Lieutenant Johnson and three of his men from the fort to assist with the preparations, and—"

"No," Myrtle answered quickly. "You are most kind, but I've hired some of the locals to help. We shall have everything ready." She knew the presence of English soldiers in the castle was the last thing she needed, especially since the Scots still didn't trust her.

"Enter," she called when there was a knock at the door. She was about to put a more discreet distance

132

between herself and her guest, but for some reason Addison shook his head and held her next to him. Urisk came in. He carried an empty silver tray. "Katie said I was to fetch the glasses, my lady."

Myrtle felt guilty as Urisk watched her, while Addison continued to hold his arm about her shoulders. "Thank you, Urisk," she managed, telling herself she was being silly. Perhaps it was because Addison and she hadn't been together in such a long time. Yet there was something about this castle atmosphere that made her unusually shy with her English suitor.

Ian picked up the almost empty decanter and one glass. When he turned back to the couple snuggling on his couch, he studied Lady Myrtle intently for a few seconds. He saw the signs of strain near her eyes, the pinched look on the soft skin about her mouth. "Time for bed, lady Myrtle."

"What the devil does that cheeky sod mean?" Addison demanded, coming to his feet. When he swayed to the right, he was forced to grab the edge of a nearby tea table. Staggering over to Urisk, he gave the taller Scot a combative look, before peering back at Myrtle. "Bald and disfigured, with the br—brains of a four-year-old, you said. Well, I think the colossal shit's got more advanced maneuvers on his mind."

Myrtle was no longer sleepy. As often happened of late, she found her back to Urisk and a defensive expression on her face as she confronted Addison. "He meant nothing. I have told you Urisk would never harm anyone. He merely blurts the first thing that comes into his head. Since I've been here, he knows I'm usually in bed by now. Urisk is merely noting the routine is different tonight." She placed her hands on the Englishman's silk-covered arms. Pungent fumes surrounded her. If anyone needed to retire to his bed, it was Addison, so he could sleep off his stupor. Yet she sensed any more references to bed

133

would set him off again.

"Please take the tray back to the kitchen, Urisk," she said over her shoulder. "Then you have my permission to retire. The captain and I will see to ourselves, thank you."

Ian pressed his lips together behind his mask. Gripping the edges of the silver tray, he gave a silent bow and left. It rankled, to hide behind this Englishwoman's protection; it gnawed at him the way he'd found Addison with his arms about Myrtle. It irritated him the way Barrington treated the Scots like an inferior race he'd bested alone.

Suddenly Ian heard a loud male voice, then a female voice coming from the sitting room he'd just vacated. Captain Barrington was dropping his aitches again. The mask hid a wicked grin. As ordered by her ladyship, Ian continued toward the kitchen. The image of the lovebirds squabbling rather than cuddling on *his* sofa pleased the laird of Kilmarock no end.

"But, Addison, please try to understand, I promised my father I would have a care for his clansmen." Myrtle tried to hold onto Addison's leather trunk, but he pushed her hands aside. For over an hour they'd had this heated argument. It finally ended with Addison storming up to his rooms. Now he was packed and ready to leave. "At least stay the night, as planned. It is dark out, and I do not think it wise to ride alone to—"

"If you cared anything for me," the officer countered in icy rage, "you would leave this cursed country after Mother and Twilla visit. The bans could be posted, as you promised, and—"

"I made no such promise." She closed her eyes as she sought to reason with the Englishman. "It is true, I never imagined settling my Scottish obligations

134

would take this long, but until I've seen to my tenants' futures, I cannot think about my own. Believe me, I do not wish to remain in Kilmarock Castle one day longer than necessary," she added, thinking of the hard tasks ahead. She came to her full height. "I gave my word to my late father, and these people need me."

"Need you?" scoffed the brown-haired man. "These filthy Scottish rabble will plunge a knife in your ribs at the first opportunity. And there won't always be an elm tree or British patrol in the area to stop the point of a dirk from ripping that naive heart out of you. I'm tormented by the picture of you facedown out on the moors, blood spurting from your chest, with all your—"

"Addison, please, I don't . . ." Her words drifted off. All color drained from her face at his graphic description. Didn't he know how afraid she felt, how alone? Since Barrington wanted her as his wife, why couldn't he be her friend now?

Clearly unmoved, Addison said, "Have the laird's ghost protect you, then, if you are so obstinate. I shall return with my mother and sister as planned next week. Perhaps a few days on your own will improve your disposition, then you'll listen to reason."

"The laird's ghost and I are no longer enemies," she said, prepared to show him she would not be cowed by him or anyone. She'd pleaded with him to stay; he wasn't going to, so the hell with him. "Would you like your picture back now?"

Looking beyond her head, Addison became more unfriendly looking when he spotted Urisk walking their way. "I've no intention of continuing this rumpus in front of a servant, and one with a puerile brain at that. It isn't like you to be so childish just because we've had a difference of opinion. You know perfectly well I want you to keep my picture just where it is on your night table upstairs. I'm sure by my next visit I'll forgive you for this quarrel; right now it's best I return to the fort. For one thing," he added, a sardonic twist to his lips, "I cannot abide that lumbering dimwit hovering about us. Here, rattlebrain," he ordered Urisk, "take my bag and bring my horse around. I'm leaving."

Ian gave a proper if exaggerated bow, then brushed past Myrtle to carry out the officer's instructions.

Chapter Eight

Outside her door, Ian stood trying to persuade himself to ignore the Sassenach's condition. She wasn't anything to him, he reminded himself. If she was unhappy, she'd probably leave all the sooner, which was exactly what he wanted, wasn't it? The image of her large eyes, the strain on her face, came to mind. Glad Barrington had left, Ian couldn't deny he'd had some part in it. First the horse comment, then the spilled gravy, and finally his remark that Myrtle should be in bed. Knocking at her door, Ian called himself every kind of a fool for checking on her.

Brushing at the moisture near her eyes, Myrtle walked over to the door. "Is that you, Katie? I . . . I'm ready for bed. Will it not keep until morning?"

Something touched him at the catch in her soft voice, the unmistakable sound of a woman trying to hide that she'd been crying. "It's Urisk. Please, may I see you?" he whispered, close to the door.

Oh, dear. Was he worried he'd be fired or sent away because of her fight with Addison? Children were sensitive to such things. Slowly she unlocked the door and opened it. The coldness from the hallway caused her to tighten the shawl about her shoulders. "Just for a moment, Urisk. You should be asleep."

That night he'd used words to comfort her in his bed from the hidden panel in his room. Right now he faced her tearstained face, the pain in her blue eyes, and he felt undone by her defenselessness. She was in bare feet and high-necked garment, and her straight brown hair streamed about her shoulders; she appeared more fragile than he'd ever seen her, despite her height and full figure. But what could he say to comfort her? He was Urisk, not Ian. As a mental defective, Urisk could not tell her the words she needed to hear. "I was worried," he blurted, his frustration causing Urisk's voice to sound more agitated. "You've been crying."

Forcing aside her own concerns, she took Urisk's hands in her own. "Just a little. It's because I'm tired, that's all." She gave him a self-deprecating smile. "I must be far louder than I thought to have you hear me through the door." When he moved closer to her, her features relaxed as she inhaled that pleasant scent of oatmeal soap. He'd removed his neckband and waistcoat before coming here. Dressed only in his white shirt, green breeches, and unbuttoned outer coat, it was clear he'd been preparing to retire for the night. "What made you come upstairs, Urisk?"

What had nudged him while he'd sat on the edge of his bed just now? he wondered. Intent on sleep, he'd come up here instead. Was it the memory of a lost look in her eyes after Addison left, the result of their quarrel? Or was it the anger he'd experienced when he saw Barrington nuzzle her ear while they sat on the sofa after dinner? Ian knew he had to say something, for he could not continue to stare down into those lovely eyes and not do something he knew would endanger his clan—like taking her in his arms, and the devil with the politics that separated them. "That redcoat doesn't like me."

Oh, now she understood why he needed to see her.

He was afraid, poor darling, frightened she might not be able to carry out her duties here as new owner. And of course, her weakness in crying just now probably made him more uneasy. He was so tall and strong, she had to remember Urisk was a child in mind and heart. She took his large yet graceful fingers in hers and caressed them as she often did to reassure him. "Dear Urisk, I will take care of you," she promised. "I will keep you safe here in Kilmarock Castle for as long as you live."

Ian wanted to shout to her this was not what he meant at all. Hell, it was *her* safety in these highlands, not his own, that worried him right now. He remembered his shock and outrage when Gavin showed him the large black-handled knife Lachlan had removed from the tree near Fiona's cottage. Was it one of his disgruntled clansmen taking matters in his own hands to rid the Sinclairs of this Sassenach? He groaned in frustration.

"Oh, Urisk, remember I have made the Scot's promise to protect you. Do not worry that I would ever abandon you," she added, thinking he still fretted about his future. With an attempt to get his mind off his troubled thoughts, she asked, "May I see Mortimer again?"

Aware tonight he'd make no headway into straightening out this quandary, he sighed and thrust his hand into his right coat pocket. Mortimer gave an impatient squeak to be pulled abruptly out of the warm softness of his master's livery coat. Myrtle was treating him like the bairn she thought Urisk was, and Ian Sinclair was a dead man to her. His pet mouse must have sensed his grim mood, for Mortimer just sat in his open palm, craning his neck warily up at both of them.

As she used a finger to gently pet his tan-colored head, Myrtle could not resist cooing at the friendly creature. "Mortimer, you are just like Robbie; you like to have your ears rubbed. May I hold him, Urisk?"

He placed the pink-eared mouse in her hands. "He and Robbie like ye. Yer gentle with dumb animals."

Was he thinking of himself? she wondered, and it saddened her to realize how cruelly Urisk had been treated as a little boy, before Ian's father had found him on a deserted road one night. Distracted, she wasn't paying attention to the mouse in her hands. Mortimer became playful suddenly and scurried up her arm, which caused her to gasp in surprise. When she reached for him, the little imp changed course and went higher, to the ruffles about her neck.

Ian was too late reaching around her back to take his rambunctious pet. Mortimer dived behind the loose-fitting neckline.

Alarmed, but trying not to show it, Myrtle fumbled with the three cloth-covered buttons at her neck. "Please . . . oh, my . . . Urisk, can you help . . . ?" She tried unsuccessfuly to get hold of the squirming animal. "Mortimer," she snapped at the misbehaving mouse.

"Hold still," said Ian, behind his mask.

"I don't think he can hear you." Her voice rose an octave as she wiggled and used her hands in a futile attempt to dislodge the intruder.

"I was talking to you, not the mouse," Ian pointed out. Aware her hopping about wasn't helping matters, with an impatient grunt, he grabbed her by the waist and used his right hand to make a pragmatic search down the open neck of her bed gown. His fingers first latched onto a warm breast, then onto his rowdy pet. "Got ye, Mortimer." He pulled out the mouse and quickly slid him back into his coat pocket. "Sorry," he said, unable to keep the amusement from his voice. Her complexion resembled a ripe tomato.

140

With shaking fingers, she attempted to redo the buttons of her gray nightgown. "You were only trying to help me. I asked to hold him; the fault was mine." The touch of Urisk's warm fingers on her breast just now had sent a wave of fire through her veins she'd never experienced before. His left hand was still about her waist, and she felt the muscular strength of his shoulder as he continued to hold her. When he began stroking her back, Myrtle's arms dropped to her sides. The shawl fluttered to the carpeted floor at her bare feet. Looking up at him seemed more important right now than bending to retrieve the shawl. She searched to see those eyes that always looked out from dark shadows. For an instant she wanted to know their color, yet neither of them spoke. She was unable to stop herself from reaching up to touch his shoulders, then moving to caress the left side of the soft leather covering his face. But suddenly he pulled back from her.

"I'm sorry," she whispered. "Did I hurt you?"

"No."

Then Urisk must have felt alarm, she decided. What must he think of her after she'd warned him against Jean Mackenzie? Wasn't she acting right now like that forward Scottish girl?

Ian read the mortification on her features and was tempted to explain he'd pulled away because he'd felt his own healthy body respond to their close contact. The touch of her warm naked breast, the scent of roses in her hair, the curvaceous feel of her figure through the slip of material covering her—he'd been a hair's breadth from taking her in his arms to slip that maidenly nightgown off her shoulders so he could take one of those hard pink nipples in his mouth and cover her full breasts with kisses. And he couldn't help thinking about her kindness to him and the way she'd begun to help his clansmen with food and supplies. She was a hard worker, often

141

driving herself beyond what was prudent. Was it possible they'd been wrong about all those derogatory things they'd heard of this woman? He scrutinized her expressive eyes for the truth he needed. How could this enchanting woman destroy the Sinclairs? Perhaps he could trust her with the truth of his identity. "Lady Myrtle, there is something I must tell—"

His words were cut off when Angus rushed through the open doorway of her study.

"My . . . lady," he puffed, then stopped to catch his breath. "There's a carriage just arrived. Man said his name is Cyril Layton. He says I was to fetch ye." Angus's white brows rose in disbelief. "I remember him here before, but surely ye canna mean to see him at this hour!"

Immediately Myrtle's whole expression changed. She retrieved her paisley shawl from the floor. "Oh, my clerk made it." Racing back to her desk, she grabbed the letter and folded it. "He was supposed to arrive by the end of the week, but Cyril has always been an employee who could work miracles. My father doted on him, and I can see why. I'll dress and be downstairs directly. Please give Cyril something to eat and drink."

Angus scratched his head. "What will I do with the trunks?"

"Trunks?"

"Aye, my lady, the Sassenach doonstairs said he'd persuaded the countess dowager to hand them over for ye."

"Oh, bless Cyril, he knew how much I needed more clothes." Heaven only knew when Barbara would have shipped them. Myrtle went to her wooden wardrobe and pulled out one of her day dresses. "Please, Angus, tell Cyril I'll be right down." Her cheeks were flushed as she hustled Angus and Urisk out of her room.

142

* * *

Hugging the short, plump gentleman, Myrtle couldn't hide her happiness. "Oh, Cyril, it is wonderful to see you."

"Quite," said the clearly embarrassed clerk. Pushing his round wire spectacles up further on the bridge of his nose, Cyril came to the point. "If you give me the letter now, my lady, I should be grateful to start back at once."

Myrtle's eyes widened. "But . . . I realize you must be fatigued after the long ride. You know you're welcome to stay the night, Cyril."

The older man shook his wig-covered head after a furtive glance about the huge stone entryway. "If it's just the same to you, my lady, I'd prefer not to stay the night."

She knew her employee must be recalling that night Tom had found the bloody sheep's head in his bed. Could she blame him for wanting to leave? Of course, she had hoped for a friendly guest from home for a few days. "Certainly, Cyril. While Urisk and Angus unload the trunks you've been kind enough to bring, I will give you the item I wrote about. Please come upstairs to my study."

On the alert, Ian had come up the back stairs to station himself behind the panel in his old bedroom. He was waiting for Myrtle and her clerk, the edge of the wooden wall open just enough for him to view and hear the exchange unnoticed.

When they arrived in her study, Myrtle reached into the pocket at the side of her gown and retrieved a folded letter. "I did not give you this downstairs, for you will know by its content that secrecy is vital. Though simple Urisk and the Thomsons seem trustworthy, they are still Scots and would never understand why I must do this. If things go as I've planned, my business here will end shortly, and I will

143

return home to Chelmsford. Read it, then put it in a safe place. Do not let this letter out of your sight, Cyril. No one else is to read it until you hand it in private to King George, do you understand?"

Gravely, Cyril took the missive, opened it, and read it. If he was shocked by its contents, years of working for this lady's father schooled his features. He refolded it and placed it in the leather pouch he carried in his hand. There was a strap on the handle that he attached around his right wrist. "No one but George of Hanover will open this letter next," he promised her. Before leaving, Cyril turned back near the door. "You will have a care, my lady," he said. "I . . ." His squeaky voice drifted off.

Myrtle knew this was Mr. Layton's way of showing his concern. "Thank you so much for doing this for me, Cyril. You do not know how important it is to have one person I can trust."

The older man looked like he might say something, but he only bowed formally. "My lady, I shall send word to you of His Majesty's reply as soon as I receive it." Then he left.

Miss Prescott walked into her bedroom to glance at the late earl's portrait again. "Oh, lion eyes," she whispered to the Sinclair's portrait, "if only you were here. I could use your advice so much."

When she left her rooms, Ian pressed the iron button to close the panel. He sat down on the cot near the rough wooden table, sick at heart at what he'd heard between the Englishwoman and her clerk. How could he have been such a blind fool? he shouted at himself. If Angus hadn't interrupted with the arrival of that Cyril fellow, he would have spilled everything to her just now, told her the laird was alive. Was it the reflection of the loch in her eyes, her sense of humor, or the endearing way she had of taking his hands in hers when she wished to speak seriously to him? They'd almost blinded him to her

144

true nature. The Sassenach was writing secret messages to King George. Gavin and Jean Mackenzie were right—this English bitch meant to sell the castle and lands without a care for the tenants. Hadn't she said she hoped to finish this business shortly and return to England? She'd probably mate with that English officer, then old squire Barrington would have Sinclair lands anyway. Why had he fought seeing the truth? She meant to destroy his clansmen. What the devil was wrong with him? The battle inside tore at his guts. With the two attacks on her life, he'd begun to feel protective of her. But now this mysterious letter to the King . . . "Curse you, Jonathan Prescott," he said aloud in his torment. "Why did ye lie to me?"

The silence of the small room pressed against his mind and heart like the stone slab that marked his grave outside the castle.

Holding the heavy leather bag of coins, Lady Myrtle walked by the young stableboy and mounted the chestnut mare herself. She hooked her right leg over the pommel of the sidesaddle and took Lily's reins in her gloved fingers. "I remember Lachlan Mackenzie taking me to the croft where Fiona lives, past where the boulders narrow, isn't it?"

"Aye," said the Scot. "But I was told ye would always take one of the Mackenzie brothers with ye when ye ride oot."

For a new employee, this lad had been briefed thoroughly, but by whom? "There isn't time to go scrounging about for Andrew or Lachlan. Besides, I carry a pistol with me." She touched the leather saddlebags that contained Addison's silver-handled gun. "Let go of the bridle," she ordered. Digging her heels into the mare's sides, she went off in a flurry of dust.

145

While inspecting the repairs done on her stables in preparation for the cattle that would soon arrive, Myrtle had been irritated to learn the cattle had arrived but had been mistakenly diverted near Fiona's cottage, not here at Castle Kilmarock, where they were supposed to be dropped off. Understandably, the Englishmen were adamant about being paid first before they turned over their four-footed cargo. She could just envision the scene of fierce but penniless Scots in need of cattle confronting her equally distrusting English herdsmen. If tempers flared and a skirmish ensued, the last she wanted was to have English soldiers, who patrolled the area, interfere and make matters worse. Thank God Fiona had taken a chance in sending over one of the boys to tell her.

Out of breath and disheveled, Myrtle arrived at the site. From the looks on Scots and English faces, along with the shouts and expletives hurling back and forth, she feared she might already be too late.

"Hello," she called, waving, forcing a lightness in her greeting that belied her nervousness. Her gaze lit on the Scot with the familiar grizzled hair about his shoulders. "Gavin, I've brought the money!" she shouted above the din. Making her way among the crowd, she thought it expedient to stay on Lily until she could make a path through the reddish-brown cattle and angry mob. When Gavin spotted her, his scarred features showed his relief as she held up the bag of coins.

"Her ladyship has brought yer cursed money," Gavin growled to the equally angry Englishmen.

Gavin stalked over and assisted her off the horse. It was then that he looked behind her. "Where are Lachlan and Andrew?"

Reminding herself she was in charge here, she answered, "They're working at the crofts, where I wish them to be." Ignoring his scowl, she walked

146

past Mr. Mackenzie toward the crowd. "Which one of you is Trevor Jones?"

The oldest Englishmen in the group came forward. He brushed off a few layers of dust from his work coat and breeches. "I am, my lady. Blimey, it's good to see you. Thought these Scots were fixin' to murder us."

She handed him the large sack of coins. "Didn't my clerk give you the note of instructions I made for you? I spent hours mapping out your route."

Taking the gold coins in the leather pouch, Trevor nodded. "Yes, but me and the lads got a little off course—the rocks and all. I asked a young Scot we met on the road for directions, and he pointed out the fastest way to Kilmarock Hall. We was all so wary of coming up in these treacherous highlands—into the enemy camp, you might say—guess we didn't pay proper attention to the Scot's directions. Thought we were done for, that we did. Be good to get back home. These tattered folk wouldn't let us pass. Said the cattle was meant for them and here they'd stay. Cor, there's been so many cattle raids by these highlanders, I didn't know if these men were brigands or your own tenants. I was ready to tell Mike to break out the rifles afore you came. Bunch of bleedin' heathen," he spat.

"Well," Myrtle tried to soothe, grateful that Mr. Jones's voice hadn't carried to the Scots in the distance. "There are extra coins in the bag for you and your men to repay you for this unfortunate mishap. Thank you for making this hard trek so quickly." She held out her hand.

Looking overcome by her charm, though Myrtle knew it was more likely the extra money, Trevor Jones pumped her hand with enthusiasm. When he grinned up at her, she noticed a few missing teeth.

"Cor, Cyril said you was a game one. Say," the Englishman went on, after he spotted the scarred features of Gavin Mackenzie over her shoulder. "You sure you'll be all right after we leave? Me and the lads could see you back to the castle."

Suppressing a chuckle, she suddenly saw the humor of the situation with her Sinclair clansmen on one side and her fourteen English workers on the other. The driver in the wagon looked ready to shout for the rifles. Departure seemed the best solution. "You go along now, Mr. Jones; I shall be fine. These people are my friends," she added, deliberately making her voice carry to both sides.

When the wagon and the men on horseback were out of sight, Myrtle turned toward her tenants. "I explained the cattle would be arriving. While I appreciate that you refrained from raiding your own property before it got here, I should have been outraged to learn you'd harmed my employees."

"Gavin said we were to wait until ye came," muttered one of the men in the front row.

Immediately, Myrtle gave Gavin an appreciative smile. At least he'd trusted her enough to give her the opportunity to straighten things out. "Thank you, Gavin. Now, let's work out the division of the cattle among all the families. I've brought the listings with me," she added, walking back to get the leather satchel draped over Lily's saddle. "Let's get to work."

After they finished, Myrtle rode over to Fiona's cottage. Though weary, she decided this was a necessary call. The auburn-haired woman answered the door. Her expression told Myrtle nothing.

Her ladyship gave the young woman a tentative smile. "I came to thank you for sending me word this morning. You helped me defuse a volatile situation. I never would have forgiven myself if anyone had been harmed in a confrontation."

Fiona appeared amazed by the Englishwoman's gratitude. "'Tis certain the Sinclairs would have suffered if any Sassenachs were injured, let alone killed. The redcoats would have come down on us like a nest of bees."

"Well," Myrtle added, "I don't wish to take up any more of your time. But thank you again, Fiona."

Perhaps it was the tiredness in her blue eyes or the dust she noticed on the Englishwoman's skirt, but Fiona stopped her. "Wait . . . I mean, will ye nae want some tea? I've just put the kettle on for myself. Ye are welcome to some, if ye care."

Like a thirsty traveler in the desert, Lady Myrtle grasped this rope of friendship with both hands. "Oh, I should like some tea very much, Fiona." When she saw the shorter woman's face relax into a smile, Myrtle gave a silent prayer of thanks. It was a start. Tying her mare to a nearby wooden fence post, Myrtle followed Fiona into the two-room cottage.

Unlike many of the cottages Myrtle had seen, Fiona's had wood floorboards covering this room, and the furnishings were simple but comfortable. There were a table and bench near the hearth. A rocking chair, patched, and an overstuffed sofa stood next to the wall that probably served as Fiona's bed. Myrtle tiptoed over to the side of the room where Jamie slept soundly on a small cot. "He's beautiful," she whispered.

"Aye, wee Jamie is that, and a little devil of mischief, to boot," said his clearly proud mother.

Over tea, Myrtle was able to learn that Fiona was, indeed, an accomplished seamstress and lady's maid. The Rosses had served the Kilmarock women for generations as personal maids. The disclosure gave her an idea. Setting her cup and saucer down on the table, Myrtle tried to choose her words carefully. She knew Lachlan worried about Fiona and Jamie living so far away from the other crofts. "Fiona, now that most of the farm repairs are near completion, I am trying to get Kilmarock Castle in order. While I am used to waiting on myself, I was not able to bring my maid with me from London. Since you are skilled with such responsible duties and used to be part of the late laird's household—" She stopped when she saw a sadness enter the girl's gray eyes. Never had Myrtle meant to hurt her with this memory. She cleared her throat. "Even on a trial basis, just to see if you liked it there again, I wonder if you would consider helping me."

Fiona smoothed down the front of her mauve gown. "Even if I did consent to be yer maid, I'd nae leave wee Jamie."

Myrtle's eyes mirrored her surprise. "Oh, Fiona, I meant the offer to include your son." Her features softened. "It would be wonderful to have the little boy at Kilmarock Hall. Even for the smallest castle in Scotland, at times it seems a huge, lonely place. I gather it was not always so."

Fiona sighed. "Och, I can remember parties and masks when I was growing up in the castle with my parents. My grandmother and mother served the late earl's mother. The Countess of Kilmarock was a sweet lady. Firm, but fair. Aye, she doted on her husband and sons, always happiest just to stay home. We played knights and damsels in the great hall. Even Ian, who was a few years older than the younger boys, would join us. Yer father's summer visits were always a time for fishing, hunting, and parties."

It reminded Myrtle how much she'd missed her father during those summers he'd spent here in the Highlands. Why hadn't he allowed her to come with him, even once? Forcing herself to the matter at hand, the taller woman said, "Will you give my offer some thought, Fiona? Take a few weeks to consider it, then tell me your answer, all right?"

The Scottish woman studied Myrtle for a few seconds. All the Mackenzies, save Jean, seemed to like the lass. She took in Myrtle's plain gown and tightly pulled-back hairstyle. Habit caused Fiona to calcuate the changes needed to enhance the buxom Englishwoman's looks. She had good bones and a firm, full figure, but she needed more shape to her gowns, and definitely brighter colors. The straight hair needed cutting in a softer style.

Myrtle hoped she hadn't put the younger woman off. She thought of Addison's few criticisms on her appearance. "I admit I could use your expert advice of choosing gowns and fripperies. You probably already realize I show little interest in such things." Her voice was cheerful when she admitted it. "I should be most grateful if you'd consider teaching me."

"Ye'll be criticized by many in the clan for taking me in." Fiona's gray eyes turned defensive. "I'll nae explain anything aboot my past to you or anyone. If I come, ye must take me and Jamie as we are, no questions."

"Certainly. And you will be under my protection." Her back straightened. "Anyone who seeks to harm or slander you or your son will have to deal with me first."

Obviously touched by the older girl's words, Fiona came to a decision. "Aye, then, in about two weeks me and Jamie will move back to Kilmarock Castle."

Myrtle could not hide her joy. "Thank you, Fiona. Please tell Lachlan when you wish to come over, and I will be sure to have wagons and workers here to help you with the move." She named a salary for her new maid.

"Nae, 'tis too much. Twenty pounds a year is what I got three years ago as servant."

Myrtle brushed her protests aside. "No, I will pay you the amount I stated. Besides, there's many renovations to be done on the new owner of Kilmarock Hall," she said, comfortable poking fun at herself.

Fiona found herself laughing with Myrtle. Lach-

Ian might be right . . . Myrtle Prescott wasn't like the other English. Her wry humor just now reminded Fiona of Jonathan Prescott's easy manner. "Aye, it's agreed, then," Fiona concluded, putting her hand out to shake the taller woman's to seal their business agreement.

Angus and Katie looked as worried as their employer. Ian had been pacing back and forth near the front of the stables for hours. He wanted to mount Sian and charge after her to be sure she'd not been harmed. The memory of the two attacks on her life gnawed at him. Despite his doubts last night, this morning, when he'd found out from the stableboy that Myrtle had ridden out alone, he'd felt distraught. Just the other day he'd told her to take one of the Mackenzie brothers with her whenever she rode. And he'd made certain all the servants knew of the directive through Gavin Mackenzie. God, what an irritating woman, he thought, thrusting his hands behind his back once more.

"The boy said she took a pistol with her, ye know the one she keeps in the drawer upstairs?" said Angus.

It did not placate Ian. "All the good it would do her from a swift knife attack in the forest. The Sassenach is as useless as a bairn around firearms, I'll warrant."

Katie's lined face became more strained. "Well, her ladyship does have a way at settlin' arguments between folks. I'm sure she'll be able to straighten out the business between the Scots aboot the cattle."

"If the lass made it up the ridge," Angus added in a low voice.

"I think the Sassenach has a lion's courage," Katie offered her worried employer.

"And a mule's stubbornness," Ian snapped, his nerves close to breaking.

Riding swiftly back home through the hills, Myrtle wasn't prepared when someone swooped down on her from a boulder and tumbled her off Lily's saddle. "Mother of God," she screamed, certain death was imminent. "Please, let me go." She struggled, but the assassin held her facedown on the hard ground. She heard him suck in his breath, but his hold on her continued. Jabbing her elbows behind her, she heard him groan, then he rolled off her.

Scrambling to a seated position, Myrtle's terror-filled eyes focused on her attacker. A year or so younger than herself, he was thin for someone so strong. Dressed in nondescript brown shirt, coat, and breeches, he sat a few feet away, just watching her.

"Another of my tenants sent to kill me, I see." Shivering with reaction, the Englishwoman clutched her gray cape about her arms. "Which clansman are you?"

"I'm nae a Sinclair, if that's what ye mean," said the wiry Scot, his young face showing affrontedness. "Ye must be Lady Myrtle Prescott, then, the Sassenach all the Sinclairs are talking aboot."

If the man meant to kill her, what was he waiting for?

Keeping his right side away from her vision, the Scot seemed to read her uncertainty. "Are ye nae even goin' to thank me for savin' yer life, my lady?"

"Thank you?" she sputtered, shakily getting to her feet. "When you are here to murder me, finish off those failed attempts by the Sinclairs?"

His brown eyes narrowed. "I told ye, I'm nae a Sinclair. And it would have been easier for me to avoid discovery by ignorin' yer situation, especially with redcoats and Sinclair clansmen aboot." He bit his lower lip, then winced as if physical pain assailed him. "If I'd really meant to kill ye, Sassenach, ye'd be dead already." He pulled out a long dagger from the

153

leather belt at his hip. "A clean slice across yer white throat when I landed on yer horse would have done it."

Her stomach lurched.

Something relaxed in the man's brown eyes, and he replaced his dirk. "But yer right, lass, ye do have an enemy." Turning his brown head to the right, the man gritted his teeth and pulled a bloody arrow from his upper right arm. "I made out the figure of a man with bow and arrow high on the ridge above ye. He had his mark set on ye, like a hunter after an unsuspectin' partridge."

Horrified, Myrtle lost most of her wariness and rushed over to the Scot. She saw the blood seeping around his torn coat. "Oh, my God," she cried, and automatically looked around.

"Nae," said the man. "He and the horse are miles away by now. Wasn't time for me to do anything but jump for ye."

Bandages, she needed—without hesitation, Myrtle turned her back, bent down, and began tearing the ruffled material of her inner petticoat. Using water from the nearby brook, she wet some of the strips, then efficiently cleaned and bandaged the man's arm. "It's deep, sir. We must stop the bleeding."

He watched her determined features as she worked over him. "You've got a healing touch, Sassenach."

She saw him grin. Everything showed on his youthful face, and she was no longer afraid of him. Lily munched grass in the distance. "If you can sit my horse, I shall take you back to Kilmarock Castle to see to that shoulder. It may need stitching, I fear."

He looked her in the eye. "Nae, my lady, I must be away from here before I'm spotted."

"By the English soldiers?"

"Or the Sinclairs," he answered, before getting to his feet. "Dinna worry, we Scots walk more than we ride. I've survived worse than an arrow in my arm."

So young, just how many skirmishes had this Scot encountered? "But . . ." she got up to stand next to him. "You must know how grateful I am for your rescue. Surely, if you are under my protection—why would my tenants wish to harm you?"

"Because my name is Duncan Knox of Clan Knox," he answered.

"Then what are you doing on Sinclair lands?"

His boyish face split into a grin. "I'd just finished keeping an appointment again with a certain lady— a lady of Clan Sinclair. As you've no doubt heard, the Sinclairs and Knoxes are not exactly on speaking terms."

Myrtle remembered all the derogatory comments she'd heard about the Knoxes from her clansmen. Yet, meeting this good-natured lad who had just suffered injury to save her, she wasn't sure they were correct. "Yes, I do understand, Duncan. The Sinclairs can be a perplexing, stubborn people," she admitted, thinking of all the trouble she was having getting them to trust her. "It couldn't be easy having a Sinclair girl as a sweetheart."

As he walked over to assist Myrtle back on her horse, Duncan Knox gave her an enigmatic smile. "I have a way to get my lassie to come around to my way of thinking," said the soft-spoken Scot. "Besides, with five sisters, and herding sheep all day, I like the company of a spirited woman."

From atop her horse, Myrtle looked down into his pleasant face. "I promise not to tell anyone of this meeting, but if I can ever be of help to you or your lady, you have but to ask."

Clearly moved by her declaration, Duncan bowed to her. "Thank you, my lady," he said. "Please have a care riding back now. I'll watch from the ridge until I know you've made it safely out of the thickest part of the forest."

Two hours later, when Myrtle Prescott finally

returned to Kilmarock Castle, she found Urisk waiting for her outside the stables. Angus Thomson was a few feet away, looking uneasy. She smiled immediately. Things had turned out well. The Scots had their cattle, her English employees their money, she would have a new maid soon, and she'd met Duncan Knox—best not think about that arrow right now. "Hello, Urisk. How nice—" Her words were cut off when she was lifted roughly off her horse.

"I told you to take Lachlan or Andrew with you when you went out," the Scot thundered, holding her firmly by the shoulders.

She had never seen Urisk like this. "It is sweet of you to be concerned about me, and I appreciated your suggestion, but—"

"Suggestion? *Merde! Les filles sont connes,*" he shouted behind the opening in his leather mask.

"Girls are *not* idiots," she countered, translating his French.

"Damn it to hell, it was an order, and I assure you, madam, I am used to having my directives carried out. Of all the rattle-brained—'tisn't enough ye were nearly murdered two times, ye have to try for a third?"

There had already been a third with the arrow a few hours earlier, but she wasn't about to tell Urisk.

His tirade switched to rapid Gaelic, then back to French. Myrtle made out a few of the French expletives, but she was certain from his furious tone she never wanted the Gaelic ones translated. "Let go of me this instant . . . you overbearing Scot!" she shouted, incensed to be addressed in such a manner. For all her strength, Myrtle was shocked to realize she couldn't pull away from the strong hands holding her right in front of him. "I'm warning you, Urisk, the next thing you'll feel is the toe of my shoe on one of those thick shins of yours if you don't unhand me. This is your last chance," she yelled, the two crimson

156

spots on her cheeks proving her own lost temper. "Mother of God, what's gotten into you?"

"Struggle all ye like, Sassenach, ye'll nae go anywhere until I'm finished. Ye may be used to doing as you please in London, but ye're on Sinclair lands now. By God, ye could have been . . ." His words stopped at the changed expression on her face.

No longer struggling, Myrtle looked slacked-jawed at his masked features. His angry words were forgotten as their implication hit her. Urisk, who was supposed to be slow mentally, had just spoken articulately in French, Gaelic, and English.

Chapter Nine

Breathing heavily, Ian stepped back from Myrtle. Worry during the last few hours had led to his outburst. Inadvertently, he'd just revealed Urisk was no mental defective. He must salvage what he could. Perhaps it was for the best. At least now Urisk might find out the truth of her plans for his clansmen and Kilmarock Castle.

But Angus rushed over to the two combatants before Ian could speak.

"Oh, it's happened!" Angus cried, his bony arms encircling an astonished Urisk when Myrtle stepped out of the way. "The doctors said it might happen." His elderly features were a picture of rapture before he addressed the puzzled Englishwoman. "My lady, the doctors in Edinburgh said Urisk had brain leaks."

"Brain leaks? I've never heard of—"

"Few have, yer ladyship. Course, that isn't the medical term for it. Caused by that horrible beating from the English soldiers when Urisk was a bairn. His suffering, they said, blocked his mind. Suppose it was Urisk's fretting about yer safety when he learned ye rode out alone that did it. The terrible shock, don't ye see? The doctors said a shock or reminder from the past might restore his wits. And it has," the older Scot blubbered, wiping his eyes on the sleeve of his work shirt. "I'm so overcome I dinna think I can talk more aboot it. Lord be praised."

"Yes," Myrtle agreed, then found she wasn't upset with Urisk anymore. Indeed, she felt her own eyes mist. "Dear Urisk," she whispered, coming close to give him a hug. "You are recovering, thank God. It is wonderful news."

Unsure what he felt at her genuine emotion and Angus Thomson's Covent Garden performance, words failed the laird of Kilmarock.

When she could speak, Myrtle asked, "Urisk, can you tell me who your people were? Perhaps you have relatives still alive, and we can—?"

"No," Ian answered, "there is no one left." He reminded himself he still could not trust this woman with the truth, not while she dallied with an English officer and wrote secret missives to King George. Besides, she'd still not revealed her plans for her Scottish inheritance. "I am Urisk, the deceased laird's gillie. That is all there is to know. The late Sinclair and I were raised together."

Aware Urisk seemed as uneasy as she about this change between them, Myrtle pressed for more information. "Can you read and write?"

"Aye."

"How much do you remember about your past, even the talks we had?"

"Verra little. It's clouded."

She frowned, disappointed at his reply. Yet part of her felt relieved. More than likely he didn't remember her awkward explanation of the birds and bees. "And your home is in this castle?"

"I have always had a home at Kilmarock Castle, but it is my choice to live here in secret. I go out at night, hidden from those who would seek my death if they knew the truth. If you wish me to leave, I'll go."

"Oh, no," she said, amazed by the fierceness of her

160

reply. "That is . . . if the dead laird counted you as a friend, so will I. Yet I wonder again why the Sinclair never mentioned you in his diary, nor did my late father ever speak of you."

"After Culloden," Ian said truthfully, "there were many English who would have wished to see me hanged for treason if they knew of my existence. Ian Sinclair kept my whereabouts secret from all save the Thomsons and Gavin Mackenzie. Jean Mackenzie found out by accident, but she'd nae betray me or any of the clan, I'm certain."

Not sharing his confidence in the dark-eyed Jean, Myrtle looked down at her dusty brown shoes. "You wear a mask and wig; is that part of the disguise, too?"

He touched the soft white leather covering his face. "No, the mask and wig are necessary and must remain."

She took this to mean Urisk was indeed disfigured from smallpox and needed the wig and mask. It occurred to her that Urisk probably fought with Gavin Mackenzie and Ian's younger brothers at Culloden. And he did say the redcoats would kill him if they found out the truth. No wonder Urisk kept hidden behind these stone walls. Urisk might now be just the person she needed to answer many of her questions. Thoughts again of dead Ian Sinclair filled her with both warmth and sorrow. The realization that Urisk knew his master well and could now communicate as an adult caused hope to blossom within her. From Urisk she could learn more about Ian Sinclair, then she might understand how best to help his clansmen.

When Myrtle took Urisk's hand in hers, it felt different this time, yet she still experienced the vulnerability of the faithful servant before her. "Urisk, I should like us to continue being friends. Rest easy, for I still mean to keep the Scot's promise I made to you. When Addison returns in a few days with two of his relatives, I believe it would be best in front of them if you continue in the guise of—"

"Yes," Ian replied, not pleased to learn Addison was coming back. "I shall play my role of village idiot."

She heard the bitterness in his voice. "If I appeared upset just now, it was from the amazing but pleasant surprise of learning your mind is no longer damaged, dear friend."

Ian felt a twinge of guilt at the open pleasure she took in his well-being. The gentleness of her tone and those expressive blue eyes of hers unnerved him with their trust and open gift of friendship. He found it difficult to remain passive as usual when she caressed his fingers. Strands of honey-brown hair ruffled about her shoulders and where her dowager hairstyle had liberated itself from those cursed pins. Yes, he thought, he'd been right to snatch that red bolt of silk from the wagon before it was sent to the crofts. Through a reluctant Jean, Ian had persuaded Fiona to make the gown. He wanted to see red silk against the soft, pale skin of Lady Myrtle Prescott's Rubenesque figure.

"I said, can we not be friends, Urisk?"

Ian blinked, unsettled to realize of late his thoughts often sauntered toward more intimate scenes than camaraderie with this tall, well-endowed woman. He looked down to see *he* was clasping *her* hands, not the other way around. When he felt her gently pull back, he released his firm hold on her slender fingers. "Friends," he repeated mechanically.

"Urisk, I did not mean to worry anyone by riding out alone," she explained, as they walked up the stairs to enter the keep. "At the time, the urgency of the message from Fiona prompted me to race out. It would have taken too much valuable time to get one of the stableboys to fetch Lachlan or Andrew.

Besides, they are put to better use helping their clansmen with the needed repairs to their farms. I will reassure Katie I'm unharmed, then . . ." her look was intense. "Please, you must tell me all you know about your late master."

"Oh, I think I've got one." When Myrtle pulled on the wooden pole in her hands, the string bent forward.

Sitting next to her on the edge of the rocky bank, Ian smiled behind his mask as he took in her animated features. With just a pink ribbon holding her long hair away from her face, she had her shoes and stockings off, as he did. "Here, I'll reel the whale in for you. Careful, or ye'll pitch headfirst into the burn." Wading into the clear water of the pond, he went for the string of her line and held up the small trout. "'Tis a behemoth you've caught."

"For my first time fishing, I think the poor animal deserves liberation." When she stopped giggling, she saw Urisk free the trout and wade back up the embankment. From his bare calves, she could observe the dusting of light hair about his strong legs below his breeches. Though his face was deformed behind his mask, Urisk's body was strong and well shaped. Her face heated at her blatant perusal. During the last few days when their work was done, she'd persuaded Urisk to begin telling her more about Ian Sinclair. Today, it had been his idea to take her on this walk in the hills to show her the burn and the lovely purple mountains high above Castle Kilmarock. Glancing to the right, she saw the pink-flowered stork's-bill growing in a crack in one of the rocks. On their walk here, she'd been enchanted by the sweet-smelling grass and fragile pink and white flowers growing in the meadow. "I can see why my father loved visiting the laird's Highlands, Urisk. How lovely it is here."

163

Sitting down on the grass next to her, Ian felt warmed by the look in her eyes. "I could eat a horse," he said, reaching for the wicker picnic basket. "Teaching you to fish is hard work."

"I could tell you were suffering," came her tart reply. "Poor darling, I should have asked Katie to cook a side of beef for you."

As they put out the cold chicken, bread, and cheese, Ian admitted he was enjoying himself. He took two bottles of claret from the bottom of the basket, tied a rope to them, then placed them in the cold water of the burn to chill. "For a Sassenach, yer company dinna seem to make me as ill as I thought," he said, imitating the broad Scottish accent that only surfaced with his strong emotion.

"Well, I've enjoyed being in your presence, now that we can discuss things," she admitted with a saucy grin. "Perhaps if you're feeling nauseated, you'd best fast." Before he knew what she was about, Myrtle snatched the chicken leg out of his hand and raced behind a huge boulder. "They say abstinence is good for the soul. Probably make you more mannerly to your elders."

For such a large man, he was graceful as he got up and walked unhurriedly over to her. "I'm a few years older than you, wee kelpie. Hand over my lunch."

"At least you're physically older than I," she countered, shoving the chicken leg behind her back. "But you are years behind me in politeness."

He stood with his hands on his hips, watching her dart from side to side behind the rock.

"My, this chicken leg does look delectable," she said, waving it over her head. Myrtle moved to the right, then left, just out of his reach as he circled her. "I always thought the Scots were expert trackers," she tossed, having fun.

"Patience has its advantages," said her companion. He looked down near her feet. "Don't move," he warned, all humor leaving his voice. "There's a badger near your pretty toes. He looks ravenous."

With a cry of alarm, she looked down.

It was just the second Ian needed to capture her by the waist. In an easy motion he had the chicken leg in his left hand and the sputtering Englishwoman firmly under his right arm.

"There wasn't any badger," she accused, squirming against the strong arm about her waist. Her toes came off the ground as Urisk clamped her against his muscular side. "You tricked me!"

"A lesson in distraction tactics." Grinning behind his mask, he took a large bite out of the chicken leg. "Umm, you were right. 'Tis delicious."

Myrtle felt the corners of her mouth turn up as she craned her neck to look up at him. "All right, you win. I know when I've been bested. Your arm must be aching. You can put me down now."

"You're just a pleasant armful, lass," he said truthfully. "I like your figure."

Pleased yet still shy with this new Urisk, Myrtle looked demurely down at the ground. "Come, you must be hungry. Let's resume our lunch."

Yes, he admitted it; he liked holding her. She was tall and shapely, and smelled enchantingly of roses and spring. Reluctantly he set her bare feet back on the ground. Lost to the open look of sweetness in her face, he saw shock enter those blue eyes suddenly.

She held her hands to her cheeks in alarm. "Redcoats," she whispered, peering over his shoulder. "Don't move. There are two of them watching us. I'll handle everything. Stand perfectly still."

Ian felt sweat break out beneath the leather covering his face. Without a weapon, save his dirk, which he'd carelessly tossed in the bottom of the wicker hamper, he cursed himself for not taking more precautions. Yet this hidden spot high in the hills had always been free of outsiders. "Be careful," he whispered to Myrtle as she walked slowly behind him. He readied himself for a fight with these intruders, if necessary. Dressed as they were, Ian knew he and Myrtle looked like simple peasants. Perhaps it would help them out of this dangerous situation.

"Oh, fear not, Urisk. I shall protect you," she said quietly behind him—just before she lifted her right foot and kicked him squarely on the seat of his breeches.

Whirling around, fright gave way to another emotion when Ian realized what had happened. "Ye . . . English brat," he snapped.

She laughed outright. "God, I enjoyed that." She bent over as another fit of giggles assailed her. "You know, Urisk, it was almost a religious experience, kicking you in the rump."

"I'll give ye a religious experience, Sassenach," Ian threatened. He tossed the chicken bone to the ground and charged after the laughing young woman.

"See, I learn quickly," she threw over her shoulder. "Distraction tactics." When Urisk's longer legs caught up with her and he grappled for her waist, this time he pulled her into his hard chest. "I don't know what came over me," she said, trying to catch her breath. "I—I'm usually considered polite and meek. Everyone in London says so, and that includes the Woman's Auxiliary of St. John. Must be the highland air. Are we even now?"

"Not quite." Though he wanted to kiss her, Ian knew his mask made it impossible. "I wonder if you are ticklish," he mused aloud. As he continued to hold her, his right hand went to her ribs to find out.

"Oh, stop! Please," she begged, laughing and wiggling at the same time. "All right, I yield. I'm . . . so . . . sorry I booted you in the backside."

Her hands latched on to his neck. "Stop. This is

unfair; you're bigger than I am." She never meant to, but her hand brushed the back of his head. The leather ties must have come loose in their roughhousing, for she felt the strings pull away. Immediately Urisk jumped back from her.

As his mask floated to the ground, Ian reached out, but missed. He peered at it on the ground, knowing Myrtle now realized the rest of the truth. Slowly he bent down to pick it up. He glanced back at Myrtle, ready to see her shock and anger.

However, when he saw her face, Ian was the one astonished. She was standing with her hands clasped in front of her, and her eyes were closed.

"You must tell me when you have retrieved the mask, Urisk. Then I will open my eyes."

It wasn't relief or joy he experienced. Ian retied the leather straps behind his powdered wig. When he walked over to stand in front of her, he saw the dark brown lashes against her smooth skin, the straight Prescott nose, firm chin, a pinkish hue from the sun across her upper cheeks. "My lady, why did ye nae look?"

Keeping her eyes shut, she answered. "I gave you my oath that I would not look upon your face until you asked me. I could not break my promise."

Her forthright answer unnerved him. It forced him to admit it—just now he'd wanted her to see his face, to end this deception between them. What was happening to him? This woman was his enemy, wasn't she? Yet there was something about her that stirred him, touched his feelings in a way no one ever had. But could he trust her?

"Ye can open yer eyes now," Ian said, his words almost gruff, though he intended the opposite.

Never had she been so playful with a man until this afternoon. "I . . . Urisk, I'm sorry if I—your mask—I should not have been so rough with you. I suppose I don't know my own strength."

He quelled the urge to laugh. The kick from her bare toes was no more than a tap; it had been her high-spirited impudence that had stunned him, the way she'd looked when she'd bested him. God, he'd wanted to kiss her warm, smiling lips. He shook his head. "You did no damage to my person, lass. 'Twas probably the threat of redcoats that unsettled me."

Then she recalled how Urisk had been cruelly beaten by redcoats as a child, and she derided herself for her thoughtless game. Poor lad, he was probably still terrified of English soldiers. "Oh, Urisk, truly I do ask your forgiveness. I never meant to bring up bad memories for you. We are new as friends. Please be patient with me."

He took her hand in his and led her back toward the spot for their lunch. "Aye, we both have much to learn about friendship, my lady."

With the gallant offer of his arm, the Scot helped her settle on the green and black plaid he'd spread out on the ground for them.

Myrtle stretched out her bare legs on the soft wool tartan, tucking her simple gown about her. She ran her fingers across the familiar crossbar pattern, while Urisk went over to pull the two bottles of wine from the pond.

After removing the cork from one, he took two large earthenware cups from the hamper and poured wine into each. When Myrtle took her cup from him, he saw the sadness in her eyes. "I'm not angry over your impish trick, Sassenach."

Her thoughts were elsewhere. "Urisk," she whispered to him, "was this one of Ian's plaids?"

When he'd shoved the wool tartan into the basket, Ian had never anticipated this. "Aye, it belonged to the laird."

She rubbed her right hand over the Scottish cloth once more. "Oh, Urisk," she said, fighting tears, "I will always regret I wasn't able to help him, to somehow reach him before he killed himself. The despair, the loneliness he must have felt. May God grant his valiant soul peace."

Moved by her genuine sorrow, Ian felt that twinge of guilt again and sought to squelch it. "The laird was nae a one for sentiment. He wasn't a saint, I can tell ye that. Now, drink your wine and eat."

Of course, poor Urisk didn't need these morbid reminders of his lost friend, she told herself. Without hesitation, she reached into the basket to pull out fresh bread and cheese. She cut Urisk a large piece of each and handed it to him on a checkered napkin.

"Umm," she said, taking a sip of the cool wine, "I was thirsty. I've never been on a picnic like this before. And it's spring," she added, trying to lighten both their moods.

As the contented hour went by, they ate their fill of simple food. With amusement, Myrtle realized Urisk did have a workman's healthy appetite. He polished off the cheese, chicken, and bread in record time. When he offered her oatcakes, she declined. "No more room," she said. Oatcakes were his favorite, she remembered, as he popped one after another into his mouth. "Oh, I don't think I should have another glass," she protested when Urisk filled her cup to the brim once more. She put a hand to her mouth and giggled. "In truth, dear Urisk, as I told you that time you brought me laced tea, I'm not used to spirits."

"Just have what you want," he said, stretching his long legs out in front of him. "Are you comfortable?"

"Yes, thank you." She inhaled the sweet May air. "Spring has always been my favorite time of year. I remember from his diary, Ian loved the spring, too." After she took another generous swallow of the tantalizing wine, a dreamy look came into her eyes. "Oh, I do wish I had met Ian Sinclair. He must have been a wonderful, fascinating man. He was the handsomest man I've ever seen, from his portrait

169

in my bedroom. I only wish Papa had let me come with him one of those summers. I could have met Ian."

Ian read the pain behind her words. "I'm sorry he didn't bring you along to meet the laird."

Memories washed over her. For the first time since her father had died, she sensed genuine friendship. Urisk was someone with whom she could trust her inner thoughts and feelings. "It wasn't until after Papa died I realized that while I loved him, I was also angry at him." She looked at Urisk, comforted in his presence as he sat listening, the position of his body showing attentiveness but not judgment. "Confident I'd look after the town house in London and our large farm in Chelmsford, he visited his friends, the Sinclairs, every summer. Papa said it was too arduous a journey for a girl, yet I knew it was because he wanted this time alone. My stepmother and her daughters are not bad sorts, really, but now I can admit there were a few occasions when I felt vexed with him for leaving me behind to deal with them alone."

"Stepmother?"

"Why, yes. You see, my mother, Jane, died when I was young, and Papa married Barbara, a widow with three young daughters. The girls are pretty and petite," she said without malice. "I know they will make splendid matches soon. But I never really fit in. While I'm content as I am, my stepmother, along with Papa at times, despaired of my ever finding a husband willing to take me on. Truth between us, Urisk, I confess I seem to scare men away with my eccentric ways, as Barbara calls them. Barbara has pointed out to me often that my height and—" she looked down at herself without criticism—"gargantuan frame," she added, totally at ease, "appear to frighten potential suitors off. My, that is tasty wine. Is there any more?"

170

Amused that she wanted a third tumbler, Ian got up and retrieved the second bottle. So, he thought, shrewish Barbara was only Lady Myrtle's step-mother. Things Jonathan told him about Myrtle began falling into place. He poured more of the ruby liquid into her empty cup, then returned to his place opposite her.

"That is one thing I admire about the late laird," she declared, her voice sounding fuzzy. "He was kind to his clansmen, a fair ruler, but he wasn't anyone's doormat." She frowned, trying to remember what she meant to say. "A Scot with the width of those shoulders and muscular legs, square jaw, golden eyes like a lion's—Ian wouldn't be intimidated by Lady Myrtle Prescott." She thought for a moment. "Do—do you think I would have frightened him?" she asked, her face crumpling.

Ian had to stifle the laughter that threatened. Foxed, Miss Prescott was parading a side of herself he'd never glimpsed before. "I think the laird would have found ye verra interesting."

"You see," she rattled on, "I've been told I can be rather uppish with potential suitors, but it's really just nerves."

"And what qualities would you seek in a potential husband?" he couldn't resist asking. When she blushed after a hiccup overtook her, Ian hoped she couldn't see his shoulders shake.

The Englishwoman took another swallow, then thought for a few minutes. "It isn't just that Ian Sinclair was handsome, it's what he was inside that I've come to admire." The wine, balmy air, and complete trust in her friend, Urisk, loosened Myrtle's tongue. "A wonderful man of honor, wit, charm— brave, yet a man of sorrows. It breaks my heart to think how alone he felt. You must have been devastated when the Thomsons found his body. I've spent many evenings standing near his grave, just

171

thinking about him, praying his soul has finally found peace."

Having placed the stone marker there himself to add proof to the tale of his demise, Ian was taken aback by the extent of her probing into his life and death.

She tried to move the conversation back to more amusing topics. "I'm certain the Sinclair could have taught the string of English suitors Barbara paraded through our London pa-par-living room," she slurred, "a thing or two about *amour*. Knew most of the pansy-dressed fops were just after my money and title. Now, Ian Sinclair, there was a real man, a man who knew his way around a female's mind and anatomy. *Hic*—I bet no woman ever left his bed unsatisfied." She sniffled into her half-empty cup. "It mu-must have been close to heaven to be in his arms, Urisk."

"I wouldn't know," said the Scot.

Her melancholia shifted when she blurted, "Urisk, is it true Ian Sinclair once made love to three dairymaids at the same time, all while grouse hunting?"

The wine in his mouth went in the wrong direction. The Scot choked before a coughing fit nearly strangled him. "Who in blazes told you that ribald tale?"

Nonplussed, Myrtle set her cup down on the ground and hugged her bent knees. "Addison told me that evening after we dined. He said I defended the deceased laird and his clansmen without knowing all the facts. Come, tell me, Urisk. We are friends, with no secrets between us. Is it true?"

"As with most gossip, the tales are exaggerated."

"In whose favor?" she countered, an impudent grin spreading across her flushed face.

"Well, nosy kelpie, Ian was seventeen at the time, and the *one* was a comely widow of thirty who instigated the pleasant encounter."

Myrtle appeared pleased with herself. "I'll wager she was plump. I can tell from the late laird's two books of French erotica he liked full-figured women," she mused aloud. "I've studied both novels closely, and I've learned a great deal about his preferences. Most illuminating."

Ian thought he was too old to blush, but the heat on his face and ears proved he wasn't. "I hardly think this is a suitable topic for an English maiden."

"Oh, don't be such a fusspot, Urisk. I mean, it isn't as if he could hear us or anything. *Hic*—besides, I found Ian's attitude toward voluptuous women refreshing. Being one myself, I'm only sorry I'll never find a man like Ian to try out some of those illustrations. Oh," she added, then placed a hand to her less than prudent mouth. "Can't believe I said that. I pro-probably would have scared Ian off, don't you think?"

The sun on her long brown hair brought out its golden highlights. Ian touched the soft leather covering his jaw. "I don't think the laird would have been frightened away, my lady."

"You're just being kind. Even though he was your best friend, one can't really know how a man will act until he's pressed against the wall."

This time the Scot did chuckle. "Though you are a fine armful, wee kelpie, I hardly think the Sinclair would have been intimated by your size or your bossy manner."

Her mind back on other things, she said, "The Parisian ladies must have been well pleased with him. His diary entries were quite entertaining. Never knew there were so many uses for whipped cream and strawberries."

The Scot fidgeted against the hard boulder at his back. "Ian's salad days in France changed to more sobering times as he grew older."

173

"Yes, he did have to take on too many responsibilities at such a young age, poor man. Urisk," she asked, after a few silent moments, "what is a kelpie? You've called me that before."

He gestured toward the burn. "A kelpie is a water spirit."

"It's a compliment?" she asked hopefully.

"Sort of," Ian answered. "It suits you today, for a kelpie is often a mischievous spirit, changing her features from shy mouse to naughty temptress with lightning speed. It keeps a man confused, in danger . . . and utterly enchanted."

The huskiness of Urisk's voice sent shivers down her spine. "No one ever called me a temptress before. I like it," she added with uncomplicated honesty. "You know, when I was younger, I used to dream about being a seductive si-siren—difficult word, isn't it? *Hic*—but I could never get the expression right. You know, that world-weary pout about the lips, and limpid pools in my eyes."

When she saw Urisk place his head in his hands as his shoulders moved, Myrtle thought she'd hurt him by dwelling on the fine qualities of his late master. Immediately she reminded herself that this sensitive Scot was now her responsibility. As her employer, he might feel obligated to return her—if she were to reach out right now and . . . The one time she'd felt his face across the soft leather of his mask, she hadn't experienced anything abhorrent. Of course, he was bald. She wouldn't want to hurt him if she wasn't able to school her features enough at his disfigurement. No, she had given her word. What was the matter with her this afternoon to speak so boldly about Urisk's deceased master? She watched him as he dropped his hands to his knees, before he placed his back against the base of the boulder once more.

The ribbon holding her hair in place had slipped off, and Ian wasn't going to tell her. A warm breeze

174

ruffled her straight hair about her shoulders. The flowered-print gown she wore was better than most he'd seen her in thus far. He looked deep into her blue eyes. "Are you in love with Addison Barrington?"

The question was so direct and unexpected, it flustered her. "I—I hardly think it is any of your bus—"

"Come, my lady, you have wandered uninvited into the laird's sexual exploits and preferences; surely my question deserves an honest answer. As you have pointed out, we are friends who can keep each other's confidences."

She peered down at her bare toes and tightened her arms about her knees. "I have told Addison I do not believe I love him. Yet he has always been very kind to me, usually accepting me as I am. He says his love will be enough for us both."

"Will you accept his offer of marriage?"

"I don't know," she answered honestly. "He knows of my determination to keep my promise to my father. It is clear we disagree on that point, but I believe I can persuade him to see my side when he visits next week."

Ian groaned inside at the prospect of seeing the English soldier again. The vision of Addison kissing Myrtle's soft neck flashed across his mind. It sparked that new emotion again—the one he'd never felt before over a woman. "What are your plans for the tenants and lands?" he demanded.

For the second time this Scotsman surprised her with his boldness. Myrtle wondered if she could share these plans with him. If he told Gavin and the others, which he was bound to do before she'd heard back from the King, all might be for nothing. Her clansmen's disappointment could lead to more anger against her. She needed time right now. "I am still working things out," she hedged.

Irritated, Ian saw, and even somewhat inebriated,

Lady Myrtle Prescott clearly wasn't going to open up to him on this subject. He folded his arms across his chest while he brooded at the still surface of the water ahead.

Suddenly sleepy, Myrtle closed her eyes and rested her head on her knees. "He had lion eyes," she murmured.

"What?"

"The laird," Myrtle answered. "His golden eyes reminded me of a proud, majestic lion's."

She was back to Sinclair again, he thought, both amused and exasperated. He knew she needed a short nap after her uncharacteristic consumption of heady wine. The blathering was starting again. "Lady Myrtle?"

"Hmm?" She managed to open her eyes.

"Come over here." He held open his arms to her. "You need to sleep before we make the trek down the mountain."

It seemed the most natural thing in the world right now. She got up a little unsteadily, then walked the few paces over to Urisk. "You really are a thoughtful friend, Urisk." She gave him a groggy smile. "Are you certain you wouldn't mind if I just closed my eyes for a second?"

"I dinna mind. Makes more sense than if you took a wrong step and fell off the cliff on our walk home." He heard her contented sigh as she snuggled up next to him. Automatically he placed his right arm about her shoulders and wrapped the edges of the wool plaid about her. "Comfortable?"

"Oh, yes, thank you, Urisk. For such a big man, you're really very cozy. I feel quite strange. Must be the high altitude."

More likely the claret, he mused, but remained silent.

"Urisk?"

"Yes, wee kelpie."

176

"I feel I can tell you anything."

"I hope you always believe you can trust me," the Scot added, thinking of their uncertain futures.

"Urisk?"

He held her close. "You should rest, not talk," he whispered close to her ear. After brushing a few tendrils of the silky brown hair away from her cheek, he looked down at her, aware she was smiling again even though her eyes were closed. "All right, what is it?"

"Last night I even dreamed about Ian Sinclair. I've never felt that way about anyone before. My heart was racing, my face flushed. I was quite shocked when I woke up and remembered just how . . . how explicitly I could imagine Ian and me . . . together. Do you have dreams about girls that way?"

"Sometimes." He remembered his own body's reaction each time he thought of this buxom woman the way she'd looked bathing in that brass tub in his room.

"It left me quite unsettled. "Do . . . do you think there is something wrong with me? I mean, if I told you exactly what the dream was, it would startle you as much as it did me when I woke up."

Behind his mask he looked down at the woman nestled in his arms. He inhaled the scent of her tea rose soap. "No, little Sassenach, there is nothing wrong with you. Go to sleep now. Let your thoughts travel where they will. It's a lovely May afternoon, and you are safe. Rest."

The soothing tone of his voice acted like a balm to her. "Well, just for a minute."

For over an hour Ian sat watching the sleeping woman in his arms. Something was changing in his feelings toward Myrtle Prescott, and it did not altogether please him. Though she might not be his enemy, he still knew he couldn't trust her. She's been reared with that class of arrogant English aristocrats

177

who saw his Scottish clansmen as a conquered race of barbarians. Though intelligent, she seemed to have a blind spot where Barrington was concerned. If she married Addison, Ian knew his clansmen would suffer. But how to keep her from wedding the English captain? This afternoon convinced him she was awakening sexually to the ghost of Ian Sinclair. His smile faded when he realized the impossible implication of her growing desire for the late laird. As Urisk to her, how could he hope to compete with his own ghost?

Chapter Ten

Carrying the wicker basket in one hand, Ian could tell Myrtle was used to walking. He'd been correct about the view of her shapely legs in the—no, best not think of that tub again, for he knew it would lead to an uncomfortable walk, the result of his usual response to that image. "You don't have to race, lass."

Stopping, Myrtle looked back at her companion. "I'm just sorry I kept you up there so long. Your poor arm—how uncomfortable for you—how boorish of me. Over an hour. I cannot imagine what got into me to sleep so soundly." Her smile was rueful. "But I enjoyed this afternoon very much, Urisk. Thank you for showing me your beautiful highlands."

"I enjoyed it, too."

"Oh, Urisk," she added, concern etching across her face. "I hope we don't run into anyone. I'm supposed to keep you hidden. Perhaps I should scout ahead first when we come out of the glen."

"Nay." He grabbed her arm, forcing her to slow her pace when she would have darted ahead. He remembered he still hadn't found out who was trying to kill her. "Ye'll stay right next to me, do ye ken? I'll nae have you goin' aboot alone from now on. And that's nae a suggestion."

Tempted to argue, she found herself chuckling. Besides, she knew by the way his Scottish accent had become more pronounced that this was an emotional subject to him. He was being protective, sweet man. "You know, Urisk, now that your mind is healing, you certainly have changed."

He released her arm. "Liked me better as the village idiot, did you?"

"You were less autocratic then," she countered, giving him an impertinent look. She walked before him but stayed just ahead as he'd ordered. "How's that?"

He heard the amusement in her voice and shared her playful mood. "Lady Myrtle, you remind me of a certain wee mouse I have as a pet at the keep—you have Mortimer's winning ways—just before he steals a piece of cheese from my hand."

"Then you had best be wary of my sharp teeth," Myrtle said, after his longer legs caught up with her. When he took her hand to help her down the stony path, she made no protest after he went on holding it as they descended the steep hill.

Viewing the tan stones of Kilmarock Castle in the distance, the Englishwoman couldn't help feeling sad their idyllic afternoon was over. It had been so comforting to leave her present problems behind for a few hours. "Your secret spot in the Highlands is an enchanted place," she mused aloud. "It almost makes me wish I could stay up there in the glen."

The wistful look on her face made Ian aware of how small her soft hand felt in his. He stopped walking. She stood before him. For a tall, sturdy lass, her ladyship needed looking after.

As she continued to search the shadowed area where his gaze seemed to consume her, Myrtle's blood raced through her veins at his touch. His warm breath fanned her cheek. He bent toward her, almost

180

as if he intended to kiss her. She closed her eyes, waiting for him.

He stepped back abruptly.

Myrtle wanted to cry out in protest, tell Urisk she wanted him to kiss her, to take the bloody mask off and—she forced herself to begin walking again, this time without Urisk's hand holding hers. Her promise to him nudged her sense of honor. She was English and his employer. Besides, she knew it wouldn't be the same as her dream. Urisk's direct questions caused her to describe the man she desired. Urisk didn't know her mind and heart were already taken. This afternoon, in the deceased laird's beloved highlands, Myrtle had experienced it more powerfully than when she'd studied Ian's portrait and read his diary.

When he yanked himself back from the dangerous precipice of his emotions, Ian reminded himself of who this woman was and the obligations he shouldered. There was no room in his life for spring folly. It had been a mistake to bring her on this picnic. For all her pragmatic attitudes toward organizing his clansmen, Myrtle Prescott was a romantic when it came to men. He'd deluded himself into believing he could easily seduce the inexperienced lass into confiding her plans for his clansmen and lands.

However, as they continued walking in silence, Ian wasn't sure just which of them had been seduced this afternoon.

Three days after their walk in the highlands, after supper one evening, as Ian watched the lady sip her tea, he couldn't help admiring the small changes in her attire. Packed away were the dowdy gowns she'd first brought with her. The dark green silk dress she wore tonight accentuated her healthy beauty. Her rich brown hair had recently been trimmed to set off her high cheekbones. Emerald earrings and green ribbons at her throat added to the alluring costume. "My lady," he said, continuing to study the English-woman who sat across from him on the overstuffed chair, "I hope you will not think I've forgotten my place if I tell you how lovely you look tonight." He was captivated when a pinkish hue tinged her features.

"Thank you, Urisk. It is Fiona's doing. She is a marvel with knowing how to choose the line and color of a gown." Her smile became self-effacing. "My stepmother ignored my directive to send more of my serviceable attire and had the trunks Cyril brought packed with a few of the dresses she'd sent for me from Paris last year." Smoothing the shimmering fabric with her hand, Myrtle added, "I own I was still in my rebellious stage, for I refused to wear any of them until now. Fiona says my stepmother has excellent taste. I wrote Barbara last night and thanked her for sending them."

Her blue eyes softened when she looked at Urisk. Instead of the tea she drank, Urisk sipped a small glass of cognac. "Extraordinary, it took my discovery that Ian preferred ladies in bright-colored gowns to make me realize I was using my resentment of Barbara's attempts at digging up a husband for me to blind me to her good qualities."

For the past week this Englishwoman had taken to sending for him when her work was done. She always offered him oatcakes and any liquid refreshment he desired, making no comment that the laird's former servant preferred a glass of cognac over ale in the evening. At first Ian was amused by her barrage of questions about the deceased Sinclair's life, and his tastes in music, reading, politics, and art. Part of him enjoyed these evening conversations. It was a pleasant surprise to discover Myrtle was a witty, well-read woman, interested in a variety of topics. Yet a part of him began chafing in his role of Urisk.

And in the late evenings, when he took his customary walk outside undetected, Ian was disconcerted to find Lady Myrtle again at her vigil near his grave. Despite himself, he began worrying about her. Obviously Myrtle Prescott was grieving over the dead chief of Clan Sinclair.

On such a pleasant May evening, no fire was needed. She appeared more pensive this evening, Ian thought. He looked about the room, taking in the tasteful new furniture that had arrived yesterday. At least he should be grateful she was restoring the castle. But was it merely to get a better price when she sold it? The Englishwoman was pleasant to his clansmen—Gavin confirmed it, but there was still a cool wariness about her when she interacted with them. For their part, they didn't yet trust her, and the earlier tales of her intentions couldn't be denied. So far, he'd been frustrated in not being able to get her to tell him her plans. Stubborn wench, he thought, then placed the half-empty crystal goblet on the new mahogany table in front of him.

Myrtle looked up at his abrupt action. "Is there something bothering you tonight, Urisk?"

"No." Friend or enemy, it wasn't something he could just ask her tonight, especially since she'd already refused to confide anything to him on this one subject. Wouldn't her actions, not words, tell him? But there wasn't time to wait and see. She might marry Addison, and—

"Come, tell me, I know you are agitated. We are friends," she reminded, placing her empty teacup next to his glass. "Are your rooms comfortable?"

"Yes."

"Has someone mistreated you?"

"Damn it, I'm nae a bairn who needs to hide behind a woman's skirts for protection."

Oh, dear, she hadn't meant to insult him. She'd enjoyed the last few days, taking charge of the renovations, finalizing her plans on her Scottish obligations. And she admitted it, Urisk was pleasant company. The deceased laird had obviously seen to Urisk's education and polish. Thinking about what might be bothering the Scot, she sat back against the wing chair. Dressed in the livery coat and breeches she'd given him, he got up quickly and began pacing back and forth, his hands thrust behind his back. "Urisk, I want to help you, but I can't if you do not confide in me."

In only an instant, it seemed he was standing over her. Ian gripped the arms of her chair. "Confidences work both ways, Sassenach."

Refusing to be intimated by his uncharacteristic behavior, her chin moved northward. "That sounds clever but unenlightening."

"Why will ye nae tell me what you mean to do aboot the laird's clansmen and lands?"

Her hands tightened in her lap. "In business matters I make it a practice to keep my own counsel until I am certain of the outcome. My father showed me how many of his colleagues who blathered plans of their investments prematurely only lived to regret it when countermeasures were taken against them by unscrupulous people."

"Unscrupulous, am I?" He pulled back from her chair as if she'd punched him.

She got up and walked over to him. "Of course, I did not mean you."

"Yet you do not trust me with the truth."

A defensive edge entered her voice. "You must understand, I've had more experience in these political and business dealings than you."

"I resent your patronizing tone."

When he placed his hands on his hips in a clear gesture of defiance, Myrtle lost some of her congeniality. "And I begin to resent your arrogance, sir. Kindly remember, I am the owner of Kilmarock Castle and lands. Any decisions concerning it or Clan Sinclair are mine alone to make."

His old sitting room suddenly felt too small for the two of them. It was clear she meant to remind him he was merely a servant in this house. "Bloody hell," he swore in frustration. "I need another drink." Turning his back to her, he walked over to the table and grabbed the cut glass decanter.

"No, Urisk," came the voice behind him. "By your surly manner, I think you've had too much liquor already. You have my permission to retire."

Nearly overturning the amber liquid in the decanter, Ian set it down on the table with a resounding clank. He whirled about to confront the woman who stood at his back. Her haughty expression scorched his frayed nerves. No one in his twenty-seven years had ever addressed him in such a way. This was his castle, his land, and he was about to take another glass of his own bloody cognac. Yet this snip of an English brat dared order him to bed like a misbehaving bairn? Through the slits in his mask, he glared down at her. "Ye are dancin' on verra dangerous ground, hellcat."

Not the least fazed by his words, Myrtle added the cold edge to her voice that had catapulted many a bumbling suitor on his way. "It is you, sir, who tarry on shaky terrain if you think my regard for your past injuries or my solemn promise to protect you will cause me to overlook your insubordination. In both my houses in England I never tolerated an inebriated servant browbeating or hiccupping about my guests. I'll remind you that company will arrive at the end of the week. For your own protection, I believe it would be wiser for you to maintain a low profile around Captain Barrington."

"Rest assured I will revert to my role as simple-

185

ton," he said sarcastically.

Didn't he realize it was for his own good? she thought. For all Addison's closeness to her, he was still a dutiful English officer. If he had the faintest inclination Urisk had fought at Culloden, she wasn't sure even Addison's affection for her would dissaude him from arresting someone he believed guilty of treason against the King. Why was Urisk being so . . . so belligerent this evening? "While we are on the subject of company, Urisk, let me remind you again to watch your habit of swearing. Mrs. Prescott and young Twilla are not use to coarse barnyard language."

"With a jackass for a son, I'd have thought his mother would be fluent in such talk. Hell, just what I need—more Sassenachs overrunnin' the place."

"That will do, Urisk," Her bosom heaved with suppressed indignation.

Taking a menacing step toward her, Ian caught himself. He couldn't risk saying or doing what he wanted right now. He was Urisk to her, not Ian Sinclair. *"Merde!"* he shouted in masculine frustration, then left, slamming the door behind him.

For the next few days the castle bustled with activities in preparation of the Barrington visit. Yet Myrtle admitted she missed the close companionship she'd enjoyed with Urisk. A strained politeness existed between them now. To Urisk's credit, his behavior was exemplary. She'd spent her evenings going through Ian Sinclair's diary and books, studying his picture again. Sensing Urisk would not relish her company as he had before, she no longer summoned him to her sitting room after supper.

Late in the day, Myrtle was helping Katie put the new bed hangings on the guest room for Addison. "My, these frames are high," she said, stepping up to another rung on the wooden ladder. The massive carved oak posts rose to the plastered ceilings. "I like this heather pattern," she mused. Stretching to reach the wooden rod to push the gathered material over to the right, she bent too far.

"Steady!" shouted a familiar voice, before she felt the ladder stop wobbling. Myrtle looked down to see Urisk.

Katie rushed over, her arms filled with new bed linen. "Are ye all right, lass?"

"Yes, Katie, thanks to Urisk." She looked down at him, wanting to say something more to end this tenseness between them.

However, assured she was safe, he gave her a servant's proper bow. "I must see that the lads have the stables ready for your guests."

Coming down slowly from the ladder, Myrtle could only watch as Urisk straightened to that military posture and walked out the door. She heard the sounds of his boots on the stairs. If only Cyril would send word of the King's answer to her petition, she could then tell Urisk her plans. It seemed so important to him to know, she supposed he felt the late chief's loyalty to his clan. While she admired Urisk for it, all could be ruined if word leaked out to the Scots and English alike before the King acted. George of Hanover was known for his unforgiving nature if a trusted ally proved a political liability. No, she had no choice. And if His Majesty denied her petition and these volatile Scots knew ahead of time, she might find herself in the center of a full-scale rebellion. And that was the last thing she wanted— more English soldiers on Sinclair land to keep the King's peace.

Looking out the bedroom window, Myrtle saw the two carriages in the distance. Quickly she went to change into the new dress Fiona had sent over this morning. Proud of the work she and the others had

187

done, Miss Prescott felt ready to receive her first houseguests.

It took Urisk and a couple of the recently employed young footmen to unload the two carriages. Told the three Barringtons were only staying a few days, the Scot wondered why there was so much luggage.

"Bond jure, dear Myrtle," greeted the short, rotund woman with the elaborately powdered wig. Dora Barrington lifted her rouged cheek to receive the younger woman's kiss. "Oh, what a long, uncomfortable ride. If the squire hadn't insisted I take our best carriage, I'm certain I would have perished from the horrible Scottish roads. Addison will be along any moment. He insisted on a military escort. Just giving them their orders before they return to the fort. You must see to the ruts in future, my dear, though Addie tells me you will be returning to your London town house soon. Twilla," she barked over her shoulder, "come out and greet your hostess."

At eighteen, Twilla Barrington had the blond beauty that was the rage in London. "'Ere, ya big loony, watch that trunk. It's got my Paris gowns in it."

It was then Ian realized Twilla's beauty was spoiled by a whiny voice.

"Ma, tell Addie when he arrives to get one of the others to carry my things. I don't think the muttonhead can hear, either."

Nervously, Myrtle excused herself from Dora and went over to the second carriage. "Twilla, how nice to see you." She helped the younger girl down. "My, don't you look lovely."

Dressed in yellow-and-white flowered gown, an amber cloak tossed casually over her slender shoulders, Twilla smiled as one accustomed to such praise. "Addison says you've let a half-wit stay on here."

Though it was clear Twilla thought she was lowering her voice, Myrtle knew it had to carry to the

188

next croft. Twilla glanced warily at the masked Scot, who was attempting a firmer grip on her large leather trunk.

"I've brought a few of my jewels with me," Twilla told Myrtle, nearly deafening the woman with the proximity of her shrill voice, just like Dora's. "Do you think they'll be safe? I mean, Addison says all these Scots would steal the gold teeth from their mother's corpse."

Before Myrtle could defend her Scottish friend, everyone heard a trunk crash to the gray cobblestones.

Twilla's blond curls bounced up and down as she charged over to Urisk. For such a small girl, she found no difficulty in reaching up with her doubled fist to give Urisk a sharp clout on his left ear, where the powdered wig was pulled back in a queue.

"You dumb ox!" Twilla screeched, "don't you dare touch anymore of me trunks. They're the ones with the yellow tags on 'um. Y-E-L-O," she spelled incorrectly. "Can you understand that, imbecile?"

Urisk stood motionless. The Barringtons represented all the self-centered arrogance he'd come to despise in the English. And he reminded himself, Lady Myrtle Prescott was probably going to marry into this crass family.

Addison arrived in a flurry of dust before Ian could tell this ill-mannered chit what she could do with her bloody trunks.

"Addison, I thought you said the booby could understand simple commands," Twilla whined to her older brother, who sat atop his horse. "You didn't say he was deaf as well as dumb." She wasted no time telling her older brother what had just happened.

The immaculately groomed officer bounded off his chestnut stallion. "Look here, Urisk, I've had just about enough—"

"It's all right, Addison," Myrtle interjected. Her

189

habit of placing herself in front of Urisk resurfaced. "I'll handle this. I would be ever so grateful if you would show your mother and sister to the drawing room. My staff has prepared a supper with Dora's favorite French sauces."

Addison's severe expression changed as her soft-spoken words seemed to placate him. Leaning across to her, he kissed her briefly on the lips. "I've missed you, lovely Myrtle. We should never have parted so abruptly last time."

Feeling a little embarrassed to air such personal things in front of everyone, Myrtle took a step backward only to bump into Urisk's hard body behind her. "I beg your pardon," she apologized, then blushed to the roots of her brown hair. Painting a demure smile on her face, she said, "Please, Addison, can we not finish this discussion after dinner? Your lady mother and Twilla must wish to rest before we dine."

"Considerate of others, as always," gushed Addison, then took her right hand in his and brought it to his lips. "And this visit I will not leave until you give me an answer to my proposal, sweet lady."

Myrtle was puzzled to feel Urisk's body become even straighter in back of her. She heard his indrawn breath before he muttered something in Gaelic, only certain it wasn't a prayer to St. Andrew.

From Addison's thunderous expression and the malevolent stares from Dora and Twilla, they must have recognized the tone, if not the words. Myrtle glanced behind her to see Urisk standing with his fists at his sides. She knew things were heading toward a heated confrontation and laughed nervously. "My, my, just a little accident, Addison. That is all. We'll check the contents carefully, Twilla, after you're settled in. I assure you, I shall pay for any damage to your lovely things. Urisk means well, part of his disability, poor lad; his fingers do not always

190

work," she added, floundering in a sea of lies. "He has sudden attacks during which he can't hear or understand. They're called brain leaks. He's better now. Urisk is just a simple, good-natured lad."

Dora spoke first. "Oh, well, *formage, formage,* as the French say."

"Hell, they're all full of shi—"

"Urisk," Myrtle admonished.

"What did the loony say?" demanded Addison.

"Just a Gaelic apology for his mistake. Yes, that's right, Urisk, you may go help Katie in the kitchen. Fine. My, my, we're all fine, aren't we?"

"Come along, Twilla dear," said Dora, a beefy arm nudging at her sulky daughter's back. "I'll let you tell Myrtle about the present we've brought her. I've always wanted to spend the night in a real castle. How romantic, how primeval, so Scottish. It makes one appreciate the rich, tragic histories, like Max Beth."

Myrtle shot Urisk a silent warning. Thankfully, he did not comment on Mrs. Barrington's last remark. She turned back to Dora. "Oh, Mrs. Barrington, you did not need to get me a present. Your visit is gift enough."

"Ye'll need a shovel if you keep piling it on so heavy," Urisk muttered near her ear as he passed her on the way to the stairs.

"Yes, we'll have wine and tea after dinner in the sitting room. Thank you for reminding me, Urisk."

With Urisk gone, Myrtle gave her full attention to the shorter woman. "You are most generous to go to the trouble and expense, Dora."

Dora waved a pudgy hand. "Nonsense." She reached up with her thick fingers to straighten the stuffed bird on her towering coiffure. "When Addison told me you'd inherited this castle, I just knew I'd found a home for all the lovely tartans I've collected. You know my talent for decorating."

191

Uneasy, Myrtle still managed to smile. "How kind."

"It's my nature, my dear. I shall need only tomorrow, and I will decorate one of your guest rooms for you. It will be my house—castle-warming present to you. It will go with these highlands, the tragedy, the romance of Scotland. *Formage,*" she repeated dramatically.

Now you can get Heartfire Romances right at home and save

Heartfire Romance

Get 4 Free Heartfire Novels A $17.00 Value!

TO GET YOUR
4 FREE BOOKS
MAIL THE COUPON BELOW.

FREE BOOK CERTIFICATE

GET 4 FREE BOOKS

Yes! I want to subscribe to Zebra's HEARTFIRE HOME SUBSCRIPTION SERVICE. Please send me my 4 FREE books. Then each month I'll receive the four newest Heartfire Romances as soon as they are published to preview Free for ten days. If I decide to keep them I'll pay the special discounted price of just $3.50 each; a total of $14.00. This is a savings of $3.00 off the regular publishers price. There are no shipping, handling or other hidden charges. There is no minimum number of books to buy and I may cancel this subscription at any time. In any case the 4 FREE Books are mine to keep regardless.

NAME _____

ADDRESS _____

CITY _____ STATE _____ ZIP _____

TELEPHONE _____

SIGNATURE _____

(If under 18 parent or guardian must sign)
Terms and prices subject to change.
Orders subject to acceptance.

HF 112

Heartfire Romance

GET 4 FREE BOOKS

HEARTFIRE HOME SUBSCRIPTION
SERVICE
P.O. BOX 5214
120 BRIGHTON ROAD
CLIFTON, NEW JERSEY 07015

Chapter Eleven

Myrtle finally relaxed as the evening meal progressed more smoothly than indicated by her guests' arrival. Dora wore a ruffled pink gown with a large ruby-and-sapphire-encrusted brooch. Twilla was a vision in aqua blue. Aware she wasn't up on these things yet, Myrtle still wondered if the diamonds at Twilla's throat and ears, along with the large gold bracelet on her slender wrist, weren't too much for an ingenue.

When Urisk, dressed handsomely in new black livery, went to serve Addison, Myrtle noticed the captain moved warily to the side while Urisk ladled out the steaming cock-a-leekie soup. The gravy incident was clearly on the Englishman's mind. But she felt proud of the way Urisk looked and behaved tonight. Polite and attentive, he was acting superbly.

Myrtle addressed the girl next to her. "Twilla, you look charming in that aqua gown."

Patting a blond curl already in place, Twilla smiled confidently. "I'll have my seamstress make you a copy." She gave Myrtle a critical once-over. "Of course, we'll have to get an extra bolt of material to make it in a larger size."

Personally insulted by the remark to Myrtle, Ian

stood at attention against the wall, watching the four English people dine. They should talk, he decided. Twilla wore too much jewelry, and she resembled a French tart in that low-cut dress. Dora, on the other hand, had pushed her flabby frame into a pastel frock designed for a girl, not a woman over fifty. And the garish blue-and-green pin at her bosom was as big as his targe that hung in the castle's entryway. Next to these two women, Myrtle was beautiful. Fiona Ross had come by this morning with the red dress and stayed long enough for Myrtle to play with Jamie on her lap while Fiona fixed her hair. The Scot told himself he was an idiot to feel outraged that the gown he'd designed in secret for Myrtle was being worn for the first time tonight, clearly for that . . . that Barrington's benefit.

When Ian glanced back at Myrtle, he saw her animated features as she listened attentively to Addison tell another amusing story—about himself. Her brown hair gleamed in the candlelight, her blue eyes possessed a sparkle he hadn't noticed before. With an expensive but small necklace of tiny rubies about the column of her throat and matching droplets at her ears, Myrtle appeared more desirable than he'd ever seen her. And it had taken Addison's arrival to cause this change, hadn't it?

No, that wasn't true, Ian told himself. She'd begun changing as she'd learned more about Ian Sinclair. The thought made him hopeful. He continued listening to their conversation. Twilla was talking about gowns again.

"It is true," Myrtle said cheerfully, "I do not have your svelte figure, Twilla."

"You know," offered Twilla, "the right stays might improve your shape, make it look smaller."

Damn it, Ian thought, why didn't Addison stand up for Myrtle? Had she been *his* betrothed, he'd taken anyone to task for such rudeness to his lady. Besides, he fumed, Lady Myrtle's figure was perfect. She was tall, and well proportioned. Just thinking about her naked in his tub always gave him a terrific—

"Urisk!" Addison shouted. "I said, my mother wishes more salmon. Fetch it, moron, and be quick about it."

Ian saw Myrtle hold her breath as she sent him a silent entreaty not to make a scene. He went back to the kitchen without a word. "The whale wants more salmon," he told Katie.

"My lord, please, ye must not let the Sassenach officer hear ye," Katie begged. She went over and cut more slices from the large, fresh fish. "He's got a cruel look about the eyes. Heaven help her ladyship if she marries that one."

Ian made a sound of impatience behind his mask. "If Myrtle Prescott is daft enough to be taken in by a scarlet uniform and fancy words, she deserves that pompous ass. Did ye nae see the way he ogled the tops of her bosom when he passed her the salt dish? And her sittin' there, smiling innocently over to him. By the root, if she were my ken, she'd nae flaunt her person so wantonly at a man she's nae even formally engaged to."

The gray-haired woman studied her employer. "Of course, the lassie will have to wed someday. I suppose she's so grateful for his attention. Gavin did tell us she was dowdy and all."

"The stories we heard are wrong. Why, tonight, in that form-fitting dress, she is gorgeous, and—" He stopped when he saw Katie's smile. He cleared his throat. "Please tell Angus to wait on serving more liquor. I'll get the lesser wine from the cellar. Damned if I'll allow those herd of Barringtons to guzzle my vintage burgundy."

"My lord," she whispered, reaching up to pat his arm, "ye can't shut yerself off from the world. 'Tis not healthy for ye to live like a ghost who wanders aboot these halls at night. Ye canna go on much longer like this."

Ian recognized the concern behind her words. Bending down, he kissed her cheek. "I know, Katie. If I could find a way out of this maze, I'd take it." Stepping back from his former nanny, he tried to cheer her. "Perhaps if the Sassenach weds her captain, they'll all race back to London and leave us in peace."

Without another word, Ian went over to the back of the room and began shoving something on a tray. "Have a feeling I'm going to need this," he said as Katie gave him a wary look when he sauntered back through the door toward the dining room.

"We purchased that blue silk in Paris last summer," Dora Barrington went on, gesturing with her wide arms encased tightly in pink tulle. "The squire and I spent a wonderful month touring that cultured city of romance. So ahead of England, so romantic. Ah, *formage, formage*. That's where I learned to speak French so well. I studied at the Sore Bun." She gave a start when she felt a tap on her shoulders. Looking to her left, she saw the servant holding a silver platter of cheese.

"Stilton or Gouda, madam?"

Puzzled, Dora peered up into Urisk's masked face. "We're just on the first course, not dessert. Why would I want cheese now?"

"Weel, ye kept callin' out *formage*. I just assumed you wanted it, and I—"

"Urisk," Myrtle warned, aware the Scot spoke fluent French, while Dora did not. "None of us wishes cheese at this time. Kindly put it on the sideboard after you serve Mrs. Barrington her salmon."

It was a small victory, but Ian savored it as he bowed formally and carried out his orders to the letter. He returned with the salmon, then stood at attention at his post, his gloved hands at his sides. Happy to have the mask on for once, he knew it hid his ear-to-ear grin.

However, after dinner, when they trooped into the cozy sitting room, Ian felt those new feelings of displeasure float to the surface again when Addison insisted Myrtle sit next to him on the settee. Dora gave her daughter a knowing wink as they settled themselves on the new wing chairs near the unlit fireplace.

After only half an hour, Dora squeezed herself out of her chair. Imitating a yawn, she turned to her blond-haired daughter. "It must be at least eight, and I am quite done in. I can see you are, too, Twilla dear."

"'Ere, Ma, I ain't—"

"Twilla," her mother reprimanded. "Remember, Papa and I sent you to that expensive finishing school so you could recover your aitches, like Mama always remembers." She fluttered her hand at Myrtle. "No, do not get up, my lady. You two young people just sit there and talk the hours away. Twilla and I will take our *day jay moos* upstairs," she gushed in more fractured French.

Dora waddled over and kissed her son on the cheek, then patted Myrtle's hand. "So sweet," she said of Myrtle. Turning to her peeved daughter, she ordered, "Come along, Twilla."

"But Ma," Twilla whined, "it's dark up them stairs. They say this ruin is haunted by the laird's ghost. Can't the loony light our way up?"

"Lud love me," complained Addison, "take the balmy sod with you, Mother."

Myrtle bit her lower lip. "Urisk, please take the ladies back up to their rooms."

"And your services," Addison added, over his shoulder, "will no longer be needed in here tonight, Urisk." The Englishman moved closer to Myrtle across the brocade cushion. "Her ladyship and I will serve ourselves if we wish any more refreshments."

For a reason he didn't want to contemplate, the Scot did not want to leave Lady Myrtle alone with Addison tonight. Yet he knew there was nothing he could do about it now. Grabbing the brace of lighted candles from the sideboard, he proceeded to the door.

"We must have our beauty sleep so we can give you our housewarming present tomorrow," Dora told her host.

Out in the hall, Dora clutched her daughter's puny arm as she puffed up the drafty staircase. "One thing I can tell you, Twilla, once Addie marries Myrt, he'll insist she turn this heap over to your father. Can't imagine why anyone would live in this horrid place. It smells moldy, it's gloomy out in the middle of nowhere. Why she wasted good money on new rugs and furniture is a mystery. She's a deep one, that Myrtle Prescott. Reads too much. Thinks about politics and the condition of the world. Not good for a woman," Dora went on. "Addison said she's even bought those filthy tenants clothes, food, supplies to fix their cottages, and cattle. I need something to calm my nerves."

"I brought your gin, Ma. It's in my big trunk, if that addlepate didn't break it when he dropped it outside."

Dora's round cheeks reddened from exertion. Perspiration smeared the heavy powder and rouge on her face. Pulling on her daughter's arm, she panted, "Wait," clearly forced to stop halfway up the stairs. "Hearse," she addressed the masked servant.

"That ain't his name, Ma. Urisk," Twilla called, "don't go so fast."

The Scot kept walking.

"'Ere, you big loony," Twilla shouted. "Brake your arse!"

The ladies saw the servant's black-covered shoulders straighten as he came to a complete halt. He turned slowly on the step and peered down at them through the slits in his mask.

"Blimey," Twilla gasped, "that queer duck gives me the willies. Addison says he's bald under the wig and has a face as ugly as a pig's after slaughter."

When the two Englishwomen made it up to his step, Ian turned to resume walking, but Dora's voice stopped him.

"Kindly remember," she said to the towering Scot, "English ladies are more delicate than your local Scottish hags who roam barefoot about these desolate mountains." She glanced at her daughter. "Though I do not believe in such flummery as ghosts, my little girl is uneasy because of the foolish tales we've heard about this place. Tell me, my good man, is Castle Kilmarock haunted?"

"I'm only the loony, madam, I wouldn't know," Ian answered, then turned abruptly to continue leading the way upstairs.

"Of all the impertinence!" Dora grumbled to her daughter as they resumed the climb. "I can tell you, Twilla, when Addison takes over this place, that cheeky lummox Hearse, or what ever the devil his name is, will be the first sacked."

When they reached the next landing, the ladies pushed regally past the servant who held the candle. "Leave the brace with us," the squat Englishwoman ordered. "You can find your own way down those treacherous stairs in the dark. And I shall speak to her ladyship about your rude, lax behavior, I can tell you."

With sweeping exaggeration, Ian raised his arms over his head. *"Formage, formage,"* he said, in mock alarm.

"Imagine," Dora fumed at his departing back. "Ignorant peasant pretending to speak French. How dare he imitate his betters."

* * *

The next morning over their kippers, Dora complained vehemently about Urisk. Myrtle could tell from Addison's expression he wished to take matters into his own hands. "I shall see to the matter now," she said, trying to sound determined. "Urisk, I wish to speak with you in the kitchen."

Shoving the plate of steaming scones down in front of Twilla, Urisk followed his mistress out the door to the kitchen.

"Urisk," Myrtle said when they were alone, "I know the Barringtons can be a trial. I'm sorry they have been—you see," she added, patting his arm, "the squire came from the poor streets of London, built up his business with hard work. A little of the rough edges remain on his wife and children."

"It's not their being poor and doing honest work for their wealth that irritates me," Ian said, keeping his voice equally low against the people in the next room. "'Tis their attitude that all Scots are inferior and their deliberate rudeness that galls me."

"Yes, I know. But it is only for a few days. You must remember," she went on, taking the Scot's right hand in hers from habit, "Captain Barrington has influence. I do not want to give him any excuse to send more troops to Sinclair lands."

He could not hide his surprise. "Then ye dinna mean to marry him?" he asked, something brightening within him. "You merely wish to court the redcoat's goodwill for your tenant's sake?"

"Well," she answered truthfully, "that is part of it, yet . . ." Her friend deserved an honest answer. "I am fond of Addison. You cannot know him as I do. In London, after Papa died, he was wonderful, kind, came over to see me almost daily, so attentive. The Highlands do not seem to agree with him. Perhaps it is the many responsibilities he holds at the fort. Right

200

now you are not seeing the congenial young man I have known."

"Mayhap," he countered, "you're seeing the true Barrington now, away from the gaiety of a plush London parlor. Are you so certain ye wish to spend your life with such a mon?"

This was not what she'd come here to speak about. Urisk's probing questions unsettled her. "I am not sure what my answer will be to his proposal. Part of me realizes he could benefit my tenants, if so inclined. And when things are settled the way I hope," she murmured, thinking of her efforts with the King, "soon I shall be able to leave the Highlands knowing you will all be taken care of."

"Aye," answered Ian, his voice brittle. He pulled his hand from hers. "The land and castles sold to the highest bidder, and safe in your fancy town house in London, ye'd never know when we were driven off the land. Your English conscience need never be troubled how the starving bairns die when winter comes with no food to feed them, or warm clothes to keep out the cold. Ye can just tell yerself you did your best, while ye spread yer legs for the redcoat."

"That you could—!" Stung by the vileness of his words, Myrtle raised her right hand automatically.

Urisk's quick reflexes cut off her intent. "Be warned, Sassenach." He increased the pressure of his fingers about her wrist. "I've had a bellyful of ye English for two lifetimes." When he saw her struggle, fear in her eyes, he released her hand.

He'd not touched her before in any way except gentleness, but she was more unnerved by her own lack of control. Never had she been so close to striking someone in anger. What was this mysterious Scot doing to her? One minute he had her pitying his sad life and deformities; the next she wanted to break a vase over his head.

And she admitted it. It cut to realize he believed she

meant to abandon her tenants so callously. "I thought you were my friend, that you more than anyone would understand—" Years of practice with her criticizing stepmother caused her to win the battle over tears. The cool reserve came to her rescue. "I came in here to ask you to stay out of sight for the day. Dora and Twilla will be busy with decorating one of the rooms. They want it to be a surprise for me. Because I realize they get on your nerves, please stay below stairs."

"And what will you and the good captain be doing?"

She did not care for his imperious tone; nonetheless, she answered. "Addison has asked me to take him on a picnic for the day. I suppose it's his mother's doing because she wishes to surprise me later."

The Scot made no pretext to hide his displeasure at this news. "I'll stay out of sight today as ye ask, my lady, but only on one condition."

Her chin lifted. "For a gillie, Urisk, you show a decided penchant for autocratic behavior."

"Aye, and did ye nae tell Barrington whether earl or peasant, we Scots see ourselves as gentlemen?"

Despite herself, Myrtle lost some of her irritation. "Yes, I did. Don't tell me the condition is that I sleep in my cellar room?" she asked, then laughed. "Your pet mouse Mortimer and I can talk over the meaning of the universe again."

Unable to join her humor, Ian winced at the reminder of how badly he'd treated her when she first arrived. "Never that. I only ask that ye nae take Barrington to our—to the place I took you the other day. I—the laird would nae like his favorite spot trampled by an English officer's boots."

She heard the earnestness behind his request. "I promise, Urisk. In truth, I would not like anyone else in that enchanted place, either. I understand why Ian

Sinclair loved it. Rest easy, dear Urisk, for the laird's memory has become precious to me, also."

The longing in her expressive blue eyes touched him like a caress. Ian reached out to cup her lovely face in his hand.

Addison's voice near the door stopped him.

"Myrtle, come along, I want to get an early start. Mother and Twilla are already busy at the redecorating." He glanced at the taller Scot, then back at Myrtle. "Gave him a dressing down, did you?" The Englishman's voice dripped sarcasm.

The magical moment between them evaporated, and Myrtle had to turn to the Englishman watching her. Dressed in fawn-colored riding coat and breeches, Addison tapped a leather riding crop against the top of his shiny boots. "Sorry, Addison. I'm ready. Just let me get the hamper."

To his credit, Ian said nothing. However, when Addison seemed more interested in taking an inventory of the well-stocked kitchen than in helping Myrtle with the full picnic basket, the Scot went over and took the hamper out of her arms. "I'll carry it to the stables for you." It was clear that, unlike at their picnic, Addison had no intention of walking.

"Thank you, Urisk," she whispered.

Ian told himself he'd bide his time for today, help Angus with repairs to the laundry room, then he'd find a quiet spot in his wine cellar to read—anything to escape the company of those two Barrington termagants.

"When I saw this room last night I just knew it cried out for my help," Dora said, satisfaction oozing from her close-set eyes. She pulled a few pieces of ribbon from her white day dress. "Don't you just adore it?"

Myrtle felt Addison's hand at her elbow as he

203

smiled at his female relatives. "It's so . . . so innovative," Myrtle finally managed, trying to hide her reaction.

"Mama, you've outdone yourself this time. It's better than father's study," praised Addison.

"I don't know what to say, I mean—"

"No," Dora cut off. "No thanks are necessary. Each time a guest stays in this room, you must tell them about Dora Barrington, who sought only to share her God-given talents with Scotland. Oh, look at the time," she added, after peering at the silver clock on the mantel. "Twilla, we must change for dinner. Have a nice outing, my dears?"

Addison answered, while Myrtle seemed overtaken by her housewarming present. "Yes, we did not go far, but it was a lovely afternoon," he said, then gave his mother a meaningful wink. "Myrtle and I had a long talk near a sturdy oak."

"Oh, you will shock your little sister if you go on," Dora teased, wagging a thick finger at her smiling son.

Myrtle's astonishment gave way to dread. Why, oh why hadn't she insisted that Dora tell her which room she was going to "improve"? All the Barringtons had been determined to surprise her about this. Yet never had Myrtle considered Dora would choose this small bedroom next to the Thomsons. "Has . . . has anyone seen Urisk?" she asked.

"The loony?" Twilla straightened the frilly apron over her peach-colored frock. "That old Scotswoman came by once, looking kind of pale; then, when I asked her, she said Urisk was down in the cellar working. That imbecile don't . . . doesn't do too much around here, if you ask me."

So Urisk hadn't seen his "embellished" room yet. Myrtle glanced again at the red and green plaid drapes, then down at the yellow and blue plaid carpet covering the entire floor. The bedspread had been replaced with a purple, brown, and orange crossbar pattern of wool.

"Now," said Dora with pride, adding a flourish with her arm. "This is Scotland. I've captured the entire culture of the highlands, the mist on the moors, the sound of bagpipes in the glen. I can tell it's moved you, Myrt. Leaves you speechless, doesn't it?"

Inwardly blanching at the garish concoction of mismatched loud plaids on the walls, floor—everywhere, Myrtle tried to smile at her guest. "How can I let you part with all your collection of wool plaids, Dora?"

"My reward is spreading my knowledge of Scottish design to Scotland. You know," she added, moving closer to the taller woman, "I can never understand why such an uncivilized people could have such taste in wool. Ah" she finished, imitating philosophical depth, *"Sail the chair.* Such is war," as we say in French.

It was while Myrtle and her guests finished their dessert of lemon cream that the tranquility of the dinner crashed to a close.

"Merde!" traveled down the hallway to the dining room. "What in bloody hell happened to my room?" was followed by the loud sound of leather boots making a quick charge toward the dining room.

Myrtle swallowed, having dreaded this confrontation for hours. And Addison hadn't given her an opportunity to locate Urisk for a quiet talk before he saw his room. Yet she was determined to handle this situation with her usual diplomacy. "My, my, it seems," she said, after a nervous smile, "Urisk has discovered the improvements to his quarters."

Dora's mouse-hair eyebrows rose to the edge of her pink powdered wig. "I had no idea a servant occupied that room. Surely that is a room for a guest, my dear. You don't let the loony stay there?"

Twilla squeaked in alarm at the force Ian used to open the double doors to the dining room.

In his gray workman's shirt and breeches, Urisk clearly hadn't taken the time to put on an outer coat before coming here.

Ignoring the others, the angry Scot stalked to the center of the room, planted his fists on his side of the table, and leaned his imposing frame over to Myrtle, who sat watching him from the other side. His question was menacing in its quietness. "Have ye seen all that tartan tosh in my room?"

She was aware all eyes were on her; her hands shook as she folded and unfolded the white napkin on her lap. "Ah, yes. It is a housewarming present to me from Mrs. Barrington." While she'd always attempted to treat servants with respect and care, never would she have stood for such insolence from an English servant at home. Why was she allowing this Scot to intimidate her? she demanded, beginning to resent this constant position in which he placed her, where she had to act as peacemaker between him and her guests. She hadn't asked for this responsibility of Kilmarock Castle. It wasn't enjoyable to have the Scots trying to kill her. "See to your duties, Urisk. My gift does not concern you."

"Gift?" His voice rose behind the leather mask at the icy dismissal in her manner. "A sack of sheep turds would be more welcome. I canna see anything but checks before my eyes after being in the room only five minutes. 'Tis makin' me bilious." He moved back from the table and glared at the four English people. "No one even had the courtesy to ask my wishes in the matter. I would nae consider goin' into your homes and takin' oot what I wished, while adding such a putrid combination of cloth and colors that I would nae even put in a pig barn."

Dora's cheeks puffed with indignation. "How dare you—a peasant—speak of my superior skills. Addison, are you going to let this . . . this low creature insult Twilla and me?"

Addison turned on Myrtle. "My lady, I thought you said the oaf was brain damaged. It seems the loony can reason a few sentences." Addison's hazel eyes took in the masked Scot's imposing frame. "And I'm beginning to wonder, just what other duties does this Scottish giant perform for you? For the servant seems clearly to have you under his thumb."

Myrtle heard Twilla and Dora laugh and felt her face flame with embarrassment. However, it was Urisk's Gaelic expletive before he leaned over, upsetting glasses and crockery, that had her full attention. Urisk hauled Addison out of his chair, across the food-strewn table. He held the Englishman down with a Scottish knee pressed against his chest and his large hands around Addison's lace-covered throat.

"Ye gutter-minded bastard," Ian growled at the man struggling to free himself.

"No! Urisk, let him go."

The English officer's face went from red to purple as air was cut off.

Myrtle clawed at Urisk's wrists to dislodge his iron grip on Addison. Twilla raced over to punch Urisk on the arm, while Dora grabbed the bowl of lemon cream and shoved it in the masked man's face.

Forced to pull away because he couldn't see or breathe with the cream in the slits of his mask, Ian moved backward.

Dora and Twilla went immediately to Addison, who reclined against the spilled wine and sauces, rubbing his bruised throat.

After checking on Addison, Myrtle walked back around the table to shove her napkin into Urisk's hands so he could wipe the goo from the slits in his mask.

"I have had enough!" Myrtle declared to all the people in the room. "Captain Barrington," she challenged, "since you believe I'm a whore, clearly you could not wish to have me as your wife."

Addison pulled away from his clucking relatives to hurry over to her. "My dear," he said, his voice full of contrition, "I never meant those angry words." He smiled across at her, then touched one of the elbow-length sleeves of her rose silk gown. "Suppose I'm jealous of all men who adore you. And you have to admit, for a servant, this odd Scot does have more authority than is prudent."

She couldn't deny it. However, for once she did not feel immediately placated by Addison's suave manner. She pulled away to address Urisk. "I pay your salary; you are a servant here, Urisk. I am mistress of Kilmarock Castle. You do not own it, nor have you any say regarding the running of it, and that includes design choices. If you do not like your present room, sleep elsewhere. Now," she added with finality, "you have my permission to retire. Do you understand my meaning?"

Urisk saw the triumphant smiles on the faces of all three Barringtons. "Aye, I ken, Sassenach." Coldness replaced his earlier fury.

Slowly he walked out of the room. He could hear Addison making a joke of it as his female relatives jeered at his back. Ian couldn't hear what Myrtle said to them, and he didn't want to look at her. She'd taken their part, not his. What did he expect? he asked himself. Myrtle was a Sassenach. She'd just sided with her own kind, he more the fool for acting like a knight challenged when Barrington insulted her honor. Honor—the word burned his tongue. The English knew nothing of the word.

Having heard what had occurred in the next room, Katie and Angus Thomson eyed the laird with trepidation when he came into the kitchen. Even the mask could not disguise that he was still in the throes of his Sinclair temper.

"I'd nae rise early to fix breakfast tomorrow," Ian told his loyal retainers. "I have a feeling that horde of Barringtons will be departing posthaste in the morning." He turned and headed below stairs. "Mortimer, Robbie, and I will be in our cellar rooms this evening."

Puzzled, Katie stared at her husband after the earl of Kilmarock left. "But her ladyship said her houseguests would be staying until the end of the week."

Angus ran his hands through his close-cropped white hair. "Weel," he said with a chuckle, "mayhap the laird has more knowledge of tomorrow than we have."

"Now, why is he taking his pet mouse and dog down there with him? Oh, Angus, you dinna think Ian is going to do anything rash, do you?"

Laughing, Angus gave his wife a kiss on her lined cheek, then mischievously added a soft pat to her plump buttocks. "He's already outfoxed the redcoats by faking his suicide and managed to convince her ladyship he's simple Urisk. How can ye think he'd ever do anything rash?"

Chapter Twelve

It was after one in the morning when Myrtle jolted awake after hearing women's screams from the hallway. She reached for her dressing gown and slippers and dashed outside her bedroom, hardly taking time to fasten the cloth-covered buttons that went from her neck to her ankles.

Dressed similarly in their ruffled nightwear and outer robes, Twilla and Dora Barrington stood clutching each other. Addison came out of his room, hastily tying the blue satin robe about his waist that he'd thrown over his white nightshirt. His thinning hair hung limply about his shoulders. "What the deuce is going on 'ere?"

The wire cage over Dora's elaborate wig bobbed up and down as she screeched in disjointed phrases. "We barely escaped with our lives—a demon from Hades, floating about our bedroom. He was horrible; tried to murder us," Dora wailed.

Her face buried in her mother's ample bosom, Twilla continued bawling hysterically. "Told you . . . ghost of Kilmarock Castle . . ."

Myrtle went over to the distraught women immediately. With difficulty, she managed to discern that both had been awakened from a sound sleep by an intruder.

"Intruder?" Dora demanded with such force that Twilla vaulted back from motherly solace. "Blimey, it were a monster with a gory face, covered with blood, and he was dressed in the most hideous garments. Like a shroud, he wore something long decayed come back to life. And there was an infectious rat with huge, gaping jaws; not to mention that devil dog—hound from hell—stood right next to the laird's ghost. I tell you, Ian Sinclair's demented soul haunts this castle. Me and Twilla seen 'im with our own eyes," she wailed, even losing her aitches.

"Mrs. Barrington, I'm sorry you were upset this way," said Myrtle. Suspicions clawed at her, yet she tried to calm the two women. She knew by Addison's scowl in her direction he was as unconvinced as she about their assumption of a ghost. He patted his mother's shoulders, then ordered a passing servant to fetch brandy. Rather than have the ladies return to "that haunted room," Myrtle insisted they take her suite of rooms. She sent Katie for new linens.

It took over an hour to settle both women in her rooms and convince Addison it was safe enough to return to his own bed. Myrtle then took a lighted candle into the women's former room. She looked about, ready to leave when nothing seemed amiss.

Then she spotted the silhouette of an imposing figure against the back window ledge. Reminding herself ghosts did not exist, Myrtle walked cautiously over to the apparition. She raised the candle over her head.

"Good Lord," Myrtle muttered when she saw that the demon from Hades consisted of a huge orange pumpkin for a head, turnips for ears, hunks of coal for eyes, carrot for a nose—propped on a wooden beam—swathed in the loud plaid drapes and rug from the room Dora had "improved." She heard a noise near her feet and bent down to kneel on the wooden floorboards. Myrtle recognized the tan coat and pink ears of little Mortimer. When she put out her hand, Urisk's pet sat up, sniffed her fingers, then hopped up into her palm. She stood up. He'd probably squeaked and scurried about the room on cue from Urisk. "And I suppose," she said to Mortimer, "Robbie was pressed into service as the hound from hell." While she had no more liking for Dora's decorations, Myrtle saw no humor in this deliberate ruse to scare her guests.

"Getting acquainted with the demon?"

With a start, Myrtle turned to see Addison coming quietly into the room. "Ah . . . since I am to sleep here tonight, I thought an investigation of the room prudent." She slipped Mortimer into the pocket of her wrapper, for some reason not trusting the look on Addison's face right now if he got hold of anyone remotely connected with this humbug. "How are your mother and sister doing?"

"The brandy helped calm their nerves. They're asleep now. I took the third bottle to my room— could use a little soothing myself." Coming closer into the room, he eyed the prop behind her. He touched one of the pieces of purple, orange, and yellow plaid. "'Like a shroud,'" he quoted his mother, "'wearing something long decayed come back to life.'" His gaze was damning. "Never, my lady, did I think you capable of such cruel chicanery."

"Addison, you cannot believe I had anything to—"

"Don't deny it," he cut her off, holding up his brocade-covered arms. "I'm too furious with you to hear any more on the matter tonight. I'll speak to you in the morning."

After he left in a flurry of icy condemnation, Myrtle couldn't sleep. It wasn't the presence of the pumpkin dummy in the room that upset her; it was the insight into Addison's overbearing personality. Getting a glimpse of the soldier's manner just now made her

213

question how he'd be as a husband, let alone a father. When she could have used some moral support just now, especially with his demanding womenfolk, Addison had addressed her in the manner of an officer reading the riot act to a lowly private.

After she came downstairs to join her guests for breakfast, Myrtle was amazed to find Dora and Twilla in the process of packing their things for a hasty departure. At least seven uniformed soldiers sat waiting atop their horses, clearly to act as protective escort for their commander's relatives' retreat home.

Myrtle rushed over to Dora. "Mrs. Barrington, please—you cannot mean to leave. I am truly sorry for that unfortunate incident, but as Addison can tell you, it appears it was just a tasteless hoax. Please stay."

Dora craned her neck to give Myrtle a look of affronted dignity. "Twilla and I will not stay one more night to be murdered in our beds by the laird's evil ghost. My son tried explaining there wasn't a ghost last night, but I know better. Such moaning could never be made by anything living."

Myrtle looked at Addison's stony expression, found no support, then took a deep breath before speaking to the two women again. "I shall be happy to show you the room upstairs so you may see for yourself—"

"No," Twilla screamed. "I ain't settin' foot in that 'ellhole again. Ma and I are sensitive. We don't need to be hit over the head to guess when we ain't wanted. There, Ma, don't cry," she said, when Dora wiped at her eyes with a lacy pocket handkerchief. Twilla stepped back with another cry of alarm when she saw the masked Urisk come out to assist the two footmen with the luggage. "Addison, you keep that flamin' lunatic away from us!"

"He will not hurt you or mother," Addison promised his sister, then scowled as the Scot loaded

214

their trunks on the coaches. "Twilla, you and Mama were so upset last night, I paid one of her ladyship's servants to send word to the fort. Good work, Johnson," he praised the young lieutenant.

Johnson snapped to attention. "Your note said you wished us here at first light, sir."

"Perhaps your leaving would be best," Addison told his mother and sister as he walked them to their carriages. "The last thing I want is for either of you to be unhappy. Can't say I blame you for disliking this place. Contrary to your insistence, I believe it was not a ghost, and I promise you, the guilty culprit will be punished severely. I mean to show these Scots such underhanded tricks and attempts to assassinate her ladyship will no longer be tolerated."

Alarmed by his cold determination, Myrtle could only stare as the Barrington women and their numerous trunks were loaded on the coaches. However, after they left, Myrtle knew her troubles weren't over when Addison said he needed to speak to her in her library—now.

Entering the large room lined with mostly empty bookshelves, another example of the late earl's attempt to raise needed cash, Addison rounded on her without even closing the door.

"How dare you insult and frighten my mother and sister!" he raged. "Just because we have no title, my lady, is no excuse for such deplorable treatment."

"Addison, never have I felt my being an earl's daughter put me above others. And I assure you I had nothing to do with what happened last evening. I really do not know who—"

"Liar!" the officer cut her off, his black boots thudding on the wooden floorboards as he came closer.

The word made it difficult for her to keep her composure. Though beginning to suspect Urisk, she

215

had no real proof. Besides, Myrtle knew she could not trust the lad under her protection to this furious Englishman. Poor Urisk had just gotten his wits back—a blow to his head might . . . She felt queasy at the thought. "Addison, I apologize. As hostess I do bear a certain responsibility for what happened to your relatives, and you have a right to be upset. However, I can only give you my word I had nothing to do with last evening's incident." When he gave her a dubious frown but did not yell, she continued. "You must understand these Scots have reason to mistrust us. We've taken over their land, dictated their dress, forbidden them to bear arms. The presence of more English soldiers here will only make matters worse."

"I believe I am in a better position to judge the suitability of military intervention. You are to blame, my lady. No, let me finish," he commanded when she opened her mouth to speak. "You are too lax with your servants. It is something I intend to change after we're married."

"Do you not mean 'if'?"

Ignoring her question, the English officer stared across at her. "You have changed, Myrtle. I never remember you being so outspoken. These highlands have made you difficult."

Her blue eyes widened. "Perhaps these highlands suit me more than London. The Scots, though they do not trust me yet, I hope in time will learn I mean them no harm."

"As last night proved?"

"I have already told you what I know of last evening."

With a sound of impatience, Addison gripped her arms. "I will have that servant. You will hand him over to me now."

"Let me go." Myrtle struggled, more irritated than frightened. "There are many servants in this castle

216

now, Addison. Anyone might have perpetrated such flummery. Even a tenant could have made his way into the keep after dark. No one died; let the matter rest. If there is anything to be done, I will do it. You are hurting me," she complained, after a few more minutes of this intolerable treatment. The pressure from his fingers bit into the soft flesh of her upper arms.

"Stubborn bitch, you may be an earl's daughter," snapped Barrington, "but I'll soon get you to heel when I give an order. Now, summon that Scot, for I suspect he was behind that despicable trick on my defenseless kin last night. It's not the first time I've sensed that secretive giant is more than the imbecile he pretends."

"No," she stated with finality, while continuing in her futile attempts to free herself. "You are wrong about Urisk. And I will not call him. Now, let me go."

For answer, the Englishman pulled her body closer to his. "I know a perfect way to make you obey."

Myrtle was truly alarmed now by the dangerous gleam in his hazel eyes. Then something brushed her arm, and the next instant she was free. Even Addison hadn't time to react, things happened so fast.

"Yer a bully and a bastard," Urisk growled, before his doubled fist connected with Addison's face.

"Mother of God," Myrtle cried. "Urisk, run to the cellar," she pleaded, when she saw Addison struggling like a stunned spider to right himself off the library floor. Blood spewed from his nostrils. When she viewed the damage, she realized the Scot had probably just broken Addison's nose. "God, Urisk, please, I'll handle this. Run. You must get to the cellar." Tears of frustration and fear glazed her eyes when her servant shook his head.

"There are some things a man canna overlook."

Addison got to his feet with difficulty. He held his

217

white pocket handkerchief in front of his nose. The skin about his eyes was already swelling. "You're a dead man, Urisk," he muttered through a torrent of his own blood. Walking shakily out the open door, he shouted, "Johnson!"

The younger lieutenant came in immediately. Addison brushed his concern away and gave him an order. Seconds later three soldiers entered Myrtle's study along with Addison.

"Take this man outside and give him forty lashes." It took the three men to hold onto the masked Scot.

"No," Myrtle said, shoving her frame in front of Urisk. "You will not harm my servant. Addison, he came to my aid because you were being physically abusive." She didn't care if Addison's men heard her. "Urisk sought to protect me the only way he knew how." She saw the three soldiers look from her to Addison, as if they could not believe their superior had manhandled an English lady, the daughter of the late Earl of Hartford.

Having gotten his nose to stop bleeding, Addison glowered across at her. "You dare defend this Scottish scum over your own kind?"

"This man is my friend, Addison. He is under my protection. And in truth, sir, I was very close to punching you in the nose myself, but Urisk beat me to it."

Two of the soldiers started to laugh outright, but a glare from the captain quelled their reaction.

Completely out of patience with the woman who stood so protectively in front of the towering Scot, who needed three of his best soldiers to hold him, Addison shouted, "My father can go 'ang! I'm damned if I will be forced to marry you, a woman who doesn't know her place." He gave her physique a critical appraisal. "A woman with the figure of a gun deck. Had I even the remotest desire to embrace a frigate, I would have joined the Navy. By all means, gentlemen," he said to the three soldiers, "let her barbarian pet go."

The soldiers left, and this time Urisk stood close to her, almost in the manner of one guarding a precious jewel.

Myrtle was concerned only about one phrase. "Addison, what did you mean, 'forced to marry'?"

Looking disgusted, Addison explained: "My father was after this land long before Ian Sinclair killed himself. If your stubborn father hadn't been friends with the late laird, Papa could 'ave been making money with the sheepherding on this huge estate years ago. Only Jonathan Prescott maneuvered the King into letting him choose the new owner, then Sinclair committed suicide. My father said it was now up to me. I had to marry you so he could get Kilmarock Castle and the lands. Blimey, no property is worth that much aggravation. My discerning tastes, Lady Myrtle Prescott, run more to blonde, lithe beauties with waists I can span in my 'ands."

Though she knew she did not love Addison and last night had helped make up her mind not to wed him, Myrtle was appalled to learn Addison felt nothing for her except as a means to appease his tyrannical father's greed. Never had her father mentioned the elder Barrington's designs on Sinclair lands. She was aware he didn't like Addison, but why hadn't her father told her the truth? Did Jonathan Prescott imagine she wouldn't have believed him, or that in rebellion she'd want to marry Addison more? Or could it have been just another discovery her father left her to find out on her own. But what if she hadn't found out about this until *after* the wedding? The questions unnerved her. Urisk must have sensed it, for his arm came about her shoulders in support.

Myrtle said nothing as Addison went back upstairs to hastily pack his belongings. Perhaps this morning's confrontation with Addison was inevitable, but

219

Urisk's proximity right now flooded her with memories of the evening before. She moved away from his comforting arm.

"Urisk," she said, looking up at his mask-covered face. "That was a childish prank you pulled last night."

He shrugged. "I think those two squealing Barringtons scared Robbie and Mortimer more than the other way around. And you can't say you're sorry to see that cruel English popinjay out of your life."

Features set, she pointed out, "None of these issues is your concern. No matter what you thought, the Barringtons were my guests. It was not your place to take matters into your own hands, either last evening or when you clouted Addison on the nose."

"Aye," he said without remorse, "I enjoyed that punch, even if it almost cost me forty lashes."

The terror that he might have been whipped drained the blood from her face. "It is not a matter of levity," she hissed. "Don't you realize Addison would not have let the matter rest with a beating? I don't know," she said aloud, then rubbed her temple where the pink scar ached again. "I've tried to help you and your clansmen, but I'm—oh, what is the use trying to explain? If only Ian Sinclair were here," she cried, her voice full of regret. She moved toward the door. "At least I owe Addison the courtesy of saying goodbye." She didn't tell Urisk she also intended to take Addison's picture off her night table.

Ian watched her walk hesitantly up the stairs to see to the captain's departure. Pleased she wasn't to marry Addison, he'd also seen the tears in her eyes when she'd mention Ian just now. She was still grieving over Ian Sinclair's death, and his conscience bothered him. Unable to stop himself from coming to her rescue when Barrington manhandled her, Ian knew Myrtle and he could not go on this way much longer. God, he thought, shaking his head—what the devil was he going to do now?

Though he expected it, late that evening when he took his customary walk along the battlements, something snapped inside when he saw Myrtle head toward Ian's grave again. Instead of turning away, this time he raced for the stairway. He bounded down the steep steps three at a time.

Entering the area before the gates that led to the family crypt, Ian slowed his pace and took in the scene before him. The tall Englishwoman was placing a bouquet of pink and blue spring flowers on the marked boulder of his grave. "Bringing gifts, like courting a lover," he remarked with asperity.

From the censure in his tone, Myrtle discovered she was still not over her irritation with Urisk and his role in bringing matters to a head between herself and Addison. Even more amazing, she suddenly realized the romantic side of her needed these times with Ian Sinclair's memory, and she resented Urisk's interruption. It had become important to her to learn all she could about the deceased laird—study the books he'd read, talk to the people he'd known, learn his tastes in art, music, and clothes. His thoughts, his hopes, everything he was, she wanted to know. She looked down at the flowers she'd placed on the cold stone of his grave. "This does not concern you, Urisk."

His own raw emotions were too close to the surface for Ian to hear the dismissal in her voice. "Och, ye should be wed with bairns aboot ye, not languishin' over a dead mon."

"I'll just go purchase a husband, shall I?" she demanded with equal rancor. "Some malleable Englishman, no doubt, who will practice flagrant adultery every chance he gets."

His boots crunched on the ground as he walked closer to her. "Ye malign yourself too harshly." Hands on his hips, Ian stood watching the defiance enter the blue stones of her eyes. It flickered for a second.

"Please," she whispered, "I wish to be alone."

"Aye, that's the problem, lass. You've been alone too much. 'Tisn't healthy, this maudlin obsession with a dead man."

"And I suppose you know all about morose things, sequestered here, living like a hermit or specter who only roams outside these walls after dark?"

"At least I'm not turning into a fixated virgin who lives through the faded memories of man's diary and her own romantic pining for a corpse."

Spots of crimson blossomed on her cheeks. "Oh, well, if it's just a problem of never having been with a man, I can solve that quickly enough. I think men place too much significance on it, often demanding it from their brides but not from themselves. Perhaps I'll ride over tonight to the fort and ask Addison to assist me. No doubt the captain would not be averse to ridding me of my maidenhead."

Instantly Myrtle regretted her flippant sarcasm, and not just because Urisk reached out and took her into his arms.

"Nay, Sassenach," he grated through the slits in his mask, "ye'll nae go to that Englishman tonight or any other night."

"Why not?" Myrtle challenged, but she couldn't explain the reason her knees suddenly weakened and her blood fired from this man's touch. His warm breath fanned her cheeks.

"The laird would nae like it."

"As you are fond of pointing out, the laird is dead."

"Aye, but I'm flesh and blood enough," said Urisk, supporting her upper body with his hands. Gently but firmly he pressed her close against him.

Not alarmed as when Addison held her, she nevertheless felt things were out of kilter. Even through her gown and chemise her soft flesh ignited where Urisk caressed her—her back, the swell of her breasts, her hips. "Urisk . . . you forget yourself." Breathing seemed difficult as she wrangled with words, then made a motion to pull away.

The Scot shook his head and kept her his willing prisoner. "No, wee kelpie, I'm finally remembering who I am." His hand came up to stroke the softness of her brown hair. "Aye, 'tis Urisk, and I'm here, alive, nae a ghost."

Despite the inner warning that she should terminate this erotic, totally improper embrace, Myrtle found herself leaning against his muscular chest. His strong, blunt-edged fingers were massaging her neck and the area behind her ears. His arousing touch made her recall that night she'd been ill. "Oh, Urisk who are you? What is happening?"

"I'm not sure of it all myself. I only know I was verra angry just now when you mentioned going to Addison. 'Tis an emotion I've never experienced before, and I dinna like it."

She pulled back to look up at him. "You were jealous? I cannot believe it," she said in awe. "No one has ever been jealous over me before."

"Now ye know," he said, giving her a gentle shake. "Ye needn't look so pleased aboot it. It took me weeks to discover it . . . among other things."

"But, Urisk." She gained more control of her emotions. "I don't know what—I am very fond of you, but . . ." She glanced back at the laird's grave. When she pulled away from him, she felt his disappointment. "You were right just now when you said I was courting a lover. God help me, I believe I am in love with Ian Sinclair, the one man I can never have."

Affected by the suffering he read on her sweet face, Ian could find no words to comfort her. "If Ian were alive—?"

"No, it would not matter," she interjected. A sad smile curved her lips. "Even if we had met before he died, I realize Ian would not have looked twice at me. Perhaps it is my consolation, holding the gallant, wonderful man's memory close to my heart, I'll always have that part of him no one can take away from me." She turned to leave. "Thank you again for being such a dear friend, Urisk. Goodnight."

Her rose-colored gown shimmered in the moonlight as she walked up the pathway toward the small castle. The laird of Kilmarock stood watching her for a long time. Ashamed, he had to admit he couldn't say with certainty, upon first meeting the Englishwoman, he would have felt the way he did now. Yet there was something about her that captivated him, drew him to her since he'd first set eyes on her that stormy evening she'd entered Kilmarock Castle like a bedraggled waif. Her hard work to help the Sinclairs, her courage in defending those less able, her sense of humor in the face of adversity—all those things forced him to discover the real Lady Myrtle Prescott. A roguish smile curved his mouth when he admitted again he did find her figure very arousing.

He kicked a few stray pebbles with the toe of his right boot. Damn it, he thought, fighting the urge to tear off his mask and wig, charge into her bedroom upstairs, and shout the truth at her. Yet he first had to discover what she meant to do with her tenants and lands. He leaned against the cold iron gates that led to the Sinclair family graves.

Suddenly, his thoughts brightened when he reminded himself Myrtle did say just now she loved Ian Sinclair. That would make it easier when she found out the ghost was alive, wouldn't it?

Chapter Thirteen

When one of the Mackenzie cousins brought the letter the next day, Myrtle gave the astonished lad a fistful of gold coins, hugged him, then raced for her upstairs office. Her heart thudded against her chest as she prayed fervently this would be the answer she'd fought so hard to procure. Her hands shook when she broke the seal and sat down at her writing desk to read the King's reply.

When she finished, Myrtle jumped up from the chair with a boisterous shout of victory that would have rivaled the loudest spectator at a cricket match. "Oh, Ian, we've won!" she cried aloud, then laughed in nervous release. It seemed to take forever, but George of Hanover had finally answered her. With this letter and his signature and formal seal, His Majesty granted a posthumous pardon to the late earl of Kilmarock, clearing Ian Sinclair entirely from the previous, now proved unfounded, charge of treason against the Crown. Her work and voluminous documents sent through Cyril Layton had paid off. She'd shown the King that never had the laird spoken out publicly or raised his sword against the English King. As a loyal subject of His Majesty, the late earl's title was restored. In accordance with Lady Myrtle's offer, she could turn over all her legal rights on

Kilmarock Castle and lands to the late earl's successor. The King now gave her permission to appoint Gavin Mackenzie, Ian's tacksman, to the position as head of the Sinclairs.

She left the open letter on her desk and rushed to find Urisk. Since she arrived, the late laird's gillie had been pressing her doggedly to know her plans. And now, thank God, she could tell Urisk the good news. Her heart soared to realize she'd been able to give the spirit of Ian Sinclair this one gift in her power.

However, on her way downstairs, a distraught Katie Thomson almost plowed into her.

"My lady," Katie cried, "an English officer . . . murdered . . . in the clearing near the keep. His body was just found . . . a Scot's dirk in his chest. The redcoats have swarmed down on us. Oh, my lady," the elderly woman went on, clearly relieved when Myrtle reached out to support her. "We're done for now. They'll kill us all for sure."

Alarmed, Myrtle wasted little time calling for Angus to help his wife. Then she raced for the stables to get her horse. Was Addison the officer killed?

The short distance away from the castle seemed to take hours before she made it over the hill. Myrtle looked down at the clearing toward the valley below. Men, women, and children were being herded in a circle by at least seventy English soldiers. Pressing her gown-covered knees to Lily's flanks, she rushed toward them. It relieved her to see Addison come over to help her dismount. "Oh, Addison, what has happened?" After she glanced to the right, she found the answer. Lying faceup on the damp grass was the body of an English officer who couldn't have been more than twenty. His coat was stained dark red, the ground near him slick with his own blood. His lifeless eyes stared heavenward in horror. Bile rose in her throat, and she had to turn away.

"How . . . how can you be sure a Scot did it?"

Seeming to dismiss the angry words he'd spoken to her the day before, Addison steered her away from the fresh corpse. "Lieutenant Johnson," he called over his shoulder.

Instantly, the blond-haired Englishman came over. He carried something in his hand. With a sinking heart, Myrtle saw the bloodstained dagger.

"Johnson removed it from that young lad's chest, my lady. There is little doubt because of the plain, unadorned black handle that it is a Scot's dagger— certainly not an Englishman's weapon. The only English for miles around here are soldiers. The question is which one of these Scottish vipers used it. That is what I mean to find out now."

"Please, Addison, you must let me speak to them first."

"Still trying to protect your precious tenants? All right, my lady, you can go over to them, but just for a few minutes, mind."

"Thank you, Addison." Myrtle walked slowly over to where about forty of her tenants stood. Their expressions of wary hostility unnerved her for a second. Grateful that Addison was keeping his word to stay back, she now wondered if this was a good idea. "Please," she began, "if you know anything about this murder, you must tell me."

"Why should we?" demanded one of the older men from the back of the crowd. "These redcoats accuse us of a deed we dinna commit. More ill-treatment from these soldiers is all we'll get nae matter what we say."

Jean Mackenzie stepped forward. "Me father and brothers are blind to this Sassenach bitch who came uninvited to our lands. You've all heard Katie's prediction aboot this blue-eyed Englishwoman, who will either save or destroy us," the seventeen-year-old shouted. "Well, I say, she's brought nothin' but trouble since she came here." Jean pointed her finger up at Myrtle. "She means to crush us with her plans to sell the castle and drive us off the land with her English lover, Captain Barrington. There is your true enemy of the Sinclairs."

"Aye," agreed a few more. Some of the men and women moved closer to Myrtle.

The Englishwoman stepped back. "You must see that violence is not the answer. Your dead laird knew this, for he sought to keep you out of local skirmishes with rival clans, and out of taking sides in this Charles Stuart business."

"Much good it did him," shouted a woman from the crowd. "The English killed his two brothers at Culloden. Near broke the laird's heart, and then he tried so hard to help us when all the food and money were gone. It was you English that drove Ian to suicide."

"I know," Myrtle countered. "I grieve for his loss, too," she said, her voice breaking. "Yet I know that officer," she said, pointing to the now covered body on the ground to her right, "did not deserve to be murdered, for he was only patrolling this area because he'd been ordered to keep the peace and see no laws were broken."

"English laws," spat the man in the back. "We've nae murdered him, and told the Sassenach captain in charge; he'll nae believe us."

"But they say it is a Scot's dagger that killed him."

"Listen to her," Jean shouted, "the Sassenach wants the redcoats to kill us all. Ye need more proof whose side she's on?"

Myrtle could tell from the grumbling and hateful looks that things were getting completely out of hand. However, when Addison ordered his armed men to mount up and move toward her, she raised her hand in protest. "Please, Captain Barrington," she called, "stay back. I am all right."

Addison frowned, but as he watched the angry

crowd, then looked back at Myrtle, something seemed to occur to him. "Since you wish to handle this matter alone, my lady," he said, "I will comply. However," he shouted to the rabble, "I'll be back with more men in a few days to loosen your tongues." Addison then turned to his men. "We're returning to the fort."

With the sound of horses' hooves fading in the distance, Myrtle felt the crowd surrounding her grow more ugly.

"The laird would nae let things come to such a pass," yelled another Scot. "The Mackenzie lass is right. Prescott plans to throw us off the land. The Sassenach is nae friend of the Sinclairs. She's probably workin' with the captain to put the blame on us for the redcoat's murder. What shall we do with this treacherous snake?"

"Kill her!" chanted the group. Men and women grabbed her.

Terrified, Myrtle could not move from the press of angry bodies around her. Someone punched her back. The material at the right sleeve of her linen dress tore from the seams when someone yanked her. Pins tumbled to the dew-covered earth as rough hands pulled her back and forth. "Please, you must let me explain. I am not your enemy. I—" Her words were drowned out by angry curses. The suffocating smell of their unleashed rage permeated the morning air.

The tall Englishwoman crashed to her knees when a man's fist struck her hard on the shoulder. Angry hands clawed at her brown hair, forcing her up.

"Let the Sassenach go!" The loud masculine voice traveled down through the heated crowd.

Myrtle followed everyone's gaze toward the crest of the hill. A lone rider approached. Wearing the outlawed kilt, a man rode toward them, dirk and pistol in the belt across the brown coat covering his

229

chest. The wide claymore on his left hip gleamed in the sunlight. She saw reddish-brown hair clubbed back with a leather thong, then his face crashed into full view.

"'Tis a ghost!" she heard those around her whisper. For a moment, she believed it herself.

The frantic crossing and horrified gasps continued as all present felt they were seeing the laird's ghost. Even Myrtle was speechless, unsure of what or who was riding with such determination toward her. But then she looked up into the handsome face she'd studied so many times from the portrait in her room. Unlike the painting five years ago, there were lines at the corners of his eyes the last difficult years had added. However, the piercing look in those golden eyes took her breath away. She knew by the silence surrounding her that his clansmen were equally awed by the magnificence of their laird. This was not a ghost, she told herself.

And when he bent down to lift her easily up in front of him on Sian's back, the arm about her waist was firmly muscled and no apparition.

It was Ian Sinclair—he was alive! Myrtle shouted to her mind and heart. Unable to take it all in, she could only sit mutely in shock as his clear voice rang out in explanation of why the deception of his death was necessary, along with his disguise as Urisk. She could hardly make out the words he spoke to his spellbound clansmen.

"And now," Ian finished, "that this English lady has cleared my name with the King, there is no need to hide from the English soldiers."

He must have gone into her room and read the letter on her desk. His clansmen were so ecstatic, they began dancing, laughing, and crying all at the same time—rejoicing in the return of their beloved laird. The Scotsman most verbal in denouncing her earlier now told his neighbors he was certain the laird would find out who'd really killed the young English officer.

Lady Myrtle felt Ian's hand on her waist as he continued holding her across his kilt-covered thighs. While happy that the man she'd thought dead was alive, she wasn't sure of the rest of her emotions. After all, she told herself, as his clansmen cheered and came around them to grasp Ian's free hand, she'd opened her mind and heart to "Urisk." She'd told Urisk things about herself no one in the world knew, along with confessing her deep feelings for the late laird. Initial shock began turning to humiliation. And why hadn't Ian trusted her enough to tell her the truth? She'd grieved over his death, stared hours at his portrait thinking about him, wondering how to help— "Please, put me down," she whispered, desperate to be away, hidden in some safe place where she wouldn't have to look into this man's face and read the mocking laughter she expected to see.

As the crowd quieted, Ian felt Myrtle's body tense, saw the cool reserve enter her blue eyes when she turned her head just now to request he put her down. "It is a shock, lass, I know. I had not meant to spring the truth on you this way. But after I read the letter from the King, and Katie told me where ye'd gone, I had to rush here. I could not let you be harmed, for—"

Too overwrought by her own warring thoughts and feelings, Myrtle could not hear his words or the tenderness in his low voice. "That blood on the letter you sent my father wasn't even your own," she scoffed. "Probably another sheep pressed into the laird's service."

His lion eyes never flinched from her disdainful gaze. Ian held up his left arm and removed his hand from her waist to shove back the white cuff of his linen shirt. "Nay, madam," he said, "the blood oath was my own."

231

She could only gasp at the deep scar on his left wrist. It forced her to grip the front of Sian's saddle to steady herself. Though she reminded herself she was still legal owner of the castle and lands, everything had changed now.

Gavin Mackenzie arrived and pulled the pair of them off the black stallion in his exuberance. "I'm glad ye could finally tell them the truth."

Ian told his tacksman about the murder of the young officer.

Gavin rubbed his bearded jaw. "And we still haven't found out who's been trying to kill the lass." He glowered at the Scots celebrating about him. "Though my fellow clansmen almost made a job of it themselves." Mackenzie addressed them in the tone he might have used to berate one of his sons. "Ready to murder her, were ye? 'Tis ashamed ye ought to be. And who was it that gave us wagonloads of food, clothes, and supplies, and had the longhorn cattle driven up from the lowlands for us?"

Many bowed their heads at the older Scots' reprimand. "And with this pardon for the laird, Lady Myrtle proves she's nae like the other Sassenachs." Gavin looked back at a smiling Ian and somber-faced Myrtle. "You and the Sassenach should marry without delay," he advised with his usual bluntness. "Then the laird will have true legal ownership over his castle and lands once more, while her ladyship will gain the needed protection of a husband."

When neither of the couple spoke, Gavin added, "The laird of Kilmarock needs an heir, and given the times, this English aristocrat's high connections will strengthen the Sinclair's position with King George."

"Aye, Mackenzie's plan makes sense," shouted a woman from the crowd, followed by several others. "To the marriage!" many of the clansmen cried, shouting their own enthusiasm for the plan.

These Scots changed from outrage to revelry in the blink of an eye, thought Myrtle, then found her voice. "No, I will not marry Ian Sinclair." She moved away from him.

Ian watched her. While he understood some of her reservations, he smarted at her quick rejection, for just now he'd warmed instantly to the idea of wedding this tall, spirited woman. Hiding his disappointment behind a half-smile, he held up his hand for silence. "Give the lass a few days to get to know me first."

The rejoicing continued at the castle two evenings later when the laird and Miss Prescott were being served dinner in the Great Hall. The recently hired servants went about their duties, smiling more these days. The clansmen and their families sat about the long wooden table that had been in this high-ceilinged room since medieval days. This was the first social event here for many years, and everyone talked of little else but the return of their laird.

Only Lady Myrtle remained more quiet than usual. Realizing that the Thomsons, Gavin, and his daughter had been in on this deception from the beginning, in her logical mind she understood the need for Ian's daring action. Yet Ian had made sport of her, letting her go on about her feelings when she thought the laird was dead, not to mention "Urisk" pretending simple-mindedness. How he must have laughed at her sentimental declarations.

Ian ran a hand along his recently shaved face. It was good to sit at the head of his table watching his clansmen eat and enjoy themselves.

He glanced at Myrtle Prescott. It surprised him that he'd had to ask her to sit at his right so he could speak with her during dinner. Upon first entering the room tonight, she'd headed for a place as far away from him as possible. For two days now, Myrtle had hardly said four words to him. Yes, she went quietly about her duties and did nothing to discourage the celebrating of her tenants, but Ian was aware she was avoiding him.

Wearing one of his better coats of dark blue that matched his breeches, Ian tried again to put her at ease. "It is good to hear laughter again in this hall."

Her smile was polite, but held no warmth.

"Would you care for more wine?"

"No, thank you."

He could tell by the way she picked at her pigeon pie that she still wasn't relaxed in his company. When Lachlan came in with his pipes, he nodded in approval. "After dining, 'tis the custom for the laird's piper to play the guests into the sitting room."

"Guest, am I, now?" she demanded.

Ian colored at his blunder. "I did not mean you are a guest. Indeed, my lady, I am well aware you are the titled owner of this estate. If anything, it is I who am your guest in this castle. May I have Lachlan play a short piece? It's been more than a year since I heard him play."

Myrtle caught the wistfulness in his voice, saw him waiting for her permission. She smiled at the black-haired Lachlan. "Yes, please play for your laird."

If Ian was disappointed she'd left herself out of the request to his piper, he could not hide his delight to hear the Scottish melody Lachlan played as he walked slowly about the room.

In truth, Myrtle was moved by the music Lachlan played so skillfully. It was like Scotland—haunting and courageous, yet it held the sadness of a war-weary race. When the song was over, Myrtle's sense of propriety would not allow her to dismiss Lachlan without thanking him.

After all the guests departed a few hours later, Myrtle politely excused herself to retire. However,

Ian's gentle request that she join him in the sitting room for a glass of wine trapped her. Was he deliberately reminding her of the many evenings she'd summoned Urisk to talk about the late laird?

She walked to the overstuffed chair in the sitting room and sat down. The minutes went by as she stared mutely at the unlit fireplace. Words buried two days ago but never spoken threatened to choke her. Determined to remain calm, she clasped her hands in the lap of her flowered cotton gown.

Myrtle was thinking about Fiona Layton, who had moved in yesterday with Jamie. The auburn-haired young woman had cried and clung to Ian when she'd first spotted him in the entryway. After holding her until she calmed herself, Ian had taken Jamie up on his shoulders and played with the child who tugged at his reddish-blond hair, then laughed into the golden eyes that matched his own. Tears turned to laughter as Fiona saw the handsome man with the small boy. Unable to watch any longer, Myrtle had turned away from Ian and her new maid, making an excuse that she needed to check something with Katie for the feast tonight. How could Ian even allow talk of marriage between them while he had a . . . mistress and bastard son right here at Castle Kilmarock? She couldn't understand why Fiona didn't hold Ian in any negative light for his callous treatment. Just what kind of man was Ian Sinclair? she asked herself, then saw him get up from his own chair a few feet away. He was coming over. Panic seized her.

Right now he looked every inch a gentleman of property and position. There was an elegant silver stickpin at the lace below his throat. He dwarfed everything in this small sitting room. She knew he was waiting for her to speak. "My lord?"

The formality of her address disappointed him. "Please call me Ian. I believe we have passed the stage of formal address."

Silence.

"No words tonight, Myrtle? You usually have so many witty things to say."

Bounding from her chair, she confronted him. "Yes, and what long hours of laughter you must have enjoyed at my expense, watching me make a fool of myself. The flowers on your grave, the way I waxed about the laird's noble qualities. Weren't you lucky the mask hid your true reaction to me? Nothing you said was the truth, was it?"

His lion eyes captured her blue eyes of defiance. "I do wish to marry you."

"Merely to get your castle and lands back."

He winced. "While I admit, that is part of it, I honestly have become fond of you."

"Oh, yes, Myrtle Sinclair could provide hours of laughter as castle jester." Something crumpled within her. "Why . . . why the pretext about your mental state?"

Regret did show on his strong face this time. "If you recall, it was Angus who told you I was addled. He sought to protect me from the redcoats, and he knew I would have fewer questions to answer in the guise of Urisk. We Scots heard tales of the Sassenach who now had the power to destroy us. In truth, my lady, the stories we heard about ye gave us little reason to rejoice in the new English owner of Kilmarock Castle and Sinclair lands."

Yes, she understood that, especially after what Lachlan had hinted to her. "All right, I accept your role as Urisk in the beginning. But why didn't you trust me enough with the truth later?"

"The way you trusted me enough to tell me of your plans for my clansmen?"

Stung by his words, she could not think of a reply. "I'm the only one with brain leaks for being so gullible," she muttered. "While I understand Angus put you in the position of slow-wit, you didn't have to pretend you knew nothing about the differences between men and women."

His golden eyes sparked with unabashed pleasure. "Aye, I felt like a blackguard for teasing ye—but the self-loathing passed after two seconds."

She saw no reason for mirth. "I suppose I should now apologize for interrupting your tryst with Jean Mackenzie?"

He shook his reddish-blond head. "I'm glad you came into the laundry room," he said with certainty. "I like Jean, but she can be a forward minx at times, the result of being spoiled by her doting father and older brothers."

The Englishwoman lowered her gaze. "Suppose you think being made a fool is good for me."

He moved to stand toe-to-toe with her. Reaching under her chin, Ian tipped her face up toward his. This time there was no amusement in his expression. "I never thought ye a fool, little Sassenach." Her eyes reminded him of the blue, star-shaped flowers in the meadow near their secret place in the purple mountains. "Indeed, I found your explanation of the facts of life most endearing. And I shall always cherish that afternoon."

For a second she almost gave in to the warmth in those arresting lion eyes, the tenderness of his fingers against her skin as he caressed the line of her jaw— but then she remembered how emotionally naked she'd felt before this man. She stepped back. "Tell me, now that Fiona is my maid, do you plan to reinstate her as your mistress here, then have two mares to service? Jamie could have a castle full of reddish-blond-haired siblings. Why, your bastards could fill the countryside!"

His square jaw tightened as he planted his fists on his hips. "I'm warning ye, Sassenach, I shall be truly angry in a minute."

She made a dismissive gesture with her hand. "Oh,

we wouldn't want the laird to lose his temper, would we?" Her wintry gaze mocked him. "Even though you can't keep your randy cock behind your kilt, I'm suppose to feel honored at the chance to be added to your harem?" Never giving him an opportunity to answer, she added, "Well, Sinclair, you'll have to ask Fiona to help you repopulate your clan. I'm not interested in that philanthropic activity."

"Bad-tempered shrew," Ian growled, roughly taking her by the arms. "I know this isn't an easy time for you, but you'll nae say one more word against Fiona. Jamie is under my protection, as is his mother. And wee Jamie is no bastard. Fiona and Hugh Sinclair were married properly, if in secret, with me and Malcolm as witnesses. Until you arranged the pardon, it would have been dangerous if the redcoats had discovered Jamie's true identity, for he's the last Sinclair heir upon my death. That's why Fiona knew she had to keep the lad's father secret, as well as stay hidden from the others. Hugh stole the uniform of an English soldier to slip through the British patrols at night a few times to visit Fiona. He was determined to see his newborn son. And I thank God he did see Jamie before Culloden."

Much of the fight went out of her at this startling news and the pain evident in Ian's eyes. "Then Jamie is your nephew?"

"Aye," he answered, gentling his hold on her arms. Then he recalled what Jean Mackenzie had told him about Myrtle's rough treatment of the lad. "And I'll nae have ye mistreat Fiona or Jamie."

Myrtle couldn't hide her reaction. "Never would I harm either of them. If I'd meant any of your clansmen ill, I assure you, sir, I would never have stayed here these weeks and gone through all this aggravation. I could have easily ignored that promise to my father and paid someone to come here in my place. From the first attempt on my life, did I run back to London?" she demanded, anger replacing the hurt that he could think so little of her. "You believe I don't know many of your clansmen want me dead? When did I fail to defend your name or your tenants, even against the man I once thought I'd marry? You have the love of your clansmen to sustain you. I've even made enemies of many English I once thought my friends because they denounce what I'm trying to do for my Scottish tenants."

The truth of her heated words affected him. He thought of her long hours of backbreaking work alongside his clansmen, the way she'd stood before him to defy Addison, who meant to have him beaten. "Ye do not lack courage, Sassenach," he said, his voice low with contrition for his earlier accusations. His hands were gentle as he massaged her shoulders. "Could yer courage sustain you into setting aside your pride enough to wed me?"

It was the sincerity in those lion eyes that almost undid her. Of course, she recognized the need for the Sinclairs to have Ian as their laird. It would take all her diplomacy to convince George II to accept the reason Ian felt deception was necessary. Yet the biggest step of getting his name cleared had already been accomplished, she reminded herself. Her sense of duty and care for the Sinclairs fought with her hurt pride. Could Ian's fondness be enough for her? She turned away to walk slowly toward the marble fireplace. Certain this would not be anything but a business arrangement, Myrtle forced herself to face the reality she'd probably never have married for love anyway. While she'd confessed to "Urisk" she loved Ian Sinclair, the Englishwoman was positive Ian did not love her. That was the major cause of her humiliation. She pressed her hands on the edge of the cold fireplace ledge. Wouldn't she be happier in these highlands than married to Addison or some foppish Englishman in London? She and Ian could go their separate ways. But right now the thought of such a cold marriage appalled her. No, it would never work, she decided. She wasn't made of such self-sacrificing material. Another way would have to be found to help the laird and his clansmen. Gavin Mackenzie was wrong; there wasn't any need for Ian and Myrtle to wed.

Almost guessing her thoughts, Ian came silently behind her. He touched her silky hair, then rubbed his thumb along the sensitive skin of her bare neck. "And," he whispered close to her ear, "if ye consent to wed me, it will be a proper ceremony and no marriage of convenience, wee kelpie."

He sounded like a man sure of her compliance. His words chafed. She turned to face him. "Then, sir," she countered with icy control, "there will be no wedding. I have not changed my mind from two days ago. Never will I marry you, Ian Sinclair."

Chapter Fourteen

That evening, alone in her rooms, Lady Myrtle began writing a detailed letter to His Majesty. She stayed up all night to compose it, finding the right words to get George II to keep to his pardon of Ian Sinclair, now that the laird was alive. She used all her skills of persuasion to explain how, desolate at the thought of leaving his beloved Scotland, and worried over his clansmen—these things had shoved him toward the desperate act of arranging his fake suicide. Indeed, she told the King, hoping her exaggeration wasn't a mistake, Ian was probably unhinged for a time, living like a brooding phantom within the walls of Castle Kilmarock.

Before the castle staff awakened, she went downstairs to get one of the stableboys to take the sealed letter to the English fort. It would be added to one of the English dispatch pouches. As she walked by Ian's room next to the Thomsons', it occurred to her he'd never demanded his own suite of rooms back, content to stay in the room he occupied as "Urisk." Well, if everything went as she planned, soon she would be leaving this castle forever. Ian Sinclair now had his title back; soon he'd have his home and lands legally once more.

When she reached her rooms, automatically she

went again to look at the laird's portrait over the fireplace. She heard Robbie's nails on the wooden floor as he got up from his curled position to join her. He nudged his cold, wet nose against her hand. She patted his head and scratched him behind his shorter ear. "Dreams die hard, Robbie," she murmured. "I have no choice. I've got to leave," she said, a wave of sadness overtaking her. Wouldn't it be demeaning to wed a man who did not love her? Addison's words about the laird's prowess with women haunted her. For the first time since reaching adulthood, she felt inadequate in this one area of physical beauty. Until now, she'd been content with her looks and size. But when she thought of Ian, how handsome he was, it disquieted her. If she married Ian, he'd surely break her heart, for she could not look the other way while he dallied with others, like Jean Mackenzie. The picture came back at Myrtle again—the dark-haired beauty on Ian's lap, her hand at the juncture of his thighs. He hadn't been struggling to get away, she reminded herself, no matter what he'd said earlier about welcoming Myrtle's interruption.

During the next few days, as Myrtle Prescott waited for a reply from the King, she went about her duties as before. Yet she could feel a change in the servants' attitude toward her. They were warm and polite, but they deferred to their laird on matters of importance. Though she understood their loyalty would rest first with Ian, it did remind her of her precarious position here. She was an outsider.

At first she was grateful when Ian made no more effort to speak privately with her. He was courteous during those times they ran into each other or at meals, but she realized he was more interested in conferring with Gavin and his sons about matters of cattle and planting. Fiona was busy stitching new suits of clothing for Ian. When Lachlan made excuses to visit Fiona in the sewing room above stairs, Myrtle wondered if Ian would mind if the widow remarried, for it was clear that Lachlan adored both Fiona and Jamie.

Well, she told herself, going back to the account books, it wasn't her concern anymore. Soon she'd be back in London. She made up her mind to settle things with Barbara and turn the town house over to her. All Myrtle wanted now was to get back to her country estate in Chelmsford. "Oh, Papa," she whispered, setting down her quill pen to rub the tense muscles at the back of her neck. "Did you have any idea what I'd be in for, sending me here?" Of course, Jonathan didn't know Ian was alive, but how could her father believe she would be welcomed by these Scots?

The knock at her door brought her back to more sobering thoughts. "Come in."

Katie entered carrying a leather satchel. "The lad just brought this for you. Said it was urgent."

"Thank you, Katie." This answer from the King had been unusually swift. Did this mean he was as outraged as she was at first to find out Ian Sinclair had tricked them?

When Katie neared the door to leave, she turned, a concerned look on her face. "The laird is nae a bad man, my lady. He'd nae make a bad husband."

So, she mused with a sigh, everyone was trying to get her to marry Ian Sinclair. "I know, Katie, but admiring a person and marrying them are two different things. Rest assured," she told the older woman, "I am working on getting you the leader you wish, who will legally own the estate."

"'Tis nae just ourselves we're concerned aboot. Angus, Gavin, and I think ye could do a lot worse than marry the laird of Kilmarock. You're a woman in need of a husband, so the laird told us."

Ian Sinclair should mind his own business, she thought, but managed to read Katie's genuine worry

243

about her welfare. "Thank you, Katie, I will bear that in mind."

Obviously recognizing the dismissal in Myrtle's tone, Katie shook her gray head and left the Englishwoman at her desk.

Myrtle scanned the note. The King wrote he would continue to honor his pardon of Ian Sinclair. But the words following this declaration horrified her. Unknown to her, Ian had also sent a petition to the King, and George II now gave his permission for Lady Myrtle and the Earl of Kilmarock to wed immediately. The King wrote that he trusted that her unquestionable loyalty to England would ensure Ian's continued neutrality.

"That son-of-a—" Anger choked her. Appalled, she realized Ian had just trapped her into marrying him. Oblivious to the hour, she rushed out of her room, flew down the stairs, and headed for Ian's room next to the Thomsons'.

The civility of knocking seemed ludicrous, so she pushed the door open. "By God, your audacity knows no limits!" she shouted, waving the missive in front of her.

Dressed only in breeches, Ian had obviously just finished washing before bed. Beads of water glistened on the reddish-blond hairs covering his muscular chest. His wet hair was slicked back against his head.

He could not help smiling as the candlelight caught the blue sparks that emanated from her eyes. Fire and outrage—she was a bonny lass.

"How dare you petition the King on your own without telling me! His Majesty now believes it is my wish to wed you. He makes it a condition to the continuation of your pardon. Damn it, how could you do this to me?" she demanded, her voice cracking. "You once told me you were my friend."

He came close to her.

No, she wouldn't cry in front of this man, she told herself.

"I would be more than friend to you, my lady." He spoke the words patiently. "However, when I tried to woo you gently, you would have none of me. Ye left me no choice, for your stubbornness was standing in the way of our happiness."

"Stubbornness?" she choked, stepped back, only to have him follow. "You think it is mere peevishness that caused me to refuse you?"

"No, I know it was more than that, but there isn't time for us to go through the lengthy courting I'd prefer. If we do not present a united front quickly, the King will become more suspicious."

"Will you leave me no pride?" she demanded.

"I am trying to have a care of it and your person, but—"

"I told you things about myself no one in the world knows. How do you imagine I could lower myself further by—"

"I did nae think," he cut off, biting out the words, "wedding me would be so demeaning."

"You know perfectly well what I mean. You never tried to stop me from blathering on about . . . about how much the laird meant to me, letting me make a fool of myself."

"Lady Myrtle," he whispered, then took her hands in his as she'd often done when she'd thought him Urisk. "Despite my initial attempts to despise you, I found each day in your company fascinating. And do you think I was unscathed in that deception? You read my diaries, words I wrote for no one's eyes but mine. As I know you, sweet lady, you also have learned intimate details about me. To my way of thinking, we are even on that score."

But he did not love her, she shouted to herself. His firm, graceful hands caressing hers sent shivers down the length of her. She had to fight the urge to reach out and stroke the planes of his face, the muscular hardness of his chest, to feel the strength of him she had dreamed about. Then she remembered—she'd even told him about her erotic dreams! Heat suffused her face. "How . . . how can I face you as a wife when you know such intimate things about me?" Over his shoulder, she saw the sock monkey and ceramic music box she'd given "Urisk." Ian had placed them reverently at the center on his wooden dresser, almost, she thought, as if he really treasured those two simple gifts.

For the first time he did regret the necessity of forcing her hand this way, yet he knew they'd little time for ceremony now. "I promise to have a care for your feelings, wee kelpie." He patted her cheek, encouraged when she did not pull away. "Aye, it is not a conventional beginning for a marriage, but the times have robbed us of the romantic courtship I wish I could give you. I would have come to London, taken a town house near yours for a few months." He nestled her head on his shoulder and began massaging her neck and back, the area behind her ears. "We could have gone to the opera, walked in Ranelagh Gardens, ridden out in a carriage in the morning. I would have brought ye flowers and chocolates, and ye could have knitted me mittens." He was delighted when she giggled at his last remark, then pressed her face against his bare chest. "You see, little Sassenach, I'm a romantic at heart, too. My brothers despaired of me because I did not wish to fight. I'd much rather read, or fish, or . . ." A devilish smile hovered near his lips, but he did not say the words.

Her thoughts were on the things Ian had written in his diary about the arguments he'd had with his brothers. She stepped back and gave him a measured look. "But I've learned you are no coward," she defended. Her mind seemed clear of the embarrass-

246

ment that had clouded her thinking since she'd discovered that Ian Sinclair was alive. She knew there was little choice. It was practically an order from the King. He'd conceded much in pardoning Sinclair and restoring his earldom. Myrtle knew she could not risk infuriating George of Hanover by refusing to wed the man the King thought she already loved. The word made her blush again. It was true, she told herself. She was in love with a man who was merely fond of her, nothing more. But it was all she could hope for. She saw the uncertainty on Ian's face as he waited for her answer. There was no arrogance in him now, just a sadness that she was going to refuse. Had he been commanding, as Addison was apt to be when crossed, her decision would have been a direct refusal again. However, it was his trepidation and tenderness just now that had moved her in the other direction.

Lady Myrtle Prescott held out her hand. "I will marry you," she said, her tone suggesting that a business deal had been arranged. "And I remember your terms," she stated, aware that if she gave her consent now, he meant this to be a true marriage.

Though tempted to seal their agreement with a more amorous exchange than a handshake, Ian recognized how much this had cost her. He shook her hand.

"I will leave the details to you," she said, "since it will be a Scottish wedding."

He looked perplexed. "But surely you would want your stepmother and sisters present at the ceremony."

"I will ask them, but I doubt they will come."

Myrtle hid her shock when she learned how soon the wedding would take place. She'd given her word, so there was no going back now. She looked down at

Fiona's dark head as she made another adjustment on the hem of her wedding gown. Where and how Fiona had found the cream-colored silk and lace to make this lovely gown, Myrtle would never know. For days the castle and surrounding countryside had been ablaze with activity—spring flowers carted in, hunting parties organized to ensure meat for the feast, constant streams of baking, sewing, and decorating.

Katie knocked at the door and entered. Dressed in a gown of lavender, a purple wool plaid pinned at her shoulder, she carried a bouquet of white flowers with green leaves. "'Tis myrtle, my lady," she said, handing the garlands to the Englishwoman. "My," she said, stepping back, "ye make a bonny bride. Oh, I almost forget." Katie reached into the side pocket of her gown. "The laird asked me to give ye this. 'Tis a wedding present."

Fiona got up to see the gift wrapped in the soft green-and-black piece of wool.

It was a silver brooch with ruby and diamond stones set in a floral pattern. "It's beautiful," Myrtle exclaimed, holding the jewel in her palm.

"Aye," said Katie, "it belonged to the laird's mother. He said he apologizes it isn't of more value. He would never tell ye," Katie added, "but 'tis all he has left in the way of valuables."

"Oh, Katie." Myrtle's blue eyes showed how his gesture moved her. "I would have no other jewel but this. And I shall wear it at my wedding this afternoon. Fiona, would you help pin it on my gown? Could we not add a swatch of the green and black plaid, as Katie wears that pretty lavender one on hers?"

Both women looked pleased that she held the laird's gift in such high esteem. Fiona located a long swatch of tartan, arranged it becomingly across her dress, then pinned the sash with the brooch at her left shoulder.

"I think I will wear my hair down," Myrtle said, coming to a decision. "Do we have any more green and black plaid ribbon?"

"Aye, we do." Fiona looked with horror at her sewing basket when she spied Jamie down on the floor pawing through the ribbons and threads, his auburn head bent over his task. "Jamie, get out of my work basket this instant."

All three women couldn't help smiling as the toddler looked up angelically at them.

"Jamie, you go out and find Lachlan, there's a good lad," said his distracted mother. Katie picked Jamie up and carried him out with her.

"Fiona," Myrtle said casually when they were alone. "I wouldn't be surprised if we had another wedding here shortly." When her blue eyes met Fiona's, both women burst out laughing.

"Aye," Fiona conceded. "Especially, since Jamie said the other day he wanted a baby brother."

"He didn't? Oh, Fiona." Myrtle hugged the auburn-haired woman. "You know I shall miss you, but I've known for a while that Lachlan Mackenzie is in love with you. He is a fine man."

"Aye, I'll give ye that. But no one can match the laird, especially today."

With the sound of bagpipes coming from below stairs, Fiona and Myrtle headed for the great hall where the wedding ceremony was to take place. As Myrtle expected, Barbara Prescott had sent a note saying she and her daughters would be unable to attend because Myrtle's youngest stepsister was having her coming-out party. With her usual tact, Barbara wrote she thought Myrtle out of her mind to marry an "unkempt, whiskey-soaked ruffian." Her stepmother went on to point out that it wasn't good form for Myrtle to marry a man everyone thought dead. What would their London neighbors say?

The large hall was filled with spring flowers. The

clansmen were dressed in their best finery. The room was awash in a variety of kilts. In her red and white plaid gown, Fiona took her place next to Lachlan, who wore a kilt of tan and dark brown. Realizing the pride they felt in attending their laird's wedding attired in traditional but outlawed dress, Myrtle prayed no English soldiers would come near Kilmarock Castle this day.

Her fingers tightened about the fragrant bouquet in her hands. The gown rustled as she walked slowly across the flagstones toward the Episcopal priest and Ian. Gavin had never looked less fierce, with his grizzled hair tied back and his gray beard trimmed. The scar across his nose and cheek looked less forbidding when he smiled at her. However, it was Ian who captured her full attention.

Barbara's derogatory description in her letter couldn't have been more inaccurate. Ian's reddish-blond hair was tied back with a black ribbon, his green and black kilt was pinned to his left shoulder by a large silver brooch. A velvet coat and ruffled white shirt hugged his muscular shoulders. The badgerskin sporran hung from a silver chain about his waist, with the Highland dirk in the leather belt that buckled above the silver chain. She saw the hilt of the small black-handled knife at the top of his plaid hose. He looked every inch a Highland chief. She could not keep the admiration from showing in her eyes and didn't try.

Ian was captivated by her tall, full-figured beauty. Her face was radiant with the adorable blush that washed over her after he'd bent to whisper about her aromatic bouquet. "Symbol is the name," he said close to her ear, meaning her name, Myrtle, was also the clan's insignia. "Katie was right to take it as a good omen. Did ye know the bluish-green leaves are also an emblem of love?"

"No, I didn't," she answered, clutching the flowers

even closer. A question occurred to her when she saw that the men about them not only wore various-colored tartans but carried claymores on their left hips and jeweled daggers along with their formal attire, as did their laird. "Where did they get all those outlawed weapons?" popped out.

Ian smiled down at his bride-to-be. "We buried them under the heather after Culloden. Gavin believes it was to have them handy in case Charles Stuart returns again to Scotland. However, I had the Sinclairs do it because I want to know my clansmen are not completely defenseless if the English prove untrustworthy as they carry out the King's orders for peace in the highlands."

As they stood next to each other reciting their vows, Myrtle tried to remind herself she was doing this only so the laird could recover his property and be forgiven by King George for the need to arrange his false suicide. Were Ian's motives any different from Addison's greed? she couldn't help asking herself. But in her heart, she knew Ian was far different from Addison. She had seen sides of Addison he'd never displayed in London. He despised everything and everyone not English. And if his father could bully him into marriage because the squire wanted Sinclair lands, what kind of a husband would he have made? Ian, on the other hand, cared deeply for his clansmen. As she glanced at the tall, handsome Scot again and saw the highland bonnet under his arm with the sprig of myrtle attached to it, as all his clansmen wore today, she knew she admired him for being his own man. And for all this Scot had been through, didn't he deserve the wealth she could give him, along with the King's favor?

And she admitted it, as the ceremony ended and Ian's warm mouth moved gently on her cheek, she wanted this marriage.

Livery-coated servants brought in platters of

venison, salmon, and sweetmeats. When the steaming haggis was carried in, Myrtle managed to hide her trepidation as she peered down at the gray sheep's stomach that had been boiled after being filled with spices, liquor, and animal intestines.

"The choicest morsels for the laird and his bride," Gavin shouted, raising his cup of wine high in the air. "May my lord and lady have only the best of what life offers in future. And may their first bairn be a braw lad," he finished. All around them raised their cups with boisterous shouts of congratulations.

Myrtle saw that Jean Mackenzie, though dressed prettily in yellow and gray tartan gown, paid only lip service to the happier cries of the Scots about her. Her dark eyes sent a message of dislike to the new countess of Kilmarock. It was clear Jean was here only because it was required. Myrtle realized the younger girl would never be her friend. Perhaps in time, if Jean married, they could reconcile. For now, there was nothing Myrtle could say or do to smooth things over between them. Lord, Myrtle thought, Jean had almost gotten her killed when she stirred up the already hostile crowd against her before Ian came to her rescue.

Ian cut a generous piece of the spicy animal entrails. He ate most of it, then offered her a small piece. "Please," he whispered, clearly aware she was trying to hide her distaste. "It is custom, my dear, for us to sample the haggis first. If you pop this small morsel into your mouth and wash it down with the wine, it will be over quickly."

It was the sympathetic look of apology in his golden eyes that won her. "Here goes," she said, putting on a brave face. She took the morsel from his fingers and swallowed it, grateful when he was right there with a silver cup of sweet wine. She drank it down, then managed to smile. "Just like plum pudding at Christmas."

He hugged her, grateful for her cooperation. "Ye *are* a bonny bride," he said. "Will ye nae join in the highland dancing?"

"Certainly," she said, catching the spirit of the uninhibited festivities around them. "Of course, if I step on your toes, you may be crippled for life."

He accepted the challenge in her saucy grin. "Weel, I dinna think it would interfere with my ability to perform my husbandly duties tonight."

She wanted to come back with a rejoinder, but her scarlet face gave her away. No, she wasn't that comfortable with him yet. He took her hand and began walking around the hall with her. They accepted the glad tidings of his clansmen. She smiled and talked with them, too. Many of the women and children she knew by name.

Attentive, checking to be sure there was enough food, wine, and ale for her guests, Myrtle felt the hours go by quickly in the enjoyment of acting as hostess at the first real party in this castle since she'd arrived. Later, she even joined in the energetic highland reels. Out of breath and laughing, she reveled in the delight of the Scots around her, for they truly seemed happy and nothing like the dour people Addison said they were. She understood why her father loved these people. They were direct but fair, slow to call you friend; but once you are accepted, you had their devotion for life.

When Gavin asked her to dance, Ian smiled at her. "It seems my lovely wife is the center of attention tonight." As she went off with Gavin, Myrtle saw Jean walk over to Ian and boldly put her hand on his arm. The Englishwoman looked away as Ian and Jean continued to talk. After Gavin returned her to the side of the room flushed and out of breath, Fiona came over with a glass of fruit punch for her.

"Oh, Fiona, where do you all get such energy? Never will a minuet hold my attention again," she said, then took another sip of the cool liquid. Both women glanced up to find Jean dancing with Ian. Jean said something to her laird. He laughed heartily. Myrtle suddenly wondered if Ian regretted not being able to take Jean for his bride.

Fiona spoke first. "Jean's been following the laird around since she was a bairn. 'Tis clear Ian sees her only as a mischievous younger sister."

The look in Jean's dark eyes as she reached up to hug Ian after the riotous dance ended made Myrtle less sure Fiona was correct in her assumption.

Ian came over to her when the reel ended. His face was ruddy, his forehead damp from exertion. He smiled at Myrtle and Fiona. "I've nae danced in this house for many years. 'Tis good to have the old place alive with laughter and music, and beautiful ladies," he added, reaching out to place an arm around his wife's waist.

Despite her unease, Myrtle could not destroy his happiness. "Come, the food is prepared. Let us lead our guests into dinner."

The Scot's golden eyes took on a darker hue. "Aye," he said close to her ear, ruffling the soft waves Fiona had worked on. "The sooner we feed our guests, the quicker we can retire upstairs."

She tried to share his jubilant mood, but she couldn't deny the anxiety she experienced right now was more than bridal nerves.

Chapter Fifteen

Ian leaned closer to whisper to Myrtle that she could retire now if she wished.

She rose and slipped away from the large medieval hall, with the loud sounds of Scottish revelry still ringing in her ears.

When she entered her bedroom, the changes there struck her immediately. Heather filled three Chinese vases on various tables about the room. The new sheets with their embroidered initials had been scented with rosemary. Then she spotted the gossamer white nightgown on the bed.

"His lordship gave specific instructions about the room," Fiona explained, as she began unbuttoning the back of Myrtle's wedding dress.

Katie went over to retrieve the nightgown. "Why," she said, running her hand under the hem so it showed clearly in the candlelight. "'Tis thin as a spider's web, and the embroidery—oh, Fiona, you might have ruined your eyes with such delicate work."

Both ladies helped Myrtle remove her hoops and petticoats. When the frothy material was put over her head, Myrtle could not help marveling at the soft, silky way it hugged her body. Yet she felt positively indecent in such nightwear. Thank heavens Ian had included a ruffled and embroidered robe. Her hands shook as she tried to fasten the cloth-covered buttons. She saw two glasses on a silver tray next to a crystal decanter of cognac on the table near the bed. Under Ian's directions, everything had been prepared for their wedding night. Rather than putting her at ease, as he'd obviously intended, it reminded Myrtle that she was not solely in charge of Kilmarock Hall anymore.

After Fiona insisted on brushing her long brown hair, Myrtle remained at her dressing table rather than remove her robe and get into the large fourposter bed. She just couldn't face that step yet. To herself, she admitted she loved Ian, and she could not deny what she openly told "Urisk," but it was her certainty that her feelings were not reciprocated that unnerved her right now. Yes, Ian would protect her and honor her as his wife, but that was all he felt for her. Again the doubts that this would not be enough to sustain their marriage assailed her. Would he break her heart when his interests strayed elsewhere, to someone like Jean Mackenzie?

The sound of male laughter and bagpipe music shoved her attention to the other side of the door. Unconsciously, her body stiffened on the cushioned seat.

The wooden door opened. Drafts of cool air from the hallway made the candle flames inside flicker and dance, sending elongated shadows about the dimly lighted room. Ian rushed through the doorway and stood barring his clansmen's entry with his usual good-natured amusement. "I thank ye for the escort, but I believe I can find my way from here."

"But, Ian, lad, 'tis the custom," one of the kilted Scots shouted, "to be certain the laird and his bride are truly wed."

Myrtle blanched at the horrifying thought of having a crowd of well-aled Scots hovering over the bridal bed like spectators at a cock fight. The analogy made her face color all the more.

Ian threw back his reddish-blond head and joined in their ribald laughter. "Aye, but ye must remember my lady wife's nae been raised as a Scot. Better she should see us putting our best foot forward."

"'Tisn't yer foot ye'll be puttin' forward tonight, laddie," said Gavin Mackenzie.

Ian roared with mirth and pressed his kilted shoulder to the door. "Weel, I'll nae get to anything if ye keep me chatting at the threshold," he pointed out. "My buxom bride is nae in the hallway."

Clearly, they enjoyed his quick rejoinders and allowed Gavin to herd them away from the door for more bacchanalia downstairs.

Ian was still laughing when he turned to find Myrtle sitting on the cushioned stool, her back pressed against her dressing table. His golden eyes devoured her. Her rich brown hair shimmered in the candlelight. He'd been right to have Fiona make her this silky nightgown and wrapper, for it accentuated the beauty of her full figure, outlining her ripe breasts and long legs. Yet it was the hands clenched in her lap and the wariness in her large blue eyes that made his features lose some of their joviality. She was frightened, though trying valiantly to hide it, and that realization made him more determined to take things slowly tonight. He removed his sword belt, sporran, and jacket and placed them in a nearby chair with his flat highland bonnet. "Would you like some cognac?" he asked, heading over to the table next to the bed.

She didn't really want any but felt it might be wiser to dull her senses for the long night to come. "Yes, if you wish."

Used to Myrtle having a mind of her own, having enjoyed their animated discussions when she'd thought he was "Urisk," Ian felt disconcerted by this new docile Myrtle. He poured the amber liquid into each glass. When he brought hers over, he felt the coldness in her fingers as their hands brushed. He walked back and sat on the edge of the bed a few feet from her.

For some moments the laird and his new bride sat watching each other in silence, each taking occasional sips of cognac. "Would you like a wee drop more?"

"No, thank you."

Ian frowned, wondering how long this formal politeness could go on. He set his glass down on the silver tray. She reminded him of a fawn about to bolt for the thicket at the first sign of danger. He knew he couldn't undress until she was more at ease with him. He rose off the downy mattress and walked slowly across the new Oriental carpet. "I like your choice of heather pattern in the wool carpet," he said. "Ye have excellent taste in furnishings."

"But not in clothes," she added too quickly, then regretted it, for she knew he was trying to be kind. Indeed, this nightgown, the red dress and others he'd had Fiona make for her were lovely. His choice of vibrant colors, she admitted, flattered her figure. Because of her usual preoccupation with business matters and her total disinterest in clothes beyond their functional use, Myrtle realized, on her own she'd never have taken the time to choose these rich styles and colors.

"Are you warm enough?"

"No—I mean . . . Yes, I'm fine." The thought of what he might do if she admitted being cold jolted her.

When he reached out to take the empty glass from her fingers, Ian saw her recoil, then attempt to disguise it. He placed the glass on the dressing table. Was she disappointed with the reality of the live Sinclair as compared with the romantic notions she'd held when she'd believed him dead? She wasn't the only one nervous about the night to come. Would he please her? Did she hate him for his maneuvers to get her to marry him? Didn't she realize it was partly for her own protection?

Despite her rigidity, he was able to draw her up to stand before him. "My lady, if I put the white leather mask back on, will I frighten ye less?"

Aware the hands gently rubbing her were restoring the circulation, Myrtle looked up into his face and knew the answer. "No, Ian, I would have you as you are, for I take great joy that the laird of Kilmarock is alive. Yet," she added, looking down at the tops of her beaded slippers, "I am afraid. Not of the physical act, for I do not think I am a coward when it comes to . . . adversity or physical pain. However, it . . . it was different when we were friends, when I thought you were Urisk. Now, I can think only of all the things I confessed to you. I cannot deny the truths I spoke to you as Urisk. It is not that you are a stranger to me; it is because you already know how much I lo—admire you—that I feel so unprotected before you."

When he placed his fingers under her chin to cup her face toward his, he saw the threat of tears in her eyes. "Oh, Sassenach, do ye think me such a boorish fool that I would nae value and protect what ye so openly shared with me? The day ye made that Scot's promise to protect me, then gave me the stuffed toy and music box, I knew something had changed between us. But I was caught in the role of Urisk, unable to say or do the things the laird of Kilmarock wanted." He touched her pink lips with the soft pad of his fingertip. "And here you've learned all about my . . . my propensities from *Lisette Meets the Pirate Prince*. I fear you may be disappointed if I do not measure up to your prince."

Well, she told herself, it was quite true she had

definite ideas about what Ian found arousing. "My, my," she whispered, thinking of some of the passages and detailed illustrations she'd studied during her convalescence. The corners of her mouth turned upward, despite the warmth in her cheeks, when erotic pictures began flashing across her mind. Yet she recognized a touch of uncertainty in his voice, especially the way he'd reverted to his Scottish burr when he spoke. Is that what he'd meant last week when he'd said she knew in-depth things about him? Could it be possible he was apprehensive, too? For the first time since he'd entered this room tonight, Myrtle felt some of the tenseness leave her body. He was reminding her of Urisk's easygoing manner. And she enjoyed his touch right now.

"When I first came down to the hall this afternoon, I worried about the danger to you and your clansmen in wearing the outlawed tartan." Stepping back, her blue eyes devoured his tall, muscular frame. "But I must confess the kilt becomes you, for you appear a magnificent highland chieftain."

"Thank you, my dear," he said, a bit self-conscious at her praise. "And since we have begun again to trust each other with the truth, I would tell you I thought you the most gorgeous woman in the room this afternoon. It pleased me when you came downstairs wearing the brooch and plaid sash on your wedding gown." He eyed her nightwear. "Aye, and right now I am hard pressed not to take you in my arms and show you just how comely I find you, sweet lady."

She blushed at the compliment, but unlike Addison's empty flattery, Ian's tone and the look in his golden eyes reassured her he meant the words. "Your compliments warm me, my lord." With more self-assurance, she stepped closer, inhaling the pleasant, manly scent of him. She ran her right hand along his shoulder, felt the smooth material of his ruffled shirt and the soft wool of the tartan pinned at his shoulder. "The way you look in this dark green and black kilt—it makes my knees buckle," she blurted, then turned a deeper rose at the confession.

Something ignited in the lion's eyes. "I feel the same reaction when I think of ye in my brass tub." Yet he still did not touch her.

"Ian," she said, aware he was determined to give her a chance to set the pace. "I believe it would be all right if you want to . . . well, you realize we have never actually kissed."

Smiling down at her, Ian took her gently in his arms. "Aye, I'm aware of it, all right." He could not hide the edge of desire from his voice. With one arm about her waist, the other supporting her back, Ian bent his head and pressed his lips to hers—tentatively at first, discovering, learning, teasing her; then his touch became surer. She was soft and pliant in her giving response. He wanted to prolong this first kiss between them but warned himself not to frighten her.

When he released her, Myrtle sighed dreamily. Never had she felt this toe-curling pleasure from kissing Addison. "Could we do it again?" she asked.

This second time, she reached up to caress the back of his neck under the queue holding his hair. Unconsciously, she pressed the full curves of her breasts against his muscular chest. When she felt his tongue coaxing her lips apart, she experienced a new sensation. It sent sparks of pleasure through her veins. His hand now fondling her back moved down toward the fullness of her hips, then up near her breasts. Even beneath her nightgown and robe, his fingers scorched her smooth skin. Never did she want this kiss to end. Yet it was Ian who pulled away first. She saw his golden eyes flame with something she'd never beheld before. It made her feel shy, yet powerful, and she knew she wanted him to continue looking at her this way. Indeed, she wanted to know what it would feel like to touch him under—

instantly she pulled her hand away to rest against his broad back.

"What are you thinking about, wee kelpie?" he whispered close to her ear. "I saw mischief in your eyes just now, but then you ran away." He brushed the sensitive area at the base of her ear, then made a trail of feathery kisses down her neck. His tongue lapped at the fluttering pulse at the base of her throat. "Hmm, will ye nae share yer plans with yer husband?"

The enticing picture he was creating in her mind as he continued his tender onslaught made her moan and press closer against him. "I . . . I only wondered," she said, catching her breath as he went on kissing her. "I mean, I was tempted to . . ."

When she seemed unable to finish her sentence, he stopped, fearing he might be going too fast for her. However, when he looked down at her flushed face and closed eyes, felt her press those voluptuous breasts firmly against his chest once more, he knew this wasn't the case, and it pleased him. "I welcome your touch, sweet wife," he said, seeming to understand her hesitation.

Her eyes opened and in her chagrin that he'd guessed her dilemma, she said, "But Barbara told me husbands want their wives to submit, that . . . only lowborn ladies take an active part or pretend to enjoy such things."

He thought a Gaelic expletive but took her hands in his, as was their habit when one of them had something serious to say. "Darling, that may be true for English husbands, but I assure you I want you to be honest with me in both your feelings and actions. Especially at times like this." He saw her watch him with those fathomless blue eyes, and for all her intelligence and maturity, it was becoming clear that in certain areas her education had been shortchanged. "Now," he added, kissing her on the mouth, "I believe my hands were here." He placed a hand at her waist and back. "And you were about to touch me wherever and however you wish."

Though grateful for his patience, she couldn't help giggling at the way he helped her. "You really are quite wonderful."

"Just the salt of the earth, that's me." Her silver laugh delighted him. However, it changed quickly to a soft moan as he hoped it would when he began stroking her delectable body again.

Ian sucked in his own breath when he felt a feminine hand on one of his bare buttocks under his kilt.

"Oh, I did wonder what Scottish men wore under their kilts," she said, more surprised at the boldness he instigated within her, not her discovery.

His lips twitched. "Now ye know."

"Doesn't it get drafty?"

He could not suppress a smile. "Until outlawed, the kilt was worn all the time. The wool keeps us warmer than many of those tattered English breeches and thin shirts we're forced to wear now. Weel, countess, I'm relieved ye waited to find out with me, rather than go searching aboot my clansmen's persons."

She returned his good-natured chaffing. "Yes, at the ceremony, I should have danced over to one of the dark Mackenzies and said, 'Excuse me, Mackenzie, may I feel up your skirt? You see, education broadens the mind, and I need to know if you wear under-drawers.'" Merriment bubbled up inside her. "Can't you just see me doing that to Gavin?"

"Nay, I canna," he said in mock annoyance. "And, my bonny bride, ye'll confide such inquires to yer husband only in future. And 'tis a kilt, nae a skirt we wear."

"Pardon," she said not the least humbled. "Though you're sounding like a fusspot again, I'll try to remember. Groping not allowed beyond home pastures."

"Saucy wench," he called her, before his mouth descended on her inviting lips once more. This time he let his desire surface openly.

There was a fierceness in this kiss, yet she met his passion with an eager response of her own. As the possessive kiss went on and on, their hands explored where they desired. Myrtle felt her legs weaken, and she had to brace herself against his strength. It startled her—this sensation of wanting to yield to him. That wonderful experience of being cherished and desired increased when he placed his arm under her legs and lifted her high against his tartan-covered chest. She kissed his neck, then rested her head on his shoulder. "I've never felt this way before. You don't look scared of me," she teased, nipping his earlobe. It seemed preposterous right now that she'd ever confided to Urisk that the laird might have found her too intimidating.

Ian placed her carefully on the center of the huge bed. The mattress sagged with his added weight when he sat next to her. He began unbuttoning the white row of buttons, starting at her neck. "You'll always be just the right size for my arms."

"But you were puffing so," she said, "I wonder if carting me over here was too much for you." Unlike the laughter she expected, she saw desire burn in his eyes when he looked back at her.

"'Tis nae the carryin' of ye but the image of ye in the brass tub that caused my breath to race just now."

"Oh, that tub again," she said with amusement. "I meant to ask you, just what is it about me and my bath that affects you so?"

Without answering right away, Ian moved from the bed to take off his shoes, tartan hose, and the ribbon at the back of his neck. After depositing the shoes on the floor, he placed the other items neatly over the back of the chair near his sporran, coat, and sword belt. The Scot stood straight, his hands on either side of his waist. "Well, if yer determined to know all, inquisitive kelpie, every time I think of yer pink, adorable body in that clear water the first time I saw ye, I always get a terrific cockstand."

Automatically her eyes darted down to find the large protrusion that tented above his knee-length kilt. "Oh . . . my, my . . . I see," she said, then turned crimson and was forced to change her gaze to the embroidered initials on their bedspread. Well, she chided herself, she had to ask.

He came over to stand next to the bed. She kept her eyes on his plaid stockings. Then he sat next to her again. His hands were a little unsteady as he resumed the task of working down the long row of buttons of her robe. She helped him by finishing the last four buttons herself. Slipping the wrapper off her shoulders, he got up and placed it across the chair that now held most of his clothing. His eyes still on her from where he stood, Myrtle watched Ian reach for the brooch on his left shoulder, unpin it, then unwind the green and black tartan away from his body with practiced ease. Next came his lace neckcloth, before he pulled the shirt over his head after unbuttoning the three buttons at his throat. In the candlelight she saw the wisps of reddish-blond hair covering his broad chest. His legs were muscular, especially his thighs. At the juncture where his legs joined, the hair was darker near the evidence of a healthy male in the state of full arousal.

When Ian came back to her, he stretched out beside her and took her upper body in his arms. Her fears receded somewhat as he stroked her shoulders and nuzzled his face in her long brown hair.

Tentatively, Myrtle placed her hand on his thigh. She heard him stifle a groan of arousal when she caressed his skin. His arms tightened around her.

265

"Ye are learning to be a siren quickly," he said, then gasped when she moved her hand higher. The impishness in her blue eyes bewitched him.

"I am a virgin, my lord, not a lunkhead. I am well read," she added, thinking of the French novels she'd discovered in the laird's library.

He felt her lips on his nipples, before a sweat broke on his forehead.

"You did say I could touch you anywhere," she reminded, heady with this feeling of power.

One eye opened. "Aye, I canna de—deny it, God help me." For a few more minutes he allowed this exploration with her hands and mouth as she traveled about his chest and upper legs. Then he knew he had to put a temporary halt to her erotic meanderings if he hoped to pleasure her before he spent too soon. "Now," he said coming to a decision, "it's my turn."

Myrtle stopped, hoping with all her heart he'd find her to his liking. Covered or in a tub of scented bubbles was one thing. Now the time was here when he would see her, know clearly, while he might call her a kelpie, Myrtle Prescott Sinclair wasn't "wee" or small anywhere.

Ian saw the sudden panic in her eyes before she could squelch it. He'd seen a similar expression that day when "Urisk" had carried her from the kitchen up to her room and tried to tease her apprehensions away. This time he did not intend to make the same stupid blunder. Lying next to her, he reached out and moved her body to cradle her in his arms. His golden eyes devoured her from head to toe. "From the first time I saw you in that shapeless traveling gown, I found yer buxom figure verra arousing." He kissed her warm cheek, reveling in the return of a soft smile that played at the corners of her inviting mouth. "Ye remind me of a Celtic warrior princess with yer feminine muscles here—" he stroked the side of her

266

leg, then moved to her hips— "and here." He moved up her full figure to linger at her large, firm breasts. "And I found yer other side just as alluring, sweet temptress." Gently, he coaxed her on her stomach. Kneeling beside her, Ian allowed his hands the freedom to move across her curves, up along her long, sturdy legs. Unhurriedly, he massaged her skin through the thin material covering her naked body. "Easy, Sassenach, 'tis no hurry. The gratification waits for ye. Ye'll never know how many nights I dreamed of touching you this way." It pleased him to see her squirm and gasp when he began caressing the full globes of her exquisite backside.

"Oh, my. You do that very well."

"Thank you," he said, stifling his amusement. "Now, will ye turn over for me?"

When she complied, he played with the embroidered butterflies along the material of her nightgown, deliberately brushing his hands across the tips of her breasts. There was another butterfly nestled across the thatch of dark curls along the apex of her thighs. Instead of removing this sheer covering first, he bent his head, cupped one of her breasts in his hands, and raised the turgid pink nipple to his lips.

Something coiled within her lower abdomen. The area between her legs dampened. She wanted more of him, to feel his naked skin against hers. "Off—take it off," she said, wiggling to get her nightgown up over her hips. Myrtle pulled at the shoulders so intently bent over her as he continued this arousing onslaught with his hands and tongue.

Unable to ignore the frantic movements beneath him, the laird pulled back and tenderly ruffled the wisps of material over her head. Unlike his usual fastidiousness earlier, Ian felt too incited to do anything but let her sheer nightgown pool to the carpeted floor next to their bed. He heard them both gasp with pleasure as their naked chests connected against each other when his passionate wife arched up to take him in her arms.

When her swollen nipples made contact with the rough wisps of hair across his hard chest, a wave of heat surged through her. Her hands went to his back to press him even closer. A mewl of protest escaped her lips when he pulled back. But it was followed by a purr of delight when his lips and hands began working their magic against her naked body. His tongue flicked against the fevered skin of her stomach, then ruffled the curls between her legs. When he pressed his mouth to her most intimate spot, she could not keep her hands from his lion's mane as her body showed him just what his lips were doing to hers. "Please, Ian. I can't . . . I feel—I'm going to swoon."

He looked up at her. "Trust me, little Sassenach, ye will nae faint. Let me give ye the sweetest of pleasures. Yield to the feeling, dinna fight it."

When he redoubled his efforts against her softness, she felt the tension building within her. It was a scorching hunger that demanded satisfaction, yet she tried to let Ian direct her. He was murmuring endearments in French and Gaelic. His firm hands under her hips held her where he wanted her to be, making her aware she could struggle in this dance of arousal all she wished, but she would not escape him. He was her pirate prince, kissing her, loving her, just as she'd dreamed those lonely nights in his bed when she'd thought only the Sinclair's ghost would ever reside here. Right now, she could not tell him all the words, for he was seducing her far beyond reasonable thought. Her entire body tensed. "Oh, Ian!" she cried, before currents of pleasure vibrated through her veins, and she sank against the rosemary-scented sheets of their marriage bed.

When Ian kissed her this time, she tasted her own

womanliness on his lips. He brushed back tendrils of damp hair from her face. "Oh, Ian, how can I give you the same pleasure? Please, oh, please, Ian show me how."

Her eagerness to give touched him deeply. Never had he known such passion and generosity in a woman. *"Mon bijou."* He kissed the soft column of her throat.

"Oh, that feels . . . please kiss me there again." After he did, she pressed her body closer to his and whispered, "No one ever called me 'my darling' before, either in French or English. I love the way you say it."

God, she was so open with her feelings. He prayed he would not cause her pain. When one of those dear, inquisitive hands reached out to hold him, his voice was ragged when he said, "Nae, please—any other time I will want your touch there, but my dear," he added, pulling away from her a little, "I am too close to bursting before we finish this exciting journey."

Contrite, she told herself she was going to do exactly as he directed, for she wanted him to experience the wonderful sensations he'd created within her. "I'm sorry, darling. Please show me what to do, for I am determined to pleasure you."

She said it with such absorption, her adorable face a mask of resolve, he couldn't help chuckling. "Wee kelpie, 'tis not all serious work."

When he knelt between her legs, he felt her try to relax her body. He pressed the tip of himself against the welcoming moistness of her cleft. Easing gently into her slippery sheath, Ian stopped when he felt the membrane across the opening to her. Bending over her, he kissed her closed eyes, white throat, creamy breasts. He sucked each nipple in turn until it became a hard pebble in his mouth. He felt her legs go instinctively about his waist as a primal force led the way for their completed union. When she moved against him, he pulled his head back, groaning in torment. "Beloved, I can't wait if you—"

"Then do not wait, my pirate prince," she said against his fevered lips, before she darted her tongue boldly into his mouth and imitated his strokes where their bodies joined. She exhilarated in the lion's growl that came from the back of his throat before he thrust deeply into her. She felt a sting of pleasure-pain, but then only pleasure washed over her when she tightened her legs about her husband's waist and arched to meet this new, wondrous sharing between them. His body was slick over hers, and the coiling like a taut spring came at her as the hunger increased again. Only this time it was an erupting fire in her blood, more potent than when he'd kissed her with his mouth. This time his penis was kissing her womb, pulling back, then teasing the response from her she could not deny. "Oh, Ian . . . I love you," she cried, as the shattering climax broke over her.

In only a fraction of a second, Ian called out her name as he pulled her tightly against his strong body, filling her, murmuring endearments in French, lost to everything except the feel of this seductive woman in his arms. Never had he experienced anything like this. His body shuddered over and over as his release tore from his very soul.

Still breathing hard, Ian took her in his arms and pulled the coverlet over both their damp bodies. "My bonny wife," he whispered, then kissed her temple with a mixture of affection and awe. *"Mon bijou."*

Her blue eyes fluttered open for a second. "You know, you can learn a lot from novels," she said, then snuggled closer to him.

Her outrageous reference to his two erotic novels at such a time made him smile. "Sassenach, you are also an impertinent rascal."

"That's something Lisette and I have in common," she countered, before sleep overtook them both.

Myrtle awoke slowly, amazed to find it was almost noon. Never had she stayed abed so late. Then she remembered: she'd never been a bride before, either. Her skin tingled at the thoroughness with which her husband had introduced her to connubial delights. She rolled over to kiss him good morning but discovered Ian was already up and dressed, standing across the room.

This morning he wore English clothes. Of course, it was more prudent with the law against the tartan, but she sighed, missing the arousing sight of him in his Highland kilt. He looked handsome just the same, she decided, admiring the way the tight brown breeches, embroidered waistcoat, white lawn shirt, and dark jacket fit his tall, muscular frame to perfection. He was finishing the leather tie that clubbed his reddish-blond hair back from his shoulders. He smiled when he turned to find her watching him.

"Good afternoon, wee kelpie. I have to meet with Gavin and the elders today to go over plans for the planting."

"Oh." Remembering her duties, she offered, "I shall come, too."

He came over to her and sat down on the edge of the bed. "No, I can handle this." He kissed her briefly on the lips. "I'll send Fiona in to help you with your bath. A nice warm soak will help ease your lovely body after its first ride."

She felt her cheeks flush, still not used to his directness about such private matters. Over his shoulder, she could see a stack of papers on her— well, she supposed it was his desk now. It made her aware Ian must have been up for hours working, deliberately until later waiting to dress so as not to awaken her. It was considerate of him. Apparently, he needed less sleep than she did.

As he got ready to leave, Ian turned back to get an adorable view of his wife's plump bottom as she bent over to retrieve the discarded nightgown. "Mayhap 'tis better I leave before the brass tub arrives," he said, only half in jest. "We both know how your bathing affects me."

"I'll keep it in mind," she answered, a pert smile on her lips.

He remembered something. "If you go out riding, dinna forget to take one of the Mackenzies with you."

"Oh, really, Ian, I hardly think—"

"I mean it, Sassenach," he cut off, his features becoming stern. He had not been able to find out who'd tried to kill her, and now he felt even more determined to keep her safe. "That's an order, nae a suggestion."

After he left, Myrtle sat up in bed and watched the closed door for a long time. With a husband and laird, her own authority was now diminished. The sudden realization did not sit well with Lady Myrtle Prescott, new Countess of Kilmarock.

She got out of bed and buttoned her robe about her, then walked into the next room and sat down at the desk. The first item on the stack of bills and documents did little to relieve her uneasiness. It was a letter dated that morning. Ian was writing to an art dealer in London to request the repurchase of two Sinclair family portraits and one medieval icon. The second letter explained more. It wasn't the thousand-pound deposit he directed his solicitor in Edinburgh to pay this dealer that bothered her. Practical, she realized the ceremony yesterday gave Ian legal access to all her wealth and property.

Skirting the issue since their betrothal announcement, Myrtle finally faced it. Was it the romantic part

272

of her that had thought somehow Ian Sinclair would be reluctant to take her money? Of course, eventually, she anticipated persuading her proud, noble husband to accept her money, for she intended to share everything with him. The Scot's bold signature for the thousand pounds jeered up at her again. But there it was—the ink hardly dry on their wedding license, and he obviously couldn't wait to dip into her coffers as readily as he'd dipped his cock into— no, she couldn't think about last night right now.

Chapter Sixteen

"Damn his soul to Hades!" Addison Barrington cursed, when Lieutenant Johnson brought him the news. Not only was Ian Sinclair alive, but Myrtle Prescott had married the Scottish bastard in unseemly haste. Alone in his quarters, Addison could not believe his bad luck. All his family's plans to acquire Sinclair lands legally or otherwise had failed. Used to winning against odds, Barrington choked on defeat.

By God, he'd not give up this easily. Nor could he, not after his father tore him to pieces for having a falling out with Lady Myrtle. The squire had told him to take ten mistresses with trim waists if he wanted, but even if Prescott's eldest daughter had the figure of two gun decks, Addison wasn't to write his father again until it was to announce his betrothal to the late earl's daughter. Addison knew he couldn't tell the squire her ladyship was wed to the pardoned Earl of Kilmarock. No, he decided, going back to his desk. He would have to settle things quickly here before word drifted back to Barrington Hall.

His only hope was to drive the newlyweds apart. But how? the Englishman thought, tapping his quill pen against the side of his powdered wig. Ian couldn't love the wench. His prowess with women was well known throughout the highlands. What could the Scot possibly see in that English mare? The question gave Addison an idea. He reached for a clean sheet of parchment, dipped the point of the pen in the dark pot of ink. Yes, he knew Myrtle's weakest point. Ian Sinclair was in for an overdue come-uppance, and the thought made Addison smile.

The English officer began his letter to Myrtle. It would be easy for her to believe the virile, handsome Scot was carrying on a liaison with some comely Scottish girl. And he knew the wench who would cozy to his plans. He would have Jean Mackenzie brought to him this very day. Already his men had discovered that the dark-haired beauty was not overjoyed at Ian's choice of bride.

Addison began his missive with a sincere apology for his bad manners when last they'd met. He pretended not to know she was already married. Yes, that would do nicely, he thought, smiling at the thought of his rotund father embracing him with pride. The old tyrant would probably increase his allowance for this. The wheezy windbag had better, Addison mused, then cursed when his pen slipped and he had to blot a dollop of ink from the white paper. After all, he was the one who'd have the disagreeable task of mounting that big English cow to give the Barringtons a male heir.

After seeing to some details about meals, Lady Myrtle sat alone at the desk she now shared with her husband and scanned the letter that had just arrived from Captain Barrington. She felt guilty for letting her earlier irritation keep her from writing him to explain the recent changes at Kilmarock Castle. She would write him immediately to break the news gently. After all, she told herself, Addison did not love her. Yet she never wanted to hurt him. Better he should hear the truth from her first.

Yet before she set about replying to his note, she reread his final paragraph with growing discomfort:

And, my dearest Lady Myrtle, if there is any excuse for my boorish behavior, I must relate the entire truth to you, for I hope it will assist you in viewing me in a more favorable light so that I may bask in your good graces once more. I was jealous of the way you protected that fellow Urisk. Your open affection for that unworthy, even if simple-minded, Scot made me testy because he does not deserve your kindness, especially after I saw the baseborn lad rutting with Jean Mackenzie in the stables during my visit to Kilmarock Hall. For your own sweet spirit, which is as precious to me as my own, I must warn you about letting that coarse Scot take advantage of your gentle, trusting nature.

The letter ended with his most affectionate regards. Though she wanted to dismiss it as part of Ian's rowdier past, Myrtle knew it wasn't logical. While Addison only knew him as the masked, addled Urisk and clearly had no interest in a servant or a Scottish girl, Myrtle realized the complete implication of Addison's disclosure. If true, the encounter between Ian and Jean took place *after* Myrtle and "Urisk" had talked so intimately at their picnic, when she'd opened up to him, telling the Scot all she believed and felt, including her affection for the dead laird—despite all that, had Ian done more than ignore Jean's forward advances? But he'd married her, not Jean, she reminded herself. Yet she had to face it—Jean did not have a fortune, or an English title, or the ability to get a Scottish lord back in the King's good graces. Intelligent and clever, Ian probably understood her enough to know how much more receptive she'd be if she thought he cared for her, rather than hearing his true feelings. Warrior princess, he'd called her—God, how she'd fallen for his honeyed words—in French and English. No wonder he was up and at his desk probably minutes after tucking her in bed last night. Not a challenge at all for him—he probably viewed her as just another night's work, minus the stable hay!

When she got up from her chair to pace across the room, Myrtle brushed by the full-length wooden mirror on curved wooden legs. Right now she only saw the reflection of a tall woman with straight brown hair, large bust, and wide hips—nothing more. Thinking of Addison's letter on her desk, she decided it would explain why Addison was so unusually angry that day. It must have wounded him to see her defend "Urisk" after Addison accidentally discovered his despicable behavior with Jean in Myrtle Prescott's barn. Yet, to the captain's credit, he hadn't blurted the truth to her but had taken her sharp words in silence. Of course, then, the Scot was only Urisk to both of them, and his sexual peccadilloes were none of her concern. Yet . . . now, she wasn't sure what she believed or felt. They had both taken vows yesterday. Surely any entanglements with the aggressive Jean were over, weren't they?

After writing Addison a friendly, polite letter about Ian Sinclair and her recent nuptials, making certain to avoid any reference to Addison's disclosures about Jean and Ian, Myrtle went downstairs to have one of the servants immediately ride over with it to the fort.

It was just after she completed the task and turned to head to the kitchen to see Katie that Myrtle heard the voices from the hallway. She recognized Ian's baritone.

Smiling, determined not to bring up Jean, for she wanted to show him she meant to trust him, now that he was her husband, Myrtle felt her jaw drop when she saw Ian enter the keep carrying a disheveled Jean Mackenzie in his arms. When Jean craned her neck to kiss Ian full on the mouth, Myrtle prayed the floor would open up to hide her.

No such luck.

She cursed herself for not being able to hide her reaction, for when Ian glanced up to see her, his smile vanished. His complexion reddened, giving the impression of a man caught in a flagrant act of philandering.

"I . . . we . . . when I was riding home, I happened on Jean," he stammered. "Her horse threw a shoe, and she hurt her ankle with the jolt to the ground."

Jean's dark eyes didn't waver from Myrtle's. "Aye, if the laird hadn't rescued me, I dinna think I could have walked home." When she batted her black lashes up at her knight, the invalid got a firmer grip about his neck to pull herself closer to him, obviously intent on kissing him again.

Ian jerked his head back in time to avoid her lips. "Nay, lassie, ye dinna have to kiss me again in gratitude."

It was then Myrtle saw the self-satisfied smirk on Jean's face. Like a well-fed tabby, she licked her parted lips, aware Ian couldn't see her expression. It was, Myrtle thought with a sinking heart, the look of a woman who had just enjoyed a man's attentions. Had Ian made love to her up in the meadow? She could just picture the laird coming upon Miss Mackenzie—Jean looking tousled and desirable, her bare legs showing where her homespun gown bunched about her hips.

Myrtle shut her eyes against the pain such musings caused her. Yet when she opened them, Jean was still in her husband's arms. Of course, her mind taunted, Jean Mackenzie was a lot lighter to hold than Myrtle. Ian could probably carry this slip of a lass for days without so much as a grunt of exertion.

It took all Myrtle's practiced reserve to quell the sharp words that played near her lips. She directed Ian to put Jean on the cushioned bench along the wall of the entryway. Katie was summoned with her medical supplies. When Myrtle was certain Jean would be properly attended and safely driven home in her carriage, she excused herself politely and proceeded upstairs.

Even during dinner, Myrtle congratulated herself on remaining calm. Through the contents of Addison's letter, her own gnawing thoughts, and the vision of Jean in Ian's arms as they kissed, Myrtle remained the English lady she'd been raised to be. Yes, she would have a little more lamb stew. No, that was enough wine, thank you. It was amazing how civilized one could remain merely from habit.

After her evening domestic duties were complete, she left Ian reading a book on the cultivation of wheat and barley, while she made a proper good-night to go upstairs.

However, when she glanced at their bed, she came to a quick decision. No, it was too much to expect. She just couldn't share a bed with a husband who not only didn't love her, but who clearly saw nothing amiss with keeping his mistress about the castle to assuage his lust when it fancied him. Barbara Prescott would certainly think her a fool for refusing to assume a wife had no choice but to look the other way at her husband's adultery.

In private now, her outward calm departed. Oh, Ian was a smooth-talking devil, all right, she thought, impatiently pulling a quilt from the chest at the bottom of the bed. She swiped at a tear that dared appear near the corner of her eye. And she, more the fool, believed every word he'd said last night. Why had he forced her into marrying him, if he desired Jean more? Then a terrible question came

280

to her: was she part of his revenge against the English for taking everything away from him, including his two younger brothers? Did he get a twisted pleasure in knowing that Lady Myrtle Prescott, last descendant of a long line of English aristocrats, was now legally under the complete control of a mere Scottish rebel?

Holding the fluffy quilt on her lap, she dropped down on the windowseat. It was dark outside. A spring drizzle began tapping against the heavy glass panes. And she'd made it all so easy for him, telling him everything he needed to know to touch her mind and heart when he'd been "Urisk" to her.

Lost in her troubled thoughts, Myrtle did not hear the door open or Ian's shoes on the carpeted floor until he was standing in front of her. His smile made her heart leap automatically. Then she yanked herself back to reality.

"Aye, I thought I'd retire early, too," Ian said, with a meaningful look at his bride. "Even while I tried listening to Gavin and my other clansmen this afternoon, my thoughts kept returning to you." He hummed to himself as he went about divesting himself of his outer coat, cravat, and shoes. *"Viens dans mes bras, mon bijou."*

Myrtle couldn't believe he was asking her to come into his arms. And to call her "my darling" right now only caused her pain, for it reminded her of his tender lovemaking of the night before. She stayed put.

"Come, I assure you I can act as your maid. You'll discover I have a flare for doing buttons."

"And servicing women," she snapped, moving off the windowseat to stand away from the arms that reached out for her.

The joviality left his face. "What is this, Myrtle?" When she did not answer, he frowned. Then a thought occurred to him. "Oh, is it the wee kiss from young Jean that has ruffled ye?"

281

"Why should I mind if you kiss other women?" Myrtle tossed the quilt on the window seat, where she'd already decided she'd sleep this night. She would protect his pride in front of his clansmen and not give the servants fodder for gossip by vacating their bedroom. But never would she sleep in his bed again.

When he remained silent, she whirled on him. "Damn it, Ian, I told you days ago I was prepared to sign over my legal claim to Kilmarock Castle and the estate to you. This marriage wasn't necessary," she added, still smarting from Addison's letter. Ian's speed in availing himself of her money didn't help, either.

Why was she acting so prickly? Tempted to tell her the truth, that it wasn't just the material things he'd needed, Ian realized she wasn't in any mood to believe him right now. "Aye, this marriage was necessary."

Irked with this brief reply, she glanced away only to spot the stack of letters and bills on the desk they now shared. "If you'd rather use your own solicitor in Edinburgh from now on, I shall write Cyril this very night and have more of my fortune transferred directly to you. Better yet, why don't I have all my investments and jewelry converted to gold coins in one huge trunk for you? That way the laird can just grab a fistful whenever he gets a notion to buy something. Paintings and horses are so expensive, are they not?" She expected him to appear chagrined to learn she was on to him. However, the blackguard didn't even flinch.

"Those paintings had been in my family for hundreds of years. I wanted them back in the hall," Ian said, a new coolness in his voice. "The costly stallion and mare I hope to breed to replenish our stables."

"You do not have to explain yourself to me;

legally, you do have the right to *my* money." When she saw him color finally, she almost regretted the last barb, but not much. "Never fear, Sinclair, I shall not trouble you with wifely rantings. I am an Englishwoman, raised within the ton's standards where husbands, *and wives*," she emphasized, "usually go their own way after marriage. However, I shall need more time than you, it seems, to choose my lover."

The brown-haired Englishwoman plunged forward, despite the narrowing of Ian's lion eyes and the way his nostrils widened when he pressed his fists against his hips as he continued listening to her. "Of course, I would appreciate it if you could refrain from rutting on the floor downstairs. Such rolling about with your paramours in front of the servants would weaken my position as lady of the house. If you give me fair warning, I assure you, I will concede these rooms to you. Mortimer and I can always go back to our cozy suite in the cellar."

"By hell, Sassenach, ye go beyond the bounds any mon can accept, even from his own wife!" His hands returned to his sides. He stalked closer to her. "And as for ye 'choosin' yer lover, hoyden wife, that choice was made the minute ye took the vows yesterday."

She went to step back, then caught herself. "While you are free to take your pleasure where you wish?"

He took seriously the holy vows he'd made before the priest, if she did not. When the chin he'd adored slowly with his lips last evening jutted up at him in defiance, Ian felt his irritation increase a hundredfold. And it did sting his pride that he desperately needed her money and could not even afford to buy her a decent wedding present. It was one more reason why he'd been so determined to hold himself in check last night—to give her as much pleasure as he could—it was the only gift he had to give her. The disdain he read in her eyes right now left him smarting.

When he continued coming at her, she moved to the right, only to have him follow. She darted past the overstuffed chair, but the lion kept tracking her. "Stop following me," she ordered, trying to make her voice sound less skittish. "Just what do you think you are doing?"

The smile never entered his eyes. "Why, madam, I am taking my pleasure where I wish."

"Never. I shall never allow you to—I will not be another of your—I refuse."

He stopped in his tracks. "I grant, my lady," he said with icy control, "you have a right to refuse my advances, as there may be times I may not feel up to the pleasurable encounter, but right now ye say no from mere pique, nothing more, is that not so?"

It was unsettling that he read so much of her feelings. "What if it is?" she demanded. "I'm sleeping on the windowseat, and that is final." She managed to sound in full control this time. "Go mount one of your Scottish lassies in the glen, or the barn, or while you're out grouse hunting. From all I've heard of the Earl of Kilmarock, you've plowed more feminine furrows than there are rocks in the highlands!"

His golden eyes darkened to amber. "I know one sharp-tongued Sassenach in need of verra deep plowing before I seed her brown-haired furrow."

She tried but failed to keep the crimson stain from her cheeks at the way he'd turned her deliberate insult into a lurid threat against herself.

Anticipating her next move, he sprang at her before she could reach the door. Easily, he dragged her struggling form to the edge of the bed.

With a mixture of wonderment and fright, his wife saw the way his shoulder-length hair caught the light from the candles. Transfixed, she couldn't take her eyes from the planes of his strong face—just before his furious mouth swooped down on hers. His kiss was punishing and demanding—asking nothing, taking everything, as he molded her body into his. There was only force and lust in his kiss now. When she tried to pull back once, he clamped a firm hand on her hips and ground her pelvis against his, clearly making her aware of his aroused state straining against the tight English breeches.

But then his mouth suddenly gentled as he changed from conqueror to seducer—teasing, urging, countering his every motion to pull away with a playful sparring movement of his body that checkmated her completely. Myrtle found him more dangerous this way than when he'd been angry with her. Her flesh heated with each provocative touch of his hand. Despite her resolve, Myrtle's body began proving traitor, especially when he caressed her breasts through her gown and underclothes.

When he lowered his head to press his warm lips against the tops of her full breasts, Myrtle had to bite her lower lip to keep the moan of pleasure from escaping. Still relentless, her husband boldly took her hand and rubbed it across the swollen area of his breeches. She heard him suck in his breath when she would not be outdone and deliberately encircled the evidence of his arousal with her fingers. Breathing hard, he stepped back from her, only to yank on the flap at the front of his breeches. The three buttons popped to the floor, showing he was in no mood for the slow undraping of the evening before. A stab of desire quickened her pulse when he began kissing her neck and ears, while tugging the material of her gown from her shoulders with his determined hands. She, too, began experiencing this new surge of urgency. While it shocked her, she didn't pull away when his hand bunched the skirt of her gown over her hips so he could fondle the damp skin between her legs.

"Sassenach, ye are as wet and hot for me as I am for you." He found the tiny nodule of her flesh between her nether lips, then worked it back and forth until the fluid of her desire covered his fingers. He buried his nose in the scent of roses in her hair, welcoming the new waves of heat that washed over him. "I want ye like a ram takes a ewe, or a stallion his feisty mare." He licked the sensitive skin of her neck, then added a soft bite, pleased when he felt her shiver in his arms. "It's nae a quiet, gentlemanly desire, little wife."

His arousing words tormented her as thoroughly as his hands and lips stirred her body.

"I only hope I'm able to wait until I get ye out of yer clothes, temptress."

"No," she blurted at the thought of more delays, "I . . . I cannot wait, Ian. Please . . . love me now, or I shall die from this ache."

A thoroughly masculine expression of triumph etched across his handsome features, but he did not verbalize it. Instead, he tumbled her back against the softness of the bed. Through a tangle of silk gown, ruffled underskirt, and chemise, she held out her arms to him. *"Ravissante,"* he said, his voice husky. Never did he think her more desirable than she appeared right now. Knowing she wanted him added to his arousal. She was begging him to take her, and he knew at this moment he couldn't deny either of them.

When he entered her slippery cleft, she could not hold back a sound of unrestrained pleasure. Her hands rubbed his shirt-covered back. She wanted to touch more of his skin but knew she couldn't wait for either of them to undress. "Oh, is this what . . . is it like being set aflame?" she cried, then arched her hips with impatience as he entered her. "I cannot bear this wanting. It hurts so, Ian.''

When he felt her long, shapely legs clamp about him, he pushed deeper into her, tormented by the fury she was creating within his throbbing body. "Aye, wee kelpie, I feel the pain, too." He groaned in heated arousal when her white teeth bit his right shoulder through his shirt. "'Tis a tigress I married," he grated, then countered with a soft bite to the fleshy lobe of her ear. "Aye, this fierce hunger only increases each time we join." She called out his name, begging, then demanding what he intended to give her from the beginning. Her strong body thrashed beneath him, and Ian reveled in the magnificence of her— "My Celtic warrior," he called her. They pulled at each other's clothes in a frantic attempt to touch naked skin. He was more successful, as her flushed face proved when he captured her bare flanks in his large hands. She became a temptress with her fingers on the backs of his thighs and hard angles of his narrow hips. He felt her nails rake him through the material of his breeches and shirt. Never had he experienced such wanton desire. As if she weighed nothing, he got a firmer hold under the expanse of her clothes to grasp her broad hips and lift her higher in his arms. He moved her body back and forth to match the relentless rhythm of his deep thrusts.

"Ye are mine, Sassenach. Say it," Ian commanded, amazed he could pull back from her at such a moment, but he had not forgotten her earlier taunting insults.

She whimpered in frustration to be abandoned so near the precipice of their fulfillment.

"Say the words first," he repeated. Her lovely face was a picture of distress, yet he would not yield this issue between them.

She could feel the tip of his engorged shaft at the entrance of her wet lips. Squirming to force what she needed—"No, don't—I want . . ." she protested, but he held her firmly in those powerful hands and would not let her take what she desired more than her pride right now. "Mother of God, Ian, please. Yes . . . oh, yes. I want you. Please . . . please don't stop. I am yours, Ian. Only yours."

Once she said the words she could no longer deny, he resumed their lovemaking immediately. He entered her to the hilt with one deep stroke, then began riding her with the force he'd held too long in check. Myrtle claimed her release with an abandoned cry of pleasure that drove him still further into the welcoming folds of her soft, pliant body. He knew control was impossible now. The raging hunger threatened to consume him, and he delighted in the fire that burned away thoughts of Addison and his wife, all differences between Scot and English. There was only Ian and his desirable wife molding as one.

His English bride opened her blue eyes to see his handsome face contorted in the throes of passion. The mane of reddish-blond hair whipped about his shoulders with his forceful exertions. She never believed her body capable of a second release so soon, but when the lion's growl rumbled from deep within his throat, the hot jet of his seed against her womb showed her otherwise. "Oh, Ian, Ian," she cried. "I love you . . . only you."

Holding her tightly against him, it took Ian a few moments before he could speak. Drenched with perspiration from their vigorous ride, he looked down at his déshabille. The edges of his shirt were rolled up near his ribs, the leather thong once holding his hair dangled against the back of his neck, he'd torn his breeches in his haste—then he studied his wife and realized her ladyship fared no better. She was an adorable bundle of rose silk gown, lacy petticoat, and torn stays that left one breast totally out of her rumpled gown. Her lovely brown hair tumbled across the lumpy bedcovers like a dark cloud. She looked beautiful, satiated, and oh, so kissable. He pressed his lips softly to hers. For the first time since they'd landed on their bed tonight, his expression was humorous. "Come, wee kelpie, I'll undress ye for bed." He grinned at the contented smile that spread across her expressive little face. Languidly, she lifted her arms and turned for him so he could divest her of her clothes. Naked, she snuggled under the covers he pulled back for her. The dark lashes fanned against her cheeks when she closed her eyes and nestled against the downy pillow.

He placed the wrinkled underclothes and dress over the overstuffed chair, then removed his own ruined attire. He blew out the candles, then joined her in bed. When he pulled her body into his, spoon fashion, he shook his head as she wiggled her luscious bottom into his lap. He could tell by her even breathing she was fast asleep. "Sassenach, ye are a handful," he whispered to the back of her head. "But a verra lovely handful," he added, cupping one of her breasts in his hand as he held her curves close against his naked body.

With the dawn came Myrtle Sinclair's realization that she'd kept her resolve never to sleep with this man again—for just about three minutes last night. His hard body branded her where their naked flesh touched. His right hand cupped her left breast the way a child might clutch a favorite toy. Dunderhead! she called herself. What had happened to her pride? He touched her and she melted like candlewax. Nothing had been resolved concerning her . . . randy husband and the designing young Jean Mackenzie.

Myrtle began inching her way to her side of the expansive bed. When she heard Ian stir, the English-woman stopped and held her breath. God, she thought, looking down at herself under the covers, she was naked again!

She glanced too quickly over her shoulder, unprepared to find a bare chest, then a leg where he'd tossed off his side of the quilt. He wasn't wearing anything but a self-satisfied smile. It was hard to bluster about propriety and spout the other words on her mind when they were both without a stitch of clothing. Unlike their first morning together, when he had risen and dressed before she'd awakened, today was disconcertingly different. Awkwardly, she clutched the embroidered quilt to her body before she turned slowly about.

"Good morning, bonny wife," Ian greeted.

His English bride thought he resembled a dangerous, powerful lion when he stretched his arms above his head. Cinnamon-colored stubble darkened the contours of his face, but when he smiled at her again, she managed a shy greeting. However, she couldn't stifle a gasp of horror when she spotted the red marks of her teeth on his shoulder.

The laird followed the shocked direction of her gaze. He touched the fiery bite on his flesh and winced, then grinned rakishly across at her. "Aye, ye were a wild little savage last night."

No words would come from her dry throat. As she tried again, only puffs of air escaped her lips. She'd bitten him—Lady Myrtle Prescott, sedate spinster, charter and youngest member of the Woman's Auxiliary of St. John, had actually bitten a man while in the throes of passionate arousal. Not a little nip, mind you, but a deep red gouge. So aghast at such uncharacteristic behavior, she clutched the quilt about her even tighter and bounded from the bed.

It was a mistake. The unexpected stiffness in her body caused her to sit down gingerly on the edge of the bed. She felt the Scottish devil watching her.

"Aye, I rode ye hard last night, little Sassenach."

Yet his teasing words were accompanied by the tender action of easing her back against the bed pillows.

Shouldn't she get out of bed first? she asked herself, then gazed frantically at the floor, the bed, the chair—looking for a robe, nightgown—anything other than this bedquilt to cover herself. The thought of leaving the bed completely naked with Ian watching appalled her. Then her blue-eyed gaze landed on the overstuffed chair. His jacket and— God, the breeches were torn—her silk dress with the Dutch lace at the rose-colored sleeves, nestled underneath them, reminding her of his torrid lovemaking and her . . . unseemly lack of control, seemed the most accurate description of her behavior the evening before. Yes, Myrtle told herself with bitterness, she certainly put her skirt-chasing husband in his place last night. If he made love to Jean yesterday afternoon, he must have the constitution of a bull to be able to carry on the way he did last night. What the devil were in those oatcakes he ate so often?

She looked adorable, Ian thought, as he watched the pinkish hue spread upward to her face. And the way she was holding on to the quilt like a targe in front of her confirmed her modesty was causing her some discomfort on this sunny morning. Yet they were married now, and sooner or later she would have to get accustomed to his not sleeping in nightcap or leg-covering shirt, as most Englishmen did. After a brief kiss on her warm cheek, he got out of bed with no further ceremony. He made an un- hurried walk to the wooden washstand, poured out a measure of cold water, then splashed his face. He heard a feminine noise of alarm, then looked over the linen towel he was using to dry his face and hands. "Did you say something, my dear?"

"No," she squeaked, amazed at his offhand attitude in prancing about the room naked. And the sunlight streaming through the windows hid nothing of his physiology. She breathed a sigh of relief when he sauntered into the room off the office where his wide wooden wardrobe, shaving stand, and other personal items had been moved from downstairs.

She heard Angus's voice as the two men talked. Thank heavens Ian had at least thought to close the door for her. Instantly, Myrtle scrambled out of the knotted bed covers and raced to her own wardrobe. Apparently, Fiona and Katie felt newlyweds shouldn't be disturbed in the morning, another thing Myrtle was grateful for right now. The last thing she wanted was to have either Scottish women know she had slept last evening without even so much as a bed gown. Fumbling through the drawers and racks of clothes, she pulled out a new petticoat, corset, cloth panniers, rosette garters, and white stockings. No, she thought, putting the corset back. She wouldn't call for Fiona, and she'd eat a whole bucket of haggis before she'd ask Ian to lace her. After putting the chemise over her head, she sat on the edge of the bed to roll up her stockings.

Myrtle was bending over to tie a bow in one of the lacy garters about her stocking-clad thighs when Ian walked in on her. "Ah, Sassenach, ye are just as lovely in the morning from the back, too."

Startled, she felt her fingers slip, and she had to make another bow. Myrtle tugged down the cotton skirt of her shift. How did he dress so quickly? He'd clearly shaved and washed, and put on white shirt, burgundy breeches, and coat. His hair was brushed and held back neatly with a leather thong. He wore riding boots. How, she asked herself, had she ever considered this man, even masked, to be only the laird's simple gillie? He moved with the air of a clan chief, one accustomed to being in charge. Well, she was intelligent enough to realize this was not the moment to confront him. She would choose the time and place carefully, when she was fully dressed, maybe even wearing an overcoat on top of her traveling cape. Despite having on her undergarments, she felt positively undressed from the look in those golden eyes. Was Jean Mackenzie going riding with him? she wondered, but knew she would never ask.

"Have a nice ride," she said over her shoulder. However, before she could go back to dressing, her husband was at her side, gently turning her to face him.

"Ye seduced me so thoroughly last evening, I forgot until this morning what I meant to tell ye."

She seduced him! Myrtle barely hid her reaction. "Yes?" she asked, adding a sugary smile completely out of character for the former sharp-tongued spinster. Was his conscience bothering him? she hoped. Well, she'd forgive him—eventually. It wouldn't hurt him to have a few disquieting minutes. It might keep him from straying in the future. "I'm listening, Ian." She waited for his apology.

His reddish-blond eyebrows rose. Simpering wasn't a characteristic he'd ever have attributed to Lady Myrtle Prescott Sinclair, and he wasn't deceived for a second. Yet he'd have given his best suit of clothes to know what she was thinking right now. Nevertheless, he let her see the sternness on his face so she'd understand his next words were not a matter of levity. "It is this: just as I am bound to you, little Sassenach, so you are bound to me. Ye are mine. Dinna ever consider taking yer pleasure elsewhere."

Chapter Seventeen

Ian's words cut; that was her first reaction. Rather than let him see it, Myrtle turned and went back over to her dressing table. She busied herself with fixing her hair. How could he believe her capable of infidelity, no matter how hurt she felt over his indiscretions with Jean Mackenzie? And if she hadn't known of his encounter with Jean in the barn, and seen the Scottish lass in his arms, and been a witness to their kiss, she wouldn't have lost her temper and made up that pile of manure last night about choosing her own lover. When she'd thought him Urisk, she'd already told him how fragile she'd been since childhood in possessing self-confidence in that one area of female beauty. The least he could have said was, "There, there, Myrtle, I love only you; every inch of you is poetry, you're a tall, voluptuous sonnet, and I cannot live without you. Forgive me for kissing Jean Mackenzie. She's just a child compared to your woman's body and spirit."

Yes, that's what he should have told her, what she anticipated just now, along with his apology.

However, her new husband had done the opposite. He reminded her she was bound to him. Did he consider her a . . . a piece of property he owned, as accessible to him as her Prescott fortune?

The laird watched his wife as she sat before her dressing table mirror. By the quick, impatient strokes she used to pull her long brown hair back and up from her face, he knew he'd not handled this well. Yet how did she think he felt last night, one day after their wedding, to have her smugly inform him she contemplated choosing a lover? That might, indeed, be the way English marriages functioned, but she was married to a Scot, the laird of Kilmarock Castle. She was daft if she thought he'd turn his head while she cuckolded him. He admitted it now. Every time he thought of her with that . . . that Captain Barrington, he . . .

No, this was not the way to handle an English lady. She was a woman of courage and intelligence; bullying wouldn't win her. And, God help him, he did want his wife to feel the way he did about her. It still rankled that she'd not come willingly as his bride. For all her progressive ideas, was it possible she thought him beneath her because he was a Scot without wealth, a member of a conquered race that many English, like the Barringtons, thought were only a rabble of uncouth peasants? Yet, how to woo his lady wife? That was the problem. She said she loved him; how could she so easily talk of taking a lover? A complex woman, this Sassenach. When he saw her finish her hair, then rise to go over to her wardrobe, he got an idea.

"Myrtle, please wait a moment. I've a present for you." He turned and went back to his dressing room. Seconds later, he returned, carrying a wrapped parcel under his arm. "I had the material sent up from Edinburgh. Fiona and Katie used wee Jamie as lookout so that ye'd nae see what they were working on, for I wanted it to be a surprise." He placed the package in her hands.

Myrtle didn't know what to say. It felt like clothing. "Really, Ian, you do not have to buy me presents." When she saw the eagerness on his face, she walked over to the bed and set the present down, then began pulling the paper away. Inside was a beautiful riding habit of hunter green velvet. The jacket was embroidered along the feminine lapels with white myrtle flowers and blue-green leaves. The cream-colored blouse had tiny seed pearls sewn along the edge. And there was a matching tricorn with one large embroidered sprig of myrtle on the upturned brim. With all their work, dear Fiona and Katie had found time to make this. "Oh, Ian," she said, holding up the jacket and skirt, "they are beautiful. Thank you."

Her pleasure delighted him. "The brooch was my mother's, but I wanted to give ye a wedding present just from me, something new that I purchased myself."

He had access to her money now, but this gift had to have been bought long before they were married. "But . . . where did you get the money to buy such expensive material and fripperies?" Instantly she regretted her automatic inquiry, for she saw embarrassment flicker across his ruddy features.

"The money was mine; I earned it honestly."

Oh, dear, he probably meant it was the coins she'd paid "Urisk" when he worked as a servant in this castle. He was correct, it was his salary earned from hard labor on this estate. She tried to repair the damage. "Well, I must tell you, I have never owned a lovelier riding habit in my life. Would . . . that is," she added, shyly flirting with him from beneath her lashes. "Since your dress tells me you were about to go riding, may I accompany you this morning?"

"Oh, aye, I should like that verra much," Ian answered, warmed that she seemed to have dismissed their misunderstanding of the evening before. All newlyweds needed a period of adjustment, he told himself. That she was still nervous with him made

297

him feel more protective. She really was like any new bride.

When Myrtle pulled the skirt over her head, after putting on the blouse, her husband came up behind her to button the back of it for her. His hands lingered at her waist. She turned slowly to him, giving him an encouraging smile. He could be so appealing at these times, she thought, wanting to make their marriage work, too. When he looked down at her this way, she had no doubts he found her to his liking. She entwined her arms lightly about his coat-covered neck. "Thank you again for the wedding present." On tiptoe she kissed him softly on the mouth. His hand moved to support her more comfortably. Her feet came off the carpeted bedroom floor as he showed how much he enjoyed her instigating this kiss.

With a boyish chuckle, Ian placed Myrtle's feet back on the Oriental carpet. "We'd best leave for the stables now, else I'll guarantee ye'll go riding but nae with a horse under your legs."

Despite the warmth in her cheeks at his double entendre, she found herself giggling. Actually, she mused, as she grabbed her boots, marriage was turning out to be more fun than she'd ever anticipated.

Myrtle was delighted when Ian led the way up to their special spot in these purple hills, the place where they'd had their first picnic. Even though the morning air was brisk for May, she asked if they might sit on a rock to watch the fish and birds near the burn. Did it please him that she used the Scottish word for pond? When she went to sit down on a large gray boulder, he stopped her.

"It will be more comfortable for you this way." He placed the seat of his riding breeches down on the stone, then patted his knee in invitation.

Of course they were married, and it was perfectly innocent, but she couldn't pretend it didn't affect her to sit down on the formfitting breeches covering the corded muscles of his thighs. As the minutes went by, she watched the pond, saw sparrows and finches flying about the forest, breathed the scents of flowers and moist grass. She found herself relaxing against her husband's supportive chest.

Ian smiled into her brown hair when she braced her arms around his shoulders after a few more settling movements. "I promise to try and take things as slowly as you wish. Are you feeling uncomfortable right now?"

"Oh, no," she answered, turning her head to look deeply into his lion eyes. "I like being here. You know, I've never been on a man's lap before."

"Good," he said, then winked at her. "'Tis a truth, I canna deny, Sassenach." His voice became husky. "So ye see, I need yer patience, too, for my mind tells me you're my wife, but I've a side of me a lot slower in accepting that other men will still find ye verra attractive, and there's nae a thing I can do aboot it. I've never experienced jealousy before, and I dinna think I'm handling the emotion verra well."

The humility of his declaration touched her. "Yes, I daresay, we both have much to learn about being married." She patted his shoulder in sympathy.

"Of course," he said after a few silent moments, "ye are learning the physical part of being wed quickly, much to my enjoyment."

"Oh, I wasn't just talking about . . ." She stopped where she saw the wicked glint in his eyes. "Yes," she said tartly, "and you must ask me if there is anything else you wish to know on that subject."

He laughed at her quick rejoinder. "Saucy wench." He gave her a forceful hug. He kissed her pink cheek, her nose, then her impudent mouth. But he made himself pull back sooner than he wanted, remembering his promise just now. "Yer blue eyes are so lovely," he whispered, his humor now replaced with a stronger emotion. "They remind me of the loch in summer." He felt a pressure in his chest with the unwelcome thought of how his life would be now if he ever lost her. The attacks against her flashed across his mind. He took her gloved hands in his bare ones. "I swear, Lady Myrtle Sinclair, I shall protect you."

His determined expression alarmed her. "Ian, I am sure those random incidents are over. Since I wedded you, there have been no further attempts to . . . harm me." She wanted to see his boyish smile again. "It might be because your clansmen realize their laird would extract a terrible vengeance if they killed me. But more likely, they adore their chief too much to openly quarrel with his choice of outspoken Sassenach bride."

He caught the impishness in her tone, felt her tickle the area behind his left ear with her fingers. "Mayhap they feel I've got my just comeuppance in marrying a feisty Englishwoman who takes no guff from me or anyone."

"Probably," she counted. "I believe it's all those years wearing gray flannel to bed and tight corsets during the day. Stiffens the resolve. Do you realize," she rattled on, "I'm not even wearing stays right now? It's ever so much more comfortable without panniers or stays. The Scottish ladies are more practical. It gives one a new perspective on life. I can feel your legs even through my skirt, and . . ." She clamped a hand over her mouth. "Good Lord," she said, appalled at her imprudence.

Smiling, her husband patted her southern region. "Bonny wife, for the last half hour while we've been chatting away, I've enjoyed the buxom feel of your adorable bottom. Did ye nae realize one of the reasons

I suggested it was because I wanted to hold ye?"

Lost when he kissed her again, Myrtle automatically pressed her mouth to his and ran her gloved fingers along the chiseled line of his jawbone.

But suddenly the bird sounds overhead grew louder, and Ian pulled away from her. Like a lion alert to danger, he scanned the area ahead and listened. "Someone is coming."

Myrtle heard nothing. However, she could tell from his quick change from ardent lover that he did not expect intruders in their secluded spot to be friendly. She rose from his lap. While she smoothed out the bottom of her velvet skirt and readjusted a comb that had loosened with their pleasurable kissing, she saw Ian walk back to Sian. He reached into a leather saddle pouch and pulled out a flintlock pistol. As he rechecked it for powder and ball, she noticed he held the gun like one accustomed to its use. Unlike aristocrats at home, she sensed this Scottish earl had spent many days as a youth living roughly out in the open with his clansmen.

"Stay here," came his curt order. "I'll climb up the ridge and see if I can make out who is traipsing about up here. The redcoats usually don't patrol this uninhabited stretch so high in the hills."

Though she wished to do more than just stay here with the horses, Myrtle could tell from Ian's expression this was where he wanted her. All she could so was watch. For such a tall, large man, he moved with surprising grace. Shielding her eyes against the morning sunlight with her hand, she made out his dark form in the distance. Was it one of the Knoxes? If it was Duncan Knox, she could talk with him. Myrtle strained her ears to hear what he'd sensed. It took a few more minutes before she heard the sound of hoofbeats in the distance.

Ian's features were grim when he returned to his wife. "Redcoats. Nothing to do but face them."

301

Why was he so uneasy? They were merely the lord and lady of Kilmarock on their honeymoon, hiking about the highlands. Glancing down, she saw the muzzle of the pistol still in Ian's right hand, and the English law against Scot's carrying firearms struck her. "Oh, Ian, please, you must put the gun away."

He winced, clearly rankled by her reminder of the changes in his position, even though he could now wander freely about his land in daylight. "Aye," he said caustically. He went over and returned his firearm to the leather pouch Sian carried across his back. "This is my land and they are the intruders, yet I must face the King's soldiers defenseless."

She went over and placed a comforting hand on his arm. "Darling, you have always said how important to survival it is for the Sinclairs to remain neutral." When he turned to her, she let him see the pleading in her eyes. "But you must also learn to deal with the King's representatives."

He pulled back. "Ye mean grovel at their feet. Bow to them as they'd have us do?"

"No," she said, refusing to give up. "Getting along with the English does not mean you must lose your honor or pride. It means breaking with the resentments of the past, using your quick mind and charming ways to get the English to willingly leave you alone so you can carry out your duties as laird of Kilmarock. The more you and your fellow Scots confront them with that show of belligerence, the more the English representatives of King George will find ways to subjugate you."

"But, Sassenach," he said, trying to see her point, "yer father was the only Englishman I admired." He shrugged with frustration. "'Tis nae that I dinna want to try; 'tis more that I don't know if I can bend that far."

She understood the return of his thick Scottish accent meant this was an emotional topic, one he'd

302

probably been wrestling with for years. Without hesitation, she took his hands in hers. "It is a gallant start that you are willing to try. I'll show you. Please, let me speak with the head of this patrol first."

She did not know what she asked, for he knew the man at the head of the soldiers riding toward them. However, Ian remembered his earlier words this afternoon. He had to deal alone with his jealousy. "Aye, I will, but I'll be right next to ye if your plan does nae work."

"Thank you, darling," she said, letting him see how much she appreciated his concession. Myrtle turned when the sound of arriving soldiers grew louder. "Perhaps they are just up this far searching for the murderer of that young English officer."

"Could be. Gavin thinks it was probably one of the Knox Clan seeking to get the Sinclairs blamed for the murder."

Myrtle thought of Duncan Knox, who seemed at ease entering his rival clan's territory, but she said nothing. The young Scot appeared so friendly. The openness on his thin face caused her to trust him that day he'd tumbled her off Lily's back to save her from an assassin's arrow. Yet Duncan had admitted that his clan and the Sinclairs had been enemies for generations. Had she been wrong about Duncan? Well, in any case, never would she tell Ian about that incident.

When Myrtle saw that Captain Addison Barrington led the patrol of ten soldiers, she wondered if she'd been right to insist on handling this. By now, Addison must have received her letter, explaining that "Urisk" was Ian Sinclair, her husband. Never did she consider their next meeting would be with her husband and ten other soldiers about as witnesses.

Addison raised his hand for his troops to halt when he spotted her. He got off his horse.

"Hello, Captain Barrington," Myrtle greeted, trying to sound welcoming. "We did not expect to see troops up here."

He bowed to her, then greeted Ian. "Lud love me, never been up this far before. However, a herdsman past Sinclair borders told us he'd spotted the man we're looking for up here. A Scot about six foot, wiry build, brown hair and eyes. Name is Duncan Knox. Have you seen him?"

Myrtle saw her husband's body straighten, but he said nothing. "No, Addison, we haven't seen anyone here today. More cattle raiding?"

"My lady, would that poaching were all." The English officer looked at both of them. "Knox is wanted for murder. It seems there was a witness when that young officer was killed."

She managed to hide her sadness to learn that Duncan Knox was not the honorable lad she'd thought. Then, she told herself, since arriving in these highlands she'd been forced to change many of her previous beliefs.

Addison peered down at the tops of his boots. "I suppose my congratulations are in order on your recent nuptials, my lady."

"Thank you, Addison. You cannot know how much your words mean to us." She was equally grateful no one mentioned the crookedness of Addison's once straight nose, the result of Urisk's fist.

Addison's reaction was unreadable when he glanced up at Ian. "I had no idea the Sinclairs had a talent for mimicry. I thought your role of imbecile quite convincing."

With an equal show of cloaked dislike, Ian nodded. "Thank you, Barrington, I believe I carried it off well, but it is better now with His Majesty's gracious pardon and permission to take Lady Myrtle as my wife. There is nothing like a honeymoon in the highlands to make a man appreciate his good fortunes." Ian placed a light but possessive arm about his wife's velvet-covered shoulders.

Grateful that Ian managed civil conversation, her ladyship thought he was doing it up a bit brown by flaunting his pardon and marriage in Addison's face. She moved away from her husband and asked, "My lord, may I please speak with Addison alone for a few moments?"

Ian barely hid his displeasure at her request, even though he knew she'd gone out of her way to ask his permission. He recalled his agreement to let her show him how to coexist peacefully with the English. "Aye. I've a mind to walk a bit up along the ridge. Good day to you, Captain."

"Oh, and, Ian, my dear," Myrtle added, hoping she wasn't pressing her luck, "I should like to ask the captain and some of his men to dine with us next week. It would please me for the first dinner of the laird of Kilmarock and his bride to be in honor of King George's birthday, with His Majesty's trusted emissaries here in Scotland at our table. May I do so?" She held her breath, but knew bridges between Englishmen and their former enemies were often reconciled over a good meal with light conversation.

His Sassenach wife asked a great deal of a man, yet Ian managed to bite back the sharp retort on his mind. "Ye are the Countess of Kilmarock now, and ye have the running of the house. Such plans are yours to make. Now, if ye will excuse me," he finished, "I've need of that walk."

Though she knew he was not happy at this last request, she was grateful he'd gone along with her. Myrtle motioned Addison over to a more hidden area away from his troops, who were now watering their horses in the pond nearby. She watched Ian's straight back as he walked farther away. Later she would explain what she hoped to accomplish at the dinner with Addison and some of the troops from the fort as their guests. Right now, she had to concentrate on Addison.

"I can only offer you a rock to sit on," she said in way of an apology. When he smiled and sat down, Myrtle felt more confident. She sat down next to him. "Addison, we both know you do not love me. Though I am sorry there wasn't time to tell you about Ian and me firsthand, I should very much like it if we could remain friends. But I cannot blame you if you despise me. It was never my intent to cause you or your family pain and humiliation."

His hazel eyes crinkled at the corners, then he sighed. "When have I ever stayed cross with you, dear Myrtle?"

Right now he reminded her of their London days, when he'd so easily made her feel she was the most important person in his life. "Oh, Addison, thank you," she added, unable to protest when he reached out to kiss her hand.

"Though you will have to forgive me for saying I still wish it was me you now called husband, I do wish you and your laird all the happiness you deserve."

She couldn't ask for more. "It means so much to hear you say that, Addison. We have such need of you. My husband now has the King's pardon, but I fear if we are not prudent we will lose His Majesty's good graces. The Scots, as you have tried to tell me," she added, smiling at her old friend, "are indeed a stubborn race. Will you come to Kilmarock Hall on Thursday next with ten other soldiers to dine with us and talk with the elder clansmen?"

"Trying to mix politics with jovial company, eh?"

"Yes, Addison. I fear for the Sinclair's future unless they learn to work with you."

"Such a wise Englishwoman," Addison murmured. "Of course we will come. Perhaps by then I'll have that murdering Scot who killed young Smith. His family was heartbroken at the news. Only son, you see. Wonder if that Knox fellow perpetrated all those attacks against you."

"Well, I'm just fine now. No more attempts since I married Ian. After all," she said, attempting to make light of the matter, "if three attacks on such a large target failed, perhaps they're suspicious enough to think I've a mythical champion to protect me. Whoever it was probably gave up."

"I wouldn't be too sure," said her companion, before taking his leave. "Tell that husband of yours to take better care of you."

As Ian and his wife rode back down the mountain, Myrtle was aware that something bothered him. He was polite but unusually distant. After over an hour of this, she nudged her mare's sides with her knees and caught up to Sian. "Ian, I wish you would tell me what is amiss."

Ian pulled back on Sian's bridle. "Amiss?" he echoed. "I try to see your side of things. I left ye alone with Addison. I've agreed to let him and his men break bread at our table next week. But," he added, just managing to keep his tone under control, "did ye have to let him kiss you full on the mouth before he left?"

She saw his lion's sharp eyes. She should have remembered Ian also shared his countryman's skill in tracking and crouching above these rocky hills unobserved. So, he had spotted Addison's farewell. "Umm . . . I was taken unawares," she explained truthfully. "It was over before I could do anything."

"Weel," he muttered, leaning across his saddle to give her nose a tweak, "dinna expect me to overlook it if I catch Captain Beaknose nuzzling you over the punchbowl at our home next week. My Scot's hospitality dinna stretch that far."

"Oh, Ian, I do adore you," she said, overjoyed at his attempt to show he was trying to bend. "You are a darling husband," she admitted, then leaned over to kiss him directly on the mouth.

The laird reached out to caress her breasts through the material of her blouse and riding jacket. When his flush-faced wife pulled back from the searing kiss, he chuckled at her expression of arousal and confusion. "Have ye ever made love in a meadow of heather?"

Automatically she glanced at the clearing ahead. Part of her was excited at the prospect, but it was so unsheltered, without trees about it. "If you want to, I'd try, but do . . . do you think it would be private enough?"

Her combination of modesty and eagerness intrigued him. "Nae, wee kelpie, I only meant to tease you, for it is too open a field for what I've in mind. Someday, you must remind me to take you farther up the hill, where a waterfall cascades down the mountainside. In summer it would be a pleasant place to . . . picnic," he finished, clearly intending something more.

"Yes," she said, readjusting her skirt about the sidesaddle. "I shall be certain to remind you, my lord."

Comfortable with each other again, the laird and his lady continued the unhurried return to their small castle. It was only a few minutes later when they spotted the small figure of a woman in the clearing. It was Jean Mackenzie.

The girl was dressed in a print gown of beige muslin. A becoming lavender ribbon held her dark hair away from her gamine face. This day she wore sturdy brogues on her feet and carried a leather sack over her shoulder.

Jean didn't see them at first. She was looking about

as if she expected someone. When she saw the two riders, she frowned but came forward.

"Hello, Jeanie," Ian greeted with warm friendliness. "Taking a stroll alone on such a lovely day?"

Myrtle said hello.

Jean answered Ian, giving him a beguiling smile. "Sometimes after waiting all day on Da and my brothers, I like to escape to the heather to be alone for a while. The pleasures of hearth and home can be a real pain in the arse sometimes." She added a meaningful look at Lady Myrtle. "Aye, real tiresome."

Lord, thought Myrtle, she and Ian had been wed only two days. Did this minx think the bridegroom was already bored with his wife? "Ankle better, I see," commented her ladyship.

"Oh, aye," Jean agreed, then held up her skirt higher than necessary to give Ian and Myrtle a clear view of trim legs without benefit of any stockings.

Myrtle told herself that today she would not let Jean's forwardness with her husband rattle her. After all, Ian had been understanding about Addison. She owed him the same courtesy. "Can we offer you a ride home? You may have the use of Lily, and I'll ride with Ian on—"

"Oh, aye, thanks."

Before Myrtle could finish her sentence, Jean tossed Ian her sack and reached up to be placed behind him on Sian's back. The Scottish lass mounted astride and didn't appear the least interested in tugging down her dress to cover her bare legs.

Ian gave his wife a sheepish grin when Jean pressed herself deeper against his back and clasped him hard about the waist.

The Countess of Kilmarock could think of nothing to say.

"Och, Ian, ye've the best seat on a horse of all the

clan," Jean praised, nuzzling her face against the soft material covering his broad back. Boldly she reached under his open coat to entwine her arms around his shirt-covered waist.

Myrtle could tell a few hidden maneuvers were taking place beneath Ian's riding coat as Jean's small hands squirmed about the laird's body.

"There now, my lord, aren't ye more comfy on this warm afternoon with yer shirt free of your breeches?" Jean asked.

Myrtle saw Ian straighten in his saddle as Jean's warm fingers meandered about his bare midsection. A strangling sound came from the back of his throat, but no words or hint that he desired rescuing. Tempted to order the little hussy to stop pawing her husband's naked chest, Myrtle clamped her lips together. Ian was going to have the clear imprint of Jean's small breasts along his back, from the way the minx was grinding her chest into him. Hurt and angry that he made no protest against the forward chit's amorous maneuvers, Myrtle pressed her knees to Lily's flanks. "I shall lead the way. Pray, do not hurry on my account."

"We won't . . . yer ladyship," came Jean's saucy reply.

Myrtle could hear Jean's jeering laughter for a long time.

She called herself a fool for letting it bother her. It was clear Ian didn't mind letting the black-haired saucebox humiliate his wife. She increased her speed, not caring if she broke her neck along these winding hills . . . anything to be free of Jean's mocking laughter.

Chapter Eighteen

When the horse whinnied in protest at the vigorous stroke Myrtle used to brush her down, the Englishwoman looked apologetic. "Sorry, Lily." After reaching the stables, Myrtle decided to care for Lily herself and waved away the stableboy. She knew she needed to work out her outrage against Jean and Ian.

She calculated how long a slow canter would take Sian to carry the two riders to the Mackenzie cottage, and then for Ian to reach home. Frowning, Myrtle realized he should have been at the castle an hour ago.

As more time went by, her ladyship knew she couldn't wait here any longer.

Then the stable door opened. Myrtle waited for Ian to come up behind her. An understanding wife, she would smile and not mention it. A look down at herself made her regret she hadn't spent the last few hours washing, then changing her clothes to appear more alluring. She turned to greet him.

The warm smile dissipated when Myrtle saw it was not Ian but Jean Mackenzie who sauntered into the deserted barn.

"Ian said to tell ye he'll nae be home until dark. He stopped by our cottage to talk with Da and the elders."

Myrtle felt more uneasy when she spotted the stray pieces of purple heather in Jean's tousled mane of midnight curls. Gone was the lavender ribbon. "And how did you get here?"

Jean smirked. "I was dropped off."

With a jaundiced eye, Myrtle took in the now wrinkled dress covering the woman before her. Mouth deeper pink, skin glowing, Jean had the aura of a woman who'd just been pleasurably ravished. Myrtle felt as though Lily had just kicked her in the stomach. Ian hadn't even the nerve to face her right away; he'd just dropped Jean off. "Why are you here?"

"Oh, I just thought ye might need some advice."

"Really?" Myrtle watched as Jean made a to-do of raising her skirt. Jean winced as she rubbed a wide purplish bruise on the inside of her thigh. The Englishwoman gasped in horror at the savagery of the male bite on Jean's soft skin. Blood still seeped from the deep teeth marks.

"Ian does get carried away when he makes love, don't he? Of course," Jean went on, "at the time his love bite felt like a kiss, he got me so hot. I've got a matching one on my right breast. But I suppose he finds your tits too large to get hold of."

Bile rose in Myrtle's throat, but she forced herself to confront the truth: Ian had just made passionate love to this Scottish girl near that heather clearing where he'd dared wistfully confess he wanted to take Myrtle. The suspicions she'd buried deep within her mind blasted to the surface. She struggled for control. The last thing she intended was to give the wench the satisfaction of seeing her true reaction to this discovery. It confirmed her worst fears, showed her the desolation of her life with Ian Sinclair, for he now had the power to break her heart. And within two days of their marriage, he'd managed it.

"Will you tell me one more thing, Miss Mackenzie?"

312

Jean shrugged her petite shoulders. "What is it?"

"Did you and Ian make love in this barn one night when Captain Barrington was my houseguest?"

"Aye, but what's it to you? Ye weren't married then. And," she added, "Ian and I had a good laugh about ye afterward. He called ye his bovine Sassenach. Told me about your queer notions and old-maid style of dressing. Well, I feel sorry for ye, so I thought ye should know if you have a mind to keep him as a husband, best start movin' yer arse more in bed. A virile mon like the laird dinna want to make love to a cold, fat cow."

"Ian called me a cold, fat co—?"

"Aye, but dinna worry, I won't tell anyone else aboot it."

Myrtle came to her full height, forced to dig her nails into her palms to keep from bursting into tears. "As you say, we were not wed then, but it seems," she added with dignity, "it would have made little difference to the laird of Kilmarock. Even with a wife, he still seeks his pleasures elsewhere. I am grateful to you, Jean, for you have helped me make a decision tonight. It may come as a shock to you, but I did not force Ian to marry me. In truth, he wrote the King himself and trapped me into the marriage."

Jean looked unconvinced. "So ye say, but all the clansmen know he married ye only to get his castle and lands back. And he needed yer money. He's a shrewd rascal with the ladies, I give him that. Ian knew ye'd nae marry if ye discovered the truth beforehand. He's got a way of making love that makes ye forget who ye are and where ye live." Her feminine laughter echoed through the barn. "Did he kiss ye between the legs, too, until yer insides felt like boiling jelly?" she asked, her dark eyes looking up at the older woman with mock innocence.

No, she couldn't take any more of this. Unable to answer, Myrtle put a hand to her mouth and raced from the stables as fast as her shaky legs would carry her. Thankful Katie and Fiona weren't about, she ran up the stone stairs to her room and locked the door behind her.

The pain was physical in its intensity, and Myrtle had to bend over and press her arms to her stomach to fight it. She made it to the overstuffed chair and slumped down. A fist near her mouth managed to muffle the cry of anguish that emerged from deep within her heart. She made herself look at the truth with all its ugliness and deceit. Ian had never said he loved her; she'd accepted him on his terms. He'd tricked her with his disguise of Urisk, caused her to tell him she loved Ian. She'd divulged her innermost thoughts and feelings to him. Ian Sinclair had beguiled her with his first gentle lovemaking, then consumed her in the fire of his skillful, passionate joining last night. Had he been thinking of Jean all the time he'd felt obligated to serve his "bovine wife"? Did he and Jean have hours of laughter about her?

When Fiona knocked at her door, Myrtle told the woman she was resting and did not wish to be disturbed. She requested that Fiona tell Katie, since Ian would not be back until late, that her ladyship wasn't hungry and did not wish dinner.

It only took a few more minutes to work out what she intended to do. Myrtle pulled out a leather bag from the back of her wardrobe and stuffed three dresses and two flannel nightgowns into it. Then she felt Addison's picture at the bottom of the bag. She looked down at it. Addison had tried to warn her against Ian's licentious behavior. She had no one to blame but herself for being so taken in by his Scottish charm. Yet the laird would soon learn she was no whey-faced English miss who would turn a blind eye to his rakehell hobbies. At least she wouldn't stay here to watch them.

And she knew right now that, given a choice, she would not change her physical appearance for the world. Ian was cruel and inaccurate to call her those names. She liked her tall, sturdy build. It pleased her to use that strength to accomplish tasks and help those less able.

Myrtle went to her desk and pulled out a sheet of paper. The words came easily:

To the laird of Kilmarock:
Like you, I have gone to greener pastures. I'll take my pleasure where I choose, not where a hypocritical, overbearing Scottish lout dictates. I wish you and Jean well. More than two people in a bed is too awkward for my conservative English sensibilities. Therefore, I leave this castle and everything in it to you. Cyril will work out the details of settlement. Financially, you and your clansmen will find me generous. With my honor, however, I yield nothing.

She signed it *"Lady Myrtle Prescott,"* letting him realize she no longer considered herself his wife and intended legally to make it so.

It was ironic that she realized the best place for him to find her note was directly at the center of their bed. She placed the flowered brooch that had belonged to his mother on top of the written message, leaving the green velvet riding habit next to it. Swiping at the tears in her eyes, she waited until she was certain she could descend the stairs unnoticed. She slipped out to the stables and led Lily quietly out to tie her in the secluded area near the gate of the family crypt. It made only a slight impression on her that the stone marking Ian's false grave had been removed.

Myrtle knew she could not spend one more night in their bedroom. No, she wouldn't give that Scot the chance to seduce her into his arms again. Hadn't she proved how untrustworthy she was in keeping her resolves the evening before? His strong, graceful fingers touched her, he whispered French words of love to her, and she melted in his arms. With Lily out of the stables, he'd assume she had ridden out of his life for good tonight, and that would be the end to it. Tiptoeing back into the keep, she carried her leather bag down to her cellar room.

"Welcome home," she muttered, realizing her first and last evening here would be spent on the low cot in this cellar. When she heard a familiar squeak, she went over to the table to find Mortimer contentedly munching on a large piece of cheese. She reached out to take him in her palm and pet his silky ears. "Your master is a lunkhead," she said, then sniffled. Returned to the table, Mortimer went back to his cheese.

Setting her bag next to her traveling cape, Myrtle went over and stretched out on the hard cot. She forced herself to rest, knowing she'd have to be up before daybreak and out of here. Then she'd ride to the fort to arrange transportation back to England. Never would she set foot in these highlands again. She'd kept the promise to her late father. The Sinclairs would benefit from her money, and she would make an excuse to the King so he would continue his good favor toward them. But it was over between her and Ian. Sadly, she knew she would love Ian Sinclair until the day she died. The inner strength that had always sustained her made her realize, with time at least, this bleeding wound inside would heal. Ian would take all of three minutes to regret her leaving. "Probably feel relieved to be rid of me. Mortimer," she whispered down to the mouse now curled up near her bag. "You have my permission to bite your master on the arse at your first opportunity." Then she turned over on her side to face the damp wall.

*　　*　　*

Bone-weary from the long ride and the hours arguing with Gavin and the elders of his clan, Ian arrived back at Kilmarock Hall late that evening. Too tired to eat, he shuffled upstairs, trying not to awaken his wife. In the morning he'd tell her about his successful attempt to get the clansmen to agree to sit down next week with the English soldiers who were coming to dinner. He glowed at the mental picture of his wife smothering him with grateful kisses when she learned he'd managed to pull this off. The persistent little Sassenach was going to get them all taking each other to their bosoms.

After pulling off his dusty boots in his dressing room, he entered their darkened bedchamber. He smiled, promising himself he'd make slow, tender love to her in the morning before he informed her of his surprise about the clan's concessions. After the torment she'd caused him when he'd witnessed Addison kissing her earlier, he'd felt the need to teach her a short lesson. That was why he'd not protested when Jean had dared sneak her determined way under his shirt to hold onto him. And Jean's fondling of his chest had been less than that lengthy kiss his lady wife had received from Addison. Now, perhaps she would understand such dangerous games had no place in their marriage. Automatically going to his side of the bed, Ian pulled back the quilt and slipped in. However, when he reached for her warm body next to his, he felt only the cold sheets. As he pulled his hand back, it brushed against velvet, then cold silver and stones of a piece of jewelry over a folded paper.

What was going on? Grumbling when his bare toe thudded against the edge of the wooden side table, Ian limped back to his room for tinder and flint. He lit a candle and returned to their bedroom, grabbing first the note in Myrtle's handwriting.

As he read the bold scrawl, Ian felt heartsick and confused, then something else stirred within his Scottish blood. *"Merde!"* he bellowed, then crushed the offending missive in one large hand.

Tying a linen towel about his hips, Ian stormed from the room to search the upstairs. Nothing. He charged downstairs to the kitchen, awakening the Thomsons, Fiona and wee Jamie, along with the rest of his sleepy-eyed household in the process. No one knew the whereabouts of his wife. They all assumed her ladyship was fast asleep upstairs.

With a string of French and Gaelic curses that left the high ceilings blue, Ian raced back upstairs to his dressing room. He threw on a pair of work breeches and a shirt, and tossed on one of the old coats he'd used as Urisk. By the time he'd pulled on a pair of gray stockings and some scuffed boots, the memories of the two attacks on Myrtle's life were tearing at him. Automatically, he went back to their room and grabbed the jeweled dirk from the leather sheath over the headboard. He walked to the chest in his dressing room and pulled out his brown leather sword belt and claymore.

"The stables," he shouted, then raced out. Angus, in stocking cap and nightgown, trailed after him. With dread, Ian saw that her horse was gone, proving she'd ridden out alone in the dark. Had she gone to Addison Barrington at the fort for comfort? The thought twisted something in his guts. "I'll get Gavin to ride with me, for he's the best highland tracker in Scotland," he told Angus.

"But, my lord, what could have made the lassie leave, and alone at night? Me and Katie thought she was happy here now. Where would she go?"

With consternation Ian realized he'd let his jealousy of Addison make him want to punish his wife a little, and he'd not stopped Jean from her outrageous pranks. Myrtle had ridden away so quickly, he'd not had the chance to show her he regretted carrying the lesson too far. Sinclair, you're a damn fool, he chided himself for not remembering how fragile her feelings were in such matters.

He hurried to Sian's stall. "Come on, Sian," he told his black stallion. "If I can take another ride so tired, then ye'll have to be up to it, too." He knew no other horse in the stables could keep the pace that might be needed to catch up with her. God only knew how long she'd been out. She would want to run to someone for help . . . but who? Addison, he thought, grinding the backs of his teeth.

With each mile of hard riding, Ian's heart wrenched against his chest. Never would he forgive himself if harm came to his highland lady.

"Oh, lassie, wake up!"

Myrtle stirred, then her blue eyes flashed open. "Katie?" she asked, trying to blink the sleep from her eyes. "What are you doing here?"

"Me? Blessed Andrew, thank the Lord for me sight. The whole household's been up for hours worrying aboot what became of ye. Then it hit me," the older woman said, sitting down on the edge of the cot next to Myrtle. "Ye were never foolhardy, I told myself. Lady Myrtle is always practical, leastways, most times. Och, poor Ian."

Myrtle did not feel similarly inclined. "What do you mean, poor Ian?" she demanded, sitting up to put her gown-covered legs over the side of the cot. She still didn't understand what the ruckus was about. Now she'd have to go upstairs instead of slipping away quietly for good, as she preferred. The Englishwoman stood up and brushed the wrinkles from her old tan dress, then stomped on her traveling shoes to restore the circulation in her long legs.

319

"Why, Ian rode out with Gavin Mackenzie to find ye over two hours ago."

"Though I'm sorry poor Gavin is forced out of bed, the exercise will do Ian good. He seems to have such a boundless store of energy," she bit out, thinking of his tireless ability to make love to a variety of women. That story Addison had told her about Ian making love to three dairymaids at once was probably true, she decided.

"But don't ye understand?" Katie asked, frantically looking up at her mistress. "He's ridden out to find ye, and where do ye suppose he's headed, the one place he'd assume you would go?"

"To Addison," Myrtle whispered. And she could just imagine the welcome he'd get—a hot-tempered Scot and his tacksman charging on the fort of English soldiers to demand his wife's return. Despite her earlier anger, the Englishwoman knew she couldn't allow her husband to continue his frantic search. "Do you think Angus would ride over to the Mackenzies with me? I need to speak to Andrew and Lachlan."

"Of course," Katie answered, giving the young woman a sympathetic pat on the arm. "Ye know, a braw Scot like Ian needs a healthy, tall lass like yerself. The laird would never be happy with a puny little wife. Both of ye have strengths that mesh well with the other's."

Myrtle did not share Katie's optimism. What would this devoted servant think if she knew just what Ian was up to this afternoon with Gavin's daughter?

Aware she would make better time without the encumbrance of a dress and sidesaddle, Myrtle persuaded Lachlan to lend her a pair of his plaid trews. She was grateful that Jean wasn't about. To Andrew and Lachlan, Myrtle kept the explanations

320

short, merely divulging that Ian and she had had a slight misunderstanding. Mistakenly, Ian had the impression she'd left for the fort. Andrew and Lachlan agreed instantly to help her. Angus went back to the castle to wait, in case the laird returned.

Gavin's sons had their father's expert skills in tracking. They were able to pick up the direction of Ian and their father quickly. Myrtle realized never would she have considered riding out alone in the dark, nor did she have any trailing abilities like these two Scots possessed.

However, with Ian's and Gavin's head start, it wasn't until about three in the morning before they spotted the two riders ahead. Thank God, they hadn't reached the fort. In the clear, moonlit night, she could make out the tops of the wooden fort in the distance. Lachlan called out to his father. Instantly, Gavin and Ian turned in the direction of the male voice.

Myrtle still felt fully justified in leaving him and would not sway an inch from her plans to depart in the morning.

Ian had spent the most gut-wrenching night of his life with each minute in the saddle. Visions of his wife with a knife in her chest, stone crushing her head, or her broken body at the base of the rock-covered ravine tormented him during the last hours of difficult riding. Every muscle in his body ached. When he spotted Myrtle on her horse, with the Mackenzie brothers riding protectively on either side of her, his first instinct was to race over to take her in his arms. He wanted to smother her face with kisses, tell her he was sorry for teasing her with Jean for a few moments this afternoon, beg her to stay because he couldn't live without her.

However, when he dismounted with the others, she ignored him completely and went over to Gavin and his sons. She was apologizing profusely to the

Mackenzies for getting them out of bed and for making them endure the inconvenience of having to come after her. As she fluttered her long lashes at them, it was clear to Ian that all three Mackenzies were taken with his buxom wife. Then Ian glanced down at her attire. Red and green trews hugged her shapely hips and long legs like a second skin. When she turned her back on him, the laird couldn't miss the way the tight plaid trousers showed every curve, every separation of her generous form. She wore a leather jerkin over a man's wide-sleeved shirt; her hair was loosely tied back with a red ribbon. He had to fight the urge to charge over and tie his wool coat about her hips to hide her Celtic warrior's figure from all eyes save his own. Unharmed, she was clearly enjoying the attention of these three besotted Scots.

As this sugary reunion went on, Ian's fear for her safety galloped in another direction. His taut emotions erupted in sparks before his golden eyes. Impatiently he waved the three Scots back toward their horses, thanking them curtly and advising them to ride on. Their laird stated that he and his wife would follow later.

Continuing to pretend that her husband was invisible, Myrtle told her rescuers, "Thank you so much for your gallantry. Again, I do wish you would accept my apology."

After mounting his horse, Lachlan leaned down to her from his saddle. He glanced at the scowling laird, then back at Myrtle. "'Tis better, my lady, if ye save your soft words for yer husband, if I'm any judge of Ian's mood at the moment."

"Scottish bluster doesn't faze me," she countered, raising her voice so the Sinclair could hear. "Tonight I reminded myself I am a Prescott, Mr. Mackenzie, and we Prescotts do not quake easily before loud noises and hot air." She gave the dark-haired Scot a beguiling smile. "I do thank you again for helping me tonight. I shall see that your trews are laundered and returned to you tomorrow. You see, dear Lachlan, I knew the stable lad's would be too small for me. That is why I felt compelled to ask you for the loan, and riding astride was more practical and timesaving tonight. Goodbye, Lachlan." She knew she would never see this man again. "I want you to know I shall always keep a warm spot in my heart for the Mackenzie . . . men," she added, unable to include Jean. "Please tell Fiona I wish her and Jamie a happy life with you." She was rewarded when he reached down to kiss her hand in a gesture of devotion from a knight to his laird's lady.

Myrtle waved as the three men rode away. It was better they did not stay to realize how completely the marriage had disintegrated between Lord and Lady Sinclair. They would know soon enough after the divorce. With Myrtle's decision to move back to Chelmsford, the scandal would run its course in London, leaving her to live quietly in the country. Barbara would not be surprised. Hadn't her step-mother said no good would come from marrying a man whom everyone thought dead?

Her back to Ian, Myrtle returned to Lily. Exhausted, she wasn't about to give Ian the satisfaction of seeing how much his adultery had wounded her. The rescue was probably just a show in front of the servants and clansmen.

"Myrtle Sinclair, dinna dare get on that horse!" Ian bellowed.

She turned around, her hands moving to fists at her sides. "And don't you dare start thundering orders at me, you . . . you burly billygoat!"

Astonishment at her words distracted him for a second.

"A fine way to address me," she ranted, "after I rode here to catch up with you before you made an ass of yourself or were shot as a Scot's traitor when you and your lone companion stormed the English fort."

Relieved to find her unharmed, Ian had been standing here for what seemed like hours, trying to hold onto his temper, even when she'd rudely and completely ignored him in front of his clansmen. Her disdainful tone right now wasn't helping. He walked three more paces toward her. "Damn it, Sassenach, I nearly went out of my mind with worry during the hard ride chasing after you in the middle of the night."

"Ha," she taunted, her voice rising to meet his. "I cannot believe the gread laird of Kilmarock is such a nincompoop to think I'd ride out alone in the dark. If you were not so preoccupied with the drainpipe between your legs, a logical thought might penetrate that empty pasture between your ears."

"You dare—by God, you sharp-tongued vixen, I'll nae be talked to in that way, not even by my wife!" Like a lion stalking his prey, he moved his booted legs closer to her. "I dinna intend for either of us to return to our home until ye'd explained exactly what ye meant by that insulting note ye left me." He came to a halt and stood glaring at her, his fists planted on his hips. "I will nae wait all night."

When he came toe-to-toe with her, she met the lion's scowl with a taunting smirk. "Weel," she said, deliberately mocking his Scottish accent. "Have to say it with a hoot and a toot, for I dinna ken ye'll ever understand it if I say it in our good King George's proper English." She enjoyed his indrawn breath, signaling that her audacity was penetrating his thick Scottish hide. "To the point, Laird of Kilmarock, you needn't waste my time begging me to stay for fear you will lose your revenue, lands, or castle. As I wrote in my letter, I am turning Kilmarock castle and lands over to you. It was what I meant to do before you weaseled me into this travesty of a marriage. Cyril will send you a generous allowance each month for its upkeep and your clansmen's welfare. So your pretended show of husbandly concern in front of your clansmen tonight was quite unnecessary. Unlike you, I keep my vows, and the promise I made to my dying father to have a care of Clan Sinclair will be fulfilled. As to the other item—well, Sinclair, I know about you and Jean."

"Jean's got nothing to do with us. What the devil are ye blathering aboot now?"

"Don't play me for a rube," she shouted. "From the first, I should have guessed the truth. Didn't I spot 'Urisk' in the laundry room? Hell, I saw Jean holding you by your ballocks. What do you suppose I thought she was doing? Looking for loose change? Checking under the flap of your breeches for her lost virtue, was she? I know you've continued . . . rogering her," she added, using the vernacular. "Even after our wedding."

The vileness of the accusation left him speechless for a minute. His next words came out in deadly calm. "I have never made love to Jean Mackenzie."

"Liar!" She hoisted the word like cannon fire. Hadn't she seen the undeniable evidence on Jean's body?

Quelle insolence!" he snapped, reverting to his French. "Were ye a mon, I'd call ye out for that last remark." His angry eyes held her defiant gaze. "By St. Andrew, ye go too far with your viper's English tongue!"

"Not far enough, Sinclair, for swallow the rest of it: I am leaving for England in the morning. I am divorcing you. You are free to marry Jean or set her up openly in the castle. I care not to hear your plans for Kilmarock brothel. Addison will arrange my transportation back to England."

The mention of Addison had the same effect as gunpowder tossed on a bonfire. He grabbed her roughly by the shoulders. "Listen well, hellion, for I'll say this but once." His loud baritone cut through the darkness. "Ye'll nae be leavin' me tomorrow or any other day. There'll be no divorce. And as for Addison, ye'll nae cuckold me with him or any other mon, do you ken?"

"Let go of me, you big Scottish oaf. If I want, I'll . . . I'll have Addison at the fort and . . . every redcoat in the place. I . . . I'll write a novel and call it *Myrtle Meets the Entire English Army*, with naval subtitles and strewn with phallic illustrations. You can have Jean . . . and your dairymaids. And I'll learn to service three men at a time if I want to, all while I knit mittens," she added, thinking of Ian's grouse-hunting scenario. "At least," she continued, struggling to free herself, "Addison knows how to keep his cock in his breeches once in a while." She aimed a kick at his booted calf, missed, then succeeded on the second try. However, he seemed impervious to the blow and tightened his strong hands over Lachlan's shirt covering her arms.

They were both breathing hard from the struggle, for Myrtle was no wisp of a lass. Her anger increased when she couldn't free herself. Until now, she'd always assumed her strength was superior enough to get her out of any difficult situation. "You should go back to wearing the kilt, English law against it or not. Wearing a kilt would save you time, for you could whip out your John Thomas quicker than having to fumble with those buttons on your English breeches. Listen, Sinclair, I'm warning you," she huffed, forced to take a deep gulp of night air, "let go of my arms."

"And I'm warning you, Sassenach, I've had enough of your gutter language and arrogance for one night. We're going home."

"Not on your life," she yelled, knowing she would never set foot in Kilmarock Castle again. If she wanted to make this break as planned, Myrtle knew she had to do it tonight while her inner strength stayed with her. "I'm through listening to your lies, while you call me unflattering names behind my back and jeer at me with your paramours." She sagged against him, purposely giving the impression a faint was imminent. As she expected, his hold loosened on her.

"Myrtle," he said in alarm, then berated himself for his uncharacteristic roughness with a woman.

She took expert advantage of the minute to double her fist, pull back her strong right arm in an arc, then plant a solid punch on the Laird of Kilmarock's unprotected jaw. His body snapped back with the impact, and she found herself free from his hands at last. As she watched the astonishment contort his features, she couldn't believe how marvelous she felt. Of course, the knuckles across her right hand ached from the contact with his iron jaw, but it was worth it. It was a shame she hadn't done this sooner, for it made her feel at peace with the universe, like receiving a blessing from above. She saw his expression turn to pain as he touched the growing red lump at the edge of his face. Served him right for acting like a dockside bully. "I'm no country bumpkin to be pawed and ordered about. I'll not play the whore for you, then look the other way while you spill your seed into Jean or any other available piece of tail your eager hands can grab. Your vanity is bruised, that's all, because an English earl's daughter dares admit you are not to her liking. Well, Sinclair, I don't give a bloody damn *what* you think. I'm giving you more than you deserve by letting you have my money."

Dismissing him from her mind, Myrtle turned her back on him and headed for Lily. She wouldn't think about her broken heart now. There would be months in England to cry over Ian, the man who'd never loved her, the Scot who'd played her for an English fool. "The fort is just ahead. I can see to myself without your escort. You have my permission to go back to Castle Kilmarock . . . or to hell; which you choose makes not a whit of difference to me."

Ian couldn't believe she'd dared punch him, but the throbbing along his face proved it. And the words she'd just shouted at him? His smoldering eyes never left her as he unbuckled his sword belt and threw it to the ground. He charged at her. All practiced niceties he'd learned at the French court dissipated. She had one foot in Lily's stirrup before he clamped a hand on her wrists and yanked her down. This time he was prepared for her initial reaction. "That's right, brat, struggle all ye like. But 'tis time ye learned how a Scottish laird tames a shrewish English wife."

She could hardly believe the strength he used on both her wrists from just one of his hands. Her boots came off the ground under his right arm. "Put me down, you randy lummox!" she commanded. "I'm warning you, Sinclair. I'll give you another lump on your face." She wiggled her frame upward and swung her right fist to prove her point, but Ian jerked his face back just in time to avoid her blow. "Damn you, let me go." His tugging and hauling her about made her even more incensed. The ground stopped spinning beneath her when he came to an abrupt halt. For the first time tonight her anger was replaced by alarm when she saw him raise his left leg to brace it on a flat gray boulder. Before she could blink, the wind was knocked out of her with the force he exerted to toss her facedown across his upraised left knee. Blood rushed to her head. Her thick brown hair tumbled over her face. "Don't you dare lay a hand on me. These are Lachlan's trews, and he expects them returned in the morning," she yelled over her shoulder. "I'll never forgive you if you ruin his riding breeches. Now, let me up at once." She pushed upward only to feel Ian's left hand shove her back down.

"Weel," said the Laird of Kilmarock with menace, "then I'll have to make certain I dinna damage Lachlan's clothes." Without hesitation, he held her across his thigh while he used his right hand to skim down the woolen pants to the back of her knees.

"No—wait—I didn't mean . . . !" When a breeze of cool night air fanned her backside and upper thighs, all practicality deserted her. "Addison, help!" she screeched, illogically hoping the captain could hear her at the fort in the distance. "Addison!"

"'Tis the wrong name," growled her husband, then raised his open palm and swung down to land across the fleshy curve of her rump.

"You Scottish . . . bastard!" she screamed.

However, the forceful descent of his broad hand on her naked derrière stifled her angry shouts by the time the eighth swat landed, and the entire expanse of her well-rounded seat smarted with pain.

"Never punch me in the jaw again, Sassenach." His hand connected with her hot skin. "And, as I treat you with respect, never call me a liar. And finally, as I told ye before, ye'll nae be leavin' me tomorrow or any other day, do ye ken?" he demanded, punctuating his question with one last swat on the center of her flaming backside. As quickly as he began the chastisement, he ended it. Setting her back on her feet, he tugged the woolen trews up to her waist.

Holding her by the wrist with one hand, the Scot bent down and retrieved his claymore and belt from the ground. He'd removed the heavy broadsword earlier so it would not injure her when she landed across his knee. Ian then pulled her behind him and began walking toward their horses. When he chanced a glance over his shoulder, he had to fight the desire to comfort her, especially when he saw how hard she grappled against the urge to cry. However, he reminded himself how worried he'd been tonight, and how angry; but mostly he'd been wounded by the filthy accusations she'd hurled at him. Those words had cut at his insides harder than the blow she'd dealt his cheek. No longer angry with her now, he wondered why Jean just snuggling up to him on Sian's back this afternoon had set Myrtle off to behaving like a virago. Jean hadn't kissed him the way Addison kissed Myrtle, and he'd been forced to overlook it. She wasn't being fair to say such vile things to him, taunt him with Addison, then expect him to look the other way when she blithely informed him she was leaving, and to hell with their marriage vows.

When they reached the horses, Ian turned to his silent wife. "Now, ye have a choice. Ye can give me yer word to ride back with me with no more of yer shenanigans, then ye can use yer own horse, else ye'll ride in front of me on Sian's back." He saw a mutinous look enter the blue ice of her eyes, but it was clear she was thinking over her options.

Myrtle would have given her fortune right now to have Addison's loaded pistol in her hands. She eyed the basket-hilt claymore Ian wore with such ease against his left hip. No, she might hate the man before her, but she wasn't a murderess, even if her rear end felt like a brazier. She'd die rather than give him the satisfaction of knowing it. He wasn't hurting her now with his hand encircling her wrist, but she couldn't get free either. "I'll ride on Lily's back. You have my promise," she said, loathing the idea of riding in front of him or being within twenty feet of this Highlander right now.

He nodded, but before she could turn to mount Lily herself, as she expected, Myrtle felt his hands at her waist, and he lifted her quickly onto Lily's back. The sudden contact of her stinging bottom with the hard leather saddle made her wince. She opened her eyes, dreading the self-satisfied amusement she was certain she'd find in his lion eyes. However, when the Englishwoman looked down at him, he was watching her as if he wore the white mask as Urisk again, and she could not tell what he was thinking.

Never had he struck a woman or child in anger before. But this Sassenach got under his skin like no one else ever had. He couldn't—wouldn't—lose her, not to Addison nor any man. Yet he wasn't proud of himself at the moment. Shrugging out of this thick wool coat, he told his wife to lean forward on the stirrups.

What now? she thought, but this masterful Ian she'd never seen before tonight caused her to obey. When he arranged the thick coat over the saddle, then gently pressed her back down on Lily's back, she was dumbfounded. One minute he was whaling the living daylights out of her; the next he was treating her like fragile china. She started to thank him for this unexpected gesture, then clamped her lips together. What was the matter with her? she shouted at herself. No one in the world, not even her father, when she was child, had ever treated her this way. And it didn't matter if Ian was carting her back to the castle, she told herself, as they made their silent way back down the mountain. He couldn't lock her away. This wasn't the Middle Ages.

He kept the pace so sedate that she almost fell asleep once, but his hand on her arm steadied her, kept her from falling off Lily's back.

"We're almost home," he whispered, giving her shoulder a gentle pat. "I know you're tired, but I thought the slower ride would cause less discomfort to your bot—I mean . . ." He left the sentence unfinished when he saw the cold fury in her eyes as she glared across at him.

Chapter Nineteen

When they arrived at the castle, it was already morning. The household was up and about. How could she face them? Myrtle wondered. And she was dressed in breeches. Would they all howl with laughter to see the recalcitrant English lady-of-the-manor being hauled back home by her Scottish husband? Ian must have sensed her reluctance to dismount, for he swung off Sian's back quickly, walked over, and lifted her down.

Myrtle's legs felt rubbery from the unaccustomed long hours in the saddle. It forced her to grip the pommel of Lily's saddle to keep from crumpling at Ian's feet, which would have certainly made her humiliation complete.

Ian saw the motion. She looked as exhausted as he felt right now. "Come, I know ye'd never forgive me if I carried ye upstairs in front of our servants, so rest yer frame against me. I'll support ye about the waist, and we'll walk into the keep together."

Why was he being so attentive? These frequent shows of tenderness always made it hard for her to stay angry with him. Too worn to argue, she concentrated on putting one booted foot before the other.

When they entered the hallway, Katie and Fiona

rushed over. A surge of guilt washed over Myrtle at the worried expressions on their faces.

"We're both just tired," Ian explained, forcing a half smile. He leaned over and whispered something in Katie's ear that Myrtle could not make out.

In their rooms, his fatigued wife didn't even protest when Ian removed all her clothes.

"Ye'll notice, madam, how carefully I fold Lachlan Mackenzie's clothes," he said, a spark of his usual humor coming back.

She didn't say anything, not even when he picked her up and slipped her naked body under the quilt. The bed and fluffy pillow felt too comfortable. She yawned, then reminded herself she could now give her iron-handed husband a piece of her mind in the privacy of their chamber. Well, it would have to wait until later, for she was too weary to shout at him now.

After only a moment, Ian could tell by his wife's even breathing that she was asleep. He removed his own clothes and decided a bath would have to wait, for he needed rest more than washing.

When he climbed in next to her, Ian stayed on his side of the bed, for fear she'd wake and remember how furious she was with him.

Myrtle's erotic dream continued. The heat between her legs became more intense, causing her to rub against the source of friction once more. *"Umm,"* she purred, as the pleasurable sensations went on. "Oh, yes, harder." She burrowed her face closer to the warmth, inhaling a familiar, musky scent. Her nose twitched when one of his hairs tickled her. Slowly the sleepy mist lifted and she realized it wasn't a dream. Her blue eyes flashed open. Ian was holding her, his skillful hand nestled between her thighs.

"Bonjour, mon bijou . . . amour de ma vie."

She saw the combination of arousal and amusement in his golden eyes. How dare he call her his darling, true love after last night? Like a scalded cat, Myrtle pulled away from him, but the demon only laughed, before reaching out to lift her effortlessly up, then down on top of him. The current that jolted through her when her womanly curves connected with the hard contours of Ian's naked torso flustered her. She struggled in a futile effort to pull free.

"Oh, I like that," he teased.

When the tips of her full breasts brushed along the light mat of fur across his muscular chest, she stopped moving. Her actions were giving them both too much pleasure. "Let go of me," she insisted.

He made a face of mock innocence. "I merely wish to check you over to be sure you've no lingering discomforts from last night." Boldly, he cupped both cheeks of her bottom and pressed her closer to him. He let his hands roam freely over the round flesh, down to the tops of her thighs, then up along her spine, to rest gently on the crest of her derrière again.

Not sure how long she could take this close fondling and stick to her intentions, she raised her upper body. "I am fine. The area you seem so concerned on checking this morning doesn't hurt at all."

"Good," he said, trying to be equally honest. He reached under her stomach to move his fingers playfully across the area he'd been arousing earlier. "I do not mean to leave my lady in discomfort elsewhere, either, by abandoning a task before it is finished."

Squirming wouldn't free her, as her attempts proved. When he parted his own legs slightly, she gasped at the blatant proof that he was also affected by their intimate contact. "Please, let me go." No, she could not bear this final humiliation—that he should now find out, despite everything, that she still desired him, that he could easily make her woman's

335

body yield to him through his expert skills as a lover. And she continued loving him, God help her, for this realization caused more anguish than she'd ever experienced in her life. "Please, Ian, don't do this to me."

Her husband stopped immediately when he heard the suffering in her voice, then saw the tears in her blue eyes. He felt confused, disturbed by her response. He'd only sought to give her pleasure just now, to right things between them. He sat up and let her move away from him, but insisted she sit next to him with the quilt pulled up about her. "I canna let you shut me out again, Sassenach. No English reserve this time. Ye must tell me what torments you so."

"Why can't you understand how humiliating all this is for me?" she demanded, unable to keep the tears from running down her face. "Will you leave me no pride?"

The frustration showed on his face. "Darling, I only sought to show you how much you do mean to me, to give you pleasure before we talked things out between us."

She shook her head. "No, we have nothing more to say or share together. I tried to tell you last night," she added with despair. "I know you do not love me. Jean Mackenzie has your heart. You have your castle and lands back; you don't need me. You never did."

He was shocked to learn she believed this. "How . . . how can you think I don't love you, need you?"

No longer crying, she met his appalled expression with a level stare. "Never, not once, did you say you loved me."

"But I thought you knew by the way I acted." He could not hide his own pain at her accusations. "Since you entered Kilmarock Hall, is there nothing you remember, nothing you can recall in my actions, either as Urisk or Ian, that showed how much I love you?"

Unbidden, the visions of the past came to her. She thought of how he'd taken care of her when she was sick, the happy hours she and Urisk had spent talking and sharing their ideas and feelings, the tenderness he'd shown when he first made love to her, and his easygoing way of getting her to laugh with him. And she admitted it—she *had* said some horrible things to him last night. Then she spotted the purplish swelling on his jaw as he sat patiently waiting for her to speak. He'd hurt her pride, not really her body, with that paddling last night, for this morning she wasn't in any discomfort at all, whereas, from the look of the large lump on his face, Ian's jaw must ache like the devil. "I suppose an apology of sorts is in order," she whispered, chagrined by her total lack of self-control the night before.

Ian sighed, misreading her words. "All right." He took her hand in his, appearing totally repentant. "Lady Myrtle Sinclair, I humbly apologize and deeply regret that you forced me to spank you last evening."

She blinked, then the audacity of his words hit her. Despite herself, she found her lips turning up at the corners. "I suppose that is the closest declaration of contriteness I'm likely to get from you, my lord. I, on the other hand, enjoyed popping you on the jaw. However, even though I believe you deserved it, I do feel a twinge of remorse because I should never have socked you so hard. My only excuse is that I did not realize how powerful a pugilist I am." His answering grin and the way he caressed her fingers told Myrtle that he, too, enjoyed this verbal banter between them.

However, the Englishwoman knew this changed nothing. She realized that the seriousness of her expression caused his smile to vanish. "Ian, though you just said you love me, how can I believe you when the facts speak for themselves?" Then she told him exactly what Jean Mackenzie had confessed. She left nothing out, including the cruel names Jean said he'd called his wife.

His reddish-gold eyebrows rose in astonishment. He knew his wife would never make up such lies. He saw the suffering it caused her to relate the words, yet he knew he couldn't stop her, for he had to know everything. When she came to the part where Jean had shown Myrtle the proof, Ian finally understood the reason for his wife's behavior, for the filthy words she'd hurled at him, words he knew she'd never used before in her life. "By God, darling, 'tis the biggest fool in Scotland ye married."

Then he did believe her, Myrtle thought, grateful for this, at least. "Then you have to realize why I must leave. Even . . . even though I cannot deny loving you, I will not be a true wife to you while you carry on with other women." She lifted her chin. "I will never be that desperate for a man, and I deserve better."

"Aye, ye do, sweet Myrtle." Without another word, despite his own nakedness, Ian got up on his knees and reached over his wife's head for the Sinclair dirk in the leather sheath over the headboard.

Good Lord, she thought with alarm, was he going to murder her instead of allowing her to just divorce him?

When he settled back down next to her, the jeweled Sinclair dagger clutched in his right hand, Ian winced at the fear he read in her eyes. "My God, wife, do ye still believe I'd harm ye?" When she did not answer, he closed his eyes against the sadness this caused him. "Myrtle, describe again what ye saw on the inside of Jean's thigh."

"Oh, Ian," she protested, "please, I told you once!

Why do you wish to punish me by making me recite it again?"

He ran his free hand through his reddish-blond mane, his own nerves close to breaking. "Just do it."

All right, she would; but dagger or not, she was getting out of here the minute she finished reciting it again. "I saw it clearly. It was a wide bite from a man's teethmarks. While Jean seemed to enjoy it, to me it looked very painful, for the wound went deep. It was still bleeding. There," she sniffed, "does that please your male pride?"

"Do you remember our quarrel a few days ago, and how it ended?"

Her face flushed at the recollection of his primitive, glorious lovemaking. "Yes, of course I remember? But what has that to do with—?"

"Think, wee kelpie," he said, entreating her with his golden eyes. "Never in my life have I felt so aroused, so out of control—no, dinna look away," he pleaded, reaching to cup her warm face back to his. "It was the first time I lost completely the ability to reason, to pause one second to think, to hold back. Ye made me want to ravish you, brand every inch of your seductive body with my lips and hands," he admitted, holding nothing back from her. "It was also the first time I've made love to a woman without even removing my clothes."

Embarrassed, Myrtle still could not tell where he was leading. "But what has that to do with Jean Mackenzie and you?"

"Just this, my darling: the next day, did you find any such bruises on your delectable little body?"

"Of course not. I mean, I did experience a slight stiffness in one or two areas, but . . . certainly not. I never had such savage, mauling gouges on my skin," she added, indignant he would even think she'd stand for such brutality.

"Exactly, and do ye think, no matter how far gone I was in my arousal, and believe me, you saw me at my worst, I'd ever risk damaging any inch of your lovely figure that I adore? If ye recall, I was the one who had a deep bite or two out of my shoulder the next morning from a certain seductive wife's sharp teeth. No, wee kelpie," he said, putting his arm about her shoulders when she looked rebuked. "I enjoyed the arousing passion that burst from ye like a blazing fire. Yer a proper lady to the world and a lioness when ye make love, and I'd have you just the way ye are." Then his expression became more serious. "In the throes of passion, when I was out of my mind from the wanting of ye, when I've never felt so out of control, I dinna manifest it in the way Jean was marked. Do ye not see? It could not have been me that made love to her. I left her in the glen as she asked, the minute ye rode out of sight from us. I canna guess where the lassie went or who she met, but it was nae me."

Myrtle bit her lower lip, wanting to believe him. She searched her mind and heart, trying to sort out her troubled thoughts and feelings. It was true that as long as she'd known this man, he'd never behaved brutally toward her or anyone else. Ian had made love to her gently, then once in anger—using the skills of his mouth and hands, he'd not left an inch of her unattended, but she had to admit it. That savage bite Jean had paraded as a trophy from Ian Sinclair did not reconcile itself with what she knew of the man next to her.

Reverently, Ian held up the jeweled dagger that had belonged to his father. He spoke the words slowly, carefully, so there was hardly any Scottish accent at all. "I give ye my sacred vow, by the iron of this cross, since the night you first entered my castle, I have never made love to any woman except you. Nor will I ever love or share my body with any woman, save my beautiful wife, Lady Myrtle Sinclair. And may the point of this blade pierce my heart if ever I break my promise." He kissed the cross of the dagger where the blade and hilt met, then somberly replaced it above their bed.

When he turned to look at his wife, her expression was neutral. Those large blue eyes watched him. Ian got up from their bed and went toward his dressing room. Despair gnawed at him. This was all he could give her. If she did not believe him now, or love him enough to stay, the Laird of Kilmarock knew he would never force her.

"Ian!" His wife jumped out of bed and rushed to him. "Oh, Ian, I believe you," she cried, reaching for him in hopes he'd hold her. "Please don't go, don't leave me."

His arms crushed her to him. He felt moisture in his eyes. "Oh, my fiery wife, I love you." He kissed her lips, long and hard, letting her see the fierceness of his love and desire.

When Myrtle pulled back, for fear she was going to swoon, she held onto his shoulders. "My, that nearly scorched my ears," she confessed, then laughed up at him. "Oh, darling, I first fell in love with the ghost of Kilmarock Castle, then dear Urisk became my trusted friend." She looked away from his lion eyes for a second. "Of course, I delighted in the return of Ian Sinclair, but at first, I dearly missed Urisk, for he was someone with whom I could share my inner self. I . . . I want my friend back, Ian."

Cupping her chin in his hands, Ian gently tipped her face up to his. "Can ye nae tell Ian what ye would have told Urisk?"

The love she saw in his golden eyes almost took her breath away. Suddenly, her tender, humorous friend and her proud, brave husband were reconciled within this one man holding her in his arms. "Yes, I think I can tell you. It is this, Ian: you are now the laird and my husband, but if I am to remain as your wife here, I cannot continue just as an ornament, a bed partner."

He held her a little away from him so she could look up into his face. "But I thought to protect you, keep you safe."

Myrtle shook her head. "No, Ian, I need work. Cosseting doesn't suit me." Encouraged when he continued listening, she went on. "There are so many areas in which I can help you—the account books, ordering supplies from London and Edinburgh, drawing up plans for diversified crops that will increase our yields. I've had years of experience running my farm in Chelmsford."

He thought over all the improvements she'd made thus far. The women of his family had always been more content to stay within these walls with their sewing, arranging parties. His mother had been relieved to have his father handle all the burdens of running the estate. Yet Ian admitted that Myrtle was unlike any woman of his acquaintance. "And you *did* promise to show me how I can get along with the other Sassenachs," he added, encouraged that they were working out things between them. "Aye, I'll try to change my attitude, and the bold fact is, my lady, my clansmen and I do need yer talents. The crops were so poor last year, I took to raiding cattle from the redcoats late at night."

Myrtle remembered Addison telling her some of his men had spotted the eerie ghost of Kilmarock charging across the moors after midnight. Never did she want her husband placed in that dangerous position again as the only way to feed his starving clansmen. "Oh, Ian," she said, pleased by this effort he was making because he knew how much sharing his life meant to her. "Thank you. There is so much to do, I'd like to begin right away."

He chuckled at her exuberance. "But yer to have a

342

care when ye go about these highlands, Sassenach. I won't bend on that point."

She strained her body to plant a kiss on his lips. "I promise never to ride out alone. You've just made me so happy, I couldn't possibly refuse you such a small request."

"I'd like to make ye even happier, wee kelpie." Provocatively, he ran his hand down her back to the swell of her hips.

"Well," she teased, twining her arms about his waist. "As long as you know how wonderful I am now, it's all right." She pulled back, letting him see the love in her eyes. "Thank you again, for giving me that," she said, eyeing the jeweled dagger now returned to its place on the wall. "You'll never know how close I came to turning my back on Scotland forever."

"Aye, I think I do," he said, equally serious. "And it still turns my blood cold to think I might have lost ye, my bonny wife."

"Oh," she said, her manner full of contrition, "are you cold? Come, get back under the covers."

He let her lead him back to their bed. She clucked over him, tucking the covers about him, much to his enjoyment. "Och, I've a much better way to warm us," he teased, pulling her eager body against his. "Isn't that better?"

"Yes," she admitted. "I hoped you'd take my hint." She bent down and kissed his neck, then flicked her tongue across the nipples of his chest. She heard him groan. "Now you know why I like it so much." Her hand brushed down his flat stomach to the juncture between his thighs. She heard him suck in his breath when her hand encircled him. Ever so slightly, she moved her fingers up and down.

"God . . . and S—Saint Andrew," pushed between his teeth as he fought for control from her arousing touch. "Ye'll drive me mad, temptress."

"Perhaps just a little, lion eyes." After continuing more of her ministrations, Myrtle stopped and moved forward on her knees to crouch next to him. "Would you mind if I tried something different?"

Cautiously, he opened his eyes. "Madam, ye already have me at a decided disadvantage. Don't tell me I've got to grovel some more?" Her musical laughter filled his ears, and he reached out to caress her ripe breasts with his large hands. "So sweet, so beautiful," he murmured, happy to hear her murmuring in contentment as he entered into her playful attempt to initiate this new closeness.

"Oh, no," she said, then pulled back from him. "I am going to make love to *you*, for a change. And I shall keep your here for . . . for a month, if it takes that long to show you just how much pleasure I can give you. I'm going to be successful as a seductress if it's the last thing I do."

"Lord," he groaned in mock horror, "I'm a dead man."

She glanced down below his waist. "From your raging cockstand right now, my lord, I believe you are far from dead."

He couldn't hide his surprise at her quick repartee. "Can this forward minx be the shy little English lass I wed, the same wee mouse who turned scarlet at the mere thought of sleeping without thick gray flannel to hide her alluring body?"

Mischief showed on her face. "Yes, lion eyes," she whispered close to his lips. "It is the same, but do you mind if I've changed a little?"

"Never, for I delight in yer ways, temptress." He kissed her but used his tongue to show her they had far more important matters to complete, and right now talking wasn't one of them. He ran his hands along her figure. "Aye, a bonny handful."

Feeling close to losing control, she nipped the flesh near his ear.

He had just enough self-mastery left to advise, "If ye plan on doing this yerself, *mon bijou*, ye'd best be at it now, or I swear I'll toss ye beneath me to end this torture ye're forcing me to endure."

Her plan. "Yes, I want to be Lisette tonight," she confessed. Slowly getting to her knees, she shifted her weight to straddle his hips. "I enjoyed this part in the novel best, where Lisette ravishes the pirate prince." Myrtle rubbed her slippery cleft along the hardness of his right thigh. His fevered skin and wisps of cinnamon-colored hair dampened from her moisture. Seductively, she moved her hips closer to where she knew he craved, but rocked back just before she touched the tip of his penis.

After a few minutes of this torment, Ian growled in frustration and grabbed her undulating hips in his hands. "Lisette had better complete what she started verra soon," warned her fully aroused husband, "else the pirate prince is going to turn her across his knee."

Not the least intimated by his threat, Myrtle giggled, then positioned herself directly over him. "Oh, Ian, it's fun to be a siren." She sat down slowly, grateful for his assistance when he guided her gently down to a sitting position. "Is that better, pirate prince?"

As she raised herself up and down in tender, giving pleasure, Ian let her see and hear the gratification she was giving him. "You are a sorceress, a temptress, a s—siren," he bit out. "I would be yer husband, friend . . ." When he arched up to meet her descent, he grinned when she gave an unexpected squeak of pleasure. "And yer lover. Oh, I like that, too, the little sounds ye make when I enter you."

"Ian," she whimpered, feeling the coiling in her loins which forced her to increase her speed as she pressed down on him.

He looked up to see the combination of mounting

345

desire and exertion on her face. Ian wanted to help, but she'd said she wished to do this alone.

Puffing with the difficult effort, her face now bathed in sweat, Myrtle had to stop a minute. "Heavens," she panted, "I . . . I never realized this position was such hard work. How ever do you manage it, Ian?"

Despite the pain in his throbbing flanks, he couldn't keep the rumble of rich laughter from bursting from his chest. They were both aroused to the point of physical discomfort, yet the guilelessness of her question at such a moment filled him with mirth. "Dearest wife," he said when he could speak, "I love you." Still joined to her, Ian moved his upper body to take her in his arms. "Would ye mind if I finished this?"

"Oh, I wish you would. It seems I need more practice, for I'm near worn out . . ."

With great care, Ian switched their positions and placed her beneath him on their large bed. Holding the weight of his upper torso by his arms, he entered her with one swift motion, delighting in the way she automatically arched her hips to meet him.

"Oh, my, that's so much better. You know, Ian, you're quite proficient at that."

He didn't laugh this time. "Only because I love you, and that makes it so important to serve ye well, beloved."

Then their words ceased as the pirate prince carried his Lisette to their special place where waves of delightful pleasure awaited them.

For the rest of the week and into the next, the laird and his lady settled into the routine of running their household, helping their clansmen, and sharing those private moments that only couples in love experience. At those times, even if they were having dinner and servants were about, their eyes would meet and time would stand still for Ian and his countess.

Overjoyed that he had been able to convince Gavin and many of the clansmen to meet with Addison, Myrtle set about drawing up the menu and readying the great hall for the important company.

It was just two days before the Scottish clansmen and English soldiers were to meet when Ian interrupted her while she helped Fiona in the sewing room upstairs.

"Enter," she called.

Dressed in a new brown coat and breeches, Ian walked in.

Her automatic smile of greeting vanished when she saw how drawn he appeared. Myrtle put down the white cloth she'd been embroidering. It was for Fiona's wedding dress. In a few months she would marry Lachlan Mackenzie.

"'Tis time, Fiona."

The auburn-haired woman nodded to her laird.

Confused by the somberness on Fiona's features before she left, Myrtle turned to her husband. "Ian, what is the matter?"

"Come, my dear." Ian offered her his hand. "We have visitors in the great hall."

She got up and smoothed down the skirt of her yellow silk gown. "But I don't understand. Who is here?"

His unusual grim expression made her follow him immediately.

Halfway down the stairs, Ian turned to her. "Today you will learn more of what it means to be the wife of a clan chieftain. You are to stand next to me but say nothing, do you understand?"

Now she was truly uneasy. "Yes," she answered, suddenly glad for his warm hand on her cold fingers as he led them into the medieval hall. Today it lacked

347

the gaiety that had permeated this huge room at her wedding banquet.

When Myrtle spotted Gavin and his sons, she smiled in relief. However, after noting all the servants lined on both sides of the room, Fiona's white face as she stood next to Lachlan, Katie with her eyes downcast, Myrtle felt her contented expression vanish. What was going on?

It was after Lachlan went over to the iron sconce at the back of the room and threw a rope over it, then secured it with a knot, that Myrtle knew why she'd been summoned here . . . and it chilled her to the bone. She followed the line of cord downward and recognized the petite form and wavy black hair that fell down the bare back of Jean Mackenzie. Her brother was securing her slender wrists to the thick rope that stretched her arms above her head. Lachlan stepped away, his face as cold as the gray flagstones at Myrtle's feet.

When she pulled back involuntarily, Myrtle felt her husband's firm hand on her elbow. How had this occurred? Myrtle thought back to the day Ian had given her his sacred vow. Yet everyone here, save herself, must have known this was going to happen, even though she'd assumed the confidential matter had been settled quietly between her and Ian. With each step toward the center of the hall, her legs felt weighted with iron. Finally, Ian stopped walking.

Gavin Mackenzie stepped forward. "My lord, since Fiona is soon to be wed to Lachlan, she has asked to stand here with the Mackenzies. Do ye give yer permission?"

"I do," Ian answered.

"Then," Gavin went on, "as head of my family, it falls to me to carry out the sentence of thirty lashes against my daughter, Jean, this day—"

"My God, you cannot," Myrtle interrupted, un-

348

able to stop herself. Instantly, she felt all Scottish eyes on her. Some appeared more shocked at her outburst than concerned that a young girl was going to be brutally beaten. Myrtle turned to her husband. "Ian, you cannot mean to let this—" She could not believe the harshness of his features. It cut the words from her lips.

"You are the laird's wife now, madam," Ian snapped at her. "You must learn our Scottish ways of dispensing justice." With unbending resolve, he walked her away from the others for a moment. His golden eyes became amber stones when he addressed her privately. "If it had not been for Jean's lies, you wouldn't have tried to leave me, and I would never have thrashed you."

"Lord, Ian," she said, keeping her voice low in front of the others, "that spanking didn't hurt a bit . . . Well, at least by the next morning I felt nothing," she amended honestly. "I daresay we were bound to come to loggerheads sooner or later, as I'm sure we will in the future. Besides, it was nothing compared to what Gavin intends to do. There is no comparison between the two."

But Ian would not be dissuaded. "Even if what you say is true, when I think I might have lost you forever because of that treacherous little viper's lies, I think the punishment by our law is too lenient." Obviously considering the matter settled, the lord of Kilmarock took Myrtle's arm and led her back. He turned to his tacksman. "The countess apologies for her outburst. We must excuse that our ways are still new to her. Pray continue."

With a determined seriousness, Gavin spoke again. "To my shame and that of her family, it was Jean Mackenzie who lied and schemed to break up the marriage between our laird and his lady wife. For bearing false witness against another, along with nearly destroying the sacred bond between man and wife, our law is clear and the punishment is deemed just and merciful."

Without another word, Gavin removed the studded leather belt across his chest. He folded it in two with the heavy buckle wrapped about his huge fist.

Myrtle saw Jean look over her bare shoulder. Even her usual defiance crumpled when she viewed the thickness of the leather sword belt that would soon be marking the smoothness of her slender back. Yes, Myrtle agreed Jean had done terrible things, almost ruining their marriage, but . . . She felt her stomach heave as Gavin pulled back his arm.

Without warning, Myrtle wrenched free from the gentle hand Ian now had on her elbow and raced toward Jean. Automatically, the Englishwoman stepped in front of the smaller girl to shield her with her own body. She closed her eyes tightly and gritted her teeth, ready to receive the lethal bite of leather on her gown-covered back. The horrible sound of the belt whistled through the air.

But nothing landed on her body. Myrtle heard the sound of a male grunt behind her, then someone lurched forward into her. She turned to find Ian Sinclair hovering over her.

"My God, I . . . !" Gavin's face was a mask of horror. "My lord, God forgive me, I dinna mean to strike ye."

Ian winced when he straightened his broad shoulders, then waved away Gavin's apology. "I'm all right."

Her back now to Jean's, Lady Myrtle held up her hands to the assembly. "Please, since I am mainly the injured party here, I beg you not to do this. What Jean did was wrong, but no one died, and my husband and I have reconciled. If you beat this girl, I shall never forgive myself. And it will only result in Jean hating me more, something I do not wish. All the Sinclairs must stay together for the benefit of the clan. Please," she repeated, "this severe punishment, though I know you view it as just, is against everything I believe. Such angry force only serves in teaching our children that violence is the solution to our problems."

"My lord," Gavin complained to Ian, who had been listening along with the rest of them to Myrtle's impassioned words. "Is yer wife to decide this important matter? What do you decree?"

Ian studied Myrtle for a long moment before he spoke. "As my lady wife just pointed out, the injury was done directly to her, indirectly to me. And if Countess Sinclair chooses to pardon Jean Mackenzie, it is her right to do so."

For as long as she lived, Myrtle knew she could never love her handsome husband more than at this moment. Her blue eyes tried to tell him silently how much this meant to her. "Then that is an end to it," she said.

"Saint Andrew's balls," Jean muttered, when Myrtle inadvertently stepped back and bumped into her. "Will ye move your wide arse off my back? I can hardly breathe. Hell, any more Sinclairs galloping to my aid, and I'll suffocate."

It was clear only Myrtle heard Jean's words. The Englishwoman looked at her husband, who was hovering anxiously over her, then saw herself protecting Jean, then took in Jean's outrageous remarks, which were hardly overflowing with gratitude. Suddenly, Myrtle couldn't help it, but the farcical nature of the situation struck her, and she burst out laughing. Not a soft titter, mind you, but a boisterous guffaw. Never had she met anyone like these Scottish highlanders before.

Angus rushed over. "Ian, lad, I think yer poor wife's hysterical. We scarit the English lass so."

The appalled looks on the Scottish faces around her at such a solemn moment, along with Angus' words, only caused her to laugh all the louder.

"Madam," her husband hissed near her ear, "do you mind telling me what is so hilarious?"

Resting her head against his comfortable shoulder, grateful for his role in saving Jean, she shook her head. "My wonderful husband." Then a fit of giggles overtook her again. "I dinna think I can," she answered, playfully mimicking his Scot's accent.

Chapter Twenty

"Please," Myrtle managed, in an attempt to control her amused reaction. "One of you, untie Jean."

Lachlan walked over and performed the task. "Ye got off lighter than ye deserve," he told his younger sister.

Ignoring her brother's words, Jean went directly over to Myrtle.

The laird intercepted her with a quick movement to stand in front of his wife. He glowered down at Jean. "As your brother correctly pointed out, Miss Mackenzie, my gentle wife has saved you, but nothing will save you from my wrath if ever you harm her again, either physically or with that vicious tongue of yers."

Jean's dark eyes read the seriousness of Ian's vow, clearly realizing their relationship, even the innocuous one, would never be the same. "Aye, I ken what ye mean, my lord. But I . . . I ask to speak with your lady away from the others."

Myrtle heard the genuine entreaty in Jean's voice. Gone was her earlier bluster. "Please, Ian," she whispered behind her husband's back, "you can keep your eyes on me if we stand over there." Tempted just to step to the side of him, Myrtle knew Ian had already conceded much to her this day, and she wished to show her respect and honor of his position as laird of their clan.

Nodding in agreement, Ian moved away from his wife. "But just for a few moments."

When they were alone, Jean looked down at her bare feet. "I . . . I thank ye for stopping Da from whipping me."

"I had no choice, Jean, for I would have derived nothing but sorrow from such action."

Jean's dark head snapped up as she took the measure of the blue-eyed Sassenach. Clearly, she accepted the truth of Myrtle's words, for she continued. "There's something I think ye should know. I never took money for it, even when that redcoat offered me a bag of coins if I'd make ye believe the lie that the laird and I were lovers."

"Addison Barrington had a hand in this?" She looked up to find her husband watching her, then forced a smile to reassure him.

"Aye," Jean answered. "But I did it for my own reasons, and the manner of it was my idea. I thought I hated ye, Sassenach."

"I am not your enemy, Jean."

Something changed in the petite girl's dark eyes for a second. "Weel, I found out the laird is besotted with ye, and he'd never look at me now. Besides," she finished, her usual cockiness returning, "I've already picked out the mon I intend to marry. He was supposed to speak to Da today, but now he'll arrive at the cottage and nae find us," she said, looking worried.

"Oh," Myrtle answered, "I am sure a man in love will find—"

There was a commotion outside the hall.

"Ye can't go in there!" one of the servants shouted, frantically racing after a trim-figured man, dressed in simple coat and breeches. The intruder carried a lethal-looking dagger in his right hand.

Myrtle saw Jean's face brighten immediately. Her own blue eyes widened when she saw Duncan Knox scan the room. When he found the girl standing next to the Countess of Kilmarock, he came over.

"It's all right," Myrtle told the horrified servant. She heard the mumbled protests, saw the hostile glances from her clansmen. Ian appeared ready to order the man thrown from the castle battlements, but then the laird's eyes met hers. He seemed to read the entreaty, for he dropped his hands to his sides and said to the two footmen, "Do as her ladyship says."

It gave her the courage to add, "Please let him enter."

Jean bolted toward Duncan and threw herself into his arms.

Gavin Mackenzie sprang after the man, his two sons close behind. "Here, ye devil's spawn, Knox, unhand my daughter."

Duncan pushed Jean behind him and raised his dagger threateningly to the three Mackenzies. "Stay away from us, Mackenzie."

In a split second Myrtle was rushing toward the scene, intent on stopping bloodshed between the two rival clansmen. Automatically, she reached out to stay Duncan's hand, which held his knife. "Please, Duncan, we must talk this—"

"Step back, all of ye!" shouted the laird of Kilmarock. "Right now, by God!" Even without a weapon, Ian's towering frame and commanding presence were enough to get almost everyone to comply. It was Lady Myrtle who appeared rooted to the spot, her words and actions cut off.

"Put the knife doon, lad," Ian said in a quieter voice. "Ye'll nae be harmed."

Duncan looked unconvinced. He held onto the weapon and continued shielding Jean behind him. "I love Jean. We mean to wed with or without yer

355

permission." As if to show agreement, Miss Macken-zie encircled her arms about Duncan's waist and held onto him like a limpet. Duncan eyed the taller man warily. "I heard from one of the Mackenzie servants ye were aboot to beat my Jean. Why should I believe ye?"

Myrtle spoke up, moving closer, despite the warning scowl from her husband. "Please, Duncan, put the knife away so we may talk. I give you my word, you and Jean will not come to any harm here."

Where he would not trust her husband, Duncan's brown eyes relented at Myrtle's open gentleness. Slowly, he placed the long knife back in the leather sheath attached to the belt across his chest.

A sigh of relief went about the room.

"Weel," snapped Ian Sinclair, apparently unable to hold back addressing his wife until a more private moment, "having aged me ten years when ye went chargin' over to protect Jean, ye'll be pleased, no doot, to learn ye just took another decade from me by hurling yerself toward Knox's dagger."

Myrtle felt her pale cheeks suffuse with color at his scolding tone in front of all these people. "Really, my lord, I was merely attempting to disperse a poten-tially dangerous situation. Suicide was the remotest thing from my mind."

"Really?" her husband countered. "From where I stood, madam, it looked exactly like you were intent on making me a widower." When her chin moved northward at him, the laird's fists went to his hips as he added, "Mayhap ye'd like me to have Angus pitched in the loch, while young Knox here holds my claymore over his head, just so ye can try for another ten years while ye bustle aboot as the rescuing angel of Kilmarock Castle!"

First it started as titters about the room, as many of the Scots tried to stifle their mirth. Even Duncan's and Gavin's shoulders shook. Before long, loud male and female laughter echoed throughout the hall.

"Ian," said Gavin, "yer Sassenach wife is a game one, all right. Got the pluck of six highlanders."

Ian returned the other man's grin. "Aye, I give ye that, Mackenzie. Now, if she'd only learn to obey me once in a while, just so I dinna forget who's the laird of Kilmarock here," he stated, adding a martyr's wistful sigh. "Suppose it's just a cross I'll have to bear."

Feeling unusually meek at the moment, yet grateful things had relaxed in the room, Myrtle tried to remind herself it was because Ian loved her and feared for her safety just now that he'd given her a verbal dressing-down in public. And it still gnawed at her conscience that her poor husband had taken that cut from Gavin's sword belt in her stead. A shy smile brightened her features, but she remained silent.

When things settled down, Ian spoke first. "Now," he told the servants in the hall, "please go back to your duties."

While Myrtle took Jean and Duncan to the other side of the room, after ordering ale, wine, and a light repast for them, Ian spoke to Gavin, Lachlan, and Andrew out of earshot. However, as Myrtle poured wine for the two guests sitting on wooden benches at the end of the long table, she heard occasional shouts from Gavin and her husband.

"Da will never give us permission to marry," a forlorn Jean said. She moved her full wineglass back and forth across the surface of the ancient oak table.

Myrtle touched the girl's arm. "Jean, I know Ian will do all he can to help you and Duncan."

"But how can ye defend yer sister?" they heard Gavin bellow at Lachlan. "She almost broke up the laird's marriage. I've no quarrel she should be married, but nae to a Knox. I'd have my daughter wed a real mon, not one of our clan's bitterest enemies.

Why, Duncan's nae even a mon! He's only a skinny scholar who spends his time reciting poetry."

Ian broke in between father and son. "The wiry Scot, Duncan follows the long line of tradition of the Knoxes as bards of their clan."

From her position, Myrtle saw the full-bearded Gavin shake his fist toward the Scot sitting next to his daughter. The countess reached for her crystal wineglass, sadly fearing this was going to be a long afternoon.

"Wiry," yelled Gavin, "I'd give ye that, Ian, but the oak-wearing Knox has verra little muscle to him."

Jean patted Duncan's thigh. "Dinna let me father's bluster bite ye, darlin'. You've plenty of muscle where it counts. Hung like a bull, ye are."

"Jean!" Duncan admonished. "Nae in front of the laird's wife."

A strangling sound wrenched from Myrtle's throat when the spicy wine shot down the wrong way. She coughed, then wheezed as tears formed in her eyes. Now she knew it had to have been Duncan who'd so thoroughly made love to Mackenzie's daughter that afternoon Jean had tried to make her believe Ian was her lover. And now Myrtle knew what Knox had meant when he'd hinted the day he'd saved her from the arrow that he had ways to get his lass to come around to his way of thinking. "Good Lord," she said, then coughed again.

"She's turnin' purple," Jean commented, then reached about and gave Myrtle a hearty thwack between the shoulder blades.

"Much . . . obliged," Myrtle managed. She looked over to see Ian and the three other men staring at her as if she'd had another odd attack. Giving them a jaunty wave and smile, she called over, "I beg your pardon, gentlemen. Wine went down the wrong way."

They resumed their discussion; however, an hour

later the four men came over to Myrtle and the couple next to her. When the Englishwoman saw her husband's grim expression, her heart sank. Lachlan and Andrew appeared torn as they stared silently at their father's determined, angry face, then at the crumpled little face of their dark-haired sister.

"Come on, Jeanie, we're goin' home." Gavin scowled at the stone-faced Duncan. "Ye stay away from my daughter, else those traitorous Knoxes will be needin' a new bard."

The bench scraped against the gray flagstones when Duncan bounded to his feet. His brown eyes did not flinch as he stared up at the gray-haired giant. "I heard ye tell the laird ye love Jean. I dinna believe it, for ye're willin' to sacrifice her happiness just to keep alive an ancient feud that serves no purpose. Ye know Jean would leave ye all and come with me now if I asked her, and that fear is tearin' the guts out of ye, Mackenzie, isn't it?"

"Ye oak-spawned—" Lachlan and Andrew, on either side of their father, held him back from Duncan Knox.

"Nay, Da," said Lachlan, "let him go."

"Dinna be scarit, Mackenzie," Duncan said with bitter irony. "For Jean knows 'tis nae my way, for I'd have her as my wife wed to me in front of both our families."

When Duncan turned sadly back to his teary Jean, Myrtle saw the wrenching finality in the look that passed between the two lovers. She was on the verge of crying herself.

"I tried, Jean," said Duncan in a low voice. "Ye should have let me end it when I begged ye to leave."

Jean shook her head from side to side in protest, clearly unable to speak.

Jean's head shot up as she glared at Gavin from her seated position. "Will ye nae even care what I want, Father?" It was the first time she hadn't called him

Da. "Does it mean nothin' to ye?"

Duncan shook his head and prepared to leave.

Myrtle watched the six people about her. Wasn't anyone going to stop this tragedy? She couldn't believe they were all going to let it end this way. Jumping up, she raced for the bard of Clan Knox. "Duncan, wait. Don't leave."

"Merde, there she goes again," Ian muttered, with a mixture of exasperation and acceptance. He walked over to position himself between Myrtle and Duncan, with the three Mackenzies on the other side, just in case. If brawling erupted, the laird intended to be ready to pluck her out of harm's way.

As Gavin saw Jean join them, he looked at the laird of Kilmarock in frustration. "My lord, it was all settled. Can ye nae do a thing to control yer wife?"

Ian looked thoughtful, rubbed a hand across his chin. "Aye, I could," he drawled straight-faced, "but the stone floor of this hall is too cold and uncomfortable to do it right here."

Jean and Duncan exchanged a knowing look; Lachlan and Duncan grinned. Even Gavin lost some of his usual dourness.

Though shocked by her husband's lewd reply, Myrtle was too concerned with the matter at hand to comment on it. "You all let stubborn pride and past grievances rule your lives," she said, addressing the Scots surrounding her. "When Captain Barrington and his soldiers arrive here tomorrow, how can any of Clan Sinclair hope to sit down to discuss peaceful solutions to the problems and tensions in the highlands if you cannot even make peace among yourselves? Oak or myrtle; soldier, farmer, shepherd, or bard—what is the difference when we're all dust? I thought you Scots a people of honor and bravery," she continued her voice beginning to sound weary. "Yet with this obsession to continue these bitter feuds between the clans, I'm ashamed to call myself

Countess of Kilmarock. Will you prove many in England right, who say you are a backward and barbarous people?"

The displeased faces of Duncan, the Mackenzies, and her husband told Myrtle she'd probably gone too far. Yet she was too tired of their squabbling and ruining lives like Jean's and Duncan's to regret her words.

"But the Knoxes are cowards, all know it," Gavin said, in the manner of one stating an obvious fact.

Duncan's right hand went to the hilt of his dagger. "And all know the bragging Mackenzies are without honor," the thinner Scot countered.

Gavin went for his own dagger. "No mon, least of all a Knox, can say that lie and live."

Myrtle wedged herself between the two threatening men. "Will you oafs stop—" Two masculine hands gripped her upper arms. With a shriek of alarm, the Countess of Kilmarock sailed upward, then found herself placed on her feet to the left. Turning, she got a quick glimpse of Ian's angry visage.

Clearly astonished that the laird's wife would be so imprudent as to thrust herself in the middle of a knife fight, Gavin Mackenzie stepped back first. The scar across his face was more prominent against his ashen features. "By the root, lass," he said, forgetting to address Myrtle properly, "I might have killed ye."

"Well," she shouted, "you might also have killed Duncan, or he you. I've had enough of your idiot quarreling, and—"

"And I've had enough, wife," thundered Ian, "of your constant attempts to gain immediate access to the family crypt outside this keep. I'm verra near choking ye myself right now."

However, Myrtle was in no mood this time to meekly step aside. His words implied she was responsible for all those past attempts on her life. "I

361

never asked to have that stone thrown at my head, or the knife, and certainly not that arrow," she finished, equally incensed.

"Arrow?" Ian echoed, his golden eyes sharp.

Oh, bother, she thought, compressing her lips. She hadn't meant to blab that. "Err . . . it was nothing."

"What arrow?" Ian's words came out slow and deliberate.

Myrtle knew Ian was more dangerous now than when he'd lost his temper. Then she thought of something. "Yes, why not tell you?" she said aloud. "Could have been a Sinclair trying to get rid of me, anyway." She told them about the incident, then looked at Duncan. "Please, Duncan, roll up your right sleeve."

"Nae, my lady, 'tisn't necessary."

"Yes, Duncan, it is, for I want to show these Sinclairs how wrong they are to accuse you of having no courage or honor. Please, for me. Besides," she added, her usual humor coming to the surface. "If you don't, this husband of mine is liable to strangle me right here." She saw Duncan smile before he rolled up the sleeve of his linen shirt.

Myrtle pointed to the deep scar on his upper arm. "There is the proof that Duncan Knox took the arrow meant for me. If he hadn't tackled me to the ground that day in the forest, I would have been murdered. He could have ignored the situation, for I was nothing to him, and he knew the consequences if you Sinclairs caught him on their land. I am proud to call this man my friend." Myrtle saw the blood leave her husband's face when he viewed the evidence. She wanted to rush into his arms to comfort him. Would he ever forgive her for her interference here? It was clear none of these men was used to having a woman take charge in these matters. Oh, Ian, she thought, trying to tell him with her eyes how much she loved him and needed his understanding right now.

"A word alone, Gavin," Ian said, then put a comrade's arm on the older man's shoulder.

Myrtle held her breath as the two talked for a few moments in low tones.

"Da looks like he's coming around," Lachlan told the others.

"Least he isn't shouting," added Jean, brightening a little. She slipped her hand in Duncan's.

Finally, Myrtle saw Gavin shrug his shoulders. He said something and Ian smiled, looked at her, shook his head, then threw back his reddish-blond head and laughed loudly. Well, Myrtle told herself, even at her own expense, if it brought about a peaceful settlement, she'd gladly let them all laugh at her.

When the two men walked back over, it took all her self-discipline to remain silent and allow her husband to handle things. Myrtle was trying to show Ian she had no intention of undermining his authority here as laird.

"Duncan Knox," Ian addressed, "it is only proper that you ask Gavin Mackenzie for permission to wed his daughter."

Duncan stepped forward. "Gavin Mackenzie, I ask ye . . . humbly if you will consent to have the banns posted for Jean and me to wed. I promise to care for her and protect her, and she'll nae come to any harm within my clan."

Gavin looked down at his only daughter, saw how hopefully she watched him as she awaited his answer. He took Jean's small hand and placed it in Knox's. "Aye, I give ye my permission."

When Ian held out his hand to wish congratulations, Duncan took it. "Lady Myrtle is brave, and I shall never forget her kindness and courage in helping us," Duncan said with feeling. "Ye are a lucky mon, my lord."

"I know," Ian said, letting his deep feelings for the

woman next to him show in his golden eyes when he looked at her.

Warmed by such public praise, when Jean came up to her, Myrtle said, "All the best, Jean."

Jean looked down, almost as if she could not bear the Englishwoman's words. "I dinna ken how ye can say that, though I know ye mean it, after all the terrible things I did and said to ye."

Myrtle sighed. "Jean, I am still learning how to be a laird's wife. God knows I keep making mistakes, as my long-suffering husband can attest. But as I grow older, I've learned nothing but decaying trees and bitterness reside in the places where we cling only to our old grudges and hatreds." She glanced over at Ian, then blushed a little to find his eyes on her. "I prefer to focus on the gifts I have now."

The betrothed couple walked with Myrtle to the door, while Ian had a final word with the Mackenzies.

Just near the threshold, Duncan warned Jean, "And if ye ever want that part of me again that yer so fond of, Jean Mackenzie, ye'll nae let me catch you with any mon but me, nor makin' trouble for her ladyship, do ye ken?" He stood scowling down at his bride-to-be, for the first time looking the fierce highlander, not just the bard of Clan Knox.

Myrtle struggled again with that choking feeling as she fought the urge to burst out laughing. These two said the most audacious things in front of her! She could not believe how cowed and meek Jean now seemed.

Especially when the hoyden of the Highlands said, "Aye, Duncan, I ken. Ye are my lord and master now."

As Duncan and all four Mackenzies mounted their horses to head for the Mackenzie cottage to draw up the formal documents of betrothal, Ian and Myrtle waved to them.

"Well," Myrtle told her husband, "I'd best go back upstairs to finish working on the final plans for tomorrow's dinner. Company, you know," she added, reminding him Addison and his English soldiers would be here.

Angus and Katie came in from the kitchen, happy to have heard from Fiona the news of Jean's betrothal.

"Time that forward hussy was wed," Katie declared, pursing her lips.

Ian smiled. "Not in those exact words, Katie, but I told Gavin if his daughter was safely wed and in her own home with the Knoxes, she'd not be so tempted to stir up trouble between the laird and his wife."

When Myrtle made a motion to go back to her work, Ian said, "Ah, Myrtle, my dear, I need to go over the account ledgers with you. Do you mind?"

Puzzlement showed on her face. "I assure you, sir, I have gone over them very carefully. Besides, I must finalize the seating arrangements for dinner tomorrow." His expression appeared set in stone. "Now?" she repeated. Part of her felt a stab of disappointment that he might not trust her ability. After all, she'd run things for her father for years, and Ian had promised to give her a free hand in helping to run the estate here. Did her interference this afternoon change his mind?

His face looked unusually imperious for a second. "Yes, I need to check them with you *now.*"

Myrtle heard the command in his voice. She felt Katie and Angus watching them. "Of course, my lord, as you wish," she consented, moving by him to walk up the stone stairs to their apartments.

Once in their rooms, she headed toward the office desk. She heard the sound of his leather shoes on the floor behind her. Myrtle sat down, opened the center drawer, and pulled out the leatherbound account book.

"First," demanded her husband, as he leaned over the desk, "tell me what caused you twice to break into such hysterical laughter that my clansmen thought ye were taking leave of your senses."

Let him know, then, she decided, still smarting from his lack of trust in her ability to handle their finances. She told him what Jean had complained after Myrtle had rescued her from her father's sword belt, then what Jean and Duncan had said to each other in her presence.

As Katie and Angus passed the closed door of their laird's master bedroom, they heard the loud laughter of Ian Sinclair.

Katie's motherly expression came back into her eyes. "Och, 'tis so comforting to hear the castle alive with the laird's rich laughter again."

Angus gave his wife a dour expression. "Aye, but I canna think what's so side-splitting aboot an account log."

"At the time," said Myrtle, after her husband's shoulders stopped shaking, "I didn't have your advantage of privacy to vent my reaction. I mean, there I was, heartsick over Gavin's loud remarks against Duncan's unworthiness, and Jean pops out with that remark. No place to run and hide; all I could do was try to hold onto my composure, pretend I wasn't there, while they said such . . . such intimate things to each other."

"Weel, I think Duncan will be able to handle Jean."

"If you are quite finished laughing your head off, I will go over these figures, which you have halted my activity of the day to see."

Reaching out, Ian closed the leather volume with a resounding snap. "The only figure I wish to go over right now is that of my wife." Without hesitation, he

366

reached for her hands and pulled her up and away from their desk. He easily lifted her in his arms and walked toward their bed.

"You mean you never wished to see the accounts?" she asked innocently, then draped her arms about her husband's neck.

"It was just a ruse to get you up here so I could seduce you."

"It's working," she whispered, then kissed his cheek.

Chapter Twenty-one

From the other side of the table, Myrtle gave her husband an encouraging smile. She was so proud of the way he was managing to speak calmly but candidly with the English soldiers and his clansmen. Love showed in his golden eyes as he looked at her, then raised his wineglass to his lips.

With Addison Barrington on her right and Gavin Mackenzie on her left, Myrtle divided her attention between both men. As the carefully prepared meal continued, Myrtle turned to Addison. "I am grateful to you, Addison, for coming here today. I can see from the talk at table between the clan representatives and your officers that we have made some important steps toward reconciliation."

"I've put in a request for a transfer," Addison said. "I'll be leaving for a post in India next month."

She could not deny it was probably better if Addison was stationed farther from Ian and herself. Relieved Jean would be marrying to live with Clan Knox, Myrtle could well understand how it might be uncomfortable for Ian to run into Addison often, as would be inevitable if the officer remained at the fort. His leaving made her decide not to bring up his role in persuading Jean Mackenzie to cause trouble between Myrtle and her husband, for it would serve no purpose now. And she was certain Jean had needed little persuading, anyway. "I do wish you all the best, Addison." Her blue eyes held his hazel gaze. "As I told you before, I never meant to cause you or your family unhappiness." Then she smiled into his eyes. "Of course, you must forgive me if I do not include your father the squire. He's clearly bullied and ranted at you since your boyhood, and I was angry to learn he coveted Kilmarock lands so much that he would force his son into a marriage he did not want."

"Lud love me, dear old Papa," Addison mused aloud without warmth. "Well, with luck, he'll soon be under the sod, where he can do more good there than he ever did me above it. Then I'll be able to resign my commission and start really living."

Though startled by the hatred in his words, Myrtle did not comment. When the blond-haired Lieutenant Johnson asked her something, she smiled and went back to the polite conversation at table.

After dessert, Myrtle reached down near her feet and picked up the item she'd placed there before her guests had come into dinner. She put the item wrapped in cotton wool quietly next to Addison's side of the table. "I wish to return this to you as a symbol that I am safe now with my Scottish clansmen, and I believe neither Englishman or Scot will need such firearms to settle our disagreements in future."

Addison pulled back the cloth to find his unloaded pistol, the one he'd given her the first day she'd arrived on Sinclair land. "Well, my lady, I accept it back, though I do not share your unwavering belief His Majesty can make peace with these Scots."

Myrtle stood up. She raised her glass. The Englishmen stood up, followed by the Scots in their best coats and breeches. "I give you a toast, gentlemen, to peace and better days for all of us."

"And to Myrtle Prescott Sinclair," Ian added, from the other end of the table, "who worked so diligently to bring this day aboot."

The Countess of Kilmarock beamed as the men on both sides of the table drank to this added toast.

However, after she sat back down and happened to glance at Gavin's bearded face, Myrtle was startled to see the way he was staring at Addison's gun.

"Captain," he said, his voice unusually soft-spoken, "'tis a fine-crafted pistol. May I see it a moment?"

Addison shrugged, then handed the silver-handled pistol to Gavin. Myrtle felt puzzled by Gavin's interest. The rest of the guests went on eating, laughing, and talking, clearly taking no interest in what was going on here.

Gavin turned the empty pistol over in his hands and seemed very intent on the handle of the weapon. "Tell me, Gavin, have ye had this gun long?"

Addison appeared affronted at the Scot's probing question, but answered, "It was a gift from my father when I entered the Army."

"As an officer, then?"

"Really, Mackenzie, I don't believe I like your tone."

Myrtle saw what intrigued Gavin, then her face crumbled in horror as she remembered the entry in Ian's diary. "Please, Addison, answer Mr. Mackenzie."

"Blimey, what the devil's gotten into you, Myrtle? Damn it, if you must know, that skinflint squire, my father, wouldn't even pay for an officer's commission for me. I 'ad to enter the Army as a bloody foot soldier."

Without another word, Gavin rose from the upholstered bench and walked the long length of the table in the great hall to bend down and say something next to Ian's ear. Then he showed him the

371

flintlock pistol in his hands.

Myrtle felt her blood chill at the expression that came over her husband's face. He whispered something to Gavin, who nodded, then returned to his place next to Myrtle.

Gavin handed the gun back to Addison. "Captain Barrington, the laird asks would ye meet with him in his library after dinner? He's verra interested in the unusual craftsmanship of that weapon, as I thought he might be."

"Of course," replied Addison, "but I can tell you right now, I'd not sell this firing piece, no matter how much your laird covets it." Admiring his own possession, Addison wrapped the gun back in the soft wool cloth. "That weapon," he told Myrtle, "has seen me through many battles. It's brought me luck."

Myrtle twisted her fingers in her lap. Though none but Gavin, Ian, and she knew what was going on, Myrtle could not believe how calmly Ian went about, talking with his guests. While he looked serious and ate no more food, he gave the appearance nothing was amiss. With English soldiers on one side and Sinclair clansmen on the other, she knew the fragile peace she'd help create here would never hold if this trouble came out openly. A carved bird appeared like any other to her. Why had she thought it was a heron? she tried asking herself.

Ian rose and left the table first. While the Scots and Englishmen went into the next room to have a farewell drink before the captain returned with his men to the fort, Gavin, Myrtle, Addison, and his aide, Lieutenant Johnson, entered Ian's library.

"My dear," Ian said, coming over to her, "I believe it would be best if you attended the rest of our guests in the next room."

His features were unreadable, yet she glimpsed the grim determination in the depths of his lion eyes. "No, Ian," she said with a firmness that surprised her. "My place is here, and I should like to remain."

He nodded, then went over to Addison. "Captain, did you fight at Culloden?"

Addison seemed surprised at such a question. "Yes, and probably so did many on both sides of that table in there," he added, nodding toward the closed door. "What has that do with your wanting to buy my gun? Tell you now, Sinclair, it isn't for sale."

"Buy the pistol?" Ian echoed, the words burning his tongue. He got to the point. "Barrington, did ye shoot my wounded brother, Hugh Sinclair, on Culloden moor after the battle ended?"

Addison looked irritated. "That was almost two years ago. How the hell would I remember? A lot of Scottish traitors died that day."

Ian shot Myrtle a warning glance for her to stay exactly where she stood next to Gavin. He walked slowly over to Addison. "I'm concerned only with one eighteen-year-old lad with hair and eyes the color of mine. My tacksman," he went on, nodding to Gavin, "saw the murder. Gavin only remembers the carved heron on the pistol belonging to the foot soldier who executed my wounded brother."

Addison belligerently glared up at the Scot. "What if I did kill him? I never knew his identity. All those tattered Scots looked the same that day. When Cumberland's own officers refused to carry out the duke's order for English justice, I saw my chance. Got a promotion to officer on the spot for it."

Suddenly, Ian backhanded the Englishman across the face, but even though his eyes showed fury, his voice was deadly calm. "For the murder of my brother, Hugh Sinclair, I challenge you to a duel to the death. I will not let the likes of you destroy the peace my wife has sought so hard to bring to my land. Therefore, we will meet at dawn in a secluded spot, and you may choose the weapons."

Addison rubbed the back of his hand against the

edge of his mouth to wipe away a trickle of blood. "Rapier," he answered, a knowing smile on his lips. "The weapon of a gentleman, needing far more skill than is required to hold that cumbersome claymore you and your rabble clansmen are used to wielding."

"No, Ian, you cannot," Myrtle cried, then raced over to her husband.

"Lady wife," Ian said, looking deep into her blue eyes.

She read everything there. Sadness consumed her when she realized she could not stop this duel. She turned to Addison. "I cannot believe I once considered marrying you."

The Englishman smirked. "Your money and high connections at court, along with my father's insistence, were the only incentives that kept me pursuing you."

Myrtle felt the outrage emanating from her husband at Addison's remark, but she pressed his arm, pleading silently for him to say nothing. She intended to learn more from Addison. She remembered Jean's confession of this officer's role in attempting to destroy her marriage. "You wanted me to fail here and go racing back to London from the beginning, didn't you?"

Addison shrugged. "You and these ignorant Scots made it so easy. I paid to have lies spread throughout Sinclair lands about how Lady Myrtle Prescott intended to drive the Sinclairs from their crofts. It did ensure you'd have a hostile Scottish reception."

"And you paid to have those attempts on my life?"

"How did you guess?" he asked, looking happily intrigued.

"Until a few days ago, I never considered it might be you. But it was the recent reminder of how Duncan had rescued me from that arrow that triggered my suspicions. The Scots here use daggers, claymores. Archery is not a sport in which they partake. Even that day when Urisk set up the targets, you couldn't resist showing off your skills, as you'd done so many times in Chelmsford when you visited me. You are an excellent archer."

He bowed, clearly proud of his accomplishments. "The rock and knife attack I paid others to do. That day of the confrontation about your cattle, I was there, dressed in work breeches and shirt, like most of the scruffy Scots. When asked, I gave Trevor Jones those wrong directions to your castle. I could have strangled you when you charged up to the glen to ward off the bloody skirmish I hoped would bring my soldiers down on your clansmen. But then I saw my chance. Only Duncan Knox happened by on his way from a romantic tryst with Gavin's lusty daughter. I intended to pay him back by getting him hanged for the murder of that young officer I drafted into my cause. In the beginning, the attempts on your life were merely to frighten you into leaving Scotland; then I wanted to make you more susceptible to my proposal of marriage. But you were a stubborn one," he said, appearing irritated at the defiance on her face as she stood in the protection of her husband's arm.

"That English officer I killed was a nobody," continued Addison. "His people are only farmers from Shropshire. I thought that was brilliant, though, for when the Scots rose up against you after they were unjustly blamed for the act, I knew they would either kill you or run you off the land. Either way, I couldn't lose. Father would have bought this place for a song with the King's blessing." His hazel eyes narrowed when he looked up at Ian. "I never counted on Ian Sinclair turning up alive. Of course," he jeered, "I shall end that unfortunate oversight tomorrow morning."

Without another word, Addison made a mocking bow to his hosts, then told the astonished lieutenant they were leaving. Johnson opened his mouth, saw his superior scowl a warning, then closed it and followed Addison out the door.

While her husband slept next to her, Myrtle slipped out of bed and walked out the door and up to the battlements outside. In her thin nightgown and wrapper she stood in her slippers looking out at the hint of sunrise. The water lapped against this back section of the small castle in the highlands. She pressed her hands against the cold tan stones, trying to fight the terror that threatened to overtake her. She knew since the King's own son had ordered Hugh to be murdered, there would certainly be no justice against Addison from the English courts. There was no other way out. It was why she had understood and not mentioned the duel again to Ian. But it was tearing her apart inside.

"Ye'll catch your death up here on the castle walk at this hour," said a familiar voice behind her.

She turned to find Ian, dressed in dark green kilt and white shirt, an English sword in the leather belt about his waist. He saw the expression in her eyes as she took in his dress.

"It is a matter of family honor, Sassenach." A smile hovered on his lips for a second. "Besides, I dinna think Addison will arrest me for breaking the law this morning."

When Myrtle shivered, Ian came closer and reached for her. He pressed her body against his and wrapped his warm plaid about her.

She knew her husband also wore his kilt because if he died in this duel, he would go down proudly to be buried as a highland warrior, no matter what English law stated.

"Come, my brave Sassenach, 'tis too cold for you up here, and . . . it is time I left for my appointment."

In the end, Myrtle persuaded her reluctant husband to allow her to ride in the carriage to the spot where the duel was to take place.

She stood silently next to Gavin. Addison was doing elaborate warming-up exercises while his aide, Lieutenant Johnson, looked on.

The May morning was lovely, and it promised to be a beautiful day, in mockery of what was about to take place, Myrtle thought, as she clutched her wool cloak tighter about her shoulders.

The combatants took their positions.

"Do ye nae intend to remove your coat, Addison?" Ian could not help asking, for the constraint of a coat could slow a man's movements.

Addison touched the bump on his nose, clearly remembering Ian's role in permanently altering the officer's once straight features. He glanced at Ian's open shirt and bare legs beneath his short kilt. "I have no intention of fighting in the almost naked manner of you uncivilized Scots."

Both men saluted, then raised their swords.

"Of course," drawled Addison, "I will try to do this slowly, since you've never fought in a battle before. It was 'coward' that even your own brothers called you, was it not?"

Ian said nothing as he focused on his target.

Lunge, parry, riposte. The sound of steel cut through the morning mist.

Myrtle bit her lip, tormented by the sounds and sights before her. The formally dressed scarlet-coated officer in wig, buttoned coat, and boots contrasted sharply with her kilt-attired husband. She had not expected Ian to be such a skilled swordsman with the light, thin rapier, but Addison was ruthless. As the duel went on, both men had cuts and were bleeding. Relentlessly, they kept up the brutal pace.

"The weasel is beginnin' to tire," Gavin said under his breath.

Myrtle couldn't tell. She'd never witnessed a duel before. To her, Addison looked dangerous. She gripped Gavin's arm.

Clearly unaware of how much pressure she exerted, the older Scot made no comment, nor did he pull away.

Suddenly, Ian saw an opening and knocked the sword from Addison's hand. It landed on the muddy ground a few feet away.

"Oh, Gavin, it's over," Myrtle murmured. But then she stared in horror as Addison reached quickly into the folds of his scarlet coat to pull out a small pistol. It was hardly in his hand before he fired it directly at Ian Sinclair.

"Nooo!" she screamed, as Ian was knocked backward by the ball's impact into his chest. Before Myrtle, the outraged Gavin, and the appalled English lieutenant could reach them, Addison gripped his sword on the ground. He charged over to his prostrate opponent, who lay facedown on the damp grass. "Now, bastard Scot, I'll send the last of the Sinclairs to Hades, where you all belong."

But Ian rolled over and landed on his feet in one fluid motion. With a Gaelic war cry, he plunged the point of a dagger into Addison's heart. The small, black-handled *Skene Dhu* had been in the top of the hose of the kilt-wearing Scot, and to Ian, Addison's pistol attack canceled all gentlemanly rules of fencing. And now he knew why Addison had insisted on wearing his outer coat.

Myrtle stared at all the blood on Ian's chest and his face—most of it his own. She saw her husband's face whiten, clearly from his wound. He swayed, but Myrtle and Gavin on each side caught him. They got him into the carriage.

Lieutenant Johnson rushed over. "My lady, the captain is dead." He said the words without emotion. "I give you my word to relate a truthful account to my superiors of what has occurred here. With your honorable Prescott name to the report, it will also weigh favorably with the King. George of Hanover is now trying to reconcile with the Scots out of political necessity. His own son's reputation of brutality at Culloden has caused enough anti-English feelings among the Scots here. Barrington did not tell you, but I have been promoted to captain, and I will be staying on at the fort. George II will not want this scandal about Hugh Sinclair's murder dredged up before the public. I vow this matter will end here," he said with feeling.

Tears in her eyes, the laird's wife leaned out her side of the carriage. "I thank you for that, Lieut— Captain Johnson."

He stepped back, clearly aware this brave Englishwoman wanted only to get her husband medical attention.

Hours later, after the doctor left, Myrtle entered their bedroom. Though it wasn't really necessary, she'd ordered a fire to keep the night chill away from her wounded husband. Ian was propped up in bed, white bandages across his left shoulder and chest. His reddish-blond hair fell about his shoulders as he rested his head against two pillows. Going over to him, she could not help worrying anew, for he looked deathly pale.

As if sensing her presence, Ian's eyes opened, and he smiled up at his wife. "Dinna fret, Myrtle, the ball has been removed, and the doctor says I'll heal. I can prove it." Ian reached under the back pillow and pulled something out. He opened his palm to show her the round ball that had been removed from his shoulder.

"Oh, Mother of . . ." A hand to her mouth, Myrtle felt her legs start to crumple under her.

Cursing himself for frightening her when he'd meant to reassure her, Ian used his good arm to encircle her waist and pull her next to him on their bed. "Oh, wee kelpie," he crooned over his ashen-faced wife as he cradled her upper body, "'tis an empty-headed ox ye married. There, now, yer safe. I'm here." He kissed her pale cheek. "Nothing to be scarit aboot."

Her blue eyes fluttered open to see the concerned features of her Scottish husband. "Next time," she said, "I'll fight the duel and let *you* wait for *me* in the carriage."

He chuckled, then hugged her close. He moved them both to a more comfortable position in the center of the bed, with his wife ending up on his lap, despite her protests that he would hurt his injured shoulder. Ian shook his head. "Adorable Sassenach, have ye nae learned I suffer more when you're nae right here with me?" He kissed her long and tenderly.

"Katie was right," he said, his golden eyes devouring her sweet face. "She told me you were meant to be the laird's wife. Your name was a good omen. If I hadn't kept alive my hatred for the English with such fervor and been so stubborn, I would have recognized I loved you the first time I saw you sleeping like a brown-haired angel on the cot in my cellar."

Myrtle caressed his face with her soft fingers. "You had many tragedies to bear, all from English hands, my love. I do understand . . . Urisk," she added, trying to tease him out of his sudden mood of regret. It puzzled her to see even Ian's ears turn a deep shade of pink at her use of the pretended name Angus gave him. "Ian, why don't you like that name?"

"I detest it," he bit out.

"But why? I don't understand."

"All right, nosy Sassenach, I'll tell ye—Urisk is the name of a satyrlike brownie from Scottish folklore."

380

She tried to stifle it, she really did, but then she lost the battle as peals of laughter overcame her. Myrtle took her prickly husband's flushed face in her hands and kissed him full on the mouth. Merriment in her sky-blue eyes, she whispered, "While you are truly no brownie, sir, I think the other description is rather apt."

Growling in mock reproach, despite his wife's halfhearted protest that he would reopen the wound at his shoulder, the laird of Kilmarock tumbled his wife beneath him. He leaned over to begin a trail of slow, warm kisses across her forehead, nose, cheeks, and the rapid pulse at the base of her throat, to the tops of her breasts. His hands wandered to her waist, then moved up along her ribs. Surprised at what he felt, he stopped for a moment to comment, "Ye're nae wearing stays this time? Can it be," he teased, "my proper, sometimes stuffy English wife is becoming a Scottish wanton?"

Her eyes danced with happiness. "Though you make me feel deliciously wicked from a mere kiss or glimpse of you dressed in your handsome kilt, my lord, I'm not wearing my corset because your doctor insisted I remove it. Though it is early, your physician tells me I'm pregnant." She was rewarded by Ian's look of astonishment as he sat back on his heels.

"Oh, my darling, bonny wife," he exclaimed, then crushed her warm body to his. "I love you." Then it registered how roughly he was treating her, and he pulled back. "I'm sorry. Are you all right?" Gently, he helped her sit up and lean back against the pillows. "I enjoy yer lovely figure so much, I often lose my head."

"I like the way you touch me," she stated, then snuggled against him. "You make me feel protected and deeply loved in your strong arms. Oh, Ian, I hope I give you a son next year."

He stroked her long brown hair as he held her close. "A bonny lass like her impudent mother will nae displease me, either." After a few silent moments, he touched her cheek again. "Jonathan Prescott did keep his promise to me. He sent the Sinclairs a gallant champion in his daughter, Lady Myrtle."

So moved by his words, Myrtle could not speak for a few seconds. She turned her head to kiss the hand that had been stroking her hair. "Thank you, Ian. That means more to me than you will ever know." The moments passed as they held onto each other.

Then she yawned behind her hand, the trials of the day taking their toll on her.

"My lady?" whispered her husband, as he went to the buttons at the back of her gown.

"Umm?"

"If you sit up a moment, I'll slip ye out of yer clothes, then ye can sleep more comfortably."

"Yes, Ian." Automatically, she followed his directive. While he unhooked her gown, she removed her stockings and shoes. When he had her out of her dress and shift, she turned to him. The white bandages across his chest reminded her. She chided herself for forgetting Ian was an injured man and needed complete rest. Tucking the covers under his side of the bed, she kissed him chastely on the forehead. "Darling, I'll sleep on the cot in the paneled room next door. I remember how it works. It's best if you rest quietly for a few days. Goodnight, my love."

Ian took a minute to realize she was in earnest. Throwing the covers back, he swung his legs over the side of the bed and stood up. He did feel woozy from loss of blood and had to grab the bedpost for support. "Myrtle Sinclair, don't ye dare press that iron button," he ordered.

At the tone of his command, Myrtle turned around, feeling both torn and confused. Of course, she wanted to stay with him, but his health . . . When he walked slowly over to her, she held up her hands. "Ian, please, you must get back into bed."

"If I have to, I'm prepared to carry ye back over to our bed," said the patient. "Of course, if every ounce of my blood pumps out of my shoulder and I die, it will be yer fault, but nobody else will ever know it. Robbie over there," he said, nodding to the sleeping dog, "and Mortimer downstairs won't say anything."

She shook her head. "Ian Sinclair, you are a rogue," she said, but she could not help smiling up at his look of pathetic resignation. "You know I'll do anything to keep you from lifting me right now in your condition."

"Oh, the room's spinning," said the Earl of Kilmarock. "Could ye help me back to bed? If I could just hold onto yer wee arm for a second."

However, she noticed wryly, instead of her arm, Ian latched a hand to each of her breasts. "Here," she said, turning to place her shoulder near his good arm. "Lean on me and I'll get us back to the bed." He didn't take his hands from her bosom.

"Leverage. Helps balance me," the laird explained.

When she got him over to the bed, she eased him back under the covers. He watched as she bent over to extinguish the candle on the side table. Sighing, he realized he'd never tire of looking at her. Even when she just performed this domestic task, it sent his blood racing.

However, as she turned to walk back to him, he made certain his features were unreadable. He felt her slip in bed next to him. She clearly felt it necessary to give him practically the entire bed, for she scrunched herself up near the right edge.

"Goodnight, my love," she whispered over her shoulder. "Pleasant dreams," she added, automatically using her fond expression.

"I'm sure they will be pleasant," said her husband—just before he lunged for her.

A squeal of surprise escaped her lips when she suddenly felt herself lifted up to land gently but fully on her husband's naked body. "Ian, my darling, your poor shoulder, you can't—" Her words were cut off as the laird of Kilmarock showed her quite effectively he could.

Later, smiling to herself, confident of her husband's love, Myrtle moved closer in his warm embrace as he slept peacefully next to her. If the child she carried was a boy, they would call him Hugh Malcolm Sinclair after Ian's brothers, she decided, just before sleep overtook her.